LIES
THAT
BIND

HOW DO YOU ARREST SOMEONE WHO DOESN'T EXIST?

CRAIG J. SMITH

A FRANKIE'S WORLD PUBLICATION
NAPA, CALFORNIA

Frankie's World
2158 Penny Lane
Napa, California 94559
www.liesthatbind.com

Publisher's Note: This is a work of fiction. Names, characters, places, and incidents are a product of the author's imagination. Locales and public names are sometimes used for atmospheric purposes. Any resemblance to actual people, living or dead, or to businesses, companies, events, institutions, or locales is completely coincidental.

Ordering Information:
Quantity sales. Special discounts are available on quantity purchases by corporations, associations, and others. For details, contact the "Special Sales Department" at the address above.

Lies That Bind/ Craig Smith. — 1st ed.
ISBN: 978-0-9994359-0-8 paperback
ISBN: 978-0-9994359-1-5 eBook
Library of Congress Control Number: 2017961227

To Denise,
who makes my world larger,
more interesting, and much more fun.

PART ONE

PART ONE

Chapter One

Officer Danny Garcia tried to add up the number of times in the past two weeks that he'd been in a fast food restaurant, watching his partner, Sean Rawlins, eat. Was it thirteen? Fourteen? Whatever the number, it amazed him that Sean managed to eat all that junk without ballooning up. Where did it all go?

"That's your third shake on this shift, dude."

Sean barely stopped slurping to reply. "Second."

"No, you had one with you when we started out today."

"Doesn't count. It was chocolate."

"Chocolate? Who cares what *flavor* it was? It was a milkshake," said Danny.

The straw still clenched in his teeth, Sean looked disdainfully at his partner. "You don't keep up on things, do you? If you did, you'd know that scientists have proven that chocolate is good for you. I might as well be working out as drinking that shake."

"You are *not* telling me that shake was healthy."

"Like drinking a V-8." Sean looked out the window, shaking his head. "And *you* want to be a detective."

"Oh, really? Someday your arteries are going seize up, man. God forbid it's during our shift and I have to rush you to the ER."

Sean hit his flat stomach with his fist. "See that? Like a drum. I'm in a lot better shape than you are, Officer Garcia. Plus, I have youth on my side."

"Youth? I'm only seven years older than you are, Sean."

"But you're in your thirties."

"Thirty-two! And my abs are just as hard as yours."

Sean shrugged and kept slurping.

"Go easy," Danny said. "You're going suck the wax right out of that cup."

Danny looked past Sean at the only other customers in the restaurant, two teenage girls sitting at a booth adjacent to theirs. Both were heavily tattooed, had multiple facial piercings, and wore black eye makeup like they got it for free. Danny judged them to be in the throes of teenage existential angst, but otherwise harmless. Still, you could make a mistake discounting the potential threat from anyone. That kind of mistake had damned near gotten him killed.

The police radio Danny had placed on the table squawked. Stopping their conversation in mid-sentence, the teens looked towards the officers. Danny glared them back to their own business, picked the radio up and lowered the volume. A citizen had reported seeing someone in her backyard, thought it was her ex for whom she had a restraining order, and was asking the police to check it out. The men groaned, hearing that she lived clear across town. When two other officers were dispatched to handle it, Danny gave Sean a fist bump.

"Hey, didn't we have a couple of calls just like this, on the same damn street if I remember right, just a few years back?" asked Sean.

"Oh yeah. You were still a rook, about a week out of academy. So it was, what, four years ago?"

"Same kind of call, too. She told him to come over both times, promised crazy make-up sex, then tried to get him busted when he showed up."

"She was hot, too. Poor bastard kept going back, thinking maybe it would be different this time." Danny chuckled. "She was worse than my ex."

"That's a scary woman right there," said Sean, pointing to the radio. "I'll call dispatch and tell them what a charmer she is so they can let the officers know what to expect."

Danny glanced at his watch. "Yeah, then let's head back to the station. It's almost midnight, and I'm ready to go home. Stay close to me in case your blood sugar whacks out on our way to the car and I have to carry you."

Sean emptied his plastic tray in the trash and then put it on top of the can. "Aw shucks, partner, listen to you." He put his arm around Danny and gave it an exaggerated squeeze. "You're worried that something bad might happen to me. You'd be lost without your partner."

Sean had the loopy grin and tussled blond hair of a golden retriever puppy. Danny almost wanted to scruff him behind the ears.

"Yeah, Sean, that's it. I don't know what I'd do without you. Let's get out of here."

They walked out into a warm Indian summer night, the kind Napa Valley is known for during Crush, the time of year when grapes are harvested. Danny used to love being outdoors, especially in the fall. These days he was a little on edge at night, not sure what the darkness might be hiding. Getting shot at, practically feeling the wind from the bullet as it blasted past his ear, still haunted him. He tried to be subtle about looking from side to side as he walked out of the restaurant.

"What are you looking for?"

"Nothing."

"You're thinking about that night, aren't you?"

Danny shrugged.

"That was a one in a million thing, Danny. There's nothing either of us could have done to stop it. You can't worry about it all the time."

"I told you, I'm not thinking about it. I'm just worried about you going into a diabetic coma. Get in the car and let's get outta here."

Sean rolled down his window and started drumming on the roof with the palm of his hand. "You want to buy me a beer after shift?" Sean asked.

"That's a hell of an offer, but I can't," Danny answered. "I've got a date with Carol tonight."

"You've got a *what*? Nobody has a 'date' at midnight—you're getting laid!"

Danny pursed his lips. "No, Sean. I'm still trying to get back on Carol's good side. Not everything is about sex."

"Still in the doghouse, huh? You're probably too old to have sex after a full day on the job anyway. Hey, you didn't eat much back there. Is it safe to take Viagra on an empty stomach? Cause if you want to stop for another burger or something, I'm cool with it."

The police radio interrupted. "Unit thirty eight: We've got a ten-fifteen at The Meadows. Can you check that out?"

The Meadows was a retirement home a mile from the Burger King, just outside the downtown area, next to the Napa Creek.

Danny sighed. "Ten-four." He turned off the mic. "Dammit."

"That's a disturbance of the peace," said Sean. "I know all those numbers are confusing at your age."

"I know what a ten-fifteen is, Sean."

"What do you want to bet its homeless guys under the bridge again? You know when they built those places right next to it, nobody was thinking about that ever happening."

"Maybe it's the homeless guys who are complaining. Some of those tenants listen to their TVs so loud, it might be bothering them."

"Seriously. Why do they do that?"

"You mean the TV volume? Because they can't hear. Don't you have grandparents? It's part of getting old," said Danny.

"You would know."

Danny knew he'd walked right into that one and let it go.

"So what does Carol see in an old guy like you, anyway?"

Less and less, Danny thought.

This promised to be a routine call. After a night of drinking, the homeless, camped next to the creek, sometimes got loud. The old bridge offered them shelter and the sense that they were alone. Police calls there mostly involved quieting the disturbance and running warrant checks. Danny couldn't remember ever turning up more than an outstanding misdemeanor charge.

He switched the mic back on. "This is thirty eight. We're on our way to the station and our shift is as good as over. Can't you give this one to Patrick and Reynolds? Over." The call and follow-up paperwork were guaranteed to make Danny at least an hour late for his date.

"Sorry, fellas. They're taking an inebriant to detox as we speak. This call is yours. Over."

"Shit," Danny muttered.

When Danny and Sean pulled into The Meadows' parking lot, they could hear loud male voices, apparently in an argument. Danny felt the muscles in his shoulders tighten and turned his head from side to side to loosen them. The voices were definitely coming from under the bridge, but he couldn't make out what they were saying.

"This is probably just what it sounds like, but check out the area around us just to be safe."

"Relax, Danny. We've done this before. We've probably been here a dozen times this year."

"Just look sharp when we're around these guys."

"Look sharp?" Sean sniggered. "Hell, I can practically smell the booze from here. It's not like these guys are going to appreciate the finer points of good police work."

Billy clubs now in their belts, Danny grabbed his flashlight and walked to the top of the bridge. Danny loved the old stone overpasses in Napa. Early in their relationship, Carol had given him a coffee table book of Napa County's historical bridges. This one, built in the early 1900s, was a single arch with a total span of less than fifty feet. In October, after months without rain, the creek bed under the bridge was dry and smooth, providing shelter and a place to sleep.

Flashlights on, Danny followed Sean, walking crab-like down the short steep bank, and peered under the bridge. Two men Danny recognized immediately were yelling at each other while gripping opposite ends of a shopping cart. They seemed to be playing tug of war with it. Two other carts, filled with a mixture of sleeping bags, clothes, and some scavenged items whose usefulness Danny couldn't fathom, were nearby. The area reeked like the homeless encampment it was: sour, unwashed bodies, mixed with stale alcohol and pungent urine. Could the guys smell all that when they were sober? Were they ever sober? They were certainly drunker now than he'd seen them in a long time, unusual this late in the month, with welfare checks still three days away.

The temperature was in the upper 50s, but the men were dressed for colder weather. One had on an oversized flannel jacket, zipped up to the neck, and fingerless gloves. The other wore black sweatpants and several sweaters, along with a Giants baseball cap, the bill turned backwards. Although he didn't look it, he was probably twenty years older than the other guy. He just hadn't been living out of a shopping cart for as long. Tough life. Their watery-red eyes were glazed and unfocused, and both men were at least a week away from a razor.

"Well, well, Mr. Perkins, Mr. Williams," said Danny, shining his flashlight from face to face. The narrow beam made them look like floating heads, and accented their red eyes. "What seems to be the problem here?"

Both men flinched as though the officers had magically appeared. Perkins, the older of the two, jutted his chin towards Williams and slurred an answer to Danny's question. "This asshole's got my cart."

"He's lying," Williams garbled. "This is *my* cart and this asshole—"

"I am not lying, you lying son-of-a-bitch!"

"Gentlemen, gentlemen—keep it *down!*" barked Sean, shocking the men into silence. He pointed his flashlight at the shopping cart between them and then from one face to the other. "Unless one of you is named Safeway, it looks to me like that cart doesn't belong to either of you, and if you don't shut up, I'll lock you both up for stealing it."

The two swayed as they stared at Sean, as though trying to figure out who he was and where he'd come from. Perkins refocused on the cart, giving it a yank with one hand as he shook a fist at Williams. The thought that one might actually try and throw a punch at the other amused Danny.

"I want you both to step away from that cart and sit down," he said, pointing to a spot on the ground with his flashlight.

Danny watched Williams seemed to contemplate the few feet he had to move, gave it a shot, and fell, landing hard before rolling over onto his stomach. "Ow!" Perkins just more or less collapsed into a heap of himself, miraculously ending up in a sitting position.

"How much have you gentlemen been drinking tonight?" asked Danny.

Williams hadn't moved since turning onto his stomach, except to curl into a relaxed fetal position with one hand under his head. Perkins looked like he was going to nod off sitting up. Neither man responded to the question. To Danny, these two were like a cranky old married couple. Although numerous warrant checks had been run on both men over the years, protocol dictated that it be done again.

Danny put his hands on the top of his belt and exhaled forcefully. "Officer Rawlins, you want to call in and see if these boys have been behaving lately? Can't risk turning them loose on the public without a warrant check."

Sean looked at Danny for a moment before responding. "Oh, right. Why don't *I* be the one to walk all the way to the car and call the station? You stay here and save your strength for your 'date.'"

"You know what? I'll go back to the car. You stay, and impress these guys with good police work." Danny walked back to the patrol car. This stop was going to make him late getting home. Carol would accept it as part of the job, but Danny knew she would worry. He didn't need any more strikes against him or the job.

Reaching through the window, he grabbed the radio and called the station. He gave the answering officer the names of the two men and asked for a warrants check. It seemed to take forever for a response. Danny sniffed at the sleeves on his shirt, wondering if any of the stink from under the bridge had stuck to him.

The car radio popped. "Unit thirty eight, come in please, over."

"This is thirty eight, over."

"Officer, are you sure about those names you called in? Can you repeat them, please? Over."

Danny confirmed the names, then waited for the report back. What he heard made no sense to him at all. Danny dropped the radio to his chest, giving himself a moment to take it all in. Then he burst out laughing.

"Officer, are you kidding me? Are you sure we are talking about the same two guys?"

The station officer confirmed his information.

"Copy that." Danny sighed. "Look, we've known these guys for years, and there is no way they could pull off any of that stuff. On a good day, they're drunk by noon. Are you positive about this?"

"Have I ever lied to you, Officer?" Danny could hear the smile in the answer. "Over."

It took Danny a few seconds to be able to respond. "Okay then. We'll bring them in. Over." He stood for a moment, staring at the radio as though it had malfunctioned. He returned it to the car and headed back to the bridge. Walking sideways down the bank to keep his balance, he joined Sean. He didn't say a word to or look at his partner; he just hooked his thumbs in his belt and stared at the two men at his feet, now passed out.

Sean cocked his head to one side. "Well? Are you going to tell me what you found out so we can finish here and leave, or are you just going to stare at these guys? There still might be time for you to buy me a beer and cry about your missed date."

"I'm afraid that's not how it's going to go tonight, Officer Rawlins." Danny studied the sleeping men at his feet. Even after all these years on the job, he didn't understand how people could drink themselves into this kind of shape. "You're not going believe this. Mr. Perkins and Mr. Williams have been busy since we last saw them, what, a couple of months ago? Between them they have warrants for fraud, theft, forgery and a whole host of other shit."

Sean snickered. "Yeah, right. And I'm wanted for grand-theft auto. You want to quit messing around, so we can wrap it up here?"

"But this part is even better," Danny said ignoring Sean's question. "A couple of days ago our friends here tried to steal about a million bucks, and got away with three hundred thousand of it."

"Come on, Garcia. You and I both know these guys couldn't do any of that stuff. And how do you only get part of what you steal? Were they too drunk to remember to take it all, or wouldn't it fit in their shopping cart?"

Danny couldn't argue with his partner, or answer his questions. The whole thing was ludicrous. He chuckled. "We're going to have to catalogue all this shit," he said, pointing to the shopping carts with his flashlight. "And if we can sober these guys up enough to get them to the station, we are about to arrest two fairly serious criminals."

"What the hell?"

Danny looked at his watch, put his hand on Sean's shoulder and forced a grin. "Like you said, partner, so much for my date."

He could only hope Carol would laugh about it.

Chapter Two

Two Months Earlier

Tim Harris stretched his right arm out in front of him, fingers splayed, looking for even the slightest movement. He stared a good five seconds.

Steady as a rock.

Grabbing his knit cap with both hands, he pulled it farther down on his head, forcing his shaggy blond hair over his ears and neck. The running shorts he wore offered little protection from the chill, and his legs were peppered with goose bumps, but it didn't matter. He stretched his neck from side to side and shook out his arms. Despite the cool temperature, he felt better than he had in months.

It was Tim's fifteenth day at New Beginnings, a drug and alcohol treatment center fifty miles northwest of San Francisco. The center was surrounded by forest for three miles in any direction. Once past the two-week mark, "clients," as the staff called them, were allowed to roam the grounds unattended for an hour each morning. This solo run was going to be Tim's first respite from constant interaction with people he barely knew and with whom he had little in common beyond having problems with alcohol. At twenty-eight, he was older than half the clients there. He beamed as he set off down the driveway. This might not be freedom, but it damn sure beat jail.

"Hey man, wait up!"

Tim looked over his shoulder and saw Jorge, another client, running towards him.

"Hey, what luck," Jorge grinned as he caught up. "Finally, a running buddy. Tim, right? This is great."

Not exactly how Tim would have characterized their meeting. "Yeah, hi. Listen, it's been a while since I've run, and I'll probably slow you down. Just go ahead, and I'll see you at breakfast."

"Hey, I've been running alone for two weeks now. I'm leaving tomorrow and would love company. If you can't keep up, I'll slow down."

Jorge was one of the best looking and most charismatic men Tim had ever met, with high cheek bones, mocha-colored skin and deep-set eyes. Tim had barely spoken to him, but watched from a distance as he interacted with other clients. Openly gay and extremely comfortable in his skin, Jorge drew people to him the way a queen bee attracts drones; they practically crawled all over him in hopes of getting noticed. Yet there was something about him that Tim didn't trust. He didn't have words for it, it was just... something. He'd purposely kept his distance.

So much for that strategy. Now he had to talk to him.

"You looking forward to tomorrow's meeting?" Tim asked. Clients who had completed their twenty-eight days shared their stories with everyone else in the house during the afternoon Alcoholics Anonymous meeting, just before leaving. It was the New Beginnings equivalent of a commencement speech.

"Yeah, whatever. I'm really looking forward to leaving though, getting back to my life. How about you? Two weeks now?"

"Day fifteen," answered Tim.

"You'll love this. Come on." Jorge started running, and Tim fell in next to him. When they rounded the bend in the driveway the land opened up to a large downhill-sloping clearing. Tim followed Jorge down the slope. They angled off the driveway and into an open, sunlit area, where they could run abreast. The mowed area ended abruptly at the forest. The transition from sunlight to shade was instantaneous, and Tim felt a slight chill. Pine needles covered the forest floor, softening the impact of his feet on the ground. He caught his stride right away, and felt like he could run forever.

"I can't believe how good it feels to be out here."

"Just wait," said Jorge. "It gets warm quick and will feel even better."

"No, I mean just being outside, not sitting in another AA meeting, talking about how messed up my life is," said Tim. "I know that's what we're supposed to do, but I'm over it."

"Trust me, in two weeks you'll be *way* over it. How'd you end up here?"

"Well, some people think I have a problem with drugs and alcohol."

"And you don't?"

It pissed Tim off every time a counselor or another client suggested that he was an alcoholic, like they knew him better than he knew himself. "No, as a matter of fact, I don't. Sometimes I party a lot, but who doesn't?"

Jorge threw up his hands. "Okay, okay. I wasn't suggesting anything, man. I'm just asking how you picked New Beginnings."

"My dad had heard about this place. I got in a jam, and this was the lesser of two evils. Coming here wasn't exactly my decision."

"If this place was the best choice you had, you either did something serious or pissed off the wrong people."

Tim had spent two weeks trying not to have this conversation and wasn't going to get reeled in now.

"A little of both, but I can't really talk about it. I made a deal that, if I kept my mouth shut, I wouldn't have to do prison time," Tim said, exaggerating the negotiating power he'd had when he got caught. The path inclined up a slight hill, covered in dead leaves. His chest heaved as he navigated the new terrain.

"I can relate to that. I overheard you say you stole something."

Tim had started to tell other clients, three or four different times actually, but had reined himself in at the last minute each time. Which sucked. His crime had been clever—hell, brilliant—and the thought that he'd never be able to talk about it to anybody felt like a cosmic injustice. It was like creating a masterpiece that you could never display. What artist could live with that?

"No, really, I can't talk about it." Tim gasped before continuing. "Besides, if somebody... found out you knew, it could... get *you* in trouble." He liked that extra touch.

"You want to slow it down a little?"

Tim shrugged off the suggestion.

"It's not the same at this place as it is out there. We're *supposed* to talk about the shit we did, especially the shit that went bad. The counselors say it all the time—'we're only as sick as our secrets.' Besides, unless you start hanging out in gay bars, you and I aren't going to run into each other after this. Come on man, what'd you do?"

In the silence that followed, Tim considered the consequences of talking. The only other person who knew for certain what he'd done was his Dad, and *he* certainly wasn't going to tell anybody. And Jorge was right—who would ever find out he'd told him? Tim could tell his story, just this once, and never mention it to anyone again. Jorge would undoubtedly be impressed, and that would be that. What were the odds of the two of them crossing paths again?

"Identity theft," Tim finally said.

"What?"

"That's what got me here. It was identity theft." Tim was panting, but just uttering the words felt good. "I stole a couple of identities...

and borrowed twenty-five thousand." And with that, it was out. Tim felt light-headed, almost giddy.

Jorge ran without responding for a moment. "You need to stop and rest?"

Tim waved him off.

"Twenty-five grand," Jorge mused. "That's not huge, but it isn't chump change either."

Tim did his best to suppress a smirk. Did he detect respect in Jorge's voice?

"How do you steal an identity?" said Jorge. "I know people do it, I just don't know how."

"I found a guy's obit on-line and sort of became him." The explanation did nothing to answer the question, but now that he was finally talking about it, Tim wanted to stretch out the story a little.

"Yeah, but what does that mean?"

"Well, I was in real estate, and had this client who was trying to buy a house but didn't have all the financing worked out. I sent him to a couple of bankers I knew, but his credit wasn't all that great and they wouldn't even talk to him. He got the idea to go to a third-rate lender—a finance company that promises money to anybody."

"Like those places that cash paychecks? They take, what, thirty-five—forty percent?"

"Yeah, sort of. I tried to talk him out of it, but he didn't see any other way he was going get the money. He didn't really think they'd make the loan and was too embarrassed to go in and ask. So instead, he filled out a loan application, had it notarized, and *faxed* it to a company."

"And they turned his ass down cold."

"That's just it—they approved the loan. Sent him a check for twenty-five grand. Never talked to him, not even on the phone."

"No shit?"

"No shit. He bought the house right after that."

Jorge shook his head and chuckled. "Damn."

They crested a small hill just as the sun started peeking through the fog. Tim leaned over, put his hands on his knees and panted.

"You gonna be okay?" said Jorge.

"Yeah, just catching my breath."

"It's downhill, then flat after this."

A small lake with half a dozen ducks and a couple of Canada Geese was ahead. Tim slowed down and silently jogged in place while watching the birds, Jorge at his side. Tim marveled at how effortlessly the birds appeared to glide across the pond, knowing that under the water, out of sight, their legs kicked frantically to produce the placid image on display.

After a few seconds, the birds lifted off the pond and flew away, as though on cue.

"Wow. How do they all know it's time to leave?" said Jorge.

"Got me," Tim answered. He turned back to the path and continued to run, Jorge following.

"Tell me more about what you did."

"So I started thinking about how to pull it off."

"Steal the money like that, right?" Jorge said.

Tim could remember exactly when the idea first occurred to him. It had been his *ah-ha* moment, an instant of almost supreme clarity, and he was proud of it.

"Well, my client got all that cash, and nobody ever laid eyes on him. He could have been anybody—they didn't know."

"I get it. Pretend to be somebody else and you never have to pay it back."

"Exactly. If you could get a loan like that, why couldn't you steal it that way?"

A slender tree branch at waist level crossed their jogging path. Tim pushed it away as though opening a gate, slowing down just a step so that Jorge could pass it easily. It made him feel… magnanimous. A small gesture, sure, but a gracious one.

"I'd racked up some serious debt and this seemed like a good way to get a lot of money fast," Tim said.

"How much did you owe?"

"Enough that I couldn't see how I was going to pay it back."

"So you stole some guy's identity to get a loan?" asked Jorge.

"It wasn't really that hard. I figured I needed two IDs—the first to get a notary's license. I go online and find someone close to my age who died in a car wreck a couple years ago. Then I go to the county's records office and ask for his death certificate. Had this elaborate excuse worked out about why I wanted it."

"What did you tell them?"

"I didn't have to say anything. Clerk goes into the back, brings me a folder with the deceased's name on it, and walks away to help somebody else at the counter. I open it, and there's a death certificate." Tim paused to catch his breath. "And big as daylight, there's his Social Security number, right on top. Under that, his birth certificate. The clerk wasn't paying any attention to me, so I took the folder and walked out the door."

"That was ballsy."

"Yeah, well, I had some liquid courage working for me. Few days later, I go to the DMV, give them his info, and boom—I've got a driver's license in his name, with my picture on it."

"Wow."

"Wow is right. You take a class at the courthouse to get a notary's license. They lecture you about the legal stuff, you take a test, and three hours later you're a notary. And that's what I did. Rather, my dead guy did."

"You get fingerprinted for that?"

Tim welcomed the question, had hoped Jorge would ask. The answer showed how well he'd thought this out. "Yeah, but so what? I wasn't going to do anything that left fingerprints."

"So they'd just sit in a file somewhere. I gotta hand it to you, man. That's pretty smart."

Tim didn't even try to hide his smile. "So now I'm ready for the next step. I figure I need some collateral that's rock solid, something a finance company won't question. If I use a piece of real estate with a lot of equity in it, they'll make the loan, sight unseen, like they did for my client."

"You own a house?"

"No, but it doesn't matter." Telling it now, Tim was reminded just how complicated it had been. All the pieces had been carefully thought out and meticulously executed. Well, except for the one mistake he'd made, but that wasn't going to be part of this telling. "I just needed to find some property that fit the bill and steal my way into owning it."

"Wait—you've lost me again."

Of course he had. That was the idea. "I stole another identity, just like before, and went back to the county to find the right piece of property. It's just like asking for that death certificate. You can research any piece of land or building you want. It's all right there, how much is still owed on it, second mortgages or liens—everything. I picked one out and added another name to it as an owner."

"How?"

"This will kill you. I just wrote the new name I'd stolen above the names of the real owners, made a copy of it and left."

"And that's it?"

"That's it. I notarized the paperwork using my first dead guy's ID, then faxed it all to a lender, just like my client. Didn't talk to a soul. They approved the loan and wired the money to the bank account I opened in the second man's name. I sent it to a bank in Santa Rosa, so I could just go and get the money."

Jorge ran on in silence. Tim looked at him out of the corner of his eye, searching for a hint of appreciation. They'd come out of the woods, and the lodge lay just ahead.

Jorge twisted his mouth. He held up his index finger as if making a point. "But why didn't you go to prison when you got caught?"

This was not the response Tim expected. "What are you talking about? I ended up here instead." Tim slowed to a walk.

Jorge took him by the elbow and stopped him. "That's a hell of a story man. You've got balls, but something doesn't make sense," he said.

Tim pulled his arm free and backed away. "What are you talking about?"

Jorge stepped forward, closing the gap between them. "If all this is true, you broke some serious laws, but somehow you didn't get busted."

Tim felt the confidence of only a moment ago ebb away. He turned and resumed running. "What do you mean, 'If it's true?' I told you, I came here instead. There're three or four guys got sent here instead of jail."

Jorge's eyes narrowed. "Yeah, but they all did petty shit. You stole twenty-five grand. That's major as far as the law is concerned. Plus, you did all kinds of other shit. You don't walk from that." Jorge's voice, soft up to now, had turned menacing. He growled with his last words, his eyes burning through Tim.

Tim felt his insides quiver. He felt lost, and scrambled for an explanation. "Look, my dad has connections. They made it go away." His breath was getting caught in his chest.

"This is either total bullshit or you're holding something back. There's no way you pull all the shit you said and don't do time behind it. What aren't you telling me, College Boy?" Jorge almost sang the question, like a schoolyard taunt.

Tim winced at the insult. It never occurred to him that he would be challenged, or that his explanation was implausible. Jorge had him jammed up, and he couldn't undo it. "It's complicated, Jorge. Not everybody gets arrested." He couldn't think of anything else.

"Everybody who does what *you* did gets arrested. You're lying about something, I just don't know what."

"Hey, I didn't have to tell you in the first place. Why would I lie about it?" Jorge had played him, and Tim had made it easy for him.

"I don't know, but I think you did," Jorge said. "You're a trip, man."

They were back at the lodge. Jorge turned his back on Tim and walked inside, shaking his head and laughing out loud.

Tim started to follow, stumbled over his own feet, and almost fell. He wanted to run, but where would he go? Better to play it cool. He followed Jorge to the dining area.

Meals at New Beginnings were served cafeteria-style in a small room off the kitchen. Most clients were already seated and eating. He and Jorge got their trays and moved down the short line to get food, without speaking to or looking at each other. Tim's ears were burning and he felt sick to his stomach. Why the hell had he blabbed?

He saw a table with only one available chair. "Hey, Adrian!" he said to an already seated client, walking towards the table as he spoke. He could hear his voice shaking.

"Mr. Tim, have a seat," Adrian said, using his foot to push out the empty chair across from him. "You okay? You're white as a ghost."

"I'm fine," Tim answered, trying to control his voice as he sat down. His armpits stank. He pressed them close to his body, trying to contain the give-away odor of fear. He broke up his eggs with his fork and almost gagged from their smell. He tried to nonchalantly glance in Jorge's direction, only to find a smug-looking Jorge staring right back at him. Tim averted his eyes as quickly as he could. All he could think about was going to prison for real. He had to calm down and figure out how to regain control of himself—and Jorge. But how?

Chapter Three

Tim checked his watch. Two minutes until the afternoon meeting was scheduled to start. He and the rest of the clients were in a semicircle facing one empty chair in front of the fireplace, where Jorge should have been sitting. The fire, usually a comfort magnet for clients, was now a heap of slowly dying embers. Tim hadn't slept much the night before. He kept thinking about how to undo yesterday's conversation with Jorge. Could he "confess" to Jorge that he hadn't really done what he'd claimed, had only been thinking about it and wanted to see how it sounded out loud? Kind of a dry run, so to speak? Tim couldn't stop worrying about all that could go bad. Jorge could talk—tell his friends about the guy he met at rehab who'd ripped off a bank and walked away from it. It could get back to the wrong people. Or Jorge might try it himself. Tim didn't think that was Jorge's style, but who knew? And if he got caught, maybe he'd give Tim up in a heartbeat. Was Jorge that kind of guy? That was the problem. Tim didn't know squat about Jorge, except having overheard someone he lived in the East Bay. He had to get to know him better. He'd planned to do so when they ran together again that morning, but Jorge hadn't shown up. Tim had looked all over the lodge for him and then, thinking Jorge might have started without him, had run the path they'd taken yesterday in reverse. But there had been no sign of the man.

"Where is he?" asked the counselor, smoothing down his goatee with one hand. His irritation was obvious. Tim sensed the counselor didn't care about Jorge, only that things were out of whack. Over two weeks at New Beginnings, and Tim still wasn't sure if the counselor's name was Don or Doug.

"Has anybody seen him?" the counselor asked again.

The clients looked at each other. "Not since breakfast," answered an adolescent looking Hispanic man, who'd arrived just a couple of days earlier. He looked too young to have screwed his life up enough to warrant being in a drug and alcohol treatment program.

"Tim, you ran with him yesterday, didn't you?" said Don/Doug.

How in the hell did the counselor know that? No secrets in this place. Everyone turned to face Tim. "Yeah, and that was the first time we ever spoke. I haven't talked to him since."

The counselor looked up towards the second floor, where the bedrooms opened onto a landing overlooking the first floor. "Hey Jorge, did you go back to bed?" he yelled. No answer.

"All right, you two," the counselor said, pointing to a couple of young men. One was a skinny kid in his late twenties, whose long hair almost covered his eyes. The guy rarely talked and constantly seemed nervous. Tim didn't know much about methamphetamine, but thought the kid fit the image of "tweaker" to a tee. "Go up there and see if he's around."

The two men ran up the stairs and into Jorge's room. One came out immediately and leaned over the banister. "He's not in here, and all his stuff is gone."

The tweaker went into his own room after checking Jorge's. "Dammit!" he yelled. A moment later, he came out and hit the top of the railing. He pushed his hair out of his face, "And I'm missing a leather jacket that had seventy-five *bucks* in the pocket!" His voice squeaked at the end. It was the most Tim had heard the kid say in the ten or so days since he'd checked in.

The other clients stared up at the two men.

"What? He wouldn't take it, would he?" said a young woman, rail thin, her arms covered in tattoos. She wore a too-large tank top, which she clutched at the bottom with both hands. "He seems like a good guy."

"I don't trust him," said another man with finality. Tim detected an accent, but couldn't figure out what it was. "Something about the way he's always studying people, checking 'em out."

Don/Doug put up his hands. "Okay, okay. When did you last see your jacket and the money?"

"I dunno. Three or four days ago?"

"Three or four days. That goes back to Saturday." The counselor held out his hand and dramatically raised his fingers one at a time, counting to himself. "We've had three clients—no, four—check out since then, and two who finished the program. That makes six. *If* somebody stole it, and I'm not saying they did, it could have been any of them." Pointing to the tweaker: "Maybe you misplaced it. Besides what were you doing with seventy-five dollars in your room? You aren't supposed to have more than twenty in your possession."

The kid shrugged. "Guess it doesn't matter now, does it?"

Money in his pocket and a new leather jacket, thought Tim. *Jorge's ready to face the world now.*

"Wasn't he supposed to leave today anyway?" Asked a tall man in his mid-twenties. Tim had observed that his wardrobe seemed to consist of one pair of jeans and two flannel shirts, which he alternated from day to day.

"Yeah," said the counselor. "Soon as he finished chairing the meeting." He pointed to the empty chair in front of the fireplace.

"Then why would he skip if he didn't steal the stuff? Looks pretty guilty to me, man," said flannel shirt.

"That doesn't make him guilty of anything," said the counselor, his fingers again at his chin. "We don't even know for sure that he's left."

"Duh. He's way gone, dude, and he's got seventy-five bucks and my leather jacket," said the tweaker, pushing his hair up and out of his eyes.

Tim knew in his gut the kid was right.

"Should we look for him?" asked a middle-aged woman.

"Yeah, let's take a quick look around." Don/Doug sounded even more irritated than before. Counselors always seemed put out when things didn't go according to plan. Tim shook his head. Jorge was gone, and looking for him was a waste of time.

"I want you to go in twos," said the counselor. "If you've been here less than two weeks, don't leave the patio area outside the back door. Everybody else, check the grounds around the lodge. I want you all back here in ten minutes." He clapped his hands, "Go!"

Clients turned and started outside. Tim hung back, then walked to the back door.

"Hey, Tim!"

Tim stopped and turned towards the counselor. "What?" he said.

"He say anything to you about leaving early?"

"No. What makes you think he'd tell me if he was?"

"Don't cop an attitude, man, I'm just asking. Go look for him."

Tim turned back to the door and headed outside. He went towards the path he and Jorge had run yesterday.

"Doug told us to go in twos," said flannel shirt, who was standing by himself at the backdoor, smoking.

So it's Doug, Tim thought, otherwise ignoring the comment. He walked outside and jogged into the woods, following the path he and Jorge had taken. In a couple of minutes he came to the pond. There were two pairs of mallards on the water, but no Jorge. *Why would he skip out?* Tim stared at the ducks. The thought of going to jail had never really sunk in, never seemed like even a remote possibility. But now...

Tim trudged back. When he returned to the back door, no one was standing outside. He walked into the lodge and the rest of the clients, all seated for the meeting, turned to him. Not surprisingly, the chair in front of the fireplace was still empty.

"I said ten minutes, Tim," said Doug. "Did you find him?"

"You don't see him, do you?"

The two men stared at each other, and Tim knew Doug was sizing him up. *Fuck you,* Tim thought. *Counselor or no counselor, I'm in no mood to be messed with.*

Doug kept his eyes locked on Tim's for a moment longer, then turned to Susan. "How about you, Susan? Aren't you leaving tomorrow? You've worked a good program. Want to speak in Jorge's place?"

Susan smiled and twirled a strand of her long brown hair around her fingers. "Sure, I can do it." She took the chair at the front.

The meeting began with the Serenity Prayer. Tim laughed inwardly at its suggestion to "accept the things he couldn't change." He sure couldn't change having blabbed to Jorge, and the outcome of doing so was way out of his hands. Tim heard little else of the meeting, lost in his own thoughts. *Jorge, you son-of-a-bitch!* He rubbed his forehead, then pounded his thigh with his fist. He looked up and caught the girl with the tank top staring at him.

I can't stay here, he thought. *I just can't.* He did the math—twelve more days until he finished the program. If he waited that long, he'd go crazy from worrying. Tim wasn't sure what he would do if he left, but it had to beat staying here, doing nothing. If he left and his dad found out, there could be hell to pay, but at least he wouldn't be behind bars. Well, probably not. Would his dad really turn him in? He didn't think so. That was a better risk to take than just staying here like a sitting duck. He had no idea what he would do, but he would leave as soon as he could sneak out.

Chapter Four

Danny knew he was compulsively fastidious. He sometimes shaved twice a day and washed his face and hands multiple times. His uniform shirt was pulled taut in the back, loose material folded neatly to keep it from bunching, all of it tucked into his underwear so that it didn't pull out during the day when he moved his arms. He carried a neatly folded hankie in his front pocket, which he used regularly to keep his shoes shined to a bright finish. He was over the top about it, still, anything less made him uncomfortable and grouchy.

"Don't make a mess in my clean car," Danny said.

Sean feigned a choke. "*Your* clean car? I believe we are both responsible for this vehicle, which, oh-by-the-way, belongs to the City of Napa."

Danny signaled a right turn. "I'm just saying, Sean, you've got a recipe for disaster on your lap, what with a chicken sandwich, fries and a shake, all laid out like a picnic."

"Disaster? Look, I *might* get a few crumbs on the upholstery, but I'm betting the Chief won't even hear about it, unless you have to tattle. And anyway, I'm also betting he wouldn't bench me for it."

"Hey, I spent the better part of an hour cleaning this thing. I found so much food I started to make a run to the Food Bank."

Sean started squirming in his seat.

"*Now* what are you doing?" asked Danny.

"Nothing. It's just hard to sit still with you all up my ass."

The squawk of an incoming radio call interrupted them. Sean grabbed the handheld before Danny could get to it.

"Great. You don't have enough going on with your hands, now you're going to hold the radio too," said Danny. He rolled his palms around the steering wheel.

The call was for a disturbance of the peace, a mile or so from their location. Sean accepted it, and a couple of minutes later Danny turned down the street where the house was located.

Like many in Napa, the neighborhood was mostly made up of homes built in the fifties, a lot of them now rentals. Even in the dark Danny could see that more than a few needed maintenance. Locating the address above the front door, Danny pulled into the driveway.

"Did you bring a lawnmower?" asked Sean. He stuffed the rest of his sandwich into his mouth and put the remaining milkshake on the floor.

"Looks like somebody should have," said Danny. The grass was a foot-and-a-half high. He heard a loud male voice coming from the house before he got out of the car. Opening the car door swept the weeds out of his way, but they sprang back defiantly when it shut.

"Sounds like the right place," Danny said.

They put on their hats and grabbed flashlights. If the porch light worked, it wasn't on.

"Kitty, I'm *talking* to you!"

"Actually, you're yelling at her," Sean said to Danny. He knocked on the front door, and the voice quieted.

"Who the hell is it?" The woman's voice sounded like it came from the back of the house.

"Napa Police," he said.

A moment passed, and the door opened as far as the security chain-lock would allow. Danny could see a middle-aged white male, the little hair he had tousled, dressed in boxer shorts and what many referred to as a "wife-beater" T-shirt.

"Is there a problem offishurs?" he asked, almost stumbling into the door as he spoke.

Even standing behind Sean, Danny could smell the booze on the man.

"We got a disturbance-of-the-peace call from one of your neighbors. Could we come in and look around?" Sean had his hands on his belt.

"Who is it?" A woman's voice yelled out from the back of the house.

"It's the police," answered the man. "Shumbody reported a dish-turbance of the peace."

"Who complained?" asked the woman.

"Sir, if you'll at least open the door, maybe turn on the porch light," said Sean.

The man looked startled, as though he'd forgotten the officers were there. "I'm sorry." He closed the door. It sounded like he was struggling to slide the security chain out of its track. He fiddled with it for a few seconds.

Sean rolled his eyes and whispered to Danny, "Should we kick it in?"

"Maybe," Danny answered. "I'm due to retire in another eighteen years, and I don't want to spend them on this porch."

The light flickered on and finally the door opened, revealing a woman, drink in hand, now standing next to the man. She was dressed in all black: tight pants which would have better suited a woman thirty pounds lighter, and a low-cut blouse that revealed ample cleavage. The bangs of her bleached hair reached her eyelids, and she wore a white pearl necklace.

"Who complained? Was it that bitch across the street? She needs to get laid is what she needs," said the woman.

"Kitty, these officers don't wan' anybody yelling," said the man. "Be quiet." He put his unsteady finger to his lips.

"Don't tell me to shut up, asshole." She moved towards the door, yelling "You got a lot of nerve, callin' the cops on us, bitch!"

Sean held up his hand and blocked her. "Ma'am, stay in the house, please. Is there anyone else here?"

"No, it's just us. He's drunk." Kitty turned her head towards her companion, then took a drink.

"Do you think you two can keep it down? If we have to come out here again, both of you are going to jail, do you understand?" asked Sean.

"I'm sho, sho sorry Officers. Id'll never happen again," said the man, his head bowed in an exaggerated show of contrition. "Kitty. Come back inside now."

"I *am* inside, you asshole. Look, we'll be quiet. Don't worry about us. I'll put him to bed.".

"Don't make us come out here again or—I mean it—we'll arrest you both for disturbance of the peace."

"No problem, Officer. I'll make sure he shuts up. Frank, go lay the hell down." Kitty closed the door, not looking at the officers again.

"Guess we showed her who was boss," said Danny.

"Can you believe those two?" Sean turned and took the two steps from the porch to the lawn. The porch light went out behind him. "Mr. and Mrs. Married Bliss."

"They weren't married." Both men had their flashlights on and were walking towards the car. Danny swept the front yard with the beam of his light.

"How do you know that?"

"She wasn't wearing a wedding ring," answered Danny.

"That doesn't mean anything. Lots of people don't wear wedding rings," said Sean.

"Lots of *men* don't wear wedding rings. Women, especially her age, usually do. Plus, she had three, big ole hulking rings on her other fingers. This is a woman who wears all the bling she has."

"You think they're single."

"I think *she's* single. He had a ring on."

"So he's messing around on his wife?" said Sean.

"Well, he *could* be a widower, still grieving over the late missus and not wanting to take his ring off just quite yet. But if pushed, I'd go with him messing around on his wife."

Sean got in the car and Danny followed suit. Both sat still.

"Anything else you pick up on, Detective?"

"His nails were dirty, like he works with his hands. She had long, well-manicured nails, maybe she does office work. But that's not detective work, it's just paying attention, good police work. You should always look at a man's hands, Sean. They tell you a lot."

"Thanks for the lesson," said Sean. "So he works outside, she works inside."

"No, he works inside too. Did you notice he didn't have a tan? If he worked outside, his arms would probably be brown and maybe his shoulders white, but he was white through and through. I'm guessing he's a mechanic."

"Is there more?"

Danny shrugged. "I'm still guessing, but I'll bet she's the office manager at the garage. His wife is either out of town or doesn't care what he does anymore."

"You really are quite the detective, aren't you?" said Sean.

"That's why I applied for the job."

"Where are you with all that?"

"Still at the top of the list. Next time a slot opens, I'm a Napa detective."

"Which you'll turn down, of course, because it would mean the end of this beautiful partnership," said Sean.

"Right. I'd give up the job I've wanted for years, just so I could ride around with you and make calls like this."

"I show you some love, and you have to make it hurt, don't you? You're going to end up a detective someday, and you'll rue the day our partnership ended."

Danny started the car. "Maybe, Sean, but I wouldn't worry about looking for another partner just yet. It could be a long time before that number one spot opens up."

Chapter Five

The Watering Hole, located out by the airport in an unincorporated part of Napa County, opened as a straight bar in the eighties. Jorge had only been there a couple of times, but knew its history. It was his kind of place. Nothing fancy, it offered little in the way of entertainment save for a juke box, pool table and the company of other drinkers. When bars in the city began to showcase DJs, dancing and a greater possibility of going home with someone of the opposite sex, the Watering Hole became less appealing to patrons, and business started to die. It took about six months for it to re-populate as a gay bar, and the frustrated homophobic owner accepted the first offer that was made on it, for considerably less than a more patient seller might have gotten. His last official act after the sale was to climb a ladder and rip down the Watering Hole sign, leaving only a few bent nails and a dark spot where the wooden plaque had been. He left with the sign under his arm, the ladder still leaning against the building. Now unadorned by a signboard, the place was referred to simply as The Hole, a double entendre not lost on the new clientele.

Jorge pulled his Porsche into the Hole's parking lot and found a space in front of the building. With a rag from the trunk, he wiped dust off the front grill and fenders. Leaning down to the side mirror, he checked for particles of food between his teeth, and brushed his short hair in place with his fingertips. It took only a couple of seconds to primp—he liked what he saw as soon as he looked. Straightening, he raised his shoulders up, back, and down. The counselors at New Beginnings wouldn't be pleased about him being here, which brought a smile to his face. He wasn't living his life for them, his boyfriend or anybody else.

For the first time since leaving rehab a few days before, he walked into a bar. He was hungry and low on cash. With luck, he'd run into people he knew, maybe somebody who'd pay for his dinner.

As his eyes adjusted to the inside lighting, he noted that the place had been remodeled since he'd last been in. It looked good: a calculated, masculine, old-west look with roughhewn pine floor and walls. Tin tiles with a dark patina finish covered the ceiling, and a full-sized stuffed Kodiak bear menaced patrons from one corner. It was a man's bar, and Jorge felt good just being there.

There were so many good-looking men inside he wondered if there were any left anywhere else in Napa County. Four guys who could have just left the gym were shooting pool. The best-looking of them, maybe the best-looking guy in the place in his tight jeans, tee shirt and cowboy boots, had just broken a rack of balls and watched as four or five fell in the pockets. Under different circumstances, Jorge would have gravitated towards him. But this outing wasn't about meeting handsome men. This was about a good meal.

Scanning the rest of the room, his eyes landed on Marcus, sitting on a bar-stool next to two other guys. Jorge had met him just before going to New Beginnings, shortly after Marcus had come out. Marcus was a far cry from buffed, instead pliable in the middle and known as a soft touch. The biggest bulge in his pants was from his wallet, which he had a reputation for taking out and opening without much prompting. Jorge's dinner was as good as served. A man at the other side of the bar leaned across it and said something near the bartender's ear, nodding towards Jorge as he spoke. Marcus, his glass at his lips, caught the gesture and turned to look in the same direction. When he saw Jorge, his eyes widened and he lowered his drink.

"Well, I'll be damned. Hello gorgeous!" said one of the two men sitting next to Marcus. He put his hand over his heart, and smiling, began patting it.

Jorge glided to Marcus, gave him a quick hug and sat next to him. "Marcus. What's up?"

Marcus did a double-take and looked towards the stool next to his. He seemed startled to be receiving attention from Jorge.

"Damn, I haven't seen you in a month. Nobody has," Marcus said, his hand now on Jorge's shoulder. "You look *great*. Where you been?" He talked louder than necessary, which Jorge figured was so other men would notice they were talking. Marcus had been chosen, and he wanted others to know it.

Jorge moved just enough to innocuously dislodge Marcus's hand. "I took a little time off from the bars. Clear my head out a bit."

"Yeah, sure. Let me buy you a drink. Bourbon up, right?" Marcus turned to the bartender, his hand raised.

"Nah, not tonight. I'll take a Pellegrino though."

Marcus did what looked to Jorge like an exaggerated whiplash. "*Water?* Seriously?"

"Come on, man. Haven't you ever skipped a day or two from alcohol?"

"Once, when I was eleven and in the hospital getting my tonsils out." To the bartender Marcus said, "Hey, another single malt for me and sparkling water for the beauty queen here." He turned to face Jorge. "You look *great*, man. You seein' anybody?"

Jorge stole a glance at himself in the mirror behind the bar, which confirmed Marcus's assessment. "Sort of, but it doesn't mean I can't look around." His eyes traveled up and down Marcus as he spoke, and he made sure the man caught him at it. Men were so easy.

Marcus brightened and sat straighter on his barstool. The bartender, his shaved head glistening almost as much as the countertop, placed their drinks on the bar. "This one's on me," he said to Jorge. He shook Jorge's hand, leaned into him and gave him a light kiss on the cheek. "Good seeing you again, beautiful. You really light a place up."

Jorge nodded and raised his water to the bartender. He turned quickly back to Marcus, his focus for now. "Truth is, I've been taking pretty good care of myself. Haven't had a drink in over a month."

"You *are* serious. You going to AA and shit?"

"I went to a program and did some meetings there."

"*You* in a program? I can't believe it. I didn't even know you were an alcoholic."

"I don't know that I am. I looked at it as a month-long vacation at a lodge in the country."

"Hey, I thought sober guys weren't supposed to be in places like this." Marcus swept his arm across the room.

"That's what they say. 'Stay away from slippery people and places,' but I'm not really worried about it. Besides, bars are where all the fun is. Where else could I count on running into a drunk like you?" Jorge winked, brushed Marcus's thigh as he spoke, watched as the man gasped for breath.

"Not at an AA meeting, that's for damn sure. Why'd you stop drinking?"

"See what sex is like sober, right?" Jorge laughed.

Marcus choked on his drink. "Holy shit! Do people actually *do* it sober?" Marcus eyed the two men to his left, who seemed to be listening. "I don't think I've ever tried."

"The guy who paid for my program thought it might help us if I was sober. It's not like I was too drunk to get it up, but I figured what the hell."

"Your boyfriend?"

"I'm not sure I'd call him that." It was too early in the evening to have Marcus discouraged.

"You're serious enough about him to give up alcohol, you must be pretty damn serious. You tell me you're monogamous and I'll fall off this stool." Marcus downed half of his drink.

"Nah, it's nothing like that, but I'm having fun. Sex is good and he's got a lot going for him."

"A sugar daddy?"

"Yeah, sort of. He's older, and he's making good money."

"An older guy, huh? Why, man? You could have anybody you want. Hell, you can take me home right now."

"Nice offer, but I'll pass," said Jorge, "at least for now." Let Marcus think anything is possible until after he's bought dinner. "Seriously though, this guy is pretty cool. He looks good. Cut, square jaw, and hung. Like a drill sergeant."

"Oh, I do love a man in a uniform!"

"He's a big man in the community, too. A wheeler-dealer. He's running a bunch of development projects. Main thing, though? He wants to take care of me. I've got a '97 Porsche Boxster in mint condition outside."

"He *gave* you a car?" asked Marcus.

"We'll see. For now it's just a 'welcome home' thing."

"He give you that jacket, too? Nice. Kid leather?"

Jorge thought of the tweaker at New Beginnings as he held out his arm.

"Soft," said Marcus, rubbing Jorge's arm longer than necessary to appreciate the texture.

"It matches the Porsche's interior."

The loud *crack!* of a rack of pool balls breaking and then scattering around the table caught Jorge's attention. He watched as balls fell in the pockets, then he checked out the man who had made the shot. A different guy than the first, but also handsome and cut. The guy was totally focused on the table until he looked up and saw Jorge. Looking away quickly, he slowly and suggestively stroked his pool cue a couple of times. Removing his hand from the cue, he broke into a toothy grin. Looking back at Jorge, he winked and ran his fingers through his hair. Jorge returned the smile. He would make a point of meeting this guy later.

"Do I know him?" asked Marcus.

Jorge switched his attention back to Marcus. "Who? The guy with the Porsche? I doubt it. I don't think you guys run in the same circles."

"Where did you meet him?"

"Gay bar in San Jose. Only he's really in the closet—way, way back there. He lives up here in the North Bay and we met when I was coming back from Monterey. When he found out I lived in the East Bay, he sort of freaked, like that's just a little too close to home for him."

Marcus wrinkled his nose. "Well, that's a drag. So you don't go out in public?"

"Not unless we go somewhere where nobody knows us. But this leaves me plenty of room to roam."

"He's okay with that?"

"He doesn't know. He's jealous, worries that I'm out fucking the entire gay community when he's not around."

"Which, of course, you are."

"Hey, I do what I can." Jorge took a drink from his water and scanned the room. "Truthfully, the jealousy thing is getting old. It seems worse since I've been home. I may move on, stay single a while. I've got to get my life together financially and all."

Marcus turned to the bartender and held up his scotch. "Better keep these coming. This conversation is starting to sober me up."

"No, really. I want to put some things in place, get some money coming in."

"What you got in mind?"

Jorge pictured Tim practically wetting himself after he'd challenged his story during their run together. "I'm still working out the details, but I've been thinking about a kind of a finance/real estate deal to get things started."

"You know, my family's been in real estate for a long time. Maybe I could give you some advice. Come on, let me buy you a drink for old time's sake and we can talk about it."

Jorge put his hand on Marcus's arm. "Nah, really. I'm doing okay like this for a while." Jorge stood up. "Tell you what—you can buy me dinner. You hungry?"

"Really? You and me? Yeah, that'd be great. And maybe we can stop by my place afterwards."

Fat chance, but Jorge would save that disappointment for dessert. He put his hand on Marcus's shoulder. "Yeah, maybe. Let's drive downtown and get some sushi. We'll play it by ear afterwards."

Chapter Six

Tim was somewhere between asleep and awake when he turned over on his side. The slight movement brought on an immediate, pounding headache. In response to the pain, he pinched shut his already-closed eyes more tightly, which only made the throbbing worse. He gasped, and the sudden burst of air rushing into his parched mouth burned his throat. He tried to swallow, but that was even more painful. When he opened his eyes, it took him a second to recognize where he was—his ex-girlfriend's sofa. "Oh shit," he muttered. He tried to sit up, almost puked with the effort, and eased back into the sofa. How did I get here? The last thing he remembered was being downtown, throwing darts in Sam's Tavern. At that moment though, *how* he got there wasn't as important as was getting up and out before Sara found him. Despite his hangover, Tim had to move quickly.

Tossing a blanket off, he saw that his jeans were pulled down around his shoes. His shirt was still on, but unbuttoned. With eyes closed, he grabbed his jeans by the waist and braced himself as he pulled them up. The exertion made the veins in his forehead throb, and he again thought he might throw up. Moving deliberately, he finished dressing, folded the blanket and placed it on the end of the couch. After looking around for anything else that might be his, he started for the front door.

"Where are you going, Tim?" Sara said as she walked into the room.

Tim jumped at the sound of her voice, which set off seismic waves of pain in his head. Sara's arms were crossed, her voice flat and expressionless. Tim hadn't seen her in months but knew her anger well. He flinched, then worried that she might have noticed and tried to play it off. "Oh, hi. I didn't want to wake you. I was trying to be quiet." Tim's mouth was so dry he thought his tongue might spontaneously combust.

Sara dropped her arms to her side and rolled her eyes. "Are you *kidding*?" She stormed to the front window and threw open the curtains.

Bright sunlight flooded the room. Tim squinted and turned away.

"It's ten-thirty, Tim." Sara flipped her hand up to the window as if to prove the point. Her voice was louder now, her anger even more apparent. "I've been up for hours. I doubt anybody in the whole *neighborhood* is still sleeping." She half laughed. "You were trying to sneak out, weren't you?"

Tim stared at his shoes. There wasn't a way to answer that question without making Sara even madder.

"You were plastered when you showed up last night."

"I wasn't *that* drunk." He knew it was a stupid thing to say as soon as it came out of his mouth. He didn't know how he'd gotten here, but Tim didn't imagine that the truth would help his case.

Sara ran her hand through her blonde hair. "Do you even remember coming over? You were shaking the door handle, trying to get in. I thought somebody was trying to *break* in. Then you started pounding on the door, calling my name loud enough for all the neighbors to hear. You could hardly stand up. I had to help you get to the couch. You were trying to take your jeans off over your shoes when you passed out."

So *that's* what happened.

"I'm really sorry I bothered you."

"*Bothered* me, Tim?" Sara scowled. "You wake me at almost two-thirty in the morning, drunk out of your skull, and pass out in my living room. You didn't *bother* me, you scared the *shit* out of me."

"Look I'm sorry, I'll leave." The pain in his throat made talking difficult.

"Oh, stop it. Come eat some cereal or something before you go. You need to get food in your stomach." Sara turned and walked towards the kitchen.

What I need is a cold beer, a little hair of the dog, thought Tim, but he figured it best not to ask for one. Instead, he followed Sara like a scolded puppy.

He was surprised to see a new, wooden kitchen table and chairs, an upgrade from the Formica-covered table and mismatched chairs she'd purchased at a yard sale after college. His mouth was too dry to comment on it.

Sara poured a cup of coffee and put it in the microwave, then opened a cupboard and took out a box of cereal. Tim noticed that she had moved the cereal boxes to a different place and wondered when and why she'd done that.

"You want juice?"

"No. Some water would be good."

He watched as Sara wordlessly opened the dishwasher and took out a glass. "Yeah, I'll bet it would." She filled it and handed it to him. "Cotton-mouth?"

Tim drained most of the glass without answering. The first sip hurt, but it was pure relief after that.

"Do you remember asking me to marry you last night?"

Was she making this up? He couldn't even remember how he'd gotten here. Sara's arms were crossed again. He thought of responses and realized most of what he could say would only make this worse.

"Guess I'm just the romantic type." He cringed as soon as he said it. Sara had turned her back when the microwave went off, but he could see her back stiffen. She handed him the coffee cup, grabbed a bowl and spoon from the dishwasher, and took a carton of milk from the fridge. "Yeah, that's it. That's the second time you've asked me to marry you, and both times you were drunk." She looked up as though considering what she'd just said. "You know what? It gets easier to say 'no' every time." She sat across from him and motioned with her eyes to the unopened box of cereal. "You should eat."

Tim doubted he could keep anything down. The cereal bowl Sara handed him was from a set she'd inherited from her grandmother. Tim had used Superglue to repair this, or another one, a year or two earlier when Sara had dropped it in the sink. That seemed like a lifetime ago.

He stopped pouring milk when the bowl was only a third full, the sight of even that making him queasy. He also figured that the more he had to eat, the longer he had to stay here. Her stare was too much.

"What are you doing, Tim?"

It took Tim a moment to realize that the question was intended in a general sense, not specific to the moment. He thought it best not to tell her that, until three days ago, he had been in a treatment program. This made him think of Jorge, which flooded him with dread, but his hangover was too big to allow much space for worrying about that.

Sara's self-confidence could be intimidating. Tim couldn't imagine her being in a compromised position, certainly not one of her own making. Six months ago his drinking had crossed the line from normal to out of control, which seemed to happen overnight. Sara had treated it as a temporary aberration and had tried to help him for a couple of months. After that, she started going to Al-Anon, and shortly after that, ended the relationship.

"What do you mean?" Tim asked, at a loss for how to answer her question.

Sara shook her head. "Are you working?"

Had it really only been a month since he'd been fired?

"I don't really want to go back to real estate." His stomach flipped. Was it the smell of the milk or the fear of getting caught in a lie?

"You were good at real estate, Tim, until you lost control of yourself. You sold a lot of houses, seemed to like doing it, and people trusted you. Bob would probably hire you again if you quit drinking."

Tim hadn't closed a deal in months. Although he had nothing to show for it, he'd spent all his money and racked up a fair amount of debt. Bob had carried him for a while, thinking he was just in a slump, but when he showed up drunk for a viewing and told the prospective buyers to go fuck themselves, Bob canned him. That was also the day he decided to steal the money.

Tim forced down a second bite of cereal while he thought about what to do. His throat was better, but his head was still pounding, and puking right there on Sara's kitchen floor was a distinct possibility. He needed to leave.

"Just because I can sell houses doesn't mean I like it. I'm not even thirty yet. I don't want to settle for some career that I'm not interested in. I'll find something, and when I do, I'll be as good at it as I was at real estate. Better, even."

Sara looked up at the ceiling and shook her head. "You know, I almost believe that? If you didn't smell like stale beer right now, I might. But you've said shit like that before. It sounds great, and I want to believe you, but it's too risky, Tim. If you quit drinking, I dunno, but now, I can't believe what you say."

Sara's eyes narrowed as she studied him for a moment. Tim squirmed in his seat.

"God, you look like you'd rather be any place but here. Maybe you should leave, Tim."

"Seriously? You mean, leave now?"

"Yeah. You slept it off, so you should go." She made no sign of getting out of her chair.

Tim stood. Ten minutes ago he'd tried to sneak out, but now that it was Sara's idea, he was conflicted. "Okay. Well, thanks for letting me stay here last night."

No response.

"I'll go." The silent walk to the front door seemed to last forever. Once outside, he immediately raised his hand to his forehead and squinted against the sunlight. The sunglasses he reached for were not in his pocket. Thinking he might have left them in the living room, he started to go back in, but thought better of it. His car was parked on the other side of the street, a few houses down from Sara's, the front end blocking about a third of someone's driveway. Head lowered, he hurried to it, hoping to be invisible to the neighbors.

Chapter Seven

Jorge had been driving purposelessly for an hour. He crossed Highway 128 and let the Porsche glide up the road to Angwin. He loved the way the rays of the sun skimmed across the brightly waxed red hood as he took turns. The top down, his foot a little heavier on the gas than was prudent, he felt good. His boyfriend, Julius—his meal ticket—was increasingly annoying, wanting to know where he was and what he was doing all the time. This was unfettered freedom.

The road, well paved and gently curving, had two lanes with pole pines and little else on either side. Driving the Porsche up the steady climb felt more like coasting. Ten minutes later, now in Angwin, he drove around the Pacific Union college campus, checking out the young, buffed students walking and on bicycles. Eye candy paradise.

Jorge looked at the clock on the dash and could see that he needed to hurry if he was to make his dinner date on time. He made a U-turn, and was well above the speed limit in moments, heading back to Highway 128. The windy road might slow him down, but it was a fun drive, especially in the Boxster.

Jorge downshifted into second as he came out of a curve and floored it. The Porsche's rear end fishtailed a little before straightening out.

The car churned through pavement the way a hungry shark goes through a school of fish and, in a few seconds, Jorge was doing seventy again. His boyfriend said Jorge looked sexy behind the wheel of the Porsche and that he was meant to drive it, but periodically reminded him it was a loan. Jorge figured he'd give the boyfriend up a long time before he'd give up the car, but that wasn't a choice he needed to make now. For the time being, he'd pay his dues and have dinner with Julius as planned. He depressed the gas pedal even further.

As he tightened his hands on the steering wheel, he couldn't help but smile. This was a powerful and responsive car. Driving it gave him a rush.

A road sign indicated another curve just ahead. Jorge downshifted at the last second, touched the brakes a couple of times, then turned the wheel. What happened next took only a couple of seconds, but it seemed like an eternity.

The Porsche drifted over the center line into the other lane. Jorge thought he still had control until the car began to glide across the pavement, the rear end skidding towards the front. In a split second, the Porsche was moving sideways, two-thirds of the way into the other lane. The wheels locked up. The car moved like a jet plane in free fall and started to do a full one-eighty. Jorge knew to hit the brakes and the gas at the same time, and the wheels regained traction. He released the gas and pumped the brakes until the car stopped.

Thank God! He sat for a moment, the rush of adrenalin pounding his ears, aware that his quick reaction may have saved his life. From facing the wrong direction, he made a three-point turn, using both lanes. Now facing the right way but in the wrong lane, he stepped on the gas. But before he could get back in his lane, a cobalt blue sports car came around the curve from the other direction, going way too fast and heading straight towards him.

"Shit!" he screamed, straightening his arms, a useless defense against the impending impact. Jorge had no time to react. He knew he was a dead man.

But instead of the expected head-on, the other car swerved and raced past Jorge's Porsche with just a sliver of space between them. Jorge gritted his teeth at the crunching sound made by the side mirrors of both cars as they collided. He heard a crash, looked into his rearview mirror, and saw the other car smashed into a tree on the side of the road.

Jorge stomped on his brakes. The Porsche slid a little, then came to a full and sudden stop. Jorge flopped back into the seat. He was panting, felt his heart pounding, and couldn't fully process what had just happened.

"Fuck, fuck, *fuck!*" He looked around. No other cars were on the road. Looking over his shoulder at the wrecked car, he saw that the rear lights were on. It was a Porsche! He hadn't noticed when it was coming at him. It was definitely speeding big time. *The driver must have lost control when he turned to miss me. This could have easily been his fault.*

Thirty yards from Jorge, the other Porsche's hood was pushed up beyond the roof. Steam from the engine rose above it. Jorge couldn't see the driver, and nothing moved inside the car. *What the fuck do I do now?* He put the car in reverse and began backing up. Suddenly, the other driver's door burst open and an emerging foot landed on the ground. Jorge gasped, jammed on his brakes and came to a stop. Other than the one leg, the driver wasn't visible. *This guy needs help.* Jorge grabbed his phone and got out of his car, but hadn't quite straightened up when another leg swung out of the car and planted itself next to the first. Jorge's heart raced. He watched as the man slowly pulled himself from the car, using the door for support, grimacing as he did. Halfway up, he fell to his knees, paused for a moment, then pulled himself upright. He turned and began moving towards Jorge, dragging one leg as he did. His face was covered in blood, but his eyes were fully visible and staring straight at Jorge.

Jorge got back in his car and closed the door. *Don't let him see your face!* He quickly adjusted his side mirror, which had been pushed in by the impact, and in it he could see in the reflection that the man had a large cut on his forehead, the likely source of the blood that covered his shirt and face. The whites of his eyes, their color a stark contrast to the mask of blood seemed to glow. Startled, Jorge couldn't comprehend what he was seeing until he realized that the guy's eyes must have rolled back in his head. The driver struggled towards Jorge's car a couple more steps, like a headless chicken still on the move, then lurched forward and fell. Jorge continued to stare. The man didn't stir.

Jorge couldn't stop watching him. *He moved – he must be alive!* The hissing of the other car's engine snapped Jorge's attention back to his predicament. A quick check showed that they were still the only two cars on the road. No one had seen the accident. No one.

Jorge turned his head from the wrecked car and looked ahead. *I can't stay here. There is nothing I can do to help. Somebody will see him and stop.* He looked in his rear-view mirror again, but the driver was still on the ground. Jorge ran his hand across his side mirror. The outer edge was rough to the touch, but there was no time to get out and look at it. He shifted into first and began to drive away, checking the rear-view mirror again. *If I don't see anybody else in a couple of miles, I'll call for help.* The speedometer reached forty when a car appeared from the other direction. *Good,* he thought, *somebody to help.* Jorge came to another curve, downshifted, and took it cautiously. When the road straightened, he looked into his rear-view mirror, saw that no one was following him, and sped up. He still had over an hour's drive ahead of him. He had to calm down, put this out of his mind, and collect himself before he met his boyfriend.

Chapter Eight

Tim had to pee. He'd been stumbling around the parking garage for what seemed like an eternity, trying to find his car. There were only three levels to the structure, and he was sure he'd been on all of them several times. But he wasn't *positive*, so he'd gone back to the top, intending to work his way to the bottom while he looked one more time. But first he had to take a leak.

Looking around and not seeing anybody, Tim stumbled between two parked cars. As he did, he lost his balance and smashed his knee on one of the auto's headlights.

"Oh, *shit!*" The pain was immediate. He reached for the injured knee, lost his balance, and fell backwards into the other car. Looking around one more time as he unzipped, he began to urinate. The sound of his pent-up stream bouncing off the pavement was as satisfying as the relief of voiding his bladder. His urine puddled, then rolled under one of the cars with the slope of the garage. Tim closed his eyes and immediately began to get dizzy. He stumbled again and peed on the side of a car. His piss bounced off the automobile's side and onto his pants. *Fuck.* He looked around again, but no one was there to see him.

Zipping up, Tim stepped back from between the two cars. The top floor of the garage was outside, and the sun, though low in the sky, was warm on his face. Exhausted from walking around, his injured knee throbbing, he sat down and nursed it by rubbing it gently. He tried to focus on the cars across from him, hoping one might be his. None of them looked familiar, though it was getting harder and harder to distinguish one from the other. It seemed like a good idea to rest for a minute, then start looking again. Gravity got the better of his eyelids. He rolled over to his side to rest for a moment.

"Hey Mister, are you dead?" The speaker's voice croaked with adolescence.

Tim tried to sit up, but couldn't. When he did open his eyes, two sets of tennis shoes and bare legs filled his field of vision. Rolling his head to the side and lifting it off the pavement, he could see that they belonged to two teenaged boys, each holding a skateboard by the wheels. One of them wore a knit cap, the other had long blond hair. Tim couldn't hold up his head any longer, and let it drop back to the pavement.

"Whoa!" said the blond, leaning over Tim. "It looks like he pissed his pants!"

"Gross," added the other youth, giggling. "This dude is fucked up."

"Totally!" said the blond.

"Fuggid. I'm OK," was all Tim could manage in response. In the shade, he was chilled, and he drew himself into a fetal position.

"What a total wasteoid," said Knit Cap.

"Hey, check this out." The blond bent down, grabbed one of Tim's sneakers and began undoing the laces. "You don't need this, do you, dude?"

Tim kicked his foot in a futile attempt to keep his footwear. "Whad da fug?" He tried to focus long enough to glare at the two skateboarders.

"Want a shoe?" The blond held it out to Tim, then turned and threw it over the tops of a half dozen cars. Laughing, he high-fived Knit Cap.

"Dude, that is hilarious!"

The blond laughed, bent down and yanked Tim's other shoe off, throwing it in the opposite direction. "This fucker won't know shit when he sobers up!" The boy abruptly quit laughing, which confused Tim.

"Get his wallet."

"What? We can't do that," Knit Cap pleaded.

"Don't be a puss. I'll do it." The blond rolled Tim on his side.

Tim flailed a hand towards his back pocket, but couldn't coordinate the move and kept missing. "Fug you, asshole."

The blond burst out laughing. "Fug *you*, asshole!" He took Tim's wallet out of his jeans.

Tim looked up and watched as the kid opened it, laughed, and showed it to his friend.

"There's two dollars here. He doesn't have jack shit." He handed one of the bills to Knit Cap and tossed the wallet to the side. Tim had to squint to see anything. He could make out the blond, looming over him, holding a dollar by the corners. He began slowly pushing and pulling it like an accordion, making it pop when fully opened, all the while staring at Tim. Tim strained but couldn't keep his eyes focused.

"The guy looks a little like your dad." Tim wasn't sure who was talking, but after a pause, he could hear the "snap" of the dollar bill.

"You're right, he does. He's a drunk, same as him, too." Tim could tell it was the blond talking. Of the two boys, he made Tim the most apprehensive. He struggled to focus, hoping that making eye contact with the boys would discourage them.

"This guy's a piece of shit. I'm gonna kick his ass."

A wave of fear overtook Tim.

"What?" said Knit Cap. "Why? That's crazy."

"Let's fuck him up! He won't remember us. My dad never remembers shit the next day."

Tim tried to push himself up, but only got a few inches before collapsing.

"No, dude, fuck that. Let's get out of here."

Tim heard one of the teens drop his board and skate away. He opened his eyes again and saw that the blond had stayed behind.

The kid leaned close to Tim's face. "I'm going kick your ass, and you can't do anything about it, fucker!" He stood up, stepped back and kicked Tim in the kidneys.

The pain was immediate and intense. "Oh, fuck," Tim groaned as he tried to roll away from his attacker.

"Did that hurt?" The blond mocked. He then leaned into Tim and breathed in his face. "I'm going to fuck you up bad."

"Please," was all Tim could manage. He closed his eyes, unable to do anything else.

"Dude, stop fuckin' around, man. We need to leave *now!*" Knit Cap's voice echoed across the garage.

"My friend's a pussy, but I'm not." The blond hissed the words in Tim's ear. Tim moaned as he tried to crawl away.

"Where are you going?" The blond snarled. "You think this is over?"

Tim's cheek burned when his attacker slapped him hard across the face. A second kick followed to the kidneys, then another. Tim gave up trying to move, sobbing softly as he laid still.

"Come *on*, dude. A car is coming. We gotta get out of here." Knit Cap's voice, more plaintive now, reverberated off the walls.

"Lucky for you, huh?" The blond hissed in Tim's ear. He felt another kick, then heard a skateboard drop to the pavement and take off. Tim grimaced and pulled his knees up to his chest. Tears covered his cheeks.

"Hey. Hey! Wake up already!"

Tim felt a hand on his shoulder shaking him. He opened his eyes and found himself inches from a stranger's face. He jerked away.

The man pulled back simultaneously. "You're in front of my car."

A woman stood a few feet behind the man, clutching a shopping bag. Both of them looked nervous, like Tim was an animal that might attack. Tim rolled over and tried to stand. It took all his strength to push himself up. He almost collapsed again from the pain in his side. His mouth was so dry it hurt. He rubbed the side of his face and felt grit from the pavement. "I couldn't find my car and stopped here to rest," he mumbled. It seemed like a ludicrous thing to say, but he couldn't think of a lie that sounded any better. It was dark outside and Tim had no idea what time it was.

The man nodded, seeming to accept Tim's explanation. "Did you look on the other floors?"

"Yeah, I think so. I thought it was up here. Maybe it got stolen."

"Are you sure this is the right garage? The Clay Street garage is a block away."

The *Clay* Street garage. He was in the wrong place! "It might be. I'll check over there, too."

The man stole a glance at Tim's feet, his brow furrowed. Tim looked down and saw white socks sticking out from under his jeans. "Where are my shoes?" He cringed as soon as he said it, his face lowered in shame.

The man moved towards his vehicle and opened the passenger door for the woman.

"Is he okay?" she said as she got in.

The man lowered his voice a bit. "I don't know, but I don't think there is anything we can do about it. He's drunk."

"Duh. That's obvious," she blurted.

Tim was sure they knew he could hear them. He could feel his blood rush to his cheeks. "I'm sorry."

The man kept his eyes on Tim and crossed in front of his car to get to his door. "Please step away from my car," he said as he got in.

Tim moved as the driver started the engine and pulled out of the space, and watched as the man drove down the ramp. He looked at his stockinged feet, turned around to search for his shoes, and received another sharp jolt of pain in his side for the effort. *What the hell's happened?* For the life of him, he didn't know how he'd gotten here. He looked at his watch. *Seven-thirty? I left the bar a couple of hours ago, I think.* He saw what looked like his wallet on the ground a few feet in front of him, and confirmed it by touching his empty back pocket. The simple movement brought on a stabbing pain. Moving slowly to minimize the throbbing, he hobbled to his wallet, slowly bent over, and picked it up. Sliding it into his back pocket, he turned his head to see if anyone was watching him. Then, like a criminal leaving the scene of his crime, Tim limped away.

Chapter Nine

Jorge pulled into the lot and parked. He reached out and ran his fingers against the edge of the side mirror again. He didn't need to see it—it was definitely damaged from hitting the other car. He glanced at his watch: 7:45 p.m. Sixty-five miles in just over an hour. Sixty minutes since that reckless driver had almost killed him. It had to have been the other guy's fault, right? Jorge wondered if the driver had gotten help. If he was okay. Fuck it, there was nothing he could do about it now. He was only fifteen minutes behind schedule but knew his boyfriend would be mad. Best to put it behind him. He avoided looking at the mirror as he got out of the car. What could he do about it anyway?

It was at least fifteen degrees cooler here than in Angwin. The elevation and dense redwood canopy contributed to that, and also made it look like the sun had already set. Jorge started to walk away from the car, but couldn't resist looking at the side mirror. Not as bad as he thought. There was a smudge of the wrong color paint on it, but you couldn't see any roughness. He spat on the spot, used the inside of his shirt tail, and rubbed it aggressively. He managed to remove all but a trace of the offending color. Julius would probably never notice it, and if he did, Jorge would deny knowing anything about it.

The path leading to the restaurant's door was covered in pine needles that crunched under his feet. The *maître d'* greeted him with a smile.

"Good evening, sir. Are you joining us for dinner?"

"Yeah, and I'm running late. I'm supposed to be meeting someone. Tall guy in his forties, gray at the temples?" Jorge looked around the restaurant as he spoke. The ceiling in the room was low, the interior walls were brick. White tablecloths covered the twenty or so tables. A gas-flamed fireplace in the back flickered steadily. He spotted his boyfriend at a table near the hearth and smiled. "I see him, thanks." Julius was staring at Jorge. He wasn't smiling.

"You're late. Again." Julius punctuated his statement by swirling his glass of scotch before taking a drink.

"I'm fine, thank you for asking, Julius." Jorge pulled out his chair and sat down hard. "If you'd pick restaurants that weren't in the boonies, I might make it on time."

"If you'd allow enough time, it wouldn't matter where we meet."

Jorge almost got up and left. It might be easier to get a job and pay his own bills than to put up with Julius's shit. He thought better of it and took a deep breath before responding. "Damn it, Julius. Are you going to start out being pissy? I've never been here before and I've been driving on twisty mountain roads for over an hour. I didn't do it to get bitched at. Would you lighten up a little?"

Julius regarded his drink for a moment, then looked up at Jorge contritely. "You're right. I'm sorry. It's been a tough day and I shouldn't take it out on you. Can we start over? Are you enjoying the Porsche?"

"Thank you. That's more like it." Jorge reached across the table and covered Julius's hand. Julius winced and pulled his hand away quickly, as if Jorge had stuck a fork in it. Jorge chuckled. "Jesus, Julius, we're in the middle of nowhere. Nobody knows you're gay."

"I told you, I'm not gay."

"Oh right, I forgot. And all that sex we have—what is that, anyway?"

Julius ignored the bait. "I'll bet you're hungry after that drive, and this place has *the* best calamari I've ever eaten. I'm going to place an order for us."

"I could do some calamari. Seriously, how do you know about this place? You live like what—eighty miles from here?"

"This place has been here since the sixties, and used to be fairly famous. A couple from church brought me here, probably twenty years ago, and I've been coming ever since."

Jorge scanned the other patrons. Judging by their age, he guessed a number of them had been here for the grand opening. It looked like an old-money crowd. The more closely he checked out the restaurant, the more he could see that the interior was tired. Autographed photos of the same man, probably the owner, in poses with B-list celebrities of bygone years adorned walls covered in dated wallpaper. I'll bet Julius doesn't know a soul here, thought Jorge. He's picked a place where he's anonymous.

"So this is where you bring young men to impress them, eh?"

"This is where I come for a good dinner. It's not about seduction for all of us, Jorge. And we are just two friends having dinner."

Jorge laughed, putting his napkin in his lap. "Yeah, you and me? We look like a couple of old friends, especially here."

"Who's being pissy now?"

Jorge sensed he'd touched a nerve. He threw up his hands in surrender. "Sorry, Julius, whatever you say."

The waiter approached the table. He was attractive, in his early twenties, clean-shaven with short brown hair. "Good evening," he said to Jorge. "Can I get you something to drink?"

Jorge looked up. "I'll have an iced tea, thank you."

"Very good." The waiter smiled and turned to Julius." Another scotch for you, sir?"

Julius's mouth was tight, "Sure. Make it a double."

"Would you gentlemen like to hear about our specials tonight?"

"Bring us some calamari to start with. We'll order when that's here," said Julius.

"Very good, sir. I'll be right back with your drinks."

Jorge pushed his plate away from the edge of the table, straightened his silverware, and looked up at Julius. The man was glaring at him. "What now?"

"Were you checking out the waiter?" Julius polished off his drink.

Jorge slumped in his seat. "Julius, don't start."

"Well, I think he was checking you out."

"He just took my *drink* order, Julius. You think everybody is hitting on me. Let it go, will you?"

"He didn't smile at *me* like that."

"He probably did. Waiters smile at everybody. They get better tips that way, Julius. He's just doing his job."

"I'd just like you to show a little discretion, is all. I don't want you hitting on everybody all the time."

"I wasn't hitting on that guy and he wasn't hitting on me. People look at each other. It's how we communicate. Can you let it go?"

Julius was quiet for a moment. "You're right again. I guess I'm more tired than I thought."

Jorge drummed the tabletop with his fingertips. *You're old, cranky and insecure is what you are.* "You said you've had a tough day. What happened?"

"It's all the construction we're doing. All four projects are coming in over budget and money is getting tight."

"Can't you raise more? That's your specialty, isn't it?"

"I wish it was that easy. Every day there's a line of people who need to get paid, and they all look to me. I spend half my time raising new money to pay old debts. It feels like a never-ending circle."

Jorge waited for more, but Julius seemed to be focused on the fireplace now. He wondered if this was leading to the older man asking him to make financial sacrifices and give up the lifestyle he was learning to enjoy. He'd give up the old man first. "It's all going to work out though, right?"

Julius looked away from the fire. "Yes, but we'll be building for a couple of years and I doubt it'll get any easier." He looked tired. "That's why I wanted to get out tonight. Coming here is a real treat—you'll see as soon as we start eating. Anyway, tell me about yourself. What did you do all day?"

Jorge could see the accident as though it was happening at the next table. He saw the driver of the other car stumble and fall. "Not a lot. I played some ball this morning. I'm in the best shape in years, and my game is all air. I practically live above the rim."

"Excuse me?"

Jorge's smile evaporated. "I'm dunking the ball, Julius. I can come from damn near the foul line and slam it. I'm blocking shots right and left. I get goal-tending calls all the time, but I don't care. My opponent knows I own him."

Julius shook his head. "I wish I could see you play sometime. Just listening to you talk about it, I can feel your passion. What else did you do?"

"Not much. Cleaned my place. Took a shower and came here."

"That took all day?" said Julius. "Did you see anybody?"

You're going there again, aren't you, old man? Jorge thought. "Julius, don't start—"

"Here are your drinks, gentlemen, and some bread." The waiter placed the scotch in front of Julius first. "That calamari will be up in a few minutes."

"Thank you," said Julius.

"I can't believe you," Jorge said, as soon as the waiter walked away. "This jealousy thing of yours is a drag."

Julius looked repentant. Jorge hated it when men showed insecurity, but for now decided to take advantage of a dominant position. "You like it that I live over an hour away from you. When we're in public you won't let me touch you. You're always looking around at everybody else. I think you worry that you'll see someone you know, and then you'll have to explain me. How *would* you explain me, Julius?"

Julius didn't answer him, but ran his index finger around the top of his glass. He looked around the restaurant as if trying to find someone.

"Hello?"

"Sorry. You're right again."

"About which thing?"

Julius stared at his glass, his lips turned up into a slight smile. "About you're living so far away. Maybe it would be better if you lived closer to me."

Jorge sat up straighter and leaned forward. "Am I hearing you right? You think I ought to move closer to you?" He sat back in his chair. "Okay, who are you, and what did you do with Julius?"

"Very funny. Look, I don't think it's working with you living so far away. I get jealous, you get angry and we end up spending too much time fighting. Maybe we should change that."

"What do you have in mind? Are you suggesting I move to Santa Rosa?"

Julius scowled. "No, of course not. That would never work."

"I knew you didn't mean it."

Julius dismissed the accusation with a wave of his hand. "I think maybe you should move to Napa."

Was he serious? Although he had mixed emotions about being closer to Julius, a free place to live in the wine country sounded intriguing. "Napa? Why there?"

"Well, it'll cut the distance between us in half. Plus, you could go to work for me."

Jorge stared at him for a moment, then burst out laughing. "Work for you? Are you serious?"

Julius tilted his glass towards Jorge. "Don't laugh. It's not such a bad idea."

"What the hell would I do for you? I mean, if you're putting together a ball team, I'm your man. But I don't exactly have any marketable skills, at least not the kind most people are looking for."

"You're selling yourself short, Jorge." Julius took a deliberate drink of scotch. "You said you went through three years at seminary, right?"

"Yeah, but that was a long time ago, and it was in Honduras."

"Doesn't matter where it was. Why didn't you finish?"

"I got tossed out for screwing one of the Brothers. Nothing happened to him, by the way, but the church thought it best if I did something else with my life. So, I'm just another college dropout."

Julius pursed his lips. "Still," he replied, "you're great with people. Hell, you're too good with them, but that's a good problem to have. Plus, you've been sober what, a month now?"

Jorge could see Julius's confidence build like a returning tide. "A little over, yeah."

"You could move to Napa. I'm there several times a week, and we'd see each other more often. It would be a lot better than having you in the East Bay."

"Again, that's great and all, but what would I *do*, Julius?"

"I think this is one of the best ideas I've had in some time. I've got just the job in mind for you, but don't worry about it right now. Let's enjoy dinner and the rest of the evening." He took a long drink.

The waiter returned with the bread and calamari. "Here we are, gentlemen. Would you like to hear about the specials now?"

"Thanks, but I know what I'm going to have. I'd like the veal piccata." Julius smiled at the waiter then looked at Jorge. "Can I suggest something on the menu for you? This place is a bit of a drive for both of us, but it has the best Italian food in the Bay Area. You are going to be glad you came."

Jorge chuckled. "You're the man with the plan. Go for it."

Chapter Ten

Tim had surreptitiously checked his watch a dozen times in the past hour. Coming to an AA meeting had been a mistake, but it was almost over, and the beer that would soothe his growing headache was only minutes away.

Hours before, he'd stopped in a tavern intending to have a quick beer. Sitting by himself at the end of a dark, wooden bar, he'd half-heartedly watched a baseball game while peeling labels off the bottles that the bartender had begun to put in front of him without having to ask. A man with empty eyes had stared at Tim from the other side of the bar. Tim put his beer to his mouth, a movement the other man mimicked. Both men took a drink, their eyes locked.

Oh shit!

There was no "other man"—he'd been looking at his own reflection in a mirror partially obscured by a row of vodka bottles. God, did he really look that bad? The undeniable realization that he did nearly shocked him sober, and he'd slid into despair. *Again? How the hell did this happen to me?* In a moment of frustration, he pounded his fist against the bar.

"You okay?" asked the bartender.

Tim briefly made eye contact with the man, attempted a smile and nodded yes. Truth was, the face he had seen in the mirror was the face of a lost soul. Sara was right. He'd been kidding himself, not her, that he had anything under control.

A spur-of-the-moment decision to attend an AA meeting instantly buoyed his spirits, but they plummeted just as quickly, since he knew that going to AA wouldn't be any different this time than it ever was. The last thing he needed was platitudes and God talk. Burning tears blurred his vision. He wiped them away and slammed his beer down onto the bar.

"We're not going to have a problem here, are we?" The bartender had his fists on his hips.

"No, no." Tim had forgotten where he was.

"That should probably be your last one today."

You don't know how right you are, Tim thought. *This should probably be my last one, period.*

Now, sobering up and sitting in a church basement with a roomful of strangers, he'd heard all the talk about a Higher Power he could take. He counted four placards with pithy inspirational messages that he'd seen at every meeting he'd ever attended. People drank mediocre coffee from white Styrofoam cups, grasping for some way out of their despair. Tim knew that empty platitudes weren't going to change anything. Sobriety had seemed like a good idea when he was sitting at the bar, but this, this whole AA scene, wasn't worth it.

Thankfully, the meeting was wrapping up.

Tim dutifully stood, clasped his neighbors' hands and joined them in reciting the Lord's Prayer. Afterward, people released hands and the meeting was over. Tim lowered his head and moved towards the door, hoping for an unobserved exit.

"Excuse me." It was the man who had run the meeting. He was looking straight at Tim.

Busted.

"You want to give me a hand with these chairs?" The man was folding and stacking them in a portable rack.

"Sure." Tim feigned enthusiasm, as though he'd been waiting for someone to ask him.

"Richard," the man said and extended his hand. "We met some months ago when you came in the first time."

Acute pain raced up Tim's side as he shook hands. He'd concluded that he must have been beaten up and robbed while in a blackout in that garage a couple of days ago. He winced.

"Did I hurt you?"

"No, I'm okay," said Tim, trying to play it off as nothing.

"Oh good," Richard said. "It kind of looked like that was painful. Cup of coffee might do you some good. People usually go to the old diner down the street after the meeting. Want to join us?"

"Uh, thanks, but I've got something I've got to do," Tim said, pointing to the door with his thumb.

"You think you could get a cup of coffee first? It's just a few blocks away. I was hoping we could talk." Richard reached for the chair Tim had folded and added it to the rack.

Talking to Richard was the last thing Tim wanted to do. Then it occurred to him that if he didn't go, he would get a beer instead, which probably wasn't such a good idea. "Well, maybe just for a few minutes."

"Perfect. If your side hurts, I can give you a ride. Can you get those empty coffee cups on the table behind you?"

Tim froze for a moment, confused by the quick segue, then turned around and picked up three Styrofoam cups that had been left on a table. "Yeah, I guess a ride would be great. I can't stay long though."

"Yeah, you said." Richard put the last chair in the rack. "All done. Let's head out."

Richard's Volkswagen van was three different colors on the passenger side alone. I might not believe in God, Tim thought, but it's going take a prayer for this thing to get out of the parking lot. He was surprised when it cranked right up.

Richard pulled into traffic. "So how long you been out this time?"

"Excuse me?"

"Drinking," said Richard. "How long have you been drinking this time?"

"I don't know. Not that long."

"You look bad."

"What did you say?"

"I don't mean to be rude, but it hasn't been that long since I saw you last. I'll bet you've lost fifteen pounds. Your eyes are puffy and red, and your skin is blotchy. You keep putting your hand on your side like something hurts, you're limping, and your breath smells like stale beer."

Tim leaned against the car door. "This is what you wanted to talk about?"

Richard checked his side mirror, turned on his left signal and changed lanes. "I'm sorry, man. I'm not trying to be a jerk. I know it sounds harsh, but you don't look so good."

Richard pulled into the parking lot of the diner and turned off the engine. "Come on, I'll buy your coffee."

Tim hadn't been in this restaurant since he was in college. The floor was still black and white checkerboard. A row of booths ran along the front window, each with a small jukebox mounted on the wall, inches above the red Formica tabletop. He and Sara used to come here at the end of a night to have breakfast and talk. Those had been happier days all the way around.

A couple sat at the counter opposite the booths, only one of which had diners. The freestanding tables in the middle of the restaurant were empty.

"Huh. I don't see anybody else from the meeting. Guess it's just you and me tonight."

Was this a set-up?

They had barely sat down when a waitress came to the table. "Hello," she said to Richard with familiarity. "What can I get you guys tonight?"

"Hi, Alice. Cup of coffee for me, please."

Alice looked at Tim.

"Yeah, me too."

Alice turned her attention back to Richard. "We've got a couple pieces left of that chocolate cake you like so much. You guys want them?"

Richard puckered his lips. "Sounds good to me. Tim, you want that other piece? It's homemade."

"Yeah, sure, and black coffee." Tim looked at the door. He could wolf down his cake in a few minutes if talking to Richard got to be too uncomfortable.

"I'll be right back with your coffees." She turned and left.

Folding his hands in front of him, Richard turned his attention back to Tim. "I love cake, but it always reminds me of one of my last drunks."

"What do you mean?" asked Tim.

"I was dating this woman who lived with her kid in the East Bay. She'd started to think my drinking was a problem, and that I should quit. What I *quit* was going to her place as much. I'd stay home and drink by myself for a few days, then sober up and go to her house."

At least I don't drink alone, thought Tim. Then he remembered seeing his face in the mirror at the bar. Well, *most* of the time.

"Sometimes I'd shave it a little close," Richard continued. "You know, quit drinking a few hours before going to her house so that by the time I got there I'd be sober. That didn't always work."

The waitress returned with two cups of coffee. Richard absent-mindedly poured sugar into his, then seemed to lose himself in the act of stirring.

Tim looked at the selection on the jukebox until he realized that Richard had stopped talking.

"What does that have to do with cake?"

"Right. Sorry." Richard put his spoon alongside his coffee. "So her daughter turned eleven, and my job was to get the birthday cake for her party. Day of, I thought I'd have a few beers, then go to the bakery. I was getting ready to go, and decided I could probably drink another one first. I mean, getting the cake then driving to her house—that could take, what, an hour? How bad could my breath smell after that?"

"I'm guessing bad enough that she could tell," said Tim.

"Worse. By the time I get over there, I'm almost two hours late and wasted. I go staggering in the living room with this cake. I must have looked scary or something. Two kids start crying right away. I start singing Happy Birthday, then tears start running down my girlfriend's daughter's face. I don't know what's happening and I yell at her. 'What's wrong with you? You should be happy that I got you this cake.' My girlfriend moves towards me real fast, and I swerve out of her way. And I drop the cake." Richard stopped talking and took a sip of coffee.

"Cake goes everywhere, on the furniture, on the kids, all over the place. Everybody freezes. It's like graveyard quiet. Then almost all the kids start crying."

At least I wasn't that bad, thought Tim.

Richard nodded his head "yes" for a moment, looking away. Tim could see that his eyes were moist.

"Man, you don't know. My girlfriend kneels down and tells the kids everything will be okay, she's going to get something to clean it up, and in a real calm voice asks me to come in the kitchen. I follow her in there and she turns on me so fast I thought she was going to hit me. In one of the quietest, angriest voices I've ever heard, she tells me to get out of her house. She's talking between gritted teeth, says she doesn't want her daughter to be around a man like me. I start to say something about helping to clean up the cake. She cuts me off, gets even more in my face and just hisses. 'Don't say a word to me. Just get the hell out of here and don't ever come back. Ever!'"

"Wow. What did you do?" asked Tim.

"Are you kidding? I got the hell out of there. I've never felt so low in my whole life. That's the last thing I remembered until the next morning when I woke up at my place. I have no idea how I drove home."

Tim remembered how bewildered he'd felt to wake up on Sara's couch. "Is that when you quit drinking?"

"Quit? Hell, I didn't get sober for another six months. I *tried* to stop but I couldn't string together more than three or four days at a time. I even went to an AA meeting, but I didn't go back for months."

That got Tim's attention. "Why did you stop going?"

"To AA? God. I mean, God didn't make me stop going—but all the talk at the meeting about God did. I felt sorry for people, having to rely on some crutch like that. People kept telling me that AA wasn't religious and that I didn't have to believe in God, but it's hard to swallow that and then hold hands with a bunch of strangers and say the Lord's Prayer. I mean, *please*. That's as Christian as it gets."

"That is *exactly* what bothers me. Every single meeting, it's nothing but God talk. Why did you go back?"

"Because I couldn't quit drinking, and I was miserable all the time. I mean, suicidal- miserable. I hated the idea of going to AA again, but I didn't know what else to do."

"Was it any different?"

"No, same as before. God, God, God. After a few weeks, I decided I couldn't take it anymore. I couldn't go to AA, and I knew that meant I couldn't stop drinking."

"But you *did* stop, right? What happened?" Tim almost pleaded for an answer.

Richard stirred his coffee before answering. "I went home after what I figured was my last AA meeting, thinking I was screwed. Had no idea what to do. I was pacing the floor, crying, totally lost. Then all of a sudden, in an *instant*, I got filled with God." Richard eyed Tim for a moment, then shrugged his shoulders.

"What do you mean, 'filled with God?'"

"I don't know how else to say it. In a split second I realized that my life was a mess, but it wasn't about drinking, it was about God. I went from feeling overwhelmed with hopelessness and fear, to feeling completely, utterly, *totally* calm. And I knew as surely as I've ever known anything, that the feeling I had was God. I didn't have any idea what was going to happen next, but I knew that everything was going to be all right. In that instant, I was completely changed, and I totally believed in Him. Or Her. Whoever." Richard shook his head like he still couldn't believe it. "And here's the kicker—I had no idea what I meant by 'God.' I could have gone out to a street corner and started preaching—I was *that* sure of what I had just felt—but I wouldn't have had a clue what to say. Still, I knew that somehow, someway, I was going be okay, and it was because of God. And I haven't had a drink since then. I haven't even *wanted* a drink."

"Here's that cake, guys." Alice stood at the table with two plates.

Tim had forgotten all about the dessert.

Richard smiled broadly. "Thanks, Alice." He grabbed his fork and pointed to his dessert. "You are going to like this."

Tim scrutinized Richard. "Yeah. So now you believe in God, just like everybody else?"

Richard spoke with his mouth full. "No. I don't really have a clue what anybody else believes. And, I don't care. I just know that there is a God, and that's been enough to keep me sober for the past eight years."

"Do you go to church?"

Richard chuckled. "Why would I go to church? That's got nothing to do with it."

"What about AA?"

"What do you mean?"

"Well, if you lost the desire to drink, why do you bother to go to meetings anymore?"

"Because those rooms are full of hope and laughter, and it inspires me. Before, when I went? I was looking for reasons not to like anything. Then I started really listening to people and realized that most of them are real, honest and sincere. Sometimes I hear the same thing over and over, but if I stop judging it, I feel better after I've been to a meeting."

Tim was at a loss for words. Richard didn't even *look* the same to him anymore, like he had somehow changed since they'd sat down. Then he realized it was *he* who wasn't the same. He felt closer to Richard than he could remember feeling to anyone. He trusted the man. And he wanted what Richard had, whatever he had to do to get it.

"I don't know what to say, Richard. Thanks for sharing all that."

"Yeah, you're welcome." He took another bite of his cake. "You going to eat that, or can I have it?"

Tim dutifully took a bite. "Wow, you're right. This is good."

"Told you."

Tim nodded.

"You ready to get sober Tim? I mean, for good this time?"

Tim considered the question, admitting to himself just how hopeless he'd felt in the bar. "Yeah. I guess maybe I am."

Richard sipped his coffee. "Good. Eat your cake. We've got a lot to talk about."

Chapter Eleven

Danny carefully lifted the sheets, so as not to wake Carol, and slid into bed. It had been a long night at work, and he was beat. He paused for a moment, listened to her breathing to make sure she didn't wake up, then moved closer to her. He leaned down and smelled the back of her neck. How anyone could sleep as deeply as she did was beyond him, but he liked having time like this, when he could simply appreciate her.

When he got home from the station, he went straight to the bedroom, took off his clothes and left them on the floor by the dresser. His shift had been slow, only two tickets issued for traffic violations to sober drivers and without incident. Cops joked that slow nights meant a potentially longer life for policemen, if the boredom didn't kill you first. Slow nights drained Danny's energy far more than busy ones. Napa was a relatively low-crime city, and boredom often hitched a ride in the back seat of patrol cars.

He spent a minute or so observing Carol. She stirred when he rested his hand on her shoulder and he lifted it until she settled. She began to gently snore. To Danny, it was the sound of innocence, an attribute in short supply among the people he encountered at work.

That it was so natural in Carol fascinated him. Her snoring sometimes woke him but never bothered him.

If his ex-wife had snored or done anything to interrupt his sleep, Danny would have used it against her like a weapon. Sadly, it was only the fights with her he remembered. They had committed to spending the rest of their lives together, but after four years he didn't know who she was. He didn't even know her enough to really miss her, but was sorry they had been so hateful to each other. With Carol, it was the polar opposite. Danny had never loved anyone as much as he loved her. He'd known Carol at a distance for years, as a friend of his ex-wife. He hadn't known her well, but he'd always liked her, in part for her directness. She paid attention. He could tell from the way she looked at people, really looked, when she was listening. He could never tell if his ex was listening to anything he said.

He hadn't seen or thought about Carol for ages when they'd run into each other, both alone, in the ticket line at the movies some months earlier. Tall, slender, and gym-buffed, Carol wore her hair long and used very little make-up. Danny thought she looked real. They chatted briefly, and he decided to join her and watch the movie she'd come to see, instead of the one he'd come for. Having company was nice, and they'd gone out for coffee afterwards.

"Have you started dating again?" Carol had asked him.

"A couple of times, different women each time. It seems really weird."

"I'll bet. Good or bad, you were married for four years and you knew what to expect. It's awkward when you don't."

"That's for sure. I know she's your friend and all, but I didn't even like her by the time it ended."

"It's okay. I haven't talked to her in over a year. It doesn't have anything to do with you, but I don't really miss her."

"Everything was predictable—including conversations and fights—and in a strange way that was comfortable. Now, even with women I like I'm a little on edge. Like I'm worried I'll say something stupid. I feel like I'm in high school."

"Well, here's a secret, Danny—women feel that way too, you guys just don't know it. So we can coast a little, watching you squirm. Some of you are cute about it, though."

After that, they had dinner together occasionally, but it didn't feel like dating. Danny simply enjoyed her company. He could relax even when neither of them was talking, instead of feeling like he had to fill the dead space. When they sat close together, he could smell comfort in her hair. They laughed. Things changed the time she took his hand in hers, though only for a minute, and he realized they were more than just friends. It had happened naturally, effortlessly. He loved that.

Carol stopped snoring. Danny waited. She stretched without waking, then exhaled deeply. He thought back to a conversation she'd initiated when they were starting to get serious. It had been after a matinee, and they'd stopped in a restaurant for a quick bite to tide them over until dinner.

"It occurred to me that you might want to have sex," Carol had said, bringing a bite of salad to her mouth.

"Wha-?" Danny dropped his fork. Lunging to catch it, he only succeeded in knocking a little salad off his plate.

"I'm sorry, that was abrupt, wasn't it?" Carol looked him straight in the eyes.

"Abrupt? No, not at all. I mean, sex talk makes sense after a good chick flick, right?" Danny took off his baseball cap and rubbed his hand over his head. "I'm sorry, I don't mean to sound like a jerk, I just didn't see that one coming," he said.

"I apologize. And I didn't know the movie was going to be that bad. You were very gracious to sit through the whole thing. Anyway, the way things are going with us, I just thought it might be time to talk about sex."

"Yeah, sure, I almost brought it up myself."

Carol laughed. "You're cute, Danny."

Danny glanced at the surrounding tables to see if any of the other diners were listening. There were a few other occupied tables, one only a few feet away, but no one seemed to be paying attention to them. "Yeah, that's me."

"I'm sorry, am I wrong? You don't want to have sex with me?"

"No. Yes. God, I don't know! What are we talking about here?"

Danny looked back at the family sitting a few tables away. They were too far away to overhear. Still, even the remote possibility made Danny nervous. An expressionless girl he guessed to be about four years old was staring straight at him. Furrowing his brows, he unsuccessfully willed her to look away.

"I'm embarrassing you," Carol said softly, looking down at her plate.

"No, no. I'm not embarrassed," he lied.

"This is a little embarrassing for me, too."

"No, you just caught me off guard. I'm not used to talking about sex until dessert." Danny said, hoping humor would help him regain his footing.

"Look, we've been going out for a while now and I think it's going pretty good. Sooner or later it's going to be time."

Danny couldn't believe how relaxed Carol seemed. He had never had a conversation like this. Sex had always just happened when it happened. "I'm sorry. Cops are trained to listen to words and nonverbal clues at the same time, but I think I'm way out of my league here. I've never had a conversation like this."

"No, *I'm* sorry, Danny. I'm making you uncomfortable, and that's the last thing I want to do. I've never had a conversation like this either, but I like you. A lot. It's just that every time I've been with somebody I like and we start to have sex, it kills it." She continued to eat her salad, seeming completely at ease.

Danny sat for a few seconds, hoping Carol would offer more explanation. She didn't.

"What exactly do you mean, 'Kills it'?"

"The relationship. It starts out great, but after a while I get uncomfortable. I get scared, I guess. I'm not really sure. I just don't seem to be able to have sex with people I really like without it screwing things up, so to speak." She laughed, a little nervously, as she took a sip of tea.

"But you seem so…together. I mean, just being able to bring this up is amazing to me."

"Trust me, Danny. I've been working up the nerve to have this conversation. So how do you feel?"

"Well, I…I don't know what to say to that. I like you too. I didn't think we would be dropping to the floor and doing it right here, but yeah, I figured that sooner or later we'd have sex. But you're saying that if we do 'it', it'll be the end of the relationship. I don't know what to do with that."

Carol nodded her head and brushed a strand of hair behind her ear. She had a half dozen bracelets on, which slid towards her elbow when she raised her arm. "It's a conundrum, all right." She took another bite of her salad. "What do you want to do?"

If someone pulled a gun and started shooting up the place, Danny would have known exactly what to do. This whole conversation, however, had him at a loss. "I don't know. Is there a manual or something for this?"

She laughed. "I like what we have. It's easy with you, Danny. I know it's my problem and in the past I've tried to fix it by myself, but it's never worked. I've talked to girlfriends, therapists, even my priest once."

How do you talk to a priest about sex? Danny wondered. *And, why would you?*

"I'm really sorry to lay this on you, but it's going be our problem if we have sex, so I figured we could try and deal with it beforehand. Together."

Danny had picked at his salad for a moment. "Look I don't know what to say right now. My marriage didn't end in divorce because of our great communication skills, and I can only blame my ex for half of it. We talked a lot, but not *about* anything, and neither of us were good listeners. We *never* had a conversation like this, not even close. I like that you and I are, but it's awkward for me."

"If it makes you feel any better, this is very awkward for me, too."

"I like you Carol, and I want us to work out, but I don't even know how to make a relationship work when the sex is easy." Then, reaching across table, "Do you think we could survive a little hand holding while I let this soak in?"

Carol had smiled and put her hand into his outstretched palm. "Yes, I think we can. I'd like that."

Watching her sleep, almost a year after that lunch, Danny thought about how much she meant to him, and his eyes watered. Just as she had promised, sex, initially loving and easy, became difficult for her and she had pulled away. But even then, they had talked about what was happening instead of hiding in silence. Eventually, Carol allowed herself to trust him, and it had brought them closer together. As she'd grown more comfortable and begun to fall in love with him, he'd gotten scared, and it had become her turn to support him. It wasn't perfect, and sometimes they fought. But they always made up, listening to each other to understand.

He closed his eyes, breathed her in, and fell asleep.

Chapter Twelve

The thud woke Danny. He rolled towards the sound and watched Carol, at her bureau, use her foot to stop a jar of cold cream that was on the floor and rolling away from her. She was in a slip, probably getting ready for church. He glanced at the clock radio—8:00 a.m.

"Good morning," Carol said, looking at him in the reflection of the mirror as she slipped an earring through a lobe. "You got in late last night."

Danny turned on his back and drew Carol's pillow onto his chest. "Two o'clock. Nothing happened all night until about eleven fifteen, then we got called for a party that was too loud for the neighbors, and after that had to take a couple of intoxicants to Detox. By the time we finished the paperwork and got out of uniform…"

"Why don't you skip church and go back to sleep?"

Danny paused for a moment. "Miss church? And risk eternal damnation? No way."

"All those years of missing church, and you think one more Sunday is going to make a difference? Get some sleep. I'll say a prayer for you."

Occasionally, Danny saw Carol as though for the first time. She looked small, vulnerable, but he knew her to be one of the strongest women—hell, people—he'd known. Being on the streets with bad guys everyday didn't faze him, but walking into a classroom bubbling over with eight-year-old energy was more than he thought he could handle. Yet she'd walked into such a classroom every day for ten years.

Danny tossed the covers aside and got out of bed. "Thanks for the support, but I probably need to go to church and plead my own case. Can't hurt, right?" He walked past her towards the bathroom, and guessed she was looking at him. He liked that she liked to see him naked. He stopped, clinched and released his butt cheeks a couple of times.

"Very cute, Officer," she said behind him. "If you're going to church with me, strut your stuff on into the shower."

The smell of bacon cooking hit Danny as soon as he got out of the shower. He toweled off, threw on a robe and walked to the kitchen. Passing the stove, he grabbed a piece of bacon and bit it in half.

"Hey, can you wait for me to finish cooking before you start eating? I might want some too, you know," Carol said.

"Ooh, feisty. I like that in a woman. Want me to pour juice?"

"Please."

"You didn't hear me come in last night?"

"I guess I was out."

"You know, that worries me a little. A man, armed no less, walks into your bedroom, gets in your bed, and you don't even know it. What if I was some perve?"

"Might be interesting."

"Ha ha. Are you making scrambled eggs?"

"No, you are making such a sacrifice, going to church and all with so little sleep, that I made you an omelet." Carol put a plate in front of him. "Eat up though. We need to leave in about twenty minutes."

Even though Carol usually seemed relaxed, Danny could still discern her shoulders drop and her face soften a little every time she walked into church. She told him the high, vaulted ceilings, stained glass windows and hymnals made her feel safe, closer to God. Danny was a little freaked out by it all. The building, and especially the thunderous pipe organ, reminded him that he was a lowly, insignificant sinner in the eyes of God.

The service over, the organist played as the acolytes and priests began the recessional. Danny and Carol exited their pew and followed them out. Danny didn't like sitting in the second pew from the front, Carol's favorite place, but it did get them out of church quickly. Danny leaned into Carol as they walked down the aisle. "He was on fire this morning, wasn't he?"

"Danny, stop it." She nudged him in the ribs. "People can hear you."

"Over that organ? Are you serious?"

Father Keenan greeted everyone at the back of the church. "Well, good morning, you two," Keenan said as Danny and Carol approached him.

Father Keenan was a slender man in his mid-sixties with thinning gray hair. His Adam's apple bobbed up and down against his clerical collar when he spoke, which Danny had pointed out to Carol. She'd told him it was tacky to mention it, even to her. But he could tell she stole glances at it when speaking to him.

"Top of the morning to you, Father," said Danny. "Another great service, as usual."

"Morning, Danny. I'm sorry if I kept you awake during the sermon."

"Oh, no problem, Father. I slept like a baby."

"Danny!" Carol punched him in the arm.

"I'm kidding, Father. I had my eyes closed but I heard every word, and it was first rate."

"It really was a good sermon, Father," said Carol. "I'll tell Danny all about it on our way home."

"Oh, now I get it from both of you, eh? I swear, I'm going to the Baptist church next week," Danny said.

"Ah, Danny, you're a good lad. Why don't you two stay for some coffee and pastries? I'll be in the parish hall in a moment."

Carol slipped her arm inside Danny's as they walked along the gravel path towards the hall. In contrast to the church with its gothic twin spires, the parish hall was a modern, one-story building.

Carol squeezed Danny's bicep. "I love you, Danny."

"I love you too. I may just keep you around awhile."

"Oh, I just melt when you get all mushy like that." Carol held Danny's arm as they walked. "You *were* falling sleep, weren't you?"

"Yeah. I was trying to fight it, but he lost me about the time the shepherd lost that sheep. I can't believe Keenan busted me like that."

A young Latino couple was walking towards them. The guy looked like he was on a mission, nervous determination ruling his face. "Do you know these two?" asked Danny. Now sure they were joining Carol and him, he nodded hello.

"Excuse me? Officer Garcia?" the man said.

"Yes? I'm sorry, have we met?"

"No, señor. I am Miguel Rodriguez."

Danny shook the man's hand. "Carol Summers, Mr. Rodriguez."

"Call me Miguel. It's a pleasure to meet you both. Allow me to introduce Maria Hernandez, my fiancée." He beamed as he put his hand on Maria's back. Rodriguez turned to Danny. "Señor, I hope I am not being rude and I am sorry to bother you, but could we speak for a moment, privately?"

"Call me Danny." He turned to Carol and Maria. "We'll see you in the parish hall in a few minutes, okay? Miguel, shall we walk?" Danny gestured towards the church.

Rodriguez walked to a small garden with two benches in front of it. He rubbed his palms together before speaking, his brows furrowing as he spoke. "It's a beautiful day, isn't it?"

Rodriguez seemed to be losing his earlier resolve.

"Yes, it is. What did you want to talk to me about?"

Rodriguez looked to each side. "Señor Garcia—"

"Please—Danny."

"Yes, Danny. Maria and I are getting married.

"Yes, you said. Congratulations to you both."

"Thank you."

"I'm not sure how I can help."

"We are going back to Mexico to get married. Most of our families live there. They don't have a lot of money to travel here, and it's important that they are at the wedding."

When Rodriguez didn't immediately continue, Danny didn't respond. He could tell the man was nervous and didn't want to rush him.

"Well, you know how the church is about marriage counseling before the ceremony," said Rodriguez.

Danny didn't have a clue how the church was about marriage counseling before the ceremony, but kept that to himself.

"We thought it would be easier to talk to a priest here at the church so we would be ready when we went to Mexico. Lots of people do that." Rodriguez waved his hand as if to dismiss what he'd said. "I'm sure you know that."

Danny nodded.

"So I asked the new priest here, Father Morales. You have met him?"

"No, actually I haven't."

"He's only been here a few weeks and usually does the Saturday service, which is mostly Latinos. I asked him if he could perform the counseling and provide us with a letter to take to Mexico. He shook his head like he was going to say no, then he said he would, but wanted four hundred dollars for it. In cash."

"They charge for that kind of thing?"

"No señor, not to my knowledge. I have other friends who have had counseling, and none of them have been charged. And he insisted on cash."

"Huh. I wonder why that is?"

"I don't know. I am not trying to cause any trouble for anybody, Officer, but it seems a little strange, and I wondered if you knew anything about it."

From señor to Officer. "Are you asking me as a policeman? I don't have any jurisdiction over what the church does unless a law has clearly been broken. I don't know if that's the case here."

Rodriguez fidgeted a little. "I am asking you because you are an officer and Latino."

Danny could feel himself blush. He probably had more in common with Carol's Anglo upbringing than Rodriguez's Mexican home life. "I can ask him about it and let you know what he says. Would that be appropriate?"

Rodriguez exhaled while shaking his head no. "I—I'm not sure, señor. I don't want to cause any trouble. That might not be good for us, especially Maria?"

Is he asking me or telling me? I wonder if Maria is illegal? Danny raised his hand. "I understand, Miguel, and I promise not to do anything that will cause you or Maria any discomfort. Give me a few days to look into this quietly, and I'll get back to you, okay?"

"Are you sure that's okay? I don't want to cause you any trouble."

"Truth is, I'm a little curious myself. Between you and me, I might need marriage counseling, and it would be good to know for myself. I'll ask for my own sake, okay?"

A broad smile covered Rodriguez's face, and he shook Danny's hand. "I knew you'd know what to do. Thank you, señor, thank you."

Danny and Miguel walked back to the parish hall. After a cup of weak coffee and a donut so stale Danny wondered if it was left over from the previous week, he and Carol said goodbye to Father Keenan and left. Carol took Danny's arm and draped it over her shoulders as they walked outside.

"Look at those Naked Ladies." Carol motioned with her head towards a stand of the tall stalks, each adorned with pink flowers. The plants started in the spring as bushy clumps of green leaves that died away without blooming, only to later yield the isolated stalks with pink blossoms in early autumn. "They are one of the last blooming plants of autumn. I love this time of year."

"You know they're poisonous, right? Also known as Belladonna?"

"Always Mister Negative."

"Well? I'm just saying…"

"What did Miguel want to talk to you about?"

"He thinks you are the most beautiful woman he's ever seen, and wanted to know if he could make a play for you."

"What did you tell him?'

"I told him you were pretty high maintenance, and I think it scared him off."

"Very funny. If it's none of my business, just tell me."

"Well, it probably isn't, but I wanted to talk to you about it anyway. Let's get in the car."

Danny strapped on his seatbelt before starting the engine. "Rodriguez and Maria talked to the new priest—Father Morales? I haven't met him. He does the Saturday Spanish service. Anyway, like all good Catholics, they're supposed to have marriage counseling from a priest and asked Morales if he'd do it."

"Maria told me the same thing."

"Did she tell you he wants four hundred dollars, in cash?"

Carol opened her mouth but words didn't immediately follow. "Oh my God, *that's* what happened. She was telling me about the counseling and said if they went to Mexico it would be cheaper. I didn't understand what she meant."

"Well, that's it. Miguel thought it was weird. He figured since I'm a cop he could talk to me about it." Danny chuckled. "And here I am blabbing it to you."

"It's not funny, Danny. The church doesn't charge for stuff like that. That's extortion!"

Danny stopped at a stop sign. "Extortion is a pretty strong word. It may not be kosher, or whatever the Catholic version of that is, but he's not breaking any laws."

"Still, I think Maria might be here illegally, and that priest might be taking advantage of it."

"Did she tell you that? I kind of got that impression from Miguel."

Carol looked out her window as she spoke. "No, it's just a hunch. Danny, what are you going to do?"

"I dunno. Want to get some lunch and drive out to the beach?"

"Now?"

"Yeah. Anyway, that's what Miguel wanted to talk to me about. He needed to bounce it off somebody, but he's clearly nervous, which made me wonder if he was worried about Maria's status. I told him I'd look into it on the QT."

"That's a good idea. Maybe you can stop it."

"Yeah, I'll talk to Keenan. I'm halfway expecting it to be a big misunderstanding that can be cleared up quickly. I mean, why would a Hispanic priest take advantage of another Latino being here illegally?" Danny pulled into the driveway and put the car in park. "So what do you think of going to the beach?"

"That's a very good idea, Officer. Let's pack a lunch, spend the afternoon. We can take a nice long walk."

"I hate to say this, but I was thinking more about a nice long nap in the sun."

Carol reached over and placed her hand on his shoulder. "Okay, Mr. Romantic—let's go nap on the beach."

Chapter Thirteen

Danny found a great deal of comfort in the law. An action was legal or illegal, punishable or pardonable, and that was it. Outside of the law, things got fuzzy. There, in legal no man's land, behavior could be despicable, wrong, or even immoral without there being any consequences. That kind of unaccountability was disturbing, and made Danny angry.

If Father Morales had tried to take advantage of a parishioner by asking for money for church services, it was a church issue. There was nothing the law should or could do about it. Danny had no control or assurances what, if any, actions the church might take in the situation. He would follow up on the accusation because he had agreed to, but he would prefer not to.

It was close to 3:00 p.m. a couple of days later when he pulled his truck into the church driveway to visit Father Keenan. The church was on a five-acre lot that a parishioner had willed to the diocese in the 1930s. Buildings and parking lots filled three-quarters of an acre, and deciduous trees another three and a half. The remainder was well-maintained gardens, with dogwoods showing off their reddish-purple foliage and bright red fruit of the season. Danny parked in a small, four-car lot outside the office building, under a canopy of dogwood branches. As a child, Danny had been taught that the spring blooms of the dogwood were the flowering reminder of Christ on the Cross: four white petals, each with rusting-nail colored tips and red-stained centers. The fall markings told of His death, both horrible and beautiful. On the ground, blue and white agapanthus were in full bloom everywhere. To Danny, the grounds of the church spoke of God's glory much more than the sanctuary, with all of its affectatious, manmade ornamentation.

Danny got out of his truck and walked towards the building. A gardener was kneeling on the grass, weeding one of the beds of agapanthus.

"Buenos tardes, mi amigo," Danny said as he passed.

"Buenos tardes, señor. It's a beautiful day."

"Yes, it is."

Once inside, Danny looked down the hallway. The sheetrock had been ripped from the right hand side of the hall, exposing the two-by-four skeletal system of the building and a large area under construction. A half-dozen workmen, engaged in a variety of noise-making tasks, seemed to be oblivious to Danny. He wondered which of the four doors on the left was Keenan's office. The howl of a table-saw ripping through plywood stopped, and in the sudden silence that followed, he heard the priest's laughter coming from the third room down the hall. As Danny reached the door, Keenan swiveled around in his chair, saw him standing there, and waved him in. He put his hand over the phone. "Danny! Have a seat. I'll only be a minute."

Danny was surprised to see Keenan in his civvies—khaki pants and a short sleeve, button-down-collar shirt. Even though Danny was out of uniform, it never occurred to him that priests wore anything other than black suits and white collars. He sat at the chair in front of Keenan's desk and checked out the room. The office looked exactly as

Danny would have guessed most priests' offices looked. Furnished enough to be comfortable, but not so much to suggest that an inordinate amount of the Sunday collections was being used frivolously. Old framed photos of past priests, their names and the dates they'd headed the church on plaques beneath them, were clustered on one area of the wall. Architectural drawings of the now-under-construction office building were on another. A small sofa covered in a muted plaid that conjured up the seventies, as well as a couple of chairs, were against the wall to the left of the desk. And of course, a painting of Jesus and a dark wooden cross adorned a third wall.

"Will I see you and Sharon this Sunday? Good, good. I look forward to it. Goodbye," Keenan said, hanging up the phone. He looked up at Danny and beamed a smile as he leaned across the desk to shake his hand. "Good to see you, Danny, especially in the middle of the week. Is Carol with you?"

"No, she's still at school."

"Well, look at this. You came to church by yourself. I'm impressed, Danny."

"Can I get a note from you on that? Carol may not believe me if I tell her I was here."

"How are things going with you?"

"Okay, all things considered," Danny said. "I think I told you I've been on swing shift for the past three months. It's still hard getting used to it and I'll be glad to get back on days."

"You did tell me. I figured that's why you nodded off in church last Sunday. I don't know how you guys do it. If I'm not in bed by nine o'clock I'm a zombie the next day. I'll bet Carol will be glad when you are back to days as well. That's got to be tough on you both."

"And all this construction has to be tough on you," said Danny.

Keenan rolled his eyes. "You don't know the half of it. We're adding classrooms, and we need it, but it's hammers and electric saws all day. I say a prayer every day that they'll finish soon."

"You're allowed to pray for that kind of thing?"

"Some days I pray for enough strong drink to help me through it all. But I doubt you came here to hear me talk about that."

Danny shifted in his chair. 'No, I didn't, actually. I want to ask you something that may sound strange."

"Strange can be good. Keeps a priest on his toes. Fire away."

"Well, it's probably a mistake. You know Miguel Rodriguez?"

"Of course. Attends the afternoon services mostly. He's getting married. I believe her name is Maria?"

"Yeah, that's what I wanted to ask you about. He spoke to me confidentially, told me he went to Father Morales about getting some kind of marriage counseling letter he could show his priest in Mexico so they could get married there."

"That's not unusual. We write a half-dozen of those a year."

"Yeah. Anyway, he said Father Morales told him that he would do it, but that it would cost him four hundred dollars, cash."

Keenan seemed to be waiting for more, then furrowed his brow. "Excuse me?"

"Four hundred bucks. Father Morales told Miguel that he needed the money to do the counseling." Danny watched Keenan closely as they spoke, wanting to see his reaction.

Keenan shook his head "no" and let out a quick laugh. "Danny, that's impossible. We don't charge people for marriage counseling or anything else."

"That's what Miguel thought too. Anyway, I told him I'd ask you about it. What do you think Morales was doing, Father?"

Danny watched Keenan's eyes for his answer. Innocent people who suddenly realized they might be accidentally giving somebody up, or that there might be more going on than they realized and thought it best to shut up, would suddenly drop their eyes and inhale, as if to catch their breath, pulling everything they'd said back inside. Danny thought of it as people circling their wagons, so to speak, protecting

94

themselves from saying anything damaging. He called it Wagon Eyes, and Father Keenan had them right now.

Keenan shook his head and muttered something inaudible under his breath. He sat up straight in his chair, his smile flatlined and the color drained from his face.

"Father? Did you hear what I said?" asked Danny.

"Yes, yes, I heard you. There has to be a mistake. What did Morales say about it?"

"Haven't talked to him. I wanted to ask you about it first."

"You should've asked Father Morales. I don't know anything about it, Danny."

"He reports to you, doesn't he? Could you speak to him about it? I promised Rodriguez I'd look into it—"

Keenan stood up from his chair. "Look, Danny, I'm really sorry but I don't know what to say. It has to be a mistake. Miguel was probably nervous about his wedding and he might not have been listening closely."

Danny almost laughed. Every time Keenan looked him in the eyes, the priest immediately looked away again. *This guy has himself so jammed up he can't even make eye contact.* "Yeah, I suppose that's possible, but Miguel seemed to be pretty sure about it," Danny said.

"You really should talk to Father Morales directly. I'm sure he can clear the whole thing up."

Keenan's smile was the definition of forced. *Why is this guy so nervous? Nobody is going to jail or anything.* Danny thought he'd push a little harder, see how Keenan responded. Sometimes angry men let their guard down. "I don't mean to be rude, Father. But if what Miguel is saying is true, it sounds like extortion." Danny was careful not to say it *was* extortion, just that it "sounded like" it. He could see Keenan clench his jaw.

"And you are starting to sound like a policeman. Are you on official duty here?"

"No, Father, I'm asking you as a parishioner. Should I be asking you as a cop?"

"There's nothing going on here to warrant that."

Danny could hear a tremble in Keenan's voice as he spoke.

"No, no of course not. But Miguel asked me in part because I *am* a cop. If there is something going on that could be viewed as illegal—"

"And you immediately jump to that conclusion?"

"No, Father. That's why I came here today. Like I said, it's probably a mistake. Father Morales doesn't have anything to hide, does he?"

Keenan sighed, seemed to collect himself, then sat back down in his chair. "Look, Danny, nobody is hiding anything. I just don't have anything to tell you. If you really want to talk to somebody about it, maybe you should talk to the Bishop."

"The Bishop? Why him?" Danny was surprised that Keenan wanted to kick this upstairs.

"He's in charge of all priests. Morales was only assigned here a couple of weeks ago. Maybe he can help you, but I shouldn't talk about this anymore. I don't mean to be rude, but I've got a lot of things to wrap up before I call it a day. Thanks for stopping by."

Keenan stood again, and Danny realized he was being dismissed. He accepted the priest's outstretched hand. "I'm sorry, Father. I didn't mean to offend you. I was just asking because—"

Keenan interrupted him. "I'm not offended Danny, but I have nothing else to say about this. Priests get accused of all kinds of things these days, and you might have touched a nerve without meaning to. I'm sure there's a logical explanation, but if you feel like you need to pursue it, you really should call Morales, or maybe the Bishop. I'll see you and Carol Sunday, right?"

"Yeah, right, Father. See you Sunday."

"Good, good." The priest sat back down, picked up the phone before Danny had even turned toward the door, and quickly dialed a number. As he walked down the hallway, Danny could hear Keenan on the phone, his voice relaxed again. "Bob? Father Keenan here. Is this a good time?"

Danny shook his head and chuckled aloud, the sound covered by the noise of the construction work. Once outside, he started towards his truck and noticed a Porsche parked diagonally across two spaces. It was a beautiful car, but that kind of entitled parking irritated Danny. He looked into the driver's side window. Immaculate in every respect. Eyeing it again from bumper to bumper, he noticed a smudge on the driver's side mirror. A closer look revealed a couple of small scratches and streaks of blue paint. He parks like this and still gets dinged, Danny thought. Serves him right.

Getting back in his truck, he thought about his meeting with Keenan. Something didn't feel right. Not one bit.

Chapter Fourteen

Tim pulled into a parking space at the grocery store and saw Sara's car one row over, as noticeable to him as if it had been on fire. His first reaction was to put his own car in reverse and get the hell out of there. He started backing up but then stopped, wondering what Richard, his AA sponsor, would say about bolting like this. Being sober the way Richard described it probably didn't include turning tail and running from something unpleasant. Somewhat reluctantly, Tim pulled back into the space and parked. Besides, there was always the chance he wouldn't see her.

That chance evaporated about thirty seconds after he entered the store, when he turned down an aisle and saw Sara, still in heels and a suit, reading the label on a box. She looked up, and they made eye contact. Even from twenty feet away, Tim could see her eyes widen. She leaned back slightly, as if to protect herself.

Like it or not, Tim was committed. "Hi Sara."

"Hello Tim." Not even a trace of a smile or a hint of warmth.

"Shopping, huh?" *State the obvious—That's real smooth*, he thought, as soon as the words left his mouth.

"Yes. I've got some people coming over for dinner and I'm kind of in a rush. Nice seeing you." Sara turned her back on him and started to push her cart away.

"Sara, wait, please." He could see her shoulders and head stiffen a little before she turned back to face him.

"Look, I know this is awkward and all, but I just want to apologize for last week. I was trashed when I came to your house. Truth is, I don't even remember how I got there. In the morning I was so hungover I was afraid I was going to puke in your kitchen."

An older woman pushed her cart past them and looked sternly at Tim at the word "puke." He lowered his head and watched her walk away out of the corner of his eye. "You were being nice to me that morning and I was a jerk in return. There's no excuse for any of it and I'm really sorry."

If Sara had any reaction, Tim couldn't immediately read it. She just looked at him.

After a pause, she spoke. "You *were* an asshole, Tim, and I didn't deserve that. Then or ever."

"You're right. I'd give anything if I could undo it."

"You at least look better than you did last week."

An opening! Tim knew to tread lightly. "I drank for a few days after I saw you. A lot, really, but I stopped. I've been going to AA. I even got a sponsor."

Sara looked down at his shopping cart.

"There's no alcohol if that's what you're looking for."

She jutted her chin towards the other end of the aisle. "I really am in a hurry, but I've got a couple more things to get. Why don't you walk with me?"

"Great! I won't hold you up."

Tim turned his cart and the two started down the aisle.

"What happened to you, Tim?"

He told her about being in the alcohol and drug program, that he'd screwed up big time to get there, and how badly he'd hurt his family. "They are trying to forgive me but probably won't fully trust me for a while."

Sara stopped at a freezer case and grabbed a bag of edamame. "How's your mom?"

Tim's mother was crazy about Sara, used to tease him that she was going to make a good daughter-in-law someday. "She misses you."

"You know," Sara said, "It really pisses me off that I can't talk to her anymore. I love your mother and it sucks. Please tell her I said hello."

"You should call her and tell her yourself. I'm sure she'd like to hear from you."

"You know I can't do that. I can't get close to your family unless we're dating." Sara raised a hand from her cart and motioned as if she were stopping traffic. "I didn't mean that like it sounded. I'm not interested in dating again."

"No, no, I didn't take it that way." He stopped at the endcap and after a quick look at his shopping list, grabbed a loaf of bread.

"Since when do you make a shopping list?" asked Sara. "You were always the original grab-and-go guy."

"Yeah, and remember some of the crap meals that used to come from it?" He waved the loaf of bread for emphasis. "Seriously, I'm trying to do a lot of things differently. I need to get my life back in order. I want to try real estate again. And even if you would consider dating me again, my sponsor says I'm not ready for a romantic relationship."

"Really? Your sponsor can tell you whether or not to date?"

Tim dropped the bread in his cart. "It's a program thing. They tell you not to get romantically involved for a year, although I doubt many people wait that long. The idea is to get grounded in sobriety before becoming emotionally vulnerable—so if something goes wrong, you don't automatically get drunk."

"I guess that makes sense. You know, you've said all this before, but something does seem different this time. I'm not even ready to see you as a friend, but let me know how it's going from time to time, okay? But if you start drinking, I don't want to hear from you. At all."

"It's a deal."

"Look, I've got to run."

"No, I know, I just wanted to say hi."

"I'm glad you did. I've got some coworkers coming over to work on a project and I have to get going. It was good seeing you, Tim." She reached up and gave him a one-armed hug. Delighted and surprised, he returned it.

"It's great seeing you, Sara. Take care of yourself." Tim smiled and began pushing his cart back towards the frozen food area. He didn't look back, so she couldn't see him beaming.

Chapter Fifteen

The officers' changing room was in the basement. A couple of dozen lockers, given to the department when Napa High School remodeled its gym, were crammed in a corner. They had arrived at the station adorned with peeling bumper stickers, decals, magic marker scribblings proclaiming undying love for a girl, car, or football team, and dents. Lots of dents. Two picnic-table benches served as the only seating. Little else differentiated the room from the storage area it had been for decades before.. The only thing new was scratch marks in the worn linoleum floor, the result of the repurposed lockers having been dragged across it. Natural light came only from narrow windows near the ceiling.

Danny's shift started at four o'clock, thirty minutes away, and he was changing into his uniform. A couple of other officers were doing the same.

"I love weekends, but the first day back is rough," said Danny, unbuttoning his shirt. "I can't wait to get off this shift."

"You guys have been on swing shift, what, a couple of months?" said one of the other officers. "Lenny and me—three years now. At least you get to do some real police work on this shift."

"Hey, I'm still a cop when I'm working days," said Danny.

"Yeah, but the bad guys are all in bed when the sun's out. Days can be so boring it feels like they last forever."

Now down to his skivvies, Danny stood in front of his locker and thought about Carol. She worried that he had a greater chance of getting hurt at night. Or worse. He *wanted* his life to feel like it would last forever.

Danny turned to the sound of Sean bounding down the steps like he was falling down them. Already in uniform, Sean fairly burst into the room and marched straight to Danny.

"There's my partner! How was your weekend, Officer Garcia?" Sean's face was ear-to-ear grin.

"Pretty good—"

"That's great. Mine was *fantastic*, truly epic. I think I met Her."

If Danny didn't know better, he'd think Sean was on speed. "Met who, Sean?"

"*Her*, man. The woman of my dreams."

Danny turned to the other two officers. "Do you guys ever have a déjà vu thing happen to you, some guy repeating himself every time you start a new week?"

"This isn't like that," said Sean.

"Like that movie *Groundhog Day*, where the same thing happens over and over?"

"Very funny, Danny, but I am telling you, this time I really did meet someone special."

"You boys talk about your little girlfriends amongst yourselves." Lenny and his partner had finished dressing for the shift. "My partner and I are going to head upstairs, find some adults to talk to."

"Very funny, guys," Sean called after them as they started up the steps to the admin area.

"Sean," said Danny, "you lasted about two weeks with the last Woman of Your Dreams. And as I recall, she dropped you for another older guy closer to her age, who was what, eighteen?"

"Very funny. And for the record, she was practically a college graduate."

"Graduate? She couldn't have been more than nineteen."

"And a half, and only nine credits shy of finishing her sophomore year. But this one is different."

"Right. This one has a note from her mother saying it's okay for you to go out with her."

Sean turned his head to the side, nodded knowingly, then began to chuckle. "I keep forgetting. Any woman under thirty is out of your league. You're intimidated by youth."

"That's it, Sean. Still, you might want to check your new girl-friend's ID, make sure she isn't jailbait."

"Do you even remember what it's like to be young, or is that just a blur in your rear-view mirror?"

"Okay, okay, I'll play along. Who is this grown-up, and how did you meet her?"

Sean closed his eyes and crossed his arms. "Actually, you might not be emotionally mature enough to understand a real relationship. I'd be wasting my words."

"Sean, your mother must be thrilled that I've taken over raising you." Danny adjusted his belt and slammed his locker shut. "I'll bet this is the One. But can we talk about your future with your new girl-friend later? Let's go upstairs and see what's waiting for us this week."

Sean ran up the stairs ahead of Danny. "You're unbelievable, you know that? I try and share something personal about myself, and you can't deal with it. I'd be better off in a K-9 unit."

"Oh, Sean, that's too easy a setup. If it'll make you happy, go get a dog."

Citizens were complaining about gangbangers on skateboards hanging around the Pearl Street garage downtown. Why otherwise rational adults thought that all teens on skateboards were hoodlums escaped Danny. But the job called for follow up when citizens had concerns. The garage was a three-story structure, open at all sides and the top.

"It's nice outside. What say we park and walk it?" asked Danny.

"Seriously? This some kind of senior exercise program?"

Danny answered with a stern glare and parked the car on the first level. Trouble wasn't likely, but the officers grabbed nightsticks as a precaution.

"I don't hear any skateboarders," Sean half whispered. Both men paused for a moment. "Nothing." He started walking. "You never did tell me about your weekend." Sean looked left to right as they walked.

"Didn't I? Do you think it had anything to do with the fact that you wouldn't stop talking about yours?"

"Okay, I show a little interest in your life, and I get sarcasm in return."

"God, you're so emotional today. Maybe *you're* the girl of your dreams, Sean."

"Hey. You don't want to talk, don't talk."

"My weekend was too damn short but, all-in-all, okay. Something weird happened at church though."

The officers reached the second level. As usual it was mostly empty, which was probably part of the appeal of it for skateboarding.

Danny told Sean about his encounter with Rodriguez and subsequent meeting with Keenan. Sean laughed when Danny mentioned Wagon Eyes.

The officers rounded the corner and reached the top level of the garage. Danny pointed to a small object ahead of him, in the corner near the steps. "What's that?" He walked a little closer.

"Looks like a tennis shoe from here," said Sean. "It's been run over a bunch." Sean pointed across the garage to another object. "And I'll bet that's its partner. Why would anybody leave a new pair of tennis shoes up here?"

"Maybe somebody besides the owner left 'em," said Danny.

"See? That kind of police work is what makes you so good, Garcia. You'll make detective in no time."

"Screw you, Sean." Danny looked around. "There's nothing going on here. Let's get back to the car. So what do you make of my conversation with the priest? I can't figure out why he got all twitchy," said Danny.

"I don't know. Some people are uptight around cops."

"Yeah, but a priest? It's not like I was going to arrest him. If anything weird *is* going on it's really none of my business."

"What if he isn't a priest?"

"Keenan? He's been there forever. You think he's spent the last forty years of his life building some kind of cover?"

"No, I mean the other guy."

Danny gave Sean a cockeyed look. "Morales?"

"Yeah. What if 'Father Morales' is really just 'Mr. Morales.'"

"Why would you say that about either one of them?"

"I don't know, it just occurred to me. What if?"

"Have you heard of guys pretending to be priests?" said Danny.

"Call it a hunch. Oh, screw it then."

Back at the car, Danny leaned across the roof and spoke. "I got a feeling Keenan isn't going to mention this to Morales, at least not right away. I might talk to him if I run into him. I told Rodriguez I'd check it out."

"Think you'll have to shoot him?"

"What? No Sean, I'm not going to shoot anybody."

"Just in case, maybe you should be packing when you go to church."

"You think I should take a gun?"

"Just in case."

"You are seriously whacked."

"I'm seriously hungry. Let's go get something to eat. I'll drive and tell you more about my girlfriend."

"You know, you worry me sometimes, Sean."

"I know, but it's so easy to mess with you."

Sean drove onto Pearl Street. Within a couple of blocks, the charm of downtown evaporated and the Wine Train station came into view. He waited at the light to turn right at Soscol, towards auto row, when a flatbed truck with a wrecked cobalt blue Porsche on its bed went through the intersection, heading in the opposite direction. Danny gazed at it absentmindedly, until something caught his eye. The front of the car looked totaled. Otherwise, it was okay, except that the side view mirror was pushed flat back against the driver's door. The otherwise bright blue mirror had red scratches on it.

He threw his arm across Sean, pointing at the flatbed. "Pull that guy over!"

"What?" Sean turned on his lights and siren, and turned sharply left, running the light. "What are we doing?"

Danny focused on the truck. "Just pull him over," he said.

"That truck? What did he do?" Sean quickly caught up with the vehicle. "You going to tell me what we're doing?"

Danny didn't take his eyes off the vehicle. "I thought I saw something."

The flatbed driver signaled and pulled over. Sean fell in behind him. He had barely put the car in park when Danny opened his door. "Stay here. Call in the plate on the wrecked car."

"The *wrecked* one?"

The car was chained at each wheel to the wooden deck of the flatbed. Its front end was destroyed, the hood up and over the windshield.

From that angle, it was practically impossible to tell what kind of car it was, but the back was completely intact. A late model Porsche Cayman.

"Something wrong, Officer?" asked the driver, looking back at Danny. "That light was green." He was a big man with a bushy beard and tattoos on his neck, including one of a tiger, its ears pinned back, teeth bared. "I wasn't speeding or nothing." Grime covered much of the driver's tee shirt and the truck's interior.

"No sir, you're fine. I just wanted to ask about the car you're taking in. Do you know anything about it?"

The driver looked over his shoulder, then scratched his beard. "Not much, other than somebody wrecked the hell out of a beautiful Porsche. It's been in the yard for over a week now. Looks totaled to me. I figured it was going to the crusher, but somebody wants it fixed. I'm taking it to Hetcher's, the Porsche shop. It's gonna cost a lot to make this car right, but it ain't my money."

"Do you know anything about the accident?"

"Not really, I just tow 'em. I did hear my boss tell some guy on the phone it was a solo. Somebody found the car and the guy driving it laying on the ground up near Angwin. He was in the hospital for a while, just got out a couple of days ago. Boss said the guy couldn't remember anything, not even leaving his house that morning. Didn't even know why he was in the hospital. Ain't that some shit? They thought he was gonna die, but he pulled out of it. Lucky son of a bitch, if you ask me."

"You got that right. He say anything else?"

"My boss? Not that I remember."

"Well, thanks for your time. Sorry to inconvenience you."

The driver grinned. "Hey, I get paid by the hour, whether I'm talking to you or driving."

"Would you mind if I took a quick look at it?" Danny thumbed back at the car.

"No, I don't care. I gotta be at Hetcher's by five, but I've got time."

Danny jumped up on the flatbed, bent down and looked at the mirror, rubbing his hand across it as he did. It was just starting to rust where the scratches were, but he was right – the marks were made from red paint.

"Son of a bitch," he muttered. He took a step towards the front of the car and inspected the hood. The rust there was the same light color as on the mirror. He guessed that the damage to the hood and the mirror occurred at the same time. The passenger side was in better shape than the driver's. Danny reached in, opened the glove compartment and found the registration. He took a picture of it, put it back in the compartment, and jumped off the bed.

Danny grabbed a business card from his front pocket and handed it to the driver. "Thanks again. If by any chance you hear anything else about the car, the wreck, whatever, would you give me a call?" Danny knew he probably wouldn't hear from the guy, but you never knew.

The driver slipped Danny's card above his sun visor and started the truck. He gave Danny a lazy salute. "No problem, Officer."

Danny patted the truck door with his palm as the guy pulled away. He went back to the car and slid into his seat. "Did you find out anything from the plates?"

"Car is registered to Robert Williams," Sean answered. "Clean driving record. I Googled him—married, two kids, early forties—he's a hot shot at Hope Springs Winery in St. Helena. Nothing weird. You find what you were looking for?"

"I don't know. I'm not really sure *what* I was looking for. Let's drive by my church."

"You feel the need to repent for giving me shit about my girlfriend earlier?"

"I can't hide anything from you, can I, Sean?"

Sean insisted that they stop for something to eat before driving to Danny's church, but Danny overruled it. It was 5:30. He worried that anybody working at church during the week would have left or would soon leave for home, and he wanted to catch as many cars in the parking lot as possible. Or at least one car in particular.

"The driveway makes a big U around the place. Just follow it," Danny said as Sean turned into the church's driveway.

"Man, this place is impressive. They use your collection money for all this landscaping?"

Danny had never thought about who footed the bills for all this.

"So, you want to explain all this again?" Sean asked.

"When I came to see Father Keenan there was a red Porsche parked next to me when I left. Absolutely mint condition, except that it had deep, blue paint scratches on the driver's side view mirror."

"Okay."

"The car on that wrecker—that blue Porsche on that flatbed? It had *red* paint scratches on its mirror."

Sean didn't say a word for moment, just nodded his head. "Well, it's amazing that you noticed and all, but so what?"

"But the colors looked the same. Don't you see? They may have scratched each other."

"Okay, but how about this as a possibility. Either of them could have been hit by a million other cars."

"It might not mean shit, but maybe they hit each other and that somehow caused the blue Porsche to drive off the road. I dunno, but we won't find out today." The officers had driven all the way around the church. "There's nobody here."

"I'm sorry Danny, and maybe you're right. But you have to admit, it's pretty random."

"Yeah, maybe it is."

Chapter Sixteen

For the next several days, Danny drove through the church's lot on his way to work. The third time he hit pay dirt.

The red Porsche was there, in the same parking space it had been in the first time he'd seen it. Or spaces. The driver had taken two again.

Danny parked next to it and registered the change before even putting his car in park. It looked, at least from inside his car, like the scratches on the mirror cover were gone.

He walked to the sports car. Sure enough, the Porsche's mirror was as spotless as the rest of the body. He rubbed his hand across it anyway, as if his eyes could be fooled. Smooth as glass. This car had been to the shop. He walked around it, not sure what he was looking for, then took his cell phone out of his jeans and called the station.

Waiting for it to ring, he squatted down and checked the mirror one more time. "Hey Joyce, it's Danny Garcia. Can you run a license plate for me? No rush at all. Listen, I'm on at four. Can I stop by your desk and get it when I get in?"

Garcia gave her the plate number and hung up. He figured he had enough time for one more stop before going to work.

"Officer Garcia, right?" Danny thought the man asking looked like a Porsche—powerful and low to the ground. He had on overalls with a Hetcher's logo and a big, easy grin. He walked with a slight limp in his right leg that didn't seem to slow him down a bit. He wiped his strong looking hands on a clean looking, salmon colored rag, then offered a handshake.

"Yes I am," answered a confused Danny, impressed with the man's grip. "I'm sorry, do we know each other?"

The man waved Danny off. "You won't remember me. You arrested my little drunk-ass brother a couple of years back. He was standing on a corner, puking on some guy's car, when you picked him up. You told him he was going to jail or detox, his choice."

"Did he make the right choice?"

"Yup, and he ended up getting sober." He pointed to the garage bay and a guy under a lift, working on a car. "Been here ever since, and he's a hell of a mechanic."

Danny didn't recognize the brother, but couldn't help but notice how immaculate his work area was. For that matter, the whole garage was clean from floor to ceiling. There wasn't an errant tool or rag in any of the six bays, all of which were in service. These guys take pride in their work, Danny thought.

"Are you Mr. Hetcher?" Danny asked.

"Oh shoot, where are my manners? Yeah, Paul Hetcher. Call me Paul, please. That's Tommy, my kid brother working on the Carrera."

"Oh, it's a pleasure to meet you, Paul. I'm glad to hear it worked out for Tommy."

"Ah, he's a good kid, just can't handle the booze. Anyway, what can I do for you, Officer?"

"I'm here about fixing a Porsche."

"You came to the right place. We'll take care of it at a good price. I owe you that much."

"No, no. I don't own a Porsche. Somebody at my church does though, a red Boxster, older model in mint condition. Had a scratch and some blue paint on the side view mirror but it's been fixed. I was wondering if the work was done here."

"Did you ask the owner?"

"Well, no, I'm not really sure who it belongs to. I'm trying to be quiet about looking right now."

Paul threw up his hands. "Say no more. It's none of my business. I know exactly what car you're talking about. Did the work on it myself. But the owner wasn't a bad guy, I can promise you. He's a priest—"

"A priest?"

Yeah. Bishop actually. Looked young for that rank, or whatever you call it. Anyway, said he probably got bumped in the church parking lot. Wouldn't be good to start accusing parishioners, so he decided to just get it fixed."

"I see."

"Looked like a simple job, right? Just buff off the scratch and repaint it?" Hetcher at his own question. "Wrong. Had to replace the entire mirror and mirror assembly. We gave him a good price, him being a priest and all. Paid cash, four hundred dollar bills. I remember 'cause they were so new they stuck together."

"Four hundred."

"Yup. Can't remember his name, but I do remember that he was a bishop. Like I said, he looked young for it."

Danny mulled it all over on the way to the station. It was a stretch to connect this Porsche to the wrecked blue one he'd seen on the flatbed, but it could be. The four hundred dollar repair charge—the same amount Father Morales had asked of Rodriguez to do marriage counseling—seemed like a strange coincidence, but if the car belonged to the Bishop, that's all it was.

Once at the station, he went straight to Joyce. "Hey, did you have a chance to run that plate I gave you?"

"Of course," she answered, as though there could be little doubt. She handed Danny a piece of paper, then pointed to it as she spoke. "Car belongs to a Bishop O'Dowd. Lives in Santa Rosa. Bought it a couple of weeks ago from a guy in Nevada who deals in old Porsches."

"So, it could have been scratched when he bought it."

"Excuse me?"

"Sorry, thinking out loud." Danny folded the piece of paper, put it in his shirt pocket and started to walk away.

"You're welcome."

"Oh, I'm sorry, Joyce. I appreciate you checking this out."

"Hope it helps."

"It might, but I'm not sure how."

Chapter Seventeen

Danny went to the station first thing the next morning and grabbed a cup of coffee in the kitchen. "My God," he said to the two other officers present. "This is worse than what we make at night."

"Same coffee," said one of the other officers. "You're just used to drinking it after it's been sitting on the burner all day and has some teeth."

Danny nodded and raised his cup. "Seen the Chief this morning?"

"In his office. Came in with a Starbucks cup."

"Smart man. That's why he's in charge." Danny dumped the rest of his coffee in the sink, rinsed his cup and put it on the dish drainer. He walked down the hall and knocked on the doorframe of the open office. "Excuse me, Chief. Gotta minute?" Some of the furniture and most of the pictures were missing since the last time Danny had been here, and the Chief's desk was as clean as he'd ever seen it. It made the office look bigger.

The Chief smiled from his desk and waved Danny in. "Hi Danny, of course I do. Please, take a seat. What brings you up to the second floor this early in the day?"

Danny shook the Chief's offered hand and sat. He respected that the Chief usually wore a uniform instead of a coat and tie. Made him look like one of the guys, a regular cop. "Thanks. I just wanted to run something past you. This may sound a little strange, but I saw two different Porsches in two different places, and I think they may have been in an accident with each other."

The Chief sat back in his chair with his arms crossed as Danny told him the story.

"The guy driving the blue Porsche, Robert Williams? He's okay now, I guess, but he apparently got hurt pretty badly and can't remember anything that happened from the time he got up. He works at a winery Up Valley, and I'd talk to him, see if maybe I can jog his memory."

"How do you expect to do that?"

It's pretty flimsy, but I thought maybe if I mention the red Porsche it might trigger something."

"Do you know who the suspected other driver is?"

"Yes sir. I saw the red Porsche at my church. Belongs to a Catholic bishop. O'Dowd?"

The Chief leaned back in his chair and whistled. "Pretty high-profile guy. Does a lot in the community to help children and the homeless."

"That's what I understand."

"I've known him since I moved to Napa, twenty years ago, although not that well. Baptized two of my grandkids. Have you spoken to him?"

"No, I've never met him."

"Did you talk to your Sergeant about this?"

"Yes sir, I talked to Sergeant Potter this morning. I told him about the Bishop and he thought I should run it past you."

"You don't have much going here, Danny, and getting the Bishop involved could be trouble. I don't like it."

"I understand how sensitive this is, Chief. I won't let it get out of hand, absolutely won't mention the Bishop and won't do anything else without checking with you and Sergeant first."

The Chief didn't say anything for a moment, then uncrossed his arms and rubbed his palms together. "All right, Danny. Go ahead and talk to the other driver and see what he says. But don't talk to anybody else, much less the Bishop, before we talk about it."

"Thank you, Chief," Danny said, standing.

"You know I'm retiring soon, don't you?"

"Yes sir." Danny waved a hand around the room. "Congratulations."

The Chief stood, grinned, and offered Danny his hand. "Let's hope this turns out to be nothing. I'd like my last days to be as hassle-free as possible."

Danny called Robert Williams, who turned out to own Hope Springs Winery, as soon as he left the Chief's office, and Williams agreed to see him whenever he could get there. Passing vineyard after vineyard on Highway 29 made this one of Danny's favorite drives. This time of year, the well laid-out rows of grapevines took on their autumn colors, as though Mother Nature organized the fall season in Napa geometrically. A couple of hot air balloons, their baskets filled with people, drifted by overhead, heading south. Danny guessed the passengers to be tourists getting a view of the Valley they would gush over when describing their vacation.

The trip to St. Helena from Napa took Danny a little under twenty minutes, and another ten to get to Hope Springs from there. He'd never been to this winery, which sat on top of a hill, surrounded by acres of vines. Williams' large office had three walls that were mostly windows and took in a sweeping view of the valley floor below. Seeing it made Danny gasp.

"Officer Garcia," Williams said, walking towards Danny on crutches. He was a short, compact man who obviously spent time at the gym. He wore an open-collar shirt, blue blazer and jeans, one leg of which was hemmed at the knee. Below that was a cast.

"Hello, Mr. Williams." Danny crossed the large space and shook Williams' offered hand. "Thank you for seeing me on such short notice."

"My pleasure. Have a seat, and call me Bob, please." Williams hobbled to a seat behind his desk and sort of plopped down in it.

"Thanks, Bob, and it's Danny. You've got an amazing view here."

"It's something, isn't it? When I work late my wife swears I'm just sitting here with a glass of wine, looking out the window."

"I think maybe I should have gone into the wine business instead of law enforcement."

Williams laughed. "You could make worse choices than this, Danny, but it isn't as glamorous as the tourists think. Crush is coming on, and we all practically sleep here for two months. Anyway, you said you wanted to talk about my accident. I've already talked to the police and am afraid I don't have much to offer you."

Right down to business. Danny liked that. "Yes. I'm glad you're okay. I understand it was bad, that you were pretty banged up and almost didn't make it."

Williams rubbed his hands together as his smile faded. "It wasn't that bad, but it scared the shit out of me, waking up in the hospital like that. I had no idea where I was or what had happened. I looked down and saw the cast on my leg. Apparently the airbags saved my life but not my ankle."

"You're okay now, besides the ankle, I mean?"

"I'll have this cast on my leg for another four to six weeks. Besides not remembering what happened, my short-term memory is a little sketchy. The doctors said I'll get it all back, but it knocked me for a loop."

"Thank God you're alive," said Danny.

"Thank God is right. When I think that I might not have ever seen my wife or two daughters again..." Williams looked at one of the pictures on his desk and shook his head as he stared at it. Danny saw that the man's eyes were moist. "Anyway, the last thing I remember about that day is tying my shoes in the morning before I left the house. I'm not sure what you want to know or how I can help."

"And I'm sorry to bother you, Bob. I'll be brief. Do you suppose another car could have forced you off the road?"

"You mean, intentionally?"

"Not necessarily. You were on a winding road, and it could have been that another car coming in the opposite direction, maybe driving too fast and drifting into your lane, might have made you run off the road. Maybe it could have hit you, just enough to force you to turn quickly."

"Do you have a reason to think that might have happened?"

Danny knew he needed to be careful. "I saw your car after the accident. Did you know there were scratches on the driver's side mirror? Looked like red paint."

"I wish scratches were the only thing wrong that car. It was one ding away from being totaled."

"Any scratches that you noticed before the accident?"

Williams looked towards the floor for a moment, then shook his head. "I'm pretty sure I didn't have any scratches on the car when I left the house. Would they have been visible from the driver's seat?"

"Probably not. You wouldn't see them unless you were in front of the mirror, maybe walking towards the car."

"If there were scratches there, I didn't see them. Red paint?"

"Yes. If a car did hit you on the mirror like that, its mirror would have to have been the same distance from the ground. Maybe another sports car, even a Porsche."

Danny looked intently into Williams' eyes for any reaction to the suggestion of another Porsche. Nothing, not even a glimmer. The man seemed genuinely in the dark about what had happened to him.

"No…I really can't remember anything. I'm sorry you had to drive all the way here for nothing and I wish I could help. It bugs the shit out of me that I can't remember any of it."

Danny waved his hand dismissively. "I'm the one who bothered you, and I apologize. Besides, it's a beautiful drive here." Danny stood to leave and Williams started to get up. "No, stay off your feet, please. Do me a favor though. If you do remember anything about that day, anything at all, would you call me?" Danny handed Williams his card.

"Of course I will," said Williams, accepting the card. "I appreciate your time."

"Looking at your car, I'm glad you still have time."

Chapter Eighteen

Some officers suspected that the newly arrived free weights had gotten 'lost' on their way to the evidence room. Others scoffed, saying weights would never be considered evidence, and accepted them as an anonymous gift. Either way, one day there were no weights in the locker room, and the next day there they were, across from the lockers.

Originally there were just over one hundred pounds of plates, but that number steadily grew for the next few days, as officers brought in weights from home. Before long, there were three hundred pounds, a bench and a set of dumbbells. Most of the officers worked out regularly at a gym but, like kids to candy, they were drawn to these weights—lifting them either before or after most shifts.

Sean and Danny had shown up early for their shift to work out. Sean stepped up to spot for Danny, who was on the bench. Danny grabbed the bar above his head and exhaled.

"You know this is only one hundred and thirty pounds?" said Sean, just as Danny was lifting the bar off the bench arms.

Danny let the bar settle back down. "Yes, Sean, I know how much weight is there. What's your point?"

"Oh, nothing. Don't let me stop you."

Danny rolled his eyes, grabbed the bar again and began to lift it.

"It just doesn't seem like much weight, and I wondered if you wanted me to add some more. Go ahead. Lift." Looking very serious, Sean took a few quick breaths, then bent his knees, put his hands under the bar, and nodded. "Okay, partner, I got you covered."

"Screw you, Sean. I like to use lighter weights and do more, faster, reps. That's the secret to building muscle tone."

"Oh. I thought it was an old guy thing. Don't lift more weight than you can eat or something."

"Smart. Insult the guy who's going to spot for you when it's your turn."

"Oh, I'm fine. This probably looks like a lot to you, but I don't need a spotter."

Danny took a deep breath and shook his head. "Sean how did you get to be so like you are? I mean, seriously." He then did twenty fast bench presses. After a pause, he did another set, then a third.

Sean added another eighty pounds and lay on the bench. "Call me crazy, but I like to put weight on the bar when I lift. But then, I've got youth on my side."

The two worked out for about fifteen minutes, then started to get dressed for their shift. Danny buttoned and tucked in his uniform shirt.

"I saw Robert Williams this morning," said Danny.

"Who? Do I know him?"

"Williams owns that smashed-up, cobalt blue Porsche we saw on the flatbed."

"Where did you run into that guy?" asked Sean.

"His place. I came in this morning and asked for the Chief's permission to go see him. Chief said yes, so I drove to Hope Springs Winery. Williams owns it."

"Seriously? You really think something is going on there, huh?"

"I don't know, something's bugging me about it." His belt now on, Danny grabbed his hat, flashlight and nightstick from his locker before pushing it shut with his elbow.

"Did Mr. Williams give you anything you can use?"

"Nada. Cast and crutches, but he's pretty much okay 'cept for a broken ankle and bad short-term memory."

"You going to drive out to the accident spot, do a little detective-style crime scene analysis?"

"After what, almost a week and a half? You fucking with me now, Officer Rawlins?"

"Pretty much," answered Sean. He closed his locker and spun the dial on the combination lock. "I don't know why I lock this. The only people who come down here are cops."

"It's because you are paranoid and insecure."

The officers trudged up the stairs to the duty sergeant. Nothing of note had happened during the day. Danny stopped in the kitchen for a cup of coffee. Pot in hand, he remembered the comment about this being the same coffee that the guys made in the morning. No way this is the same stuff, he thought. Still, he decided against drinking it. He put the pot back on the burner and set the unused coffee mug in the sink. He and Sean headed outside. Danny thought it looked like rain, which was unusual this early in the season. With Sean taking the wheel, they pulled out of the parking lot.

"So, you got another move on the Porsche conspiracy, or is it over?"

"I know you're messing with me again, Sean, but I'm telling you, something isn't right. I'd really like to talk to the bishop that owns the red Porsche."

Sean turned right on Jefferson. Schools let out a half hour before their shift started during the week, and unless dispatch told them to do otherwise, the officers often began by riding by Napa and Vintage

High Schools, just to make sure that students had gone home without incident.

Sean pantomimed talking on the phone. "Bishop? Danny Garcia here, Napa PD. Say, you didn't happen to run a guy off the road, did you? Damn near kill him, then drive away? Reason I ask, some of the guys have a bet going. I say you're clean, just wondering if I can collect."

"Yeah, I haven't really figured out how I would strike up that conversation. Maybe he'll show up at the church, do communion. I could ask him just as he hands me a wafer." Danny pointed to a small group of protesters in front of Planned Parenthood.

Sean shook his head. "I'll give them this—those protesters show up there damn near every day. You know the staff knows them by name, brings them coffee when it's cold?"

"Weird relationship all right. So, you got any ideas about how I talk to the Bishop?"

Sean turned left on Lincoln and both officers looked at the empty Napa High schoolyard. "Maybe. That thing at your church, the priest asking the guy for four hundred dollars? What if you go talk to him about that? Lead with it, and see where it goes."

Danny thought about it. "You know, Sean, that may be a good idea."

Sean tapped his forehead, "Got a lot of those up here. 'Course, I don't know how you clear that with the brass. It's none of our business if the priest wants to sleep with the guy's fiancé, much less ask him for a few hundred bucks."

"That's my partner, straight to the sex angle. I don't know though. The Chief was okay with me talking to Robert Williams about the accident. Maybe if I can show him where I'm going, he'll be okay with it."

"Or not. He might think you're crazy, kick you off the force. Then I'd have to break in a new partner."

"Yeah, well. I'm going to stop by the body shop again tomorrow morning, then I'll go to the station and ask the Chief. Good idea, Sean. I may be off to visit the Bishop."

Sean whistled. "Lions and tigers and priests, oh my!"

Chapter Nineteen

"Did he call?" Danny shook his wet hair as he walked into the kitchen, then rubbed it with a towel.

"Danny!" Carol wiped her cheek with the back of her hand. "What are you, a dog?"

"Oh, please. My hair is what, an inch long?" Danny could feel his bare feet stick to the linoleum as he walked across the floor. Carol, fully dressed with an apron on over her blouse and skirt, stood at the stove, turning over bacon and eggs on a skillet.

"Why didn't you dry off in the bathroom? And did who call?"

"The *Bishop*. I've called him, like twice now, and he hasn't called back."

"Danny, he's a busy man. He'll call you. What time did you get home last night?"

Danny hung the towel around his neck. "You really don't know, do you? God, I wish I could sleep like you do." He fidgeted with the tie of his robe, pulling it tighter. He kissed Carol on the cheek, grabbed the coffee pot from the counter and poured a cup.

She shrugged, "Sometimes I hear you come in the house, but then I roll over and go right back to sleep."

"How do you do that?" He put his coffee down and hugged her from behind, drawing her to his body.

"Danny…" Carol pulled away from him. "What is it about cooking breakfast that turns you on?"

"I don't know. The eggs, the bacon, your perfect body…" Danny leaned into her and wiggled his head against her neck.

Carol moved away again. "Hey mister. Short or long, your hair is soaking wet. This is becoming a Sunday morning routine with you. Are you trying to get out of going to church?"

Danny kissed her on the cheek again. "Me? Miss church? Please!" He released her, grabbed his coffee mug and sat down. "I live for Sunday sermons. You think the Bishop will be there today?"

"I seriously doubt it. It's a big deal when he comes to town. They talk about it for weeks beforehand." Carol put two plates on the table, bacon and eggs plus toast for Danny, half a cantaloupe for herself. She grabbed two glasses of orange juice from the counter and sat down.

"What are you talking about? He's in Napa all the time."

"I don't think so," said Carol. "What makes you think otherwise?"

"I've seen his car at church twice in just the last two weeks."

"Oh, you know what kind of car the bishop drives. And how is that?"

Danny took a bite of toast, mainly to give himself a second to think before answering. It might upset Carol to know that he'd been asking questions that related to the Bishop. On the other hand, she would be even more upset with anything but the truth.

"I think he may have caused an accident, hit and run, seriously hurting the other driver. He at least fled the scene."

Carol froze, her fork halfway to her mouth. She put the fork back on her plate. "What are you talking about?"

"When I left Father Keenan's office the other day, there was a red Porsche parked next to me that had blue paint on the mirror." Danny filled her in on everything else. Carol didn't eat a bite while he he was talking. Looking at her, he kept thinking "deer in the headlights."

"So you're going to accuse the Bishop."

"No. Much as I'd like to have that conversation and at least see where it goes, the Chief won't let me."

"Well, I'm glad somebody is being sensible."

"I'm going to talk to him about the priest at church trying to get four hundred dollars out of a parishioner to do marriage counseling." Danny used his toast to scoop up the rest of his bacon and eggs.

"But you already talked to Father Keenan about it. Besides, you said even if the Father did ask for the money, it wasn't a police matter. Now it's okay for the cops to talk to the *Bishop* about it? That doesn't make sense."

Danny stood and gathered his dishes and nodded towards hers. "Are you finished?" he asked. When Carol just looked at him, he shrugged, then put his plate in the sink. "I'm not going to ask as a cop. I'll be in my civvies, and I'll be in Santa Rosa because I'm going to REI to look at kayaks and thought, as long as I'm there, I'd talk to the Bishop."

"*Kayaks?* Danny you've never even *been* kayaking."

Danny had his back to the sink, his hands on the counter. "I've gotta have some reason for being there. Chief told me I absolutely can't be in uniform. He doesn't even want to know what happens when we talk."

"Danny, I'm very uncomfortable with all this. This is my church you're talking about, and it sounds like you are playing pretty fast and loose with something. Could this be considered harassment?"

"Not unless I say or do something stupid, and I won't. The money thing is a legitimate topic, though. I'm just asking about it because a church member asked me to. I'm not accusing anybody of anything, and I'm talking as a regular guy, not a cop."

Carol collected her dishes. "Except that you *are* a cop, Danny." She scraped her remaining eggs into the disposal while she spoke. "Rodriguez asked for your help specifically because you are a cop."

"Carol, there is nothing to worry about."

"I think there is, but let's deal with it later. You've got to get moving or we're going to be late. I don't want to walk in after the service has started and have Father Keenan look at us the way he can."

Danny stifled a yawn. "Yeah, sure, let's get ready."

"Are you awake? What time did you get in?"

"I'm fine, I got in a little after one and went right to sleep."

"Now I'm worried that the Bishop *will* be there and that there'll be a big scene with you two."

"Carol, if he is there I'll just ask if I can stop in and talk to him when I'm in Santa Rosa, that's all. If he says 'no,' I'll shoot him and we can come back home."

"Very comforting, Danny. Put some clothes on and let's go."

Chapter Twenty

Danny pulled into the circular driveway and parked behind a new Mercedes. Holy shit, he thought, checking out the place—This isn't a house, it's a *palace*. He'd been to Father Keenan's rectory with Carol before, and it was nice, but it was a third the size of this. It struck Danny as funny that the church didn't actually *pay* priests. Far be it from members of the clergy to soil their hands on a paycheck. That's for sinners like him: guys who, if they couldn't pay the mortgage, might lose their homes. Plus, the disparity between men and women applied to the church as well, with the pay that nuns *didn't* get being far less than what priests weren't paid. He couldn't imagine that the sisters in Catholic school left for a place like this at the end of a day's lessons. *And it's for this that we put money in the collection plate?*

Danny got out of his car and turned his baseball hat so the brim was in front. As he walked to the front door, he looked inside the garage windows. There were three cars, a Mercedes convertible, probably a '72 model, and a '63 Porsche 911. The third, looking like the odd man out, was a late model Toyota Rav 4.

His third call to the Bishop, two days before, had gone straight to voicemail. His voice had been flat as he spoke. "This is my third call this week, and I would appreciate a call back. A parishioner at my church shared some concerns about Father Morales that I'm guessing you'd want to know about. I'm not sure if it's a police or church matter and was hoping you and I could clear it up. I've got to run some errands in Santa Rosa and thought I could stop by your office to talk." The part about this being a police matter was a bluff, but Danny guessed it was a safe bluff.'

"Danny, I got your call yesterday. How good to hear from you," the Bishop had begun when he called Danny back the next morning. Not a word of explanation or apology for not returning the other calls. "I understand you'd like to talk and will be in Santa Rosa. I'm afraid I'm going to be traveling all week and I don't want this to get put off any longer." He said it as if it were Danny's fault they hadn't spoken before now. "Could you come to my home office as soon as possible so we can get this resolved?"

Danny rang the doorbell, wishing now that they weren't meeting here. The Bishop's turf, his big-ass, intimidating house.

He suddenly wondered if he even had the right house, a suspicion confirmed when an Asian man answered the door but dissolved when he greeted Danny with a slight accent. "Officer Garcia? Won't you please come in? The Bishop is waiting for you."

Oh, please. He has a butler to boot?

The butler turned and Danny followed him. The inside of the house, awash in art, was as opulent as the outside.

Who has statues in their frigging house? Danny stopped in front a piece that he thought was a horse, but it was too abstract for him to be sure.

"This way, please," said the butler, ten feet in front of Danny.

"Sorry," said Danny, without moving. "Is this for real?" he asked, more about the presence of the statue than about any characteristic of it.

134

"The sculpture? I'm not sure what you mean. The Bishop's office is this way." At the end of the hall, the butler opened a door, stood to the side and motioned Danny into a large room. The furnishing and decor were testosterone-steeped: dark wood, leather and brass. A virile, handsome man whom Danny guessed to be in his mid-forties sat behind a massive mahogany desk. Another sculpture, this one a life-sized replica of a ballerina—*en pointe*, arms extended towards the ceiling—stood on the floor near a large window. Even the presence of so feminine an art piece didn't diminish the fact that this was a man's office.

The Bishop stood as soon as Danny entered the room, crossed the distance between them, and extended his hand. Danny took off his baseball cap, stuck it in the back of his jeans, and shook the Bishop's hand. He was surprised to find it so soft.

"Danny, it's a pleasure. I'm Bishop O'Dowd. Thank you so much for coming to see me. We've met before, haven't we? Did you find the place all right? Would you like something to drink? Coffee, maybe?"

Wonder if I am supposed to answer any of those questions? Is he nervous or on speed? "I don't think we've met. Coffee sounds good, if you're having some."

The Bishop nodded to the Asian man. "Martin, would you be so kind?"

"This place is beautiful," said Danny. "Amazing actually. I've been in nice homes before, but this one is really something."

"Oh, this doesn't belong to me," the Bishop said, chuckling as he spoke. "This house belongs to the church."

"The church?"

"Yes. It was built in the early eighties for the presiding bishop. The contractor, a parishioner here in Santa Rosa I believe, generously donated much of the cost and had his crew build it. I'm the third bishop to live here. I sometimes *wish* this was all mine, but it will belong to someone else when I move."

"Wow. I hope this doesn't sound tacky, but it seems like a lot of house for one man."

"It may seem extravagant, but the diocese looks at it as an investment opportunity. They may never sell it, but if they do, the church will do well."

Meanwhile, you're doing extremely *well,* Danny thought. "The art alone has got to be worth a fortune. It's amazing," he said, pointing to the sculpture of the dancer.

"Thank you. Not as many originals as you might think, and most of it belongs to my family's private collection. My father made a killing in the market, as they say, and has been generous in lending me pieces. None of my relatives took a vow of poverty."

"Well, if this is poverty, you can sign me up, Father. Or do I call you Bishop?

"Whatever you wish. I'll always consider myself a priest at heart. Sit, please, make yourself comfortable. I appreciate you taking time from work to come here." The Bishop took a seat in one of the two leather chairs in front of his desk and motioned for Danny to the other, facing him.

"It's okay, I'm not on the clock. I had errands to run in Santa Rosa anyway," Danny said. He sat and the chair absorbed him, almost swallowed him. It may have been the most comfortable chair in which he had ever sat.

"I'm glad it worked out. I'm sorry I had to ask you to drive here, but it's been pretty crazy around the diocese lately. Three new priests in four months and a building fund campaign in full swing. We're expanding in four churches. I'm telling you, I've never been so busy. But listen to me. I apologize. You were kind enough to drive here and I'm talking about myself."

Martin returned with a tray of coffee. He placed it on the desk and wordlessly left the room.

"Let me," said the bishop, pouring a cup for Danny. He sat back in his chair without pouring a cup for himself.

"Aren't you having any?" said Danny, motioning to the tray.

The bishop waved at the tray. "No, thank you. You wanted to talk about something."

"Well, I go to church in Napa."

"Which of the two?"

I'll bet you called both priests and know exactly which one. "St. Michael's. A Mr. Rodriguez, one of the other parishioners, approached me after service a few Sundays ago with his fiancée. He said he'd asked Father Morales if he would do marriage counseling for them and provide a letter documenting it. The wedding is in Mexico and, apparently, it would help to do the counseling here first. I don't really understand how all that works. Anyway, Morales agreed, but wanted four hundred dollars to do it. He also said he'd need it in cash."

"Go on." The Bishop stared intently at Danny as he spoke.

What more do you need? "Well, that's it."

"I see."

"I was surprised Morales asked for money like that. Is that normal?"

The Bishop crossed his legs, brushed something invisible off his pants. "Of course not. Our priests don't charge money to do God's work."

You mean, like invoice for it. It was obvious from this house alone that church work paid well. "Well, why would Morales?"

"Danny, did you know that Rodriguez's fiancée is probably an illegal immigrant?"

You want to talk about her immigration status? "No, I didn't," Danny said, even though it didn't necessarily surprise him. "Is that relevant?"

The Bishop smiled, uncrossed his legs and leaned forward. "There's a connection. I talked to Father Morales about this. He was shocked that Mr. Rodriguez would make such an accusation. They did discuss marriage counseling, but Father Morales said he never asked for any money."

Danny stopped sipping his coffee, put the cup on the table. "He said that?"

"That's right."

"That seems strange. Why would Rodriguez make that up?"

The Bishop stood, leaned against his desk, and crossed his arms. "Danny, did you know that Morales is from Honduras?"

"Excuse me?"

"I mean originally. He was born in Honduras. There is apparently some kind of bad blood between Mexicans and Hondurans. I don't exactly know what it's all about, but it seems to be a deeply ingrained cultural thing. It's why I mentioned that the fiancée may be an illegal immigrant."

"I'm not following this at all."

"Even though Father Morales is a priest, Mr. Rodriguez may have been worried that Morales would expose her immigration status. A Honduran's way of making life difficult for a Mexican. I can't imagine why he would think a priest might do such a thing, but nevertheless, he might have wanted to beat Morales to the punch and discredit him by making up the story."

It was all Danny could do to keep from laughing. He halfway thought the bishop might start too, unable to tell such a whopper and maintain a straight face. "No offense, Bishop, but that sounds a little far-fetched," said Danny.

The bishop threw up his hands. "I know, I know. I don't understand this kind of cultural bias at all, but I see it all the time."

"Let me get this straight. You're saying that parishioners accuse priests of this on a regular basis, because they are worried the priests might expose their immigration status?"

"I understand your skepticism *and* the sarcasm, Danny. No, I don't mean that particular example per se, but I'm telling you, I've seen how these two cultures interact. I'm sorry it happened, but I can't honestly say I'm surprised."

Danny wanted to dial it back a bit. "You know I'm Mexican. Or my parents were," said Danny. "I didn't know we had any kind of thing with Hondurans."

"You were raised in a strong Catholic home, is why."

Danny didn't interrupt with the facts.

"Now, I'm sure Mr. Rodriguez is a good man in every other respect, but my experience leads me to believe that he was probably making this up. I don't know why, but like I said, I spoke to Morales, and he gave me his word that he never asked for money."

"His word."

"Yes, Danny, his word. And I believe him. I've known Father Morales for quite some time now. I ordained him as a priest. He's a good man, Danny. Have you ever spoken with him?"

"No, actually. Carol and I usually go to the nine o'clock service, and Morales preaches at the afternoon Spanish service."

"Yes. I set that service up when I took over the diocese. We've got a large Hispanic congregation, and I thought they might be more comfortable attending a service in Spanish. It's been quite popular. Anyway, Morales has been better received by the congregation than someone born in this country. They trust him. Again, I don't know why Mr. Rodriguez would make such accusations, but I can tell you with certainty that Morales did not ask anyone for money."

"Wow. I don't know what to say, Father. I'll have to take your word for it. I'm a police officer and people lie to me all the time. I can usually spot it. I didn't think Mr. Rodriguez was lying, but if you are sure that he was—"

"Danny, much as I hate to accuse any man, I'm *quite* sure. There is no point for anyone else knowing about this, and I'd appreciate it if we kept this conversation between us. Father Morales is extremely popular with the congregants, and this would only hurt Rodriguez's standing with the other parishioners."

They say that when women lie, they avert their eyes while talking, while men maintain steady eye contact, thinking that it will be interpreted as telling the truth. The Bishop hadn't taken his eyes off Danny since they'd started speaking. For that matter, he barely even blinked.

"If you say so. Well, then, I guess that's it. I'm sorry to have wasted your time."

"Don't be silly. You're not wasting my time. You thought something nefarious was going on with one of the church's priests. You *had* to come to me and I'm glad you did." The Bishop walked Danny to the office door, where Danny was surprised to find Martin waiting.

"Thank you." Danny turned to leave, then turned back. "Excuse me, can I ask you something totally unrelated? You've got some great cars in the garage and I noticed the Porsche. Do you like it?"

The Bishop looked far more relaxed, now that the subject had changed. "Again, those cars are part of my father's collection, but yes, I enjoy driving Porsches."

"You've driven others, besides that 911?"

"A few, yes. Are you thinking of buying one?"

Danny held his hands up beside his head, as if surrendering, and laughed. "Oh, a Porsche is just a dream on a cop's salary, but I wish. I was just reading about the Boxsters, especially the early models, and most of the magazines say they are pretty good cars. Do you own one of those?"

Danny could practically see the wheels turning in the bishop's head.

"I have driven Boxsters, but not in some time now."

"So you don't own one?"

"I guess owning a Boxster is something we both dream about. I apologize, Danny, but I've got a lot of work to do. Do you mind if

Martin walks you to the door?" The Bishop extended his right hand, his palm turned to the floor. Danny half wondered if the guy expected him to kiss the ring on his finger. He took the Bishop's hand and shook it.

"Listen to me, going on and on. I don't mind a bit. Thanks for seeing me like this." Danny looked for any kind of tell in the bishop's face, but saw nothing.

"I'm glad we could clear this up, Danny. I hope to see you again soon."

PART TWO

PART TWO

Chapter Twenty-One

"What are you going to tell the Chief?"

"About my conversation with the Bishop? Nothing, at least not right away. One condition of my going was that I *not* talk about it with him," Danny answered. He and Sean had responded to several calls this shift, between which Danny had filled his partner in on his visit that morning. They drove down Main Street. Danny marveled that all the restaurants were packed, with people spilling out onto the sidewalks. If the economy was struggling, it wasn't from lack of food. "Does anybody eat at home anymore?"

"Not in Napa, it seems. What about Carol? You going to tell her?"

"About my visit? That's my real problem right now. She thinks I'm stirring up shit that will make it hard for her at church—"

"Which you are."

"Yeah, but not on purpose. The Bishop was full of shit from the minute I walked in his office. If he had just blown me off about Morales, I would have let it go. Hell, I really only brought it up so I could ask him about his Porsche Boxster. And he lied about that too, big time."

"So where will you go with it?"

"I don't know. Now I feel like I have to look into both things, Morales and the car."

"One of which is none of our business and the other is total speculation on your part."

"I can't really see my next move at all," said Danny.

"Here's how *I* see it. All of this could easily go south on you. You're gonna lose your job and Carol, start drinking heavily and mope to me about it all. I don't have the time for it, Danny."

"Thanks. I'll try and keep my train wrecks off your tracks."

Sean turned and crossed the river on the Third Street Bridge. Even at night, Danny could see that it was low tide, when the river looked like a small stream cutting through a mud flat. Hard to believe that it was eight feet higher twice a day and flowed into the San Pablo Bay.

They turned right onto Soscal. A late model Cadillac with darkly tinted windows, going a little too fast, passed the officers in the inside lane. It came to a quick, jerky, last-second stop at a traffic light, a few car lengths ahead of their patrol car.

"Wow. That was real smooth." Danny chuckled.

"Those are some dark-ass windows, too," said Sean. "Can you see anything inside?"

"Not from the passenger side. But I do see that his taillight is burned out. Why don't we pull him over and let him know, have a look-see."

"It's damn near ten o'clock. He can't possibly see out of the rear or side windows," said Sean.

Danny got behind the driver when the light turned green, switched on his lights while grabbing his microphone and told him to pull over. "This one feels funny. You get the passenger side, okay?"

"Roger that," said Sean.

The officers walked to opposite sides of the car. The driver lowered his window a couple of inches and glowered at Danny.

"Good evening, sir." Danny made sure he sounded pleasant. The four men he saw in the car were big and sullen. Two were wearing sunglasses. Danny saw tough looking guys all the time, but these men looked hard, gamers who'd lost more than once. He would bet most of them had done time. "Would you lower your window and the passenger window for me?"

"Is there a problem, Officer?" asked the driver.

"Not if you'll roll down the windows. All the way please."

Sean nodded to the men as the passenger window lowered. Danny noticed him scanning the whole car. He appreciated that when Sean was on, he was on.

"Evening, gentlemen," said Sean. The men ignored him.

Although faint, Danny could smell pot. "License and registration, please."

"What's the problem, Officer?" The driver sounded annoyed.

"Probably none, but you've got a burned-out taillight."

"It's my sister's car, I'll bet she doesn't even know it. How about I tell her and fix it myself?"

"Sure, but I still need your license and registration."

The driver leaned over to open the glove compartment. Danny and Sean briefly looked at each other through the open car windows, then Sean looked into the back seat. Danny's eyes stayed on the driver, front-seat passenger and the glove compartment. Although crammed full of napkins, papers, and a few maps, it otherwise looked okay. Finding the registration, the driver handed it and his license to Danny.

"Thank you. I'm going to have to ask you three to exit the car on the passenger side," said Danny. Motioning to the driver, "You stay seated until they're all out. And take off the sunglasses, please."

"Oh man, this is bullshit," said one of the back seat passengers. "You're doing this because we're black!"

"Only looks to me like two of you are black, and that's got nothing to do with it anyway. You guys in the back seat get out first."

The men grumbled as they did. Sean stood away from them and the vehicle, his hands on his belt and near his gun. When they were out of the car, he opened the front passenger door.

"Sir? If you'll join your friends over here," said Sean.

"You can exit the vehicle now, sir," Danny said to the driver.

"This is bullshit and you know it," he said to Danny as he got out.

"Right over there," Danny said, ignoring his comment. He nodded to Sean, then stepped to the patrol car. He reached through the window, grabbed the radio and called the station. He spoke in low tones and called in the driver's information.

Dispatch responded quickly. "He's out on parole, and has missed the last two meetings with his parole officer," was the report.

"Thank you," Danny said— still in a low, even tone. "We've got four men here, and I'll bet the driver isn't the only one with a record. Have you got any units close by?"

"McPherson and Waters are relatively close. Should we send them over?"

"Affirmative. We might need the backup. Over and out." Danny leaned back in the car and started to put the radio back in its holder, all the while watching the men.

He would later say that what happened next seemed to happen in increasingly slow motion. He'd heard other people say that, and it always sounded so corny, but that's how it went down. When he told the inquiry board about it, he realized that no more than two or three seconds had passed before it was all over. He must have reacted quickly, but at the time he felt as though gravity was conspiring against him.

As Danny released the radio, he watched the driver of the Cadillac step behind another of the passengers and lift up the back of the other man's shirt.

"Sean!" Danny yelled, still leaning in the car.

He watched Sean look towards him, then reach for his weapon. The driver, a gun now in his hand, pushed the passenger to the side, and crouched down. Danny was stunned. It wasn't supposed to happen like this. Sean began turning towards the four men, but before he could face them, the driver took aim at him and fired.

Danny watched as the bullet left the chamber, heading straight for Sean. When it hit him near his shoulder, just above his heart, Sean spun around. Danny watched as his partner, now on one foot, started falling to the ground. He grabbed his own gun and tried to raise his arm, but he couldn't move it from the holster. He felt his heart beating in his chest, his temples and his eardrums. The thumping sound was the only thing he could hear. Danny watched as the driver swung his gun around and aimed it at him.

Then everything stopped completely.

Danny couldn't move. He could see inside the barrel of the driver's gun. There was something in it, way in the back, but at first he couldn't make out the image. He had to squint, then realized it was his mother, crying. She was calling for Danny's father, her deceased husband. Danny tried to answer, tried to tell her that he was there and loved her, but he couldn't say the words. Danny, so young he could only tug on her skirt as he looked up at her, was blinded by his own tears. He wiped them away and realized the face he was looking at wasn't his mother's, but his ex-wife's, distraught about their collapsing marriage. He reached for her to tell her everything would work out, but she didn't know he was there, couldn't hear him or just ignored him. He tried to take her shoulders, look her straight in the eyes, but her face was too blurry. It started to come back into focus, but it wasn't his ex, it was his brother, smiling at him. Danny hadn't thought about his brother in months, had pushed all thoughts of him away, and now he was face to face with him, eye to eye in fact. Danny wanted to speak to him, but didn't know what to say. Before he could collect his thoughts, choose the words, his brother's face suddenly exploded right in front of him. A bullet passed through the fragments of his brother's face and out the chamber of the gun, headed straight for Danny.

It left the gun barrel and began moving towards him in slow motion. Danny could only watch as the bullet just missed him, passing above his shoulder, close to his neck. He could hear it. If he could just move, he could knock it to the ground. Finally, he was able to break his imprisoned arms free, slowly raise them, and aim his own gun at the driver. He pulled the trigger, and the gun fired.

As soon as he heard his own gun go off, the action returned to real time. The driver threw up his arms and fell backwards violently. The gun flew out of his hand. Danny quickly looked at Sean, now lying on the ground, and then at the three Cadillac passengers, who seemed frozen, their mouths open. He looked back at the driver, splayed on the pavement, his gun a couple of feet from his head.

"Down on the ground and hands on your head, *now!*" Danny ran towards the other men, his gun pointed at them. He kicked the driver's gun towards Sean. The car passengers seemed to move as a single unit, hitting the ground simultaneously as though they'd choreographed it. Danny was surprised at how clear-headed he now felt. He held his gun on the men and backed up towards his partner.

"Sean? Are you okay?" Danny was yelling. "Talk to me, partner."

Sean didn't move.

Chapter Twenty-Two

Danny stared at Sean for a second, maybe two, expecting—hoping—for him to get up. Did this really just happen? What was he supposed to do now? Danny shook his head, and the cop in him took full control, pushed his emotions aside. He depressed the switch on his shoulder radio. "This is Garcia. Officer down. Sean Rawlins is down. I am on Soscol south of Oil Can Road. We need backup. Now!" He glanced at the driver. The man was not moving and a pool of blood covered the top left side of his shirt. One of the passengers lying on the ground lifted his head.

"Move and I'll blow your fucking brains out!"

The man immediately put his head back down and raised his hands a few inches off the pavement in a gesture of surrender.

"Nobody fucking move!"

They didn't.

Danny knelt next to Sean, looking back and forth quickly from him to the other men. He felt Sean's neck for a pulse. He had to move his fingers around, but found it. He's alive! Danny couldn't see any blood, but his partner's shirt was torn at the bullet's point of entry.

He wanted to check the driver's pulse but wasn't about to leave Sean until backup arrived. He kept his eyes on the bad guys while cradling Sean's head with his free hand.

"I hope you don't die, you bastard, but it's your fault if you do." Danny growled to the driver, who still hadn't moved.

Danny was startled to feel Sean's head move, and thought he had dropped him.

"Son of a *bitch* that hurts!" Sean yelled.

Shocked, Danny laughed and burst into tears at the same time. "Son of a bitch yourself, man. You're alive!"

Sean picked up his gun, which was lying on the ground right next him, then sat up and pointed it at the Cadillac's passengers. "Of course I'm alive. My head is killing me though, and I think I cracked some ribs. Shit!"

Danny stood up. "Can you stand?"

"Yeah, I can stand. Did I get shot?" Sean started to get up and fell back, breaking his fall with his free hand.

"What do you mean, did you get shot? Yes, in the chest. Your shirt's ripped and the bullet is probably lodged in your vest. You took quite a header when you fell." Danny grabbed Sean's arm and pulled him up, all the while keeping his eyes on the passengers.

"Damn! Easy, okay?" Sean pulled away and touched his shoulder. "I thought these vests were supposed to take all the impact." Sean looked at the men around him, then nodded towards the driver, who still hadn't moved. "Better see if he's alive."

Danny went to the driver and crouched beside him. The man had a pulse, although an extremely weak one. "I think he'll live. Unless you want to kill him."

"Is he the guy who shot me? Maybe I will," said Sean. "Maybe I could blame it on this headache."

Danny felt the tension leave his jaws at the sound of approaching sirens. He looked in the direction of the sound and realized that traffic on the road had slowed to a crawl. *Rubberneckers.* Looking above the cars, he could also see that the sky was clear and full of stars. It seemed incongruous with everything that was happening.

In seconds a patrol car pulled onto the shoulder, the front of the car pointed towards the scene, and came to an abrupt stop. Two officers scrambled out and drew their guns, aiming at the men on the ground.

"Where is the downed officer?" asked one of them, Sergeant McPherson. He scanned the area as he spoke.

"It was me, but I'm okay," said Sean.

"Are there any others?" said McPherson, now concentrating on Danny and Sean.

"No, just these guys," said Danny. That one needs an ambulance." He had barely finished speaking when he heard more sirens. The ambulance pulled onto the shoulder fifty yards from Danny's car and sped past the slow-moving line of onlookers. From the passenger seat a paramedic jumped out before the vehicle came to a complete stop.

"You've got an officer down?"

Danny motioned to Sean with his head. "He was, but apparently he was faking," Danny said.

Both paramedics grabbed bags and went to Sean.

"You frisked these guys yet?" said Sergeant McPherson.

"No," said Danny, "we were waiting for you."

"Let me do it," said Sean.

"Oh no. There's another ambulance coming, and you're getting in it," said McPherson.

"Come on, Sergeant, I'm all right."

Two more patrol cars, sirens blaring, showed up. The whole area was lit by flashing lights and headlights.

"You've been shot, Officer. Protocol says you're done for the night until you get medically cleared. And you, Garcia, are facing a mountain of paperwork for all this. This area is going to be crawling with cops in a few minutes. We'll take it from here. You boys have earned the rest of the night off."

"Oh, come on," said Danny, motioning towards the four men. "We'll stay and help you sort this out."

"Sorry, boys," said the sergeant. "The cavalry is here. You're off shift now."

Chapter Twenty-Three

The solitary echo of his footsteps reminded Danny of walking down the halls of school when he was a kid. The reflection from the fluorescent lights on the well-polished linoleum stayed the same distance in front of him as he moved forward. He remembered back then running faster, then slowing down, trying to outwit and overtake his shadow image. It was a no-win endeavor, but it was amusing. This walk, however, felt like punishment, a perp walk, the shadow judging his every move.

The office was two thirds of the way down the hall, as he'd been told it would be. Room 124. *L.L. Hiakawa, MD.* Danny reached for the doorknob, but stopped before touching it.

Every cop knows that shooting someone, or getting shot at, is a possibility every time he puts on his uniform. It's drilled into cadets. But it's impossible to feel any emotion behind it when it's just a hypothetical classroom discussion, much less to imagine the myriad of feelings and confusion that surface when a gun is actually fired by or at you. Some cops are over it as soon as they holster their weapons. For others, that's when emotions kick in. As a concept, gunfire had meant nothing to Danny. But the feelings he'd had since the other night were new, confusing. He needed to process them for himself, not discuss things with a stranger—and certainly not a stranger who would be scrutinizing his every word and movement, looking for something, anything, that might indicate that he couldn't do his job. But Danny had been ordered to have this talk. It wasn't his choice.

He let his hand fall on the doorknob, turned it and walked in. The receptionist looked up from her desk. He knew it was silly, but he felt embarrassed to tell her his name and why he was here. Danny Garcia, one tough and by-the-book cop, having to see a shrink. "Danny Garcia here to see Dr. Hiakawa."

"Yes, Officer, she's expecting you. I'll let her know you're here."

She?

The receptionist lowered her phone after a brief exchange. "You can go right in, Officer." She pointed to the only door in the room besides the one he'd walked in. Did she think he was too befuddled to figure that out?

A tall woman with large-framed glasses extended her hand to him when he walked through the office door. "Come in, Officer Garcia. I'm Lorraine Hiakawa. May I call you Danny? Won't you have a seat?"

She offered Danny an upholstered chair to the left of her desk, grabbed a file and took another chair directly across from him. The office looked like the old classroom it was, divided in half with a sheetrock partition and a coat of paint. Hiakawa, or somebody, had softened it up with curtains, a few posters on the wall, and the sparse furniture.

"How are you, Danny?"

Danny thought about what "relaxed" looks like and tried to emulate it. "Well, truthfully, a little uncomfortable being here. That won't count against me, will it?"

Hiakawa laughed, simultaneously adjusting her glasses. "No, it won't, and I can imagine that being sent here by a superior officer might make anybody a little nervous."

Danny wasn't comforted by her response. "I thought you'd be a man," he said.

"And did you also think I'd be Asian?"

"Well, yes. With the name, and all."

"One of my professors in graduate school suggested I use my initials instead of my first name, especially when I publish articles. He said if people thought I was a man, I'd have more credibility. I'm afraid it's still a man's world. And my stepfather was from Maui. He adopted me when I was three. Mom changed our last names."

"So you didn't take your husband's name."

Hiakawa touched her wedding ring. "No. I'd already been working for a while and it seemed easier, professionally at least, to keep my own."

"How many weeks have you been married?"

"God, is it that obvious? Just under a month. How did you know?"

"You touched your ring when I asked about your maiden name. Usually only newlyweds do that."

"Wow. You pay attention. I'm impressed."

"It's a smart thing to do if you're a cop. Might save your life."

"Yes, I suppose so. That's sort of why you're here, isn't it? You shot a man after he shot at you."

Danny straightened up in the chair. "I fired a round at a suspect after he shot my partner. He got off another round before I was able to neutralize him."

"That sounds very police-like."

"I'm a cop. We tend to sound police-like," said Danny.

Hiakawa took off her glasses and laid them on the arm of her chair. "You're angry."

Danny thought she looked older with her glasses on and wished she hadn't taken them off. She's just a kid, he thought. "No, I'm not angry, but this is awkward. You're trying to ascertain if I'm likely to screw up as a result of what happened. I'm not, not in the least, but you being a shrink makes me feel like I should keep my guard up."

"I appreciate the honesty and I understand how this may feel. I don't know if this will make you feel any better, but I'm really here for your sake. You've been through a traumatic experience, and I just want to see how you're processing it. If you need it, maybe I can help."

How could she help? Danny guessed she'd been a doctor for a year, maybe two tops. "How long have you been doing this?"

"I've been working with the police department for eight years, but I've been licensed for twelve."

"I would never have guessed that you were that old," said Danny. Hearing himself, "I don't mean 'old'…you just look younger is all."

Hiakawa laughed again. Danny liked her laugh. If he wasn't careful, he might like her. That kind of vulnerability probably wasn't a good idea.

Hiakawa spoke. "I read the report. The men you stopped were drug dealers?"

"Methamphetamines. They found about one hundred thousand dollars worth in the trunk of the car. We stopped them for a traffic violation and didn't know about the drugs. I guess they thought killing us would be preferable to letting us search the vehicle."

"Yes. I understand the man…" she looked in her file, "Charles Brooks, died of his wounds at the hospital."

Charles Brooks? Was that his name? Danny had only heard it once, when he called it into dispatch to run a warrant check. During the brief inquiry at the station immediately following the shooting, Brooks had been called either "The Shooter," or "The Driver." Charles Brooks sounded like an accountant, or somebody's neighbor, not the felon that Charles Brooks was—or had been. Not the Charles Brooks who had tried to kill both him and his partner.

"That's correct," said Danny.

"How does that make you feel?"

"You mean that he died? He shot one cop and tried to shoot another. When you do that, cops shoot back. He asked for it."

"I understand that, and I understand that what you did was one hundred percent justified, but the man is dead now, and you were part of it."

"Part of it? I pulled the trigger, so I guess that's a safe bet."

Danny hoped Hiakawa was smiling with respect and not like he'd just uttered the thing that would nail him.

"My apologies. I might be trying too hard to be sensitive to how you might be feeling."

"Officers shoot people and get shot at. It happens. But most get back to work right away and I've been on forced leave for two days."

"Yes, Danny, officers *do* get shot. But you watched a man shoot your partner, try to shoot you, and then you fatally shot him. He deserved it and anybody else would have done the same thing, but he died as a result of it. That's something some cops can't handle."

"Oh, I can. What I can't handle is being put on ice, like I've done something wrong. I want to get back to the job, but I can't until you okay it."

Well, this is partly for your sake, like I said, but I'll be honest—the department doesn't want a cop who's emotionally unstable on the streets."

Danny let her words soak in. "I understand. Let's do this."

"Thank you. I'd like to start by you telling me how you've been since it happened. How are you sleeping, have you been irritable, or jumpy—"

"You mean you're worried that I might have post-traumatic stress disorder?"

Hiakawa laughed a little. "No, I think it's a little too early to slap a label on you, but it's a safe bet that this had some impact. I just want to know how you are processing everything. When, exactly, did the incident take place?"

The "incident." That was neat, tidy.

"Three days, ago, about ten at night. We still had a couple of hours on our shift, but they had to take Sean to the hospital to be checked out and I had to start answering questions."

"What was it like?"

"You mean getting shot at, or shooting at someone?"

"Both, sort of. I'm sure you were on autopilot, but I wonder if you had any thoughts or feelings about what was happening while it was going on."

Danny thought before answering, and decided to tell her the truth. Part of that was because his gut instinct was to trust her, and part was because he worried that any lie he thought up might accidentally make him sound crazy. "I've never been in that situation," he said. "Never had somebody point a gun at me and known he was trying to kill me. I can't believe how many places my head went in that instant until I could get off a shot. They say your life passes in front of you when something like that happens. All I got were the crappy parts, the shit, how I'd let people down in my life. Things that didn't work out the way I wanted them to. I felt absolutely powerless. It seemed to last forever, and it was painful, hideously painful, but it only lasted a split second. Shooting him? Shooting him wasn't a big deal at all, tell you the truth. That was automatic and I'd do it again. He isn't dead because I shot him, he's dead because he shot at two cops. He asked for it. I'm clear as a bell on that."

"Can you tell me about the memories that came up for you?"

Danny could see Charles Brooks drop to his knees, his gun pointed at him. "It was like I could see inside the gun barrel." Danny relived the rest of it for Hiakawa. He felt no connection to his memory of the events; in fact he felt a distant, almost forced, separation from his own feelings.

"Why do you think you had all those painful memories?"

"I've thought about that. I want it to be because I was afraid Sean might die and I'd lose him, too, but I don't think I'm that gallant."

"Meaning?"

Danny threw mental dice and decided to stick with the truth. "I was worried that I might die. Kind of selfish."

"Kind of normal, Danny. A man is trying to kill you, I would expect you to think about your own life. I don't know how you could think about anything else."

"Well, why did I think of all that sad shit then?" Danny asked. "I thought I was supposed to remember all the good times?"

"Who told you that?"

"I don't know," said Danny. "That's how it happens in the movies, isn't it?"

Hiakawa smiled. "Maybe you're a bad script writer, huh? Seriously, I don't know that there are any rules here. It seems pretty normal to me that, if you were facing death, especially if it's happening suddenly and at somebody else's hands, you'd think about loss."

"I'm in love, I hope to get married, and I didn't think about *her* until it was all over."

"Why do you think that is?"

"I don't know. All the others were people really close to me, too."

"But you said all of them had painful memories associated with them. How is it with her?"

"It's good, it's very good. Carol may be the first pain-free relationship I've had."

"Carol is your fiancée?"

"Not yet."

"Well, I can't say why you thought about painful things at that time, but you did. It makes sense that you wouldn't think about your girlfriend while you were thinking about people associated with bad memories. Maybe you thought about her afterwards because you were no longer focused on loss."

"I hope that's right," said Danny. "Makes me feel a little better about myself."

"This was an extremely traumatic situation, Danny. How do you think it's affected you?"

"You mean, did it change me? Not shooting him, that didn't change me at all. Getting shot at did, but not in a way you and everybody else are worried about. It won't stop me from doing my job. It's made me focus more on my personal life, but I'm not planning any big life changes or anything. It won't change how I do the job. And I want to do the job."

"Getting shot at has to be a life-altering experience."

"I don't know how to explain that. You're not a cop. I know it's a cliché, but you don't have a partner who would put his life on the line for you if he had to. No offense, but your husband might not even do that. Not many people would—or *could*, is more like it. That man, Charles Brooks? Shot my partner. Tried to kill him. Sean drives me crazy, he's like a kid, but I sometimes think I love him more than anybody else on the planet, almost as much as the woman I hope to marry. Shooting Charles Brooks was not only automatic, it was a pleasure. It was all I could do for Sean at that moment. If I'm worried about anything, it isn't that I'll crumble if that ever happens again, it's that it *might* happen again. Next time, if I'm not on the ball, Sean could get killed. If I thought I was in any way compromised to do the job, knowing that someday something might happen and I'd freeze under pressure, you wouldn't have to tell anybody I couldn't work. I'd quit and never look back."

"I don't know that it's that easy, Danny. I know you feel okay now, but the psychological reaction to something like you've experienced could happen right away or it could take a long time to manifest. Weeks, or even years isn't unusual."

"So, are you saying I should *never* go back on the streets because something might hamper me, even though there's just as good a chance that it won't? I'm sorry Doc, but I can't buy that."

"No, I'm not saying any such thing. I just think we need to explore this a little more. Give you some idea of what to look for and tools to deal with it should you notice a change in your responses to situations. It might also help if you could confide in someone close to you who would also tell you if they notice anything different in your behavior. Maybe Carol. Do you go to church? Is there a priest you could talk to?"

Danny thought about the Bishop and Morales, and he laughed. "Well, I go to church every week, but it's not really a place of comfort, if that's what you mean."

"Could you try it?"

"Trust me, that's not going to work. Can we just let it go at that?"

"Okay. So you think you are fine."

"Personally? I don't know what I am, tell you the truth, but I don't think 'fine' is at the top of the list. That stuff I thought about was unsettling. I've got to do something about it, I'm just not sure what that something is. But work-wise? I'm okay. I am not professionally compromised. I can do my job, and I want to do my job. The sooner you and everybody else realize that, the better."

Chapter Twenty-Four

Tim was sober, had been for two months, starting the night he'd gone to an AA meeting and met Richard. Clients at New Beginnings were encouraged to attend an AA meeting every day for the first ninety days. Tim hadn't missed one yet. He still wasn't completely comfortable with all the talk about God, but it didn't bother him as much as it had. He was amazed that Sara had taken him back. Humbled that the manager who'd fired him had rehired him, and that real estate sales were going so well. Mostly he was just plain grateful. Grateful that Life seemed to be giving him another chance. This time, he was determined not to screw it up. Any of it.

He was thinking about all that while scrunching his long legs under the steering wheel. Once settled, he unlatched the two levers at the top of the windshield and with one hand put the top down. The car was Sara's, a green Miata. Tim had his gym bag on the passenger seat and planned to drive by his old high school to see if he could get into a pick-up basketball game.

As he drove past the Soriano bakery, the aroma of freshly baked bread reminded him of how much Sara loved the loaf of sourdough he'd taken home a few weeks earlier. He made a U-turn, pulled in the lot and parked. When the bell over the door rang, Mr. Soriano looked up from behind the counter. "Timmy my boy!" Soriano's eyes sparkled. He came around the counter and hugged Tim, his head barely reaching Tim's chin. Soriano was slight of build with sharp, angular features, the physical opposite of what Tim thought a baker should look like. "It's been too long. To what do I owe the pleasure of this visit?"

"The pleasure is mine, Mr. Soriano. I could smell the fresh bread as I drove by and had to stop. How's the family?"

"Ah, they're great. Did your mom tell you Marie's going to make me a grandfather again? That makes four, Timmy. How's it with you? You met the right woman yet?"

"I may have. In fact, that's why I'm here. I took home a loaf of your sourdough the last time I was in Napa, and she loved it. I think I could get away with anything as long as I keep bringing her your bread."

"So, you've found somebody and she appreciates good bread? That sounds like a special woman, Timmy. Don't let her get away." Soriano chuckled, moved behind the counter and towards a row of freshly baked bread. He grabbed two loaves, simultaneously dropped each in its own paper bag and brought them back to Tim. "Here's a sourdough. Take her this rye, too. She likes good bread, this will make her happy."

"Thanks, Mr. S. I'll do that." Tim reached into his back pocket.

"You better not be pulling out your wallet, Timmy. Your money's no good here, not today, anyway. You're getting bread for the special woman in your life. I want you to give this to her from me."

"Thanks, I appreciate that. So will she. She tastes this rye, she might leave me for you."

"Don't you think I know that?" Soriano looked over his shoulder and gave Tim a conspiratorial wink. "I love my Elisabeth. We've been together forty-eight years now, but a man's got to have a backup plan, right?" He stepped out from behind the counter and grabbed Tim by the shoulders. "Timmy you look great. I'm so glad you stopped in! You taking care of yourself?"

"I hit a rough patch a while back, but things are going good now." Tim was pleasantly startled to hear himself answer honestly, without trying to sugarcoat the past. Before, he would have lied in a heartbeat if he thought it would make him look better.

"That's a boy. Glad to hear it. Are you still in real estate? Your parents said you were doing well."

"Actually, I am. I stopped selling for a while, but I've been back at it for a couple of months now. It's a good time to be in the business."

"You're a smart one. You work hard while the market is good, save a little money so you and that special woman can have the things you want. Ah, I'm so glad you stopped in. You come back to town next time, you bring her with you, you hear?"

"It's a promise. It's great seeing you too, Mr. Soriano. Thanks for the bread."

Tim got back in the Miata and tossed the two loaves next to his gym bag. Talking to Soriano had made him feel good about himself.

Approaching the school a few blocks later, he could see that a small game was in progress. Excellent! He parked the car and looked around. The school—a plain brick building when he had attended— was now covered in thick ivy, which appeared to have been growing there for years. Tim counted five guys on the court. I'll make the sides even, he thought. Taking his tennis shoes and socks out of his gym bag, he kicked off his flip-flops and laced up, checking out the game as he did. One guy, the tallest, was dominating the boards.

As Tim walked toward the court, a player went in for what should have been an easy layup. From the other side of the lane, the tall man leaped into the air with graceful ferocity and blocked the shot, knocking it clear off the court.

Wow, nice move, thought Tim. The errant ball rolled towards him and he bent over to retrieve it. Straightening up, he started to throw it back on the court, when he got a better look at the tall guy.

"Jimmy? Is that you?"

Tim nearly dropped the ball. It was Jorge.

"It's Tim. And yeah, it's me." He face started to tingle and his stomach flipped. Be cool, he thought. "What are you doing here?"

"Well I'll be damned," said Jorge. "Look at you, man. You come out here to play some ball?"

The other men were all watching as Tim walked towards the court. He realized he still had the ball and threw it to one of them. "How'd you get here?"

"What do you mean? I'm here almost every day. I *own* this court," said Jorge, smiling and pointing at the other players, several of whom rolled their eyes. "How 'bout you? What brings you here?"

"I came here to play some ball." Nodding his head towards the building: "I went to school here."

"You live in Napa? I didn't remember that."

"No, I live in Santa Rosa now. I'm just visiting my folks. I thought you lived in the East Bay?"

"Yeah I did, but I moved to Napa a few months ago."

"Why?"

Jorge seemed to be at a loss of words for a moment, but recovered with a smile. "I heard this town needed a basketball coach."

One of the other men groaned.

"You're looking fit, Timmy."

"You too, Jorge." Real good in fact, thought Tim. It looked like he'd gained fifteen pounds of muscle.

"Hey, we're all thrilled that you guys are together again, but can we play ball?" The man holding the ball at his hip quipped. He shook Tim's hand, "I'm Alex. It's you, me and Tony here against Jorge and the other two," he said, pointing to the other men on the court. He peeled off his tee shirt. We'll be skins. First to twenty wins?" Tim and Tony nodded, bumped fists and took off their shirts.

Alex threw the ball to Tim. "Take it out!"

Tim stepped out of bounds moving the ball from hand to hand. Doing so grounded him, and lessened the shock of seeing Jorge. He threw an inbound pass to Alex, then ran up court. Alex passed back to Tim. He dribbled for a moment, then threw a bounce pass to Tony, who was breaking under the basket. It was an easy-to-read play, and Jorge stepped between the two men, stole the ball and dribbled down court. Uncontested, he laid it up for two. He caught the ball as it fell from the net and passed it to Tim.

"You've got to bring more than that out here, College Boy. That was a junior high pass. Want to try it again?"

Still with the "College Boy." Tim decided to let it slide, and to concentrate on the game. "Sorry guys," he said to his teammates. "Little stiff getting out of the car." Neither of the men said anything. Tim stepped out of bounds, passed to Tony and ran up court. He broke from his defender and moved to the perimeter. Tony threw him a pass. Tim dribbled towards the basket and Jorge stepped in front of him.

"Come on. Bring it on!"

Tim stopped for a moment, dribbled with his left hand and looked Jorge in the eye. He moved to Jorge's left and started to drive to the basket. Jorge reached in to steal the ball. It was just the move Tim was hoping for. In an instant, he turned his back to Jorge while switching hands on the ball, spun around completely and dribbled past Jorge's right side. Two steps later he was at the basket, leaped in the air, and dunked.

"Ooohh," Tony said, high-fiving Tim.

Tim thumped his chest twice with his fist. "Is that what you had in mind, Jorge?"

"Not bad." Jorge did not appear to appreciate the move as much as the other men. "Enjoy the moment, cause that's not going happen again."

"We'll see." Tim couldn't help but smile.

Jorge stopped talking after that and was all business. Fifteen minutes later, Jorge's team was up by two.

Alex inbounded to Tim, who dribbled down court. He paused in front of Jorge, then drove hard past him. Jorge could only watch as Tim went up for an easy layup.

"Tied up! Pressure is on now," said one of Tim's teammates.

"Game is to twenty. It's not over yet," answered Jorge.

Jorge threw the ball to Bill. "Inbound it." He stood in front of him with his hands at chest level, indicating that Bill should inbound to him.

Jorge dribbled towards the basket at the other end of the court with Tim running beside him step for step. Tim got between Jorge and the basket, and as Jorge went up for a layup, Tim went up with him. Jorge pushed the ball towards the backboard with one hand, but Tim blocked it hard, knocking it out of bounds.

"You're not going to win that easily," Tim said.

Jorge didn't respond. He looked angry, focused.

"Inbound it again!" Jorge flipped the ball to Bill.

Bill rolled his eyes and inbounded to Jorge, who immediately pulled up for a jumper—and missed. Alex grabbed the rebound and passed to Tony, who was at half-court. Tim broke for the lane and Tony hit him with a perfect pass. Tim dribbled twice and went up for a layup, but Jorge was with him. It was just the two of them at that end of the court, and both of them went up at the same time. No one could see Jorge when he pushed Tim's chest with one hand, hard, while raising the other to block the shot. He didn't need to block—the push knocked Tim off balance. Tim not only missed, he fell and landed on his rear end, his legs splayed out in front of him.

Jorge grabbed the rebound and headed down the court.

"Oh, do you think that might have been a *foul*?" Tim, still sitting on the court, yelled to Jorge's back.

The other men all stopped, expecting Jorge to acknowledge the comment, but he never looked back. He dribbled the length of the court, went airborne, and dunked the ball resoundingly.

"*Yes*! That's twenty and the game!" he said.

"Aw, man. That's more like prison ball you're playing," said Tim. He pushed himself up. "You could do time for a foul like that."

Jorge walked up to him, fist clenched by his sides. "What? I didn't foul you. You were charging."

"You've *got* to be kidding."

"Anybody here see me foul this man?" Jorge pointed to Tim. He looked from man to man.

"I saw Tim miss his shot and fall down," said Bill.

"Okay then," responded Jorge.

"But I couldn't see anything. I can't say that he wasn't fouled," Bill added.

"Well, *I'm* saying it," said Jorge. "Anybody got a problem with that?"

Jorge's anger shocked Tim. He looked to the other men for their reaction, and saw faces of surprise and embarrassment from them as well. All looked to Tim for his response. He knew he'd been pushed, a flagrant foul, but decided it wasn't worth an argument, and certainly not a fight. If he was still drinking, maybe, but not while he was sober.

"Okay, okay. Maybe I just lost my balance. You guys won this one," Tim said, attempting to smile as he did. Someone had to clean this up.

Tim watched Jorge's anger fade from his face. He looked from man to man, smiled and slapped Tim on the back. "Nice game, College Boy. You almost beat us."

"College Boy" bothered Tim a little when they were at New Beginnings, but now it downright pissed him off.

"Let's play again."

"Oh no, that's enough for me," said Eduardo. "I gotta Honey-Do list as long as my arm. My wife will *kill* me if I'm any later."

Tony picked up the ball. "Yeah, I have to go too, and it's my ball. Sorry fellas. Good playing with you guys. Nice meeting you, Tim. You play a good game."

The men were leaving, the skins picking up the tee shirts they'd left courtside.

"Good game, Tim," said Tony. He and Alex got into a black Mercedes sedan. "How 'bout next week, same day same time?"

Disappointed at first that they were through playing, Tim admitted to himself that he wanted revenge more than another game, and that stopping now was for the best. "Thanks for the game, guys. If I'm in town next week, I'll be here," said Tim.

"Hey, we're going out for a beer. Anybody want to join us?"

"Not me," said Jorge. "How about you, Timmy?"

"No, me neither," Tim answered. "Thanks again, guys."

"No, thank *you*," said Alex. "It was fun watching somebody who could dunk on the Father."

Jorge wagged his finger at Alex. "He got lucky today." Turning to Tim: "But you did good out there, Timmy. You brought a lot more with you than I expected."

Father? "I've played before, remember?" said Tim. "And what did he mean, 'Father'?"

"They call me The Godfather of the Court," replied Jorge, "Because it's my neighborhood."

The others were driving away. Jorge squeezed the top of Tim's shoulder. "Hey, I might have bumped you harder than I thought. If I did, I apologize."

There's the smooth Jorge he remembered. "I dunno, maybe you didn't. No worries. He resisted knocking Jorge's hand off him. "So you're still sober?" he asked.

"Been sober since I left," said Jorge. "I still go to the bars every once in a while. Got to keep up my social life, you know."

"Do you feel comfortable in a bar? I don't think I could do it."

"It's no big deal. Tell you the truth? I'm surprised how easy it's been to stay sober. I just stopped and poof—" He snapped his fingers on the word, "It was gone."

"Hey, how come you left like you did? We were all looking forward to hearing your story."

"You mean New Beginnings?" Jorge swatted his hand. "Truthfully? I was worried that I'd get all emotional. Besides, I was ready to go. How about you? Did that legal stuff catch up with you?"

Tim could feel his cheeks burn. "No, Jorge. I told you, that was cleared up when I went to New Beginnings."

Jorge laughed. He bent over, picked up a pebble, and threw it at the backboard. "Yeah, so you said. I also remember it was a decent chunk of change. What was it, twenty thou?"

"Twenty-five. But we've had this conversation. Why are you asking now?"

"I just remember thinking it was strange. I mean, there has to be *some* amount that would raise red flags with the loan officers, but apparently, twenty five K isn't it. Did you know that when you picked that number?"

"No, I didn't. It was based on what I needed. Why are we talking about this again?"

"Why not? It's no big deal, just stuff from the past."

Tim didn't buy that for a second. "What about you? What have you been doing since you left New Beginnings?"

"Keeping busy. Playing a lot of ball."

"Are you working? You said you moved here. What prompted that?"

Jorge had his arms folded in front of him and was looking at the ground. He didn't say anything for a few seconds, then dropped his arms to his side and stared into Tim's eyes. "It was good playing ball with you today. I hope to see you out here again. But you and me? We aren't going to be friends, so let's don't waste time on a lot of small talk." Jorge reached out and put his hand on Tim's shoulder. "Good seeing you though. I look forward to the next game." With that, he turned and walked to his Porsche.

Tim didn't move or say a word, he just watched Jorge get in his car and drive away. "Good seeing you too," Tim said to no one.

Chapter Twenty-Five

Sean and Carol closed their car doors and started walking towards Danny. Both were expressionless. He couldn't remember ever seeing the two of them together and didn't understand the long faces. "What are you guys doing?" he asked.

"Looking for a good cop," Sean replied from his passenger seat.

Wait, how did he get back in the car?

Oh, it was a dream. Danny wondered where it was going.

The car was a black, early eighties Cadillac. The windows were so heavily tinted that Danny could barely see Sean, wasn't even sure if it was him after all. He got out of the car and it wasn't Sean. It was his brother. *Why is he with Carol?*

The lot was filled with Cadillacs. Danny thought they were all black and didn't have windows, but it was hard to tell. For that matter, he couldn't see anything. He could somehow feel Carol, and knew she was in trouble.

"Carol! Sean! Where are you?" Danny screamed, but he wasn't making any sound, nothing at all. He started to run to where he had last seen them, but his legs wouldn't move. He leaned forward, thought he would fall over at such an angle, but his legs were rooted in place.

This was getting bad. He needed to wake up.

"Danny!" It was Carol. Where had she been a moment ago? Her arms were stretched out to him and she was visibly distraught, although Danny couldn't tell why. She was crying, sobbing. "Oh Danny, please help!" His brother stood next to her, but he was laughing.

"Where's a good cop when you need one, eh partner?" It was Sean, and he was laughing so hard now that he was doubled over. Danny thought Sean's body was mangled, misshapen somehow, but it was just a feeling he had. He couldn't see anything visibly wrong with his partner. It made no sense and that really scared him.

Danny could feel his heart pounding, and worried that it might burst out of his chest. "I've got to wake up!" Did he say that or just imagine it? He looked down at his feet, but still couldn't move them. *What the fuck?*

Carol kept crying. "Don't you care, Danny?"

"Of course I care, Carol!" Danny was sure she couldn't hear him. He felt totally helpless.

Sean had a gun in each hand, both pointed at Danny. "You're no good to anybody, Garcia." Sean fired the weapons. Thick, dark smoke from the discharges began to surround him and Carol until Danny couldn't see them anymore. Then the smoke disappeared, and he could see dozens of bullets coming at him. He tried to move again but was now completely paralyzed. "I can't wake up!"

Everything went black.

"Shit!" Danny kicked his legs and pushed himself up. He was awake now, in his bed.

"Danny!"

Danny jerked away from the hand on his shoulder and sat up. The dream was over—at least he thought it was.

"Oh shit, I'm sorry," he said quietly.

Carol turned on the lamp on her side of the bed. "Are you okay? You were moaning and kicking your legs. You're panting, Danny. What were you dreaming?"

Danny ran his hand through his hair. "I'm not sure. You and Sean were there, or maybe you and my brother. I think you needed help and I couldn't move." Details of the dream were already eluding him. He was left with the fear. "I'm sorry I woke you."

"Don't be silly. Do you want some water?"

Danny rubbed his chest with the palm of his hand, surprised by the sweat that came from it. He lifted the blankets off. "I'm okay," he said, getting out of bed and walking around to her side of it. "I'm going to the bathroom. You go back to sleep."

"Are you sure?"

"Yes, yes, I'm fine, babe. Go back to sleep."

"Okay, then. I love you, Danny." Carol leaned up to receive Danny's kiss.

"I love you too. Go back to sleep."

He turned off Carol's lamp and turned on the bathroom light. His reflection startled him. He leaned across the sink and looked at his eyes.

A month after Danny had joined the force, a young, angry man had pointed a gun in his face. The gunman had just lost his job, and his wife, and was robbing a convenience store that Danny happened into after his shift. He talked the man into letting everyone else leave the store and then into giving him the gun. Two years ago, he and Sean had found themselves surrounded by five angry gang bangers who were threatening to kill the officers because, a week earlier, another officer had shot one of their members in the line of duty. Danny managed to diffuse that situation as well, telling the men that, while he understood how they felt, killing him and Sean would lead to more deaths and more lives ruined for no good reason. Although his adrenalin had been off-the-charts high both times, Danny hadn't been afraid. It was all part of the job. He was emotionally equipped to handle tense situations, and he left the incidents behind when they were over.

Danny's dream was just that, a dream, and he knew it. Still, there was no denying the terror and total loss of control he'd felt. He looked at himself in the mirror, turning his head from side to side as he did. Everything looked normal. No reason to stay awake now. He flicked off the bathroom light, opened the door, and walked back to bed. Within seconds, he could feel himself drifting off to sleep, and jerked himself awake.

Chapter Twenty-Six

The ice cream shop, now owned by a national chain, first opened fifty years ago as a Mom and Pop store. The original eight-foot-tall ice cream cone-shaped sign still stood next to the curb, the new corporate owners' nod to the store's local history. Located across the street from an elementary school, that sign was a kid magnet, a siren call for frozen, sugary heaven, and the after-school business alone had made the store successful for all of the five decades it had operated. At 3:30 p.m., the place was full of mothers and students just out of school, most with ice cream already smeared on their faces.

"This is nice, isn't it? Just the two of us, enjoying an afternoon cone together." Sean took a bite of his cone, taking about a third of the ice cream with it.

Danny looked around. "Are you serious? There must be thirty kids in here. The noise would drown out a jet."

"Always Mr. Negative. I take you out for a treat and this is what I hear," said Sean.

"You take *me* out? *I* paid for these 'treats,' partner," said Danny.

"See? You focus on the details and miss the bigger picture. It's nice to be able to sit quietly and just relax," said Sean.

A woman with two kids, a boy and girl, stood by the cash register. The little girl reminded Danny of a picture he'd seen of his mother when she was a child, her curly hair as bouncy as the flounced skirt she'd worn. She couldn't have been more than five when the picture was taken. Danny figured less than ten seconds had passed since the store employee had handed the kids their cones, yet the little girl's chin was already covered with orange sherbet. Her mom grabbed a napkin out of the metal box on the counter and wiped it off. "Rachel, how did you get so much on you so quickly?"

He watched as Rachel's ice cream fell from its cone and onto the floor. The girl missed the spill but, as soon as she noticed what had happened, burst into tears. "Mommy!" she cried.

"Rachel, you have to be more careful," said her mother. "Ronny, share your ice cream with your sister."

"But I didn't do anything!" said a distraught Ronny.

"Don't argue, young man," said the mother. "Rachel, eat some of your brother's ice cream and stop crying." Ronny began to protest the sacrifice he was being forced to make more loudly, which made Rachel cry all the harder.

Danny gripped the edge of his table and could feel blood pulsing in his temples. He cringed at the sound of a high-pitched squeal to his left. Two boys were on the bench of the booth next to them, jumping up and down as though on a trampoline. The cones they held were melting, and Danny couldn't tell where the ice cream ended and their hands started. One of them let out another screech. Danny winced. He was starting to have trouble breathing. He started to speak, and had to strain to sound normal. "This is a special, magical moment, Sean, but I've had enough. Why don't we finish the ice creams in the car?" He got up from the booth and walked to the door.

Sean sat and looked at him as he walked away. "What do *you* think, Sean? Would you like to stay or leave?"

Danny walked outside and dropped his cone in a trashcan by the door. He got in the driver's side of the car and pulled the door shut tightly. The immediate quiet made him realize how agitated he was.

Sean followed a few seconds later. He had his cone in his right hand and used his left to close his door. When he pulled it shut, he grimaced.

"Could we have at least *talked* about leaving?" said Sean.

"Don't worry about it. What's that all about?" said Danny.

"What was what? I was enjoying my ice cream until you stormed off." said Sean.

"No, when you closed the door, you looked like you were in pain." asked Danny.

"My chest still hurts."

"From getting shot?" asked Danny.

"Are you sure he had a gun? It feels more like he used a cannon." Sean popped the rest of his cone in his mouth, then rubbed his chest where the bullet had lodged in his vest. "What just happened in there?"

Danny was quiet for a moment. "It's hard to believe that was only a week ago," he said.

"Not to me. This thing hurts all the time," said Sean.

"Do you think about it much?" Danny asked. Hiakawa had released him to work after their second session. He'd been back on the job for three days, and he and Sean had barely talked about what had happened.

"You mean getting shot? Hell, yes, I think about it. If he wasn't dead, I'd find that guy and kick his ass. Is what just happened related to that?" asked Sean.

Danny ignored the question. "Well, I got to shoot him, and that felt great," Danny said.

"Getting the third degree afterwards was about as bad. I know procedure says to investigate everything, but it felt like *we* were the ones being interrogated, instead of the bad guys," said Sean.

"Tell me about it. And having to go to a psychiatrist was over the top."

Sean chuckled, then sat quietly for a moment. "What'd you tell the shrink?"

Danny shrugged his shoulders. "The truth, mostly. I was afraid that if I tried to lie to her, she'd see through it, or I'd end up sounding worse than I really am."

"Are you okay?"

Danny didn't answer.

"Danny, this is your partner asking."

"God's honest truth? I don't know, man. I mean, I'm not paranoid or anything, but little shit bothers me. Like those kids in there. I wasn't freaking out or anything, but all that noise—I've got no tolerance for that shit."

"Well, a little of that goes a long way."

"I had a nightmare last night. I've had bad dreams before, but this one kicked my ass, man. Scared the shit out of me."

"Do I need to worry about you?"

As mercilessly as his partner teased him, Danny knew he could tell Sean anything without fear of it coming back on him. "On the job? No way. If I ever have to draw my weapon again, I'll shoot without hesitation. That whole thing really pissed me off, if you want to know the truth. Trust me, you have nothing to worry about."

"Of course I trust you," said Sean.

Danny leaned forward to start the car, stopped in mid motion, and sat back in his seat.

"What did you say to the shrink?" Danny asked.

Sean looked out his window for a moment before speaking. "We off the record here?"

It took a moment of silence for Danny to realize that Sean was serious. "What? Of course we're off the record. It's *me*, Sean."

Sean still looked out the window. "I told her that I saw him pull his gun, but I couldn't get mine out of the holster fast enough and he shot first. Told her as soon as I was hit, I went down, hit my head and blacked out."

Danny furrowed his brow. "I didn't think you saw him. I called your name when he pulled his gun. You looked at me for a split second and then he shot you. *I* feel bad because I distracted you. If I hadn't said anything, you'd have seen him and fired first."

Sean turned in his seat so he was facing Danny. "I don't think you saying something had any impact on my response to the situation, so you can let that go. To tell the truth though, I don't really know what happened. I remember pulling the car over and the two in the back seat getting out. But then I don't remember anything until I came to on the ground."

"Seriously?"

"My girlfriend says it's a repressed memory thing, like my brain went into shock and blocked it out of my mind."

"They teach that shit in high school?"

Sean rolled his eyes.

"Sorry, man, that was uncalled for. But you really don't remember anything?"

"Nothing. That's what bothers me. If I can't even remember, how could I have been effective in the situation?"

"You were totally effective, and I don't think that memory works like that anyway," said Danny. "If I understand it right, you're present and fully on your game when whatever happens happens, but your mind tries to forget it afterwards to spare you the trauma. It's like the driver of the blue Porsche? He doesn't even remember leaving his house in the morning. I think that's pretty normal."

"Man, I hope so. I want to believe I had my shit together when it went down, but I don't know," said Sean.

"And you lied to the shrink about it?" asked Danny.

"Duh. If she knew the truth, she might have kept me off the job, and I wasn't going take that chance. Getting shot had a big impact on me, too, Danny. I'm pissed that some slime ball out there might try that again, with us or some other cops. If that ever happens again, I'll drop whoever it is in his fucking tracks. It bothers me that I can't remember, but no shrink is going to keep me off the job because of it."

"Well, you definitely didn't screw anything up, Sean, and I'd tell you if you did. You looked away because I called your name as soon as the driver moved. That's all it took for him to get a shot off."

Sean looked out his window again and rapped his knuckles against the glass. "You have to promise me this stays with us," he said.

"What, are you kidding? You think I would say anything to anybody that would jeopardize my riding around with you every night? No way, man. I live for this."

"I'm serious," said Sean.

Danny waited for Sean to look at him before he answered. "So am I Sean. I trust you with my life, and that hasn't changed a bit. We're partners."

Sean paused a moment before speaking. "Good. That's how I like it."

Danny started the car and put it in reverse. "We're about three blocks from Jack in the Box. You want to go there?" asked Danny.

"You're suggesting a food run? To what do I owe this treat?"

"Well, first off, I'm not treating, but I figure we've been through a lot lately. I just want to show my partner a little love," said Danny.

"If I tell you something, do you promise to never use it against me?" asked Sean.

"Well, that's a big ask, but go ahead."

"I'm not really hungry."

Chapter Twenty-Seven

The first time they had attended church together, Danny had stopped at the first pew they came to, in the back of the church, and gestured for Carol to have a seat. Here, Danny could see everyone in the building. Carol had done a double-take, giggled, and then taken his arm and walked to the front of the church. Taking a seat in the second pew, she looked up at Danny and patted the spot next to her. Shocked, he started to explain why this was such a strategically bad location. "This is where I've sat since Daddy brought me here to be baptized," she explained. Her dad felt that the family should sit up front to show the priest and the rest of the parishioners that they were serious about being there, committed to staying through the whole service without the temptation to sneak out early that a back-of-the-church pew afforded.

At least, that's what Danny figured her dad must have been thinking when he'd picked this spot. Why else sit so frigging close? Up here, you could only keep track of a dozen or so people. What if something happened and you had to react?

Danny furtively glanced over his shoulder. He'd never liked this particular pew, and now sitting there made him nervous. Danny had counted: there were thirty pews on each side of the aisle, sixty in all. Each pew easily held twelve people. On a full Sunday, that was over 700 worshippers. Sitting in the second row as they did, he could see only twenty-four of them without turning his head. To see the other ninety five percent, he'd have to turn his head all the way around. How could he keep track of that many people invisible to him?

When he turned back to face the front, he briefly locked eyes with Carol. There was no missing the crease in her brow. He looked at the hymnal she held and mumbled another chorus. Carol studied him while they sang, which he tried to ignore.

When the recessional hymn ended and the priests and altar boys were exiting the church, Carol closed the hymnal, reached up, and rubbed the skin under Danny's nose with her thumb. "Danny Garcia. You're growing a mustache."

"Technically it's a goatee, and I wondered when you would notice,"said Danny. He took her wrist and gently pulled her hand down so that her thumb was touching his chin. He lifted the kneeling bench into place with his foot. They turned to walk into the aisle.

"Oh, I knew you didn't shave yesterday, when you scratched me. I saw you shave for church this morning and didn't think any more about it. But you're growing facial hair."

"I can't get anything past you, can I, Teach?"

"You hate beards, Danny. This just isn't like you."

"Well, a man can change, can't he?"

They reached the back of the church, where Father Keenan stood greeting everyone as they exited. "Father, nice job this morning, one of your best. I hung on every word," said Danny.

Keenan warmly wrapped both his hands around Danny's. "Well, you were at least awake the whole service. I hope to see you two in the parish hall," he said.

"Count on it," said Danny. He and Carol walked out of the church and stopped on the steps.

Carol looked at him again and shook her head. "I can't believe you with a beard."

"No, a goatee. Does it bother you?"

"I'm not really sure. I just never thought you'd grow one."

"You're worried it's going to be a chick magnet and you'll have to fight them off of me."

"That's it. That thing grows in, I won't be able to let you out of my sight," said Carol.

Stepping outside, Danny could feel fall in the air. The temperature was in the fifties. Except for the evergreens, most of the trees had lost their leaves, which formed a patchwork carpet on the ground. A slight breeze was enough to send them skidding along the sidewalk, making a seasonal rustling noise Danny loved.

"What were you looking at in church?" asked Carol.

"Excuse me?" Danny replied.

"You kept looking behind us, like you were searching for someone."

"Was I? Probably just looking at other women, showing off my new look." Danny put his arm around Carol and pointed to the parish hall with his free hand. "Let me buy you a cup of coffee. It's usually not very good, but the price is right."

"No, seriously. You looked over your shoulder practically the whole service, like you were expecting to find something. You never used to do that." She was quiet for a moment. "Do I need to worry about you, Danny?"

Carol no longer sounded playful. "What?" Danny stopped and faced her. "Is this about the shooting? You've been stealing glances at me all week. Carol, I'm telling you, I am okay. I wasn't really looking at anything in there and I'm just growing a goatee for the hell of it."

"You're sure? I know you haven't been sleeping well." She put her arm around his waist.

Danny hugged her. "What are you talking about? I sleep like a baby."

"Oh, please, you toss and turn so much, *I* can't sleep. You used to hit the bed and not move for eight hours. And your nightmare the other night was scary. I'm worried that you went back to work too soon."

"Hey, I wouldn't have been cleared to go back to work unless they were convinced I was okay. And if I wasn't, I'd tell you."

"Okay, I'm taking you at your word. How is Sean doing with all this?"

"Tell you the truth, I'm worried about him. He's been acting really immature, kind of crude—wait—that's the way he always is."

"Very funny."

They entered the parish hall. "I know you want to say more, but hold that thought and I'll get us some coffee." Danny turned and found himself practically nose to nose with Father Keenan. He gasped and jerked his head away from the priest. Blood rushed to his cheeks before he could regain his composure, and Danny worried that Keenan would notice.

"Oh, excuse me, Father."

"Sorry, Danny. Didn't mean to sneak up on you," said Keenan. He already had his vestments off and a cup of coffee in hand. "I startled you."

Danny's heart was racing. "No, my bad. My mind was someplace else."

Keenan leaned into Carol and kissed her on the cheek.

"How's my favorite new Catholic?" he asked Danny. "You look like you were just trying to get away."

"You know, I'm not a new Catholic, Father—I just haven't been to church in a while. I promised Carol a cup of that wonderful coffee you're serving."

"Some of the worst stuff I've ever put to my lips," said Keenan. "I'd say we make it to punish the sinners, but all parishioners, good and bad, drink the same stuff."

Danny chuckled. "Hey, what's with the polyurethane wall? I thought all the work was outside your office." Danny pointed to the back of the hall, which was covered from floor to ceiling with plastic tarp.

"All part of the church's growth," said Keenan. "They've knocked out the wall to expand. This room will be twice as big as it is now."

"This, plus the new classrooms? How much is that costing us?"

"Danny! That's not our business," said Carol.

Keenan held up his hand. "It's all right, Carol. The lad is asking a good question. It's costing a fortune, I'll bet, but the Bishop said the money is there. And it's not just this church getting the makeover. There are three others..."

Danny stopped listening when another priest entered the hall, this one dressed in a full collar shirt and black cassock. He knew it was Morales as soon as he saw him, even though he was nothing like the small, beady-eyed man with bad teeth that he'd pictured when Rodriguez had first talked about his encounter with him. There was no comparison between that cliché and the man Danny was looking at now. This guy was a player, someone to be reckoned with. Strikingly handsome, he emanated self-confidence. Danny could sense it from across the room. He started grinding his jaws, felt himself getting angry.

Danny interrupted Keenan, pointing to Morales as he spoke. "Excuse me, Father. Is that Father Morales?"

"Yes. You haven't met him yet? Do you want me to introduce you?" Danny could tell that Keenan was a little nervous, but that didn't concern him at the moment. His eyes never left Morales. "No, I've got this. Excuse me."

"Danny? Are you just going to walk away?" asked Carol, but she was speaking to his back.

"Father Morales." Danny's flat greeting elicited only a raised eyebrow from the young priest. "I need to talk to you. Walk with me outside for a moment?" Without waiting for an answer, Danny took the priest by the elbow and moved towards the door. "Excuse us," he said to the couple Morales had started talking to. They stepped aside, mouths open.

Morales tried to pull away, but Danny's grip was firm.

"Excuse me, I was talking to those people," muttered the priest.

Danny kept walking, still with a hold on Morales's elbow. "Yeah, well, now you're talking to me." Danny continued until they were standing outside.

Once out of sight of others, Morales jerked his arm free. "Who the hell are you, and what do you think you're doing?"

"I'll bet you know exactly who I am, Father, but just for grins, let's say you don't. I'm Danny Garcia. I'm a cop and I'm curious: What the hell you think *you* are doing?"

Morales got close to Danny's face and spoke evenly and angrily. "It doesn't matter to me what you are. I'm going back inside now, and I don't want you bothering me again. Do you understand?"

"Understand? I still don't understand why you would ask a parishioner for four hundred dollars for marriage counseling."

"What are you talking about?"

"What I can't understand is why everybody is defending you."

"You're not making any sense," said Morales.

"Sorry, was I too vague? What part didn't you understand?"

"Are you like this all the time?"

In that instant, Danny realized he probably was out of line, but he couldn't put on the brakes. "I dunno, I used to think I had plenty of time for niceties, but lately I'm not so sure, and I just don't feel like beating around the bush," said Danny.

"So that gives you the right to be rude and do things any way you want?" Morales spat out his words. "Maybe you should pay more attention to the sermons."

"Maybe you should've met Charles Brooks."

"Who is Charles Brooks?"

"Never mind, just some guy I bumped into at work." Danny took Morales's elbow again. "Let's walk over to the oak tree."

Morales shook Danny off. "No. Look, this may be how you act when you're in uniform, but this is *my* house, and you can't pull this kind of crap," said Morales.

"Funny—I thought this was *God's* House."

Morales shook his head, then turned around and walked away.

Danny put his hands around his mouth to project his voice. "Okay, but you're only making this harder on yourself."

Morales walked back to Danny and got in his face. "I don't know what you think you know. Nobody broke any laws here and this is none of your business. You're a royal pain in the ass, you know that?"

"Father! Are you allowed to talk like that?" Danny tried to sound shocked, but made no effort to hide his grin.

"Just what the hell do you think you've got on me?"

"I keep *trying* to tell you but, apparently, we've got some sort of communication problem," said Danny. "Here's the deal—both times I've talked to a priest about you trying to get money out of one of the flock, I either got iced out or patronized. Why do people think you're such a threat?"

"Who do you think you are to talk to me like this?"

"Between Keenan and the Bishop, I think the Bishop was the worst. He's a lot smoother than Keenan, but he's lying about something," said Danny.

"Look, you son of a..." Morales twisted his mouth.

"Strike a nerve, did I, Father? What are you and the Bishop trying to hide?"

It only lasted a split second. Morales's eyebrows didn't move as his eyes widened, and it's doubtful that anyone else would have noticed anything. But for Danny it was impossible to miss.

Wagon Eyes! Those two are *up to something!*

Morales's face softened before he spoke. "I am going back inside now. I don't want to hear any more about this, and if you bother me again, I'm going to the police. Do you understand me?"

"Yeah, that's a great idea, Father. Try to extort money from someone, then go to the police when you get called on it."

"Extort is a pretty strong word. Watch yourself, Garcia."

Chapter Twenty-Eight

The more he thought about it, the madder Morales got, and the faster he drove. By the time he reached his exit in Santa Rosa, he had topped ninety miles an hour.

Father Keenan had told him that a parishioner, who was also a cop, had stopped by the office and asked if Morales was trying to get money out of congregants. All Keenan did was suggest that the cop "might want to talk to the Bishop about it." So, of course, the cop did, and the Bishop told Morales that he had "contained" the officer by feeding him some bullshit story about how Mexicans and Hondurans hated each other. What kind of wimpy bullshit was that? Did either of those guys think their comments would in any way deflect the cop from his inquisition into Morales's conduct? That was just throwing gas on the fire.

He was especially surprised at the bishop, who he'd thought was stronger than that. But in the past couple of weeks, the man seemed increasingly distracted. Maybe the pressures of the job were getting to him, but that was all part of the game, wasn't it? And to feed a cop that kind of crap and think it would help? He was supposed to be a bishop, for God's sake, not some naïve pushover. Weak, just plain weak.

Morales stormed into the Bishop's house without knocking and started towards the office. Martin ran from another room and stepped in front of the furious priest, as if he could stop him, but Morales just pushed him aside. Martin's voice got higher as he pleaded with Morales to stop. "Out of my way!" Morales said, throwing the door open and bursting into the office.

"What the hell is going on? You can't knock?" the Bishop asked, jumping up from his chair. His desk was covered with loose paper that he furiously swept towards him into one disorganized pile. He took a manila folder out of a desk drawer and covered the papers with it.

"I thought you were going to talk to him," Morales fairly shouted.

Martin nervously flitted beside Morales. "I asked him to wait at the door so I could check with you first, but he pushed me." He looked at the Bishop anxiously.

"It's all right, Martin," the Bishop said, as though granting absolution. "Apparently Father Morales doesn't have time for social graces." He looked at the pile on his desk, then picked it up and placed it on the floor beside him. "Thank you, Martin. You can leave us alone." With a sigh, the Bishop turned to Morales. "Won't you have a seat, Father?" His voice dripped with sarcasm.

Morales pointed at the spot on the floor behind the desk. "What are you trying to hide?" He could feel spittle at the corners of his mouth. The Bishop took a step back from him.

Morales glared, "He came to church and accused me of lying. Hell, he accused us both of lying."

"What are you talking about? Who called you a liar?"

"Who do you think? That cop, Garcia. He practically dragged me out of the parish hall."

"I doubt he dragged you. You're a big man. What did he say you were lying about?" asked the Bishop. He moved around to Morales's side of the desk, rolling down and buttoning his shirtsleeves as he did.

"He thinks I tried to get money from a guy for marriage counseling," said Morales. "He said I lied about it and he wants to know why. Said I was in good company, that you lied too, and he wants to know what's going on between us." Morales pointed to the desk. "What the hell *are* you trying to hide back there?"

The bishop frowned. "Wh-what? Are you sure?" he stammered, ignoring the question.

"Am I sure? About the cop? Yes, it was crystal clear."

The Bishop put his palms together under his chin.

"I don't think praying is going to help right now," said Morales.

"I'm *thinking*," said the Bishop. "Something I wish you'd do more of. Sit down!" He spoke firmly, gesturing to two leather chairs in front of the desk. The Bishop sat on the edge of his desk and crossed one ankle over the other. He pressed a button on a desk intercom. "Martin, could you bring us coffee?" He released the button without taking his hand from the machine and looked at Morales. "Funny, I don't remember if you take cream and sugar," he said.

Morales shrugged without answering and slumped into one of the chairs.

The bishop switched the intercom back on. "And could you bring cream and sugar?" It looked to Morales as if the Bishop had regained his composure. "And when did this happen with the cop?"

"After the ten o'clock service," said Morales. "I usually don't go then, like we agreed, but I was in the area and I wanted to get something. Anyway, I went to the parish hall for coffee. I was talking to a couple when he grabbed my elbow. Pulled me outside and started right in."

"And did anyone hear you talking?"

"*That's* what you're worried about? That somebody else might have heard us? No, I'm not stupid. No one heard us."

"So, *did* you lie to him? Are you extorting money from a parishioner?"

"I'd say extortion is a pretty strong word," answered a sullen Morales. "As I told you right after you talked to the cop, I didn't do anything illegal."

"And I believed you then, but I'm beginning to think you really are guilty."

Morales's eyes narrowed as he scrutinized the Bishop. *He's so worried about himself that he can't see the big picture*, he thought. If the cop had any idea of what was really going on, they could both go down. "So you're going to side with the cop, huh?"

"I'm not siding with anybody, but I am disappointed in you. Why are you even *offering* marriage counseling?"

"The guy asked me for it. What's the big deal? You just tell them to listen to each other when they talk and say 'I love you' every so often," said Morales.

"Oh, it's that easy, huh? I thought we agreed you were only going to recite mass and not get involved in anything beyond that?"

"What am I supposed to do, walk away when people talk to me? I'm wearing a collar. I recite mass. People look at me, they see a priest. Some of them want to talk, so I talk."

"That's just it. You aren't supposed to talk to them about anything. You tell people they need to make an appointment with another priest, like we agreed."

"Oh, right. You try telling someone who asks you a question, 'I'm sorry, I'm not allowed to talk to you. You'll need to make an appointment.'"

"And why would you try and take four hundred dollars from somebody instead of asking me for it? What do you need with the money?" the Bishop asked.

"I don't know, I didn't feel like asking you, and I needed cash."

"For what?"

"What difference does it make? Do I have to clear everything I do with you?"

The Bishop sat in the chair next to Morales. "No, this is about I pay all your bills and keep you living the high life. Hell, you're driving my car. Which I told you was a loan, by the way. And I've told you repeatedly to play it low key at church. If anybody starts asking questions about you because of something stupid you say or do, how am I supposed to help you?"

There was a knock at the office door.

"Come in Martin," said the Bishop.

Martin opened the door and entered carrying a tray with coffee, cream, sugar, and spoons. "Where would you like this, Monsignor?"

"Here, on the table. Thank you."

No one spoke as Martin shuffled to the table and lowered the tray. He poured two cups and handed one to each of the men. "Will there be anything else, sir?"

"No, Martin. Thank you."

Both men watched quietly as Martin left the room.

"What are you going to do about it?" asked Morales.

"What am *I* going to do about what? It seems to me that you're the one who got into this mess. Are you expecting me to clean it up for you?"

"You're in it as much as I am. If anybody comes after me, it'll lead straight to you," said Morales.

"Are you threatening me?"

Morales put cream and sugar in his coffee. "I'm just saying, you and I have things going on that'll make a lot of people unhappy. If that cop keeps snooping around, things could get ugly for both of us."

The Bishop stood and walked to the window behind his desk. Hands clasped behind his back, he stood there in silence.

"Hello?" said Morales.

"Can I think for a moment?" asked the Bishop.

"Yeah, sure, if you can think of something that will help."

"This comes at a bad time. I've got a lot on my plate and don't need one more thing to juggle. These construction projects are all coming in way over budget, and the money isn't there."

"Then take more collections or something, I don't know. Why is any of that your problem anyway? So, construction costs are higher than anyone thought they'd be. It's not like you're stealing the money."

Morales could see the Bishop stiffen, practically freeze on the spot. That's when he got it. "Shit, no wonder you choked in front of the cop. You *are* stealing, aren't you?" Morales started to laugh.

The Bishop turned towards Morales, his fists clenched by his side. "How dare you insult me like that! Suggest that I would steal from the church!"

"Are you kidding? You went stiff as a board when I mentioned it and your face is as white as your clenched knuckles." Morales relaxed a bit. If the Bishop was stealing and got caught, no one would give his own little indiscretion a second's thought.

Morales couldn't believe how vulnerable the Bishop looked. It repulsed him, but it also gave him the upper hand.

The Bishop seemed to be in a world of his own; then his face softened and his fists unclenched. "What we both need is for that cop to stop asking questions, and I just had a very good idea about how to get him to stop."

"Let's hear it."

The Bishop walked quickly back to the chair next to Morales, sat down, and placed his hand on the other man's arm. "If you're out of that cop's district, he can't talk to you."

Morales shook off the Bishop's hand and stood up. "What do you mean, 'out of his district'?"

"His jurisdiction. If you're not in Napa, he can't touch you. I'll transfer you to Ukiah for a while until this all settles down."

Morales could see the wheels spinning in the Bishop's mind. *Well, son of a bitch. This is no temporary move—he's trying to get rid of me.* Morales could see his gravy train derailing. "That's your plan? You'll just pack me off and all your worries are over?"

The Bishop shook his head emphatically as he got out of his chair and stood next to Morales. "No, *our* worries. You said it yourself: this situation could undo both of us. With you gone, just for a while, it'll blow over. We're talking a few months, tops. Go to Ukiah. The church there is small. You won't even have to show up much." He patted Morales vigorously on the back, his face one big smile. "Take the car—live a little!"

That was it then. The Bishop was going to cast him out and probably stop paying for everything. Without financial support, Morales figured he'd be strapped within weeks, maybe even homeless.

"Couple of months, you say?"

The Bishop waved the question off. "At the most. You'll be back in no time."

Morales knew he had to appear to accept this without question. The Bishop had to believe that he was on board. "All right, Julius. I trust you completely. Seal it with a kiss?" Morales closed his eyes and leaned towards the priest.

The Bishop almost fell over getting out of the way. "Jorge, stop it! Martin could come in at any moment."

"Oh, right. But he wouldn't suspect you're gay or anything, would he?"

"How many times have I told you, I'm not gay?" The Bishop spat out the words, but visibly softened almost as soon as he finished. He patted Morales on the cheek. "Let's not do this. We won't see each other for a while and this is no way to separate."

"You mean I should leave soon?"

"The sooner you leave, the quicker this blows over and you come back. I'll need a little time to set this all up, but we can get it done in ten days. Two weeks, tops."

Right, and that will be the last you see of me, thought Morales. He thought about what he needed to do, and getting some cash together was at the top of the list.

Chapter Twenty-Nine

"Knock-knock." Doris walked into the Chief's office without waiting for a response. The employee with the most seniority, she had started in the department a week before the Chief had. She wore glasses and her brown hair was twisted into a loose bun on top of her head. She carried a box of donuts in one hand and steadied a cup of coffee, balanced on the box, with the other. "Wow! Are you moving things out at night? This place is starting to look empty."

"Doris! Good morning. Come in, come in." Chief Salerno waved her into the largely empty office. The walls were bare, their only adornments the dark rectangles left where pictures had hung. A half-dozen sealed boxes were stacked in one corner, each with a carefully written contents-label stuck to the outside. The bookshelves were empty.

"Twenty-seven days and counting," said Salerno, "and I'm spending nineteen of them on vacation."

"Place won't be the same without you."

"And I expect nothing less than gnashing of teeth and tearing of clothes when I leave. What's that?"

"Oh," Doris said, looking at her hands as though surprised by what they held, "I brought you a coffee and donuts."

"Chocolate-covered with sprinkles?"

She shook the box. "Your favorites."

"Doris, you don't bring me donuts unless you're bringing me trouble at the same time." The Chief removed a half-packed box from one of the chairs in front of his desk, and then motioned for her to sit down. "What is it?"

"Listen to you, Mr. Glass Half-Empty."

"The donuts, Doris," Salerno reached across the desk, grabbed one from the box, and took a big bite.

"Truth is, we've got a situation."

"We established that with the donuts." Salerno spoke between chews. He swallowed and took another bite. "Why don't you just tell me what it is."

"Well, we aren't exactly sure," Doris said, hesitantly. "It seems that a John Robinson took out a number of loans against some properties that, it turns out, he doesn't own."

Salerno waited for more. "Well?"

"Mr. Robinson is dead, sir."

Salerno popped the rest of the donut in his mouth, then took a drink of coffee. "Hmm. Taking out the loans killed him, or do we have a murder case on our hands?"

"No sir, he died about fifteen years ago."

Salerno stopped chewing. "Guess that rules him out as a suspect. Any idea what happened?"

"Well, no one is completely sure, but it seems that someone stole his identity and then took out the loans."

"I think that's a fair guess. You keep saying 'loans.' How many 'loans' are we talking about?" asked Salerno.

"Twelve. All for twenty five thousand dollars."

"Twelve? Seriously? That's..." the Chief counted on his fingers, "three hundred thousand."

"Yes sir. He actually tried to take out forty loans, but somebody figured it out after the first twelve and the rest didn't get processed."

"Quick thinkers. What company?" asked Salerno.

"Nations Financial, all from branches in Northern California."

Salerno wiped his mouth with the back of his hand and put his coffee on the desk. "Do we have more details?"

"We're a long way from the whole picture, but all the loans were taken out on Friday, and all within ten minutes of each other. The loan applications were faxed into all forty offices, and the money that was approved was sent out the same day, by wire, to three different bank accounts, two newly opened. None of the branches knew the same loan application had been sent to all of the others until twelve had been paid out."

"Why would they process loans like that?"

"Apparently that's standard operating procedure for Nations. We think these loans were rushed because it was the end of the month, and the branch managers were probably trying to make their monthly quotas. They get bonuses if they exceed a certain number. One of the Nations managers was on the phone with another one, telling him the 25K loan put him in the black for his quota. The second manager had just received identical paperwork for the same amount and from the same man. He slammed down the phone, made sure the loan was killed, and put out an alert to all the branches."

"And I'll bet the first manager shit his pants. So much for getting bonuses. If this happened all over the place, why are we getting stuck with it?" asked Salerno.

"The money was deposited in Futures Bank, here in Napa," said Doris. "The vast majority of the money was deposited in two of the three accounts. Nobody had information on those account holders until Garcia and Rawlins arrested them both."

"Garcia and Rawlins cracked the case? That's good then, isn't it?"

"Well, 'cracked' may not be the right word. The officers responded to a disturbance of the peace call on the twenty ninth."

"You mean three days ago. Saturday. The day after the loans were taken out?"

"It was just before midnight, Saturday. Technically they brought them in on Sunday. Two homeless men who had warrants out for their arrest. Garcia discovered it when he did warrant checks on them. Seems the money was in accounts in their names."

Salerno grabbed another donut from the box, took a bite and chewed for a moment. "Homeless men did this. Does anybody actually believe that?"

"No sir, but nobody really knows what to think."

"Where are Garcia and Rawlins now?"

"They've been off the past couple of days, but their shift starts at four p.m."

"Damn. I've got to go to Sacramento for a well-deserved retirement dinner that'll probably go to nine or ten. I'll drive back and be here when the officers get off shift. Make sure they know to come see me as soon as they get in. I don't even want them to take the time to change out of uniform."

"That's going to be midnight, Chief."

"Yes, too late for me to be up, and I'm not happy about it. Meanwhile, get me somebody at the bank to talk to. We've got to see where this thing is now."

Doris closed the donut box, got up, and started for the door.

"You said some of the three hundred thousand dollars was deposited in a third account. What do we know about it?"

"I guess they know whose name it's in, but it hasn't been released yet. It's very strange..." Doris looked at the Chief, as though expecting him to finish.

"And...?"

"Well, it seems that the third account had a nickel deposited in it."

"A nickel."

"Yes sir."

"Five cents. You're telling me that Mr. Robinson, who is dead, opened three accounts, split almost three hundred thousand dollars in two of them and put a nickel in the third?"

"Yes sir."

The Chief shook his head. "This, just before I retire."

"This is going to be a long day." She grabbed the box of pastries and started for the door.

"Oh, and Doris," Salerno said, stopping her, "leave the donuts."

Chapter Thirty

Tim idly stirred his coffee, watching drops fall from the end of his spoon back into the cup. He took a sip, added a little more sugar, and began stirring again. "Do you ever get tired of going to meetings?" He and Richard sat in the same booth in the corner of the diner they'd been sitting in regularly for months.

"What...AA meetings? Oh, all the time." Richard wiped his glasses with his shirttail. He had on what Tim now knew to be one of the four flannel shirts he wore all the time. "Sometimes as I'm walking out the door of my place I think, there *has* to be something better to do with my life than to go to another AA meeting and hear the same damn people talk about the same damn things. Why do you ask?"

"What do you do when that happens? Do you ever just not go?"

"No, I still go. When I get there, I tell everybody that's what I was thinking on my way over." Richard put his glasses back on and grabbed his coffee mug. "About half the people in the room give me a 'been there too' laugh."

"I just wonder if I'll always have to go," said Tim. "Don't get me wrong, I usually get something out of it, but sometimes I just feel like I can't do it forever."

"You don't have to go forever if you don't want to. All you have to do is go today, and you've already been. Worry about tomorrow, to-morrow."

"You're just walking, talking program, aren't you?" said Tim.

Richard raised his mug to Tim. "Here's to AA, one day at a time, and one more cup of coffee with you."

Richard had become Tim's AA sponsor shortly after they first met. When Tim had asked him if he would, Richard had insisted that Tim talk to his original sponsor first. It was a conversation that Tim had felt sheepish about initiating.

"Tell you the truth," the man had said when Tim brought it up, "I forgot I was your sponsor, it's been so long since you called me. Richard is a good guy. He doesn't play games, and he doesn't take any shit. He'll be good for you."

Tim and Richard attended three meetings a week like clockwork. They went to the diner for coffee afterwards at least once a week with anybody from the meeting who was interested in coming along, or by themselves if no one was. Tim told Richard things about himself that he'd never admitted to anyone else. It felt good to trust someone so completely, to get his secrets off his chest.

"Hey, I ran into a guy I knew at the treatment center," said Tim.

"New Beginnings? You never told me any of those people lived here," said Richard.

"Actually, he lives in Napa now. I went there to see my parents. Afterwards, I was looking for a basketball game, and he was on the court."

"And here are those apple pies with ice cream, gentlemen," said the waitress. "I don't know how you guys eat so much of this and stay so slim. I'd balloon up!"

"Thank you, Alice," said Tim. He hadn't known her name for the first month she had waited on them, despite the fact that she wore a nametag.

Alice set the slices of pie in front of them. "Anything else?"

"No, this is great," said Richard. He waited until she was out of earshot and then asked, "You ever wonder what this place is like any other time of day? Who comes here besides late-night drunks and sober alcoholics?"

Tim shook his and took a bit of pie. "Truthfully, I never gave it a second's thought."

Richard grinned and shook his head. "No imagination... So, who's the guy you saw?" he asked.

"Jorge. Hispanic guy. Good looking, gay, real athletic, and a real con—at least to hear him talk about it. He always made me nervous."

"Why?"

"I don't know. I always felt like he was sizing people up to see what he could get. When we were at the program, he was bugging me about the crime I committed that got me there. Wanted to know all the details. I halfway expected him to try the same thing."

"Did you tell him everything?"

Tim picked at his pie for a moment without taking a bite. He looked at his plate when he answered. "Pretty much. I wasn't supposed to tell anybody about it—part of the deal about my going to the program instead of jail—but I guess I was playing big shot."

Richard shrugged. "Well, you're not the first guy to do that. I used to pump myself up in front of the guys I ran with. We all tried to one-up each other."

"Anyway, it's been like six months since I'd seen him, and he started asking me about it again. He remembered everything I'd told him, all the details. It was amazing how much he remembered."

"Is he sober?" asked Richard.

"He says he is, but he doesn't go to meetings or anything, and he told me he still hangs out in bars."

"Well, some people can do that. I'm not one of them, but some can. Are you worried that he might try and steal some money? There's nothing you can do about it now except to worry, and that won't get you anywhere," said Richard.

"Steal that much? I doubt it. When he left New Beginnings, a client thought he'd stolen his jacket and money, but nothing ever came of it. If Jorge did it, I bet it was a spur of the moment thing. If he is a thief, he strikes me as a petty criminal."

"What makes you say that?" asked Richard.

"This might sound judgmental, but I don't think he's got the patience to plan something big."

"There you go. There's really nothing to worry about." Richard finished his coffee. "Ready to go?"

"Almost." Tim twirled his coffee cup between his hands for a few seconds before continuing. "Talking to Jorge made me realize that I'd never told you about all that."

"About all what?"

"The crime I committed."

"I thought you did. You stole a couple of identities, then 'borrowed,'" Richard made air quotes around *borrow*, "money from some property you didn't own. Is that about it?"

"Pretty much, but I left something out."

Richard studied him for a second. "Okay, why do I think the other shoe is about to drop?"

"I stole one identity and used it to become a notary public, so I could notarize the documents I needed."

"Yeah, I remember that," said Richard.

"I went to public records at the county, gave them the name of a guy I found in the obits, and got his social security number," said Tim.

"You already told me all this," said Richard.

The second identity, I started to do the same thing, but I chickened out. I gave Jorge the impression that's how I got the second ID, too, but I lied."

"Do you think you owe Jorge an apology for lying? Is that what this is about?"

"No, that's not what I'm saying. For some reason, I wasn't worried about the first ID I stole. I didn't think anybody would ever find out about that. But the second time, it felt scarier somehow."

"I'm not sure I'm following you," said Richard.

"I don't know if I can explain it. I didn't want to use some name from the obits again and have to go back to the County. It was like I'd been lucky the first time and didn't want to chance it again. I just figured less could go wrong that way." Tim fell silent.

"Yeah, go on," said Richard.

"I thought a long time about whose ID I could steal. Then, I hit on somebody I knew inside and out. Soon as it came to me, it made total sense. At least, it did at the time." Tim said nothing else.

After a few seconds, Richard rolled his hand to encourage Tim to keep talking. "And you're going to tell me who it was, right, or am I supposed to guess?"

"I know this is going to sound really bad, but I chose my father."

Richard didn't respond.

"The second identity I stole was my dad's. I took out a loan in his name."

Richard was quiet for a moment. "Seriously?"

Tim shrugged. "Yeah."

"You stole your dad's ID and used it to commit a crime?"

"Yeah, I did."

"Wow. Why haven't you told me this before?"

Tim could feel himself sink into the booth. "I wanted to tell you before, but I've been too ashamed."

"So when you got caught, the cops must have thought your dad did it. You set him up as the fall guy."

"The cops never got involved, thank God, so it never came to that. But it's a lot worse than that." Tim was barely audible.

"Worse? How could you have made it any worse?"

"The property I borrowed against? I wanted to make sure I got something with a lot of equity—and, like I said, I didn't want to risk going to the County again. Last thing I wanted was to apply for a loan and get turned down. So, I thought about properties I knew really well. My parents owned their place free and clear. It seemed perfect." Tim stopped talking for a moment and drank some of his coffee. "I picked my parents' house. I stole my dad's ID and then took a loan out against their house."

Tim could sense that Richard was trying to process what he'd just heard. Alice walked by, and Richard held up his empty cup. "More coffee, please, Alice?" Neither of them spoke as Alice filled his cup. He turned back to Tim.

"You're saying you ripped off your own parents?"

"Yup. I stole twenty five thousand from my mom and dad."

Neither Tim nor Richard spoke for a while. Richard drank his coffee, and Tim fiddled with his pie.

"They know everything, right?"

"Mom and Dad? Yeah, of course. They knew as soon as it happened."

"Well," Richard stirred his coffee for a moment, "You should have told me all this when you did your fifth step: 'Admitted to God, ourselves and another human being the exact nature of our wrongs,' but at least you're telling me now. Is there anything else you left out?"

Tim exhaled before answering. "That's it."

"This will sound weird coming from somebody who's heard a lot of recovering alcoholics admit to some strange shit, but I would never have figured you would do something like that. You're nothing if not entertaining."

Tim held up his coffee cup, tipped it towards Richard in a silent toast, and took a sip.

Chapter Thirty-One

"You've got something on your…" Sean pointed at Danny's face, then pantomimed wiping his own chin.

"Where?" Danny quickly brushed his chin. He felt his new goatee and got the setup. "Very funny, Sean." The two other officers in the locker room chuckled.

"I'll bet Carol made you grow that, hoping you'd look sexier. Maybe younger too."

"Carol did not *make* me grow anything, but, as a matter of fact, she's decided it does look sexy."

"Tell you the truth, I think it makes you look angry."

"Thanks for weighing in. I'll make sure and check with you before making any other fashion decisions."

Sean leaned in closer and spoke quietly. "Did you hear anything about those rich drunks we arrested under the bridge Saturday?" He put one foot on the locker room bench and finished tying his shoelaces.

"You mean the homeless guys who have more money than we do? Not a word," Danny answered. "There was nothing in the paper either, which is really weird. If I was writing the crime beat, I'd be all over that."

"Maybe it's too soon. It's only Tuesday afternoon. It'll probably be in tomorrow's paper."

"Are you kidding? Most of the time, we haven't finished the paperwork on a case and they've already got the story online. They report *everything* that happens. Why would they skip this?" Danny closed his locker. "This is *big*. It's weird."

"Maybe the paper is waiting to get our story. It *was* pretty impressive police work." Sean straightened his belt. "I'm ready when you are."

"Yeah, I'm sure that's it, Sean. The way we kept those drunks from passing out long enough to bring them in was the stuff of police lore. And if you'll notice, I'm dressed and waiting for *you*. Let's go upstairs and see what's going on tonight."

The transition zone from the boisterous world of patrol officers to the hushed world of administration was an enclosed, carpeted stairway. Sixteen steps separated the officers' downstairs locker room, with its linoleum floor that amplified noise, and the upstairs office area, with its inherent quietness. Danny was always conscious of the spot where the stairs swallowed locker room noise and allowed only muted conversation, making him momentarily self-conscious about his own voice. The sixteen steps prepared anyone ascending them for the quiet, orderly world of admin.

"If I'm looking at the calendar correctly, and I think I am, we have exactly two weeks left on this shift," said Sean. He was behind Danny as the two climbed the stairs. "I can't tell you how happy that makes me."

"That's if the new hires go through, Sean, and you know what a long drawn-out process it is getting hired here. Only way we get off swing shift is if there is somebody to take our place, and I'm not as optimistic about it as you are."

"Oh, that's so not fair. They've *gotta* hire somebody, and fast. I hardly ever get to see my girlfriend."

"That's true. I'll bet her parents don't let her talk on the phone, much less see boys after, what, nine p.m.?" asked Danny.

"Very funny, partner." They reached the landing and the office area. At the beginning of each shift, officers came upstairs to check in with the duty sergeant for updates and special instructions.

"She wants to meet you and Carol, by the way. I've tried to talk her out of it, but she says it's time."

"You mean *you* want us to meet her. That's a first. She clear that with her parents?" Danny asked.

Sean feigned a silent belly laugh, then turned to the woman at the desk outside the duty officer's office.

"Hello, Doris," he said. "Sergeant Potter in his office?"

"No," she answered without stopping typing.

Sean sat on the edge of her desk, which was clear except for a computer, phone, and a few pieces of paper. "Let me guess. He got sick of working indoors nine to five, and he's back out on the street mixing it up with bad guys."

Doris looked at Sean's body as if to will it off her desk. "He's sick all right. It's the flu. Chief Salerno took one look at him and sent him home before leaving for Sacramento."

"The Chief walked over here? From his office all the way down the hall?" said Sean. "I thought he said he wasn't leaving there till he retired next month."

"Actually, he came over here to talk to you two."

"Us?" said Danny. "What does he want with us?"

"Believe it or not, sometimes he does things without telling me. Sean, can you manage to get yourself off my desk?" Doris stopped typing and looked into his face for the first time.

"Oh," said Sean as he slid off. "I didn't realize you were using it."

"You should do standup, you know that?" said Doris.

Danny had always wondered why Doris's desk was void of photos or anything else that said anything about her. No pictures of children, a spouse or boyfriend, or animals. The three desks next to hers each had at least one picture. A "World's Greatest Grandmother" coffee mug sat on one desk and, on another, a stuffed toy poodle. The interior walls of the partition farthest away had half a dozen crayon drawings of stick figures pinned to it. Danny realized how little he actually knew about Doris, except that she'd sat at that desk since he'd been on the force.

"Doris, how long have you worked here?" Danny asked.

"A long time. You want I should stop doing my work and tell you all about it?"

"No, no, the show must go on. Seriously, you don't know what the Chief wanted?"

"He just said to tell you that he wanted to see you after your shift."

"After, not before? We get off at midnight," said Danny.

"I'm pretty sure he knows when the swing shift ends," said Doris, "and he said after."

"And the duty sergeant?" asked Sean.

"He's still home sick, just like he was when you started this conversation," she said.

Sean looked at Danny and shrugged. "Okay. No special instructions tonight, I guess. Let's go catch some bad guys. Always good talking to you, Doris."

"Try not to get hurt out there," Doris said, her eyes and fingers back on her keyboard.

At the end of their shift, Sean and Danny walked back upstairs to the office area, which was virtually deserted. Sean knocked lightly on the frame of the Chief's open office-door. "You wanted to see us, Chief?"

"Rawlins, Garcia, come in boys," said Salerno. He was wearing dress blues. "How was your shift tonight?"

"Fortunately, quiet," said Danny. "How was Sacramento?"

"Overcooked chicken in a mystery sauce, all served with a lot of long speeches, but tonight it was all about me, so overall it was good," said Salerno. "Last one of those I'll have to attend. So, your night was quiet?"

"Yes sir," said Danny. "Congratulations on your retirement."

"Thanks. Listen, we're going to have enough noise around here when the paper comes out tomorrow. They're going to be reporting that collar you guys made Saturday night, and I'm betting it'll be front page above the fold."

"I wondered why it wasn't in there already," said Danny.

"That makes two of us. Somebody big must have major juice with the paper. They don't sit on *anything*. Anyway, when it hits, it's going to hit far beyond Napa," said Salerno.

"You think they'll want our pictures as arresting officers?" asked Sean. "I can get my dress blues down to the cleaners and have them ready by five tomorrow."

Salerno rolled his eyes. "While that's a very unselfish offer, I'm guessing you'll be a minor part of the story, Sean, if you're in it at all." He sat in his chair and pointed to the two chairs in front of his desk. "Please, have a seat. How well do you know the guys you arrested?"

"We've been arresting them for minor stuff for years, almost always involving alcohol, but that's about it," said Danny. "What were you hoping for?"

"These guys seem to be caught up in an identity theft case," said Salerno.

The words didn't sink in immediately, maybe because the concepts of homeless and identity theft were incongruous. Then Danny felt his stomach drop. "*Identity* theft?" he asked, aware only after speaking that his voice was louder than needed.

The Chief gave him a cockeyed look. "You okay, Garcia?"

Danny composed himself. "I'm fine, sir. It's just a little over the top to think that those guys committed an identity theft crime."

"I didn't say that," said the Chief. "I said they got caught up in something. It seems that somebody else stole the money and deposited it in three accounts. Most of it was in two of them, in your guys' names. The money only stayed in those accounts overnight, then got electronically swept away first thing Saturday, before you arrested Perkins and Williams that night. Nobody at the bank knew anything until Saturday morning, and now they're trying to figure out where the money went. They seem to be falling all over themselves. I'll bet they've probably shit enough bricks to build a small house by now."

"How much got stolen?" asked Sean.

"Three hundred thousand. Whoever did it tried for more, but some of the loans got turned down."

It was all Danny could do to contain himself. He just listened.

"How many loans *were* there?" asked Sean.

The Chief chuckled and shook his head. "Forty in all, each for twenty five thousand dollars. Different branches processed twelve of them before somebody figured out that something fishy was going on."

"Anybody know who did it?" Danny practically whispered.

"Well, supposedly a guy named John Robinson, but it seems he's been dead for quite a while, so I'm thinking it wasn't him." The Chief brushed some lint off his pants.

"How does somebody pull this off?" asked Sean.

"Turns out it's not that hard. Somebody somehow resurrected Mr. Robinson and took loans out on real estate that didn't belong to him, even when he was alive. They did it all by fax and had the money wired to the three accounts."

Danny gripped the arms of his chair, hoping not to jump out of it.

"You guys hungry?" The Chief picked up the pink donut box on his desk and offered it to the officers. "Doris brought these in this morning, and I ate three of them. Two more than I need."

Sean quickly scooted to the front of his chair, reached in the box and took one. "Since you are offering, it *has* been a long shift."

"Danny? the Chief asked, offering the box to Danny.

"No, thank you. Why our guys?" asked Danny.

"Excuse me?" asked the Chief.

"The guys we arrested. Why do you suppose the money went into accounts in their names?"

"Not a clue," said the Chief. "I was hoping you might be able to help us with that. Do you have any idea how two homeless men would get caught up in this?"

"No, not them," said Sean, swallowing. He reached for another donut. "They're usually half in the bag. They couldn't do this. Trust me."

"Well, do you guys know anyone who could have?"

Danny thought the Chief looked straight at him. He focused to make eye contact. "No sir, I don't." He made sure his voice was even when he spoke.

It was the first time Danny had ever told a lie on duty. For that matter, he couldn't remember the last time he had told a lie, on or off duty. He didn't dare look at Sean, afraid his partner might say something to contradict him.

"I didn't think so, but it can't hurt to ask," said the Chief.

"You said there were three accounts," Danny said.

"Yes. This is the weird part. The third account had a nickel deposited in it."

"Sir, I'm sorry, I had a mouth full of donut and missed what you said." Sean swallowed.

"You couldn't hear because you were *chewing*? Why am I retiring? I'm really going miss it around here. Anyway, you heard right—a nickel."

"Why would anybody—" Danny started.

"Don't even ask," the Chief cut in. "It makes no sense at all. Apparently, that nickel didn't leave the account, once it was deposited.

I'm wondering if there is something about that nickel that's making the press keep this quiet. But I could be completely wrong."

"Anything else, sir?" Danny's ears were ringing, and he couldn't wait to end this conversation.

"No, but the next few days are going to be crazy around here. When the press finds out that you were the arresting officers, they'll probably be all over you."

"We know how to handle ourselves, sir," said Sean.

"I'm sure you do," said the Chief. "But just so we are clear, I don't want you talking to anybody about anything. A reporter asks you a question, even directions to the bathroom, you send them to me. Understood?"

"Loud and clear, sir," said Sean. He pointed to the donuts. "Would you mind if I had another?"

The Chief pushed the box of donuts to him. "Take the whole box, please."

"Oh no, sir, I couldn't, unless you insist," Sean said as he stood. He took the box and saluted. The Chief gave him a lazy return salute.

"Garcia?" asked the Chief.

"Sir?" responded Danny.

"Are we clear here?"

"About what, sir?"

"Are you listening to me, son? The *press* and how you won't say anything to anybody," said the Chief.

"Oh, absolutely, sir. No press."

"Thank you, gentlemen. Go get some sleep."

"Holy shit!" said Sean, bounding down the stairs to the dressing room. "Can you believe all that? This thing's got more twists than a dance contest."

Danny was only halfway down the steps as Sean reached the bottom. "Yeah. Look, Sean, there isn't much paperwork to do tonight and I've got someplace to go. You finish it, okay?"

Sean stopped and turned to face Danny. "You've got someplace to go at midnight? What, another Date Night?"

"No, I just have to do something."

Sean stopped walking and grabbed Danny's arm. "Wait. You think you know who did this, don't you? You think it's him."

"I'd say there's more than just a passing chance. Look, I'll see you tomorrow." Danny opened the back door and walked out. He could hear Sean yell to him.

"Danny, you haven't even taken off your uniform. You think maybe you should sleep on this? Don't do something stupid—"

The door closed before Sean could finish. Danny walked across the parking lot, got into his car, and drove off, tires squealing.

Chapter Thirty-Two

Always mindful of his surroundings, Danny was usually on high alert when driving late at night. Drivers were far more likely to be impaired, either because they'd been drinking or because they should have been sleeping. If he thought a driver was erratic or in any way suspicious, Danny would follow him for a while. It meant a potential traffic stop and getting home later, but at least he would know the streets were that much safer.

Tonight, however, Danny didn't notice much at all. He drove fast, *too* fast, staring straight ahead, his fingers gripped tightly around the steering wheel. Close to 2:00 a.m., there were few cars on the neighborhood streets, but Danny didn't see them anyway, lost as he was in his own thoughts.

"Blended family," he said out loud. "Yeah, right."

"Just think," his mother had said, crouching down to his level, her arms holding his then small shoulders, "Now you'll have a little brother to play with. Won't that be fun?" Her voice was soothing, but young Danny would have none of it.

"But I don't want a brother," he whined. Then, pouting, looking as angry as he could: "I want my *Father*."

"I wish your Father was still alive, too. I miss him every day, Danny." She ran her fingers through his hair. "I loved him as much as you do, but he's dead, and he's not coming back. Paul is a good man, and he'll take good care of us. He and I are getting married, and that means we're blending our families. His son is now *my* son, and your brother."

"Why do we need more people? Have I done something wrong?" Danny's lower lip began trembling. "I don't even like them."

"No, no, sweetie, you haven't done anything wrong." She hugged him. He returned her hug, tried to pull her inside his body. "Your Father was a good man, but we have to get on with our lives, Danny. I love Paul and he loves me. When adults feel that way about each other, they get married. But I love you more than anything, and that will never ever change, I promise."

"You promise?" Danny pulled back to look her in the eyes. His lower lip still quivered, and he had lost the fight to hold back his tears.

"Yes, I promise," she smiled. "I love you with all my heart. And I know it sounds hard to believe, but one day you'll love Paul, and his son too."

Danny could still see her, crouched down in front of him, looking in his eyes. The car behind him honked, and he realized the light had turned green. He was startled to see where he was; he didn't know how long he had been driving so distracted. He had the address of the house, and, even though he'd never been there, he was on autopilot.

Although the homes were not luxurious, the neighborhood was nice. Despite the darkness he could see the contrast between grass and concrete, exposed sidewalks and driveways sharply edged, bushes trimmed and lawns cut. Danny easily found the address he was looking for and pulled into the driveway. He sat behind the wheel after turning off the engine, remembering some of the good times he had enjoyed with his brother.

"Can I play football with you and your friends?" his brother had asked him.

"Nah, we play too rough for a little guy like you," Danny had answered, one hand on his brother's shoulder. "How about if you and I play some after we finish?"

Danny still remembered how dejected the boy had looked. He'd loved his new little brother almost from the moment he'd met him, despite his early determination to hate him, and was actually more interested in just being with him than he was in playing football with his friends. He watched the small boy walking away, head lowered and feet dragging.

"Hey wait!" Danny called out. He waved for the kid to rejoin the group. "Okay, come on."

The boy flew to his brother's side and hugged him around the waist.

"Hey, if you're going to play football with us, you can't hug people."

His brother stopped, but couldn't wipe the adoration off his face.

"He's going to play with us," Danny announced to the guys.

"Oh please," said one of the boys. "What's he, like six?" The others laughed.

"He's ten, and he's tough." The other boys just looked at the small boy, several shaking their heads. "And if he gets hurt," Danny continued, "I'll bust the ass of the guy that does it."

The memory gave Danny a good feeling that evaporated quickly. How did such a good kid end up fucking up so badly, hurting so many people? His own friggin' family, for God's sakes. He looked in the garage as he walked past it, saw a new sports car, and shook his head. Walking onto the front porch, Danny rang the doorbell and began pounding on the door before waiting for an answer.

Lights went on in the dark house. "Okay, okay!" said a voice from within. The porch light turned on and the front door opened. "What the hell is—Danny! What are you doing here? Come in."

Danny pushed the door open and charged in. "I thought you gave up the illegal shit when you quit drinking. Does that mean you fell off the wagon, or were you just lying the whole time?" Danny spoke between gritted teeth.

"What are you talking about? It's two in the morning. Sit down, talk to me," his brother pleaded.

"There is no talking to you," Danny said. "You'll say anything to get out of a jam, and you don't care who gets hurt."

"Danny stop. Listen to me."

"No Tim, I'm tired of listening to you. Fuck that!" He punched his brother in the face, knocking him to the floor. Danny stood over Tim, his fists clenched. "Good to see you, little brother."

Still on the floor, Tim put his hand on his eye. "Dammit, Danny!" He looked up briefly, then fell back to the floor.

"This isn't over yet, Tim, and you brought it on yourself." Danny walked out of the house, slamming the door behind him.

Chapter Thirty-Three

Danny tried to shake the pain out of his right hand while using his left to reach for the large metal mixing bowl in the kitchen cabinet. He hadn't punched anybody since high school, and couldn't believe how badly his knuckles hurt. He'd been home for five minutes, long enough to use his good hand to gingerly remove his gun belt and uniform shirt and place them on the sofa.

He pulled the bowl off the shelf, not realizing that two smaller bowls were nested inside it. The other two flew out. In trying to catch them and stop them from hitting the floor, Danny managed to knock two pans off the stove as well. It sounded to him like they all hit the floor at the same time, making enough noise to wake the dead, and surely Carol—exactly what he didn't want. He leaned into the living room and looked towards the bedroom. In a few seconds, a light came from the back of the house.

"Sorry sweetie, it's me. Everything is okay. I'll come to bed in a few minutes," he called.

After picking up everything he'd dropped on the floor, Danny opened the freezer and scooped several handfuls of ice cubes into the mixing bowl while holding it against the kitchen counter with his hip.

He sat at the table and stuck his injured hand in the ice. Soon after, Carol walked into the room, wearing her pink terrycloth robe and slippers. Danny could see from her eyes that she'd been sound asleep before his bowls-and-pans cacophony.

"It's almost three a.m." Carol yawned. "Could you make any more noise?"

He watched her eyes go to the bowl.

"Oh, Danny, you hurt your hand?" She sat next to him and took his other hand in hers.

"I did it at work," Danny said. "It's no big deal. You go back to sleep and I'll be in in a few minutes."

"I'm wide awake now," Carol said. "How did you do this?"

Danny did not want to answer. More to the point, he didn't want the conversation that was bound to follow. "I punched somebody. Really, it isn't a big thing."

"Did someone attack you? What happened?"

Danny moved his hand around in the ice. He was trying to think of a story to tell Carol that wouldn't upset her, but that would mean a lie. He decided he owed her the truth.

"I saw Tim, and I punched him."

"Tim who?" Carol asked.

"My brother," said Danny.

Carol took her hands off Danny's arm. "Your brother? Where did you see him?"

"I went to his house after work."

"His house? In Santa Rosa?"

"Yes."

"After your shift?

"Yes. I just got back a few minutes ago."

"I don't understand. You haven't even mentioned him in months. What's suddenly so important that you have to drive there this late at night and get into a fight?"

Danny sighed. "Look, this is going to take some time to explain. Let's go in the living room where it's more comfortable, okay?" He stood up, grabbing the bowl of ice. Carol just sat, looking at him. He tilted his head towards the living room, and she got up.

Carol turned on a lamp by the sofa and sat at one end of it. She pushed her hair behind her ears, crossed her arms and looked at Danny's shirt and gun belt.

"Sorry," he said, scooping up both and placing them on the floor. He sat at the other end of the sofa and put his hand back in the ice.

"So what's going on with you and Tim?"

"It's a long story—"

"I'm not going anywhere."

Exactly what Danny was afraid of. "We can talk about this in the morning if you want to go back to bed?"

"I'm wide awake. Let's talk now."

"Okay. You remember those homeless guys Sean and I arrested last Saturday night?"

"Of course. They ruined our date night. What does that have to do with you hitting your brother?"

"I'll get to that. Anyway, the Chief was waiting for us when we got off duty tonight— "

"At midnight?" Carol asked.

"Yeah. He wanted to talk about those two guys. They allegedly stole an identity and used it to borrow a lot of money on properties they didn't own."

Carol chuckled. "I'm not a cop, but please. Two homeless men did this?"

Danny moved his hand, wincing with the effort. "Nobody really believes they did it, but somebody did, and whoever it was put the money in bank accounts in their names."

"I'm not really following this," Carol said.

"I'm sorry. The point is, it was an elaborate crime that took a lot of thought. It's not like robbing some random house, where you break in and take whatever stuff you find. This took planning. It's a unique crime."

"I thought you were going to tell me about Tim."

"I'm telling you now. I told you that Tim was an alcoholic. He lost his job, his girlfriend, and a lot of money—"

"And he went to rehab. I know all that, Danny. And you've hardly mentioned him since."

"Yes. What I didn't tell you is that Tim got in a lot of trouble before he went to rehab. Big trouble. If he'd gone to trial for it, he would have gone to prison. Dad intervened and gave him the choice between going to rehab or jail. He would definitely have done time if he'd gone to court, maybe even serious time."

"What did he do?" Carol asked.

Danny took a deep breath and exhaled before answering. "Tim did the same thing these homeless guys are implicated for. He stole money on some property he didn't own."

Carol looked at Danny for a moment, then she sat up straight. "Oh my God, you think Tim did this."

"I don't think so—I *know* he did."

"He admitted that?"

"No, he didn't have to." Danny thought it best not to say that he hadn't given Tim a chance to explain anything. "But I know he did it. It's the same crime, Carol. You said it yourself: the homeless guys didn't do this. It's Tim's crime right down to the smallest details. He's guilty."

Carol put her hands to her head. "But wait, Danny. You haven't talked to him about it yet?"

"Right," Danny answered.

"Well then, it might have been somebody else. You've got to find out, and if it wasn't Tim, you have to help him."

"Carol, I'm trying to tell you, this wasn't a run-of-the-mill crime. I don't know how he thought of it in the first place—and, I have to admit, it took brains to think it up and balls to pull it off. But for somebody else to come up with the same exact crime, with all its moving parts? It just isn't going to happen."

"But it *could* happen. You can't tell me it couldn't."

Danny looked at his knuckles. He picked up the bowl and put his fist back in it. "Carol, you know what Occam's Razor is, right?"

"Yes. If there are two theories about the same thing, the simpler one is usually right. You're saying that applies here."

"He did it before, the same thing. It's his MO all the way. Odds are greater that he did it again than of somebody else pulling it off. A helluva lot better."

"Still, Danny, he's your brother."

"And that's why I don't talk to him anymore. He hurt my parents deeply, more than you can imagine. He lied to all of us, and he got off incredibly light. Once is bad enough, but this is inexcusable. This time he's going to jail for a long time."

"Can't you help him? Can't you do something to help him get off?"

"Get him off? I'm going to help put him away."

The look of horror on Carol's face surprised Danny.

"Danny, you can't do that. He's your brother, for Heaven's sake."

"He's my stepbrother, and he committed a felony. Several of them, actually. I don't want to have anything to do with him."

"Stop it. He's family and you have to help him." Carol's voice was flat.

"And you have to stop telling me how to do my job."

"I'm not telling you how to be a cop! I'm telling you how to be a *brother*, and how you treat family."

"This really isn't your business, Carol."

"That's just the point, Danny. It *is* my business, especially if you and I have any kind of future together. Tim is your family and you *lied* about him. Now you're ready to send him off to prison before even giving him a chance."

"How did I lie about him? I've hardly mentioned Tim since we've been going out." Danny was exasperated.

"You lied by omission. You never told me he committed any crime, or anything else, really. What other little family secrets are you keeping, Danny?"

"Carol, I think you are overreacting," Danny said, not even trying to conceal his anger.

"Oh, do you? Just when I thought you couldn't make this any worse. Something's happened to you, Danny. This isn't who you are and I don't like the way you've been acting lately. I don't want to talk to you anymore. I don't even want you to stay here tonight, but *that* may be overreacting. Instead, I'm going to get pillows and a blanket and make up the sofa. I don't care if you sleep here or I do, but I don't want to sleep with you tonight. And I think you need to talk to the psychiatrist again." With that, Carol left the living room.

Stunned, Danny watched her walk out. He couldn't understand what was happening. For the first time since he and Carol had started going out, he had no idea what his next move was.

Chapter Thirty-Four

"What kind of a bug you got up there?" Sean asked. He opened the glove compartment and seemed intent on finding something in it.

"Excuse me?" said Danny.

Sean kept rifling through the glove compartment. "The bug you've had up your ass all shift. I just wondered what it is."

Danny scowled without answering. A call came in on the radio. Neither officer reached for it.

"Sean, answer the damn radio, will you?"

"You won't even answer calls tonight," Sean said. He slammed the glove compartment closed and grabbed the radio. "I thought I had a Power Bar in here." He switched on the mic. "This is car nineteen. Come in please, over."

The call was about a woman who had locked her keys, and small dog with them, in her car in the Target parking lot. The officers were only a few blocks away and Sean said they'd take the call. He hung up, and the two drove in silence to the shopping center.

The driver saw them before they saw her, and began waving them over. She was older, Danny guessed late sixties, and had a cart filled with shopping bags next to her car. Danny parked at a right angle to her, in front of her car.

"I'll handle this," said Sean, opening his door. "You stay here and see if you can fish that bug out."

Danny didn't mind staying put. He was in no mood to talk to anyone. If he could count on Sean for anything, it was to be charming and help the woman out. He rubbed his left hand over the bruised knuckles of his right. *It would be just my luck*, he thought, *if I broke something punching my brother.*

"Evening, ma'am."

Danny listened to Sean through the open car windows. He could see and hear the small dog, a white Jack Russell terrier, standing in the driver's seat and barking incessantly.

"Oh Officer, I'm so glad you're here. Scooter is frantic," said the woman.

Sean looked in the car. "Did he lock himself inside?"

"No, I'm afraid I did," said the woman, missing Sean's joke.

"Well, don't you worry. We'll have Scooter out of there in a jiffy. Just let me get my tools."

Sean started for the back of the patrol car, and Danny popped the trunk open. He looked in his rear view mirror, but could see only the open trunk and a few inches of Sean's midsection. After a few seconds, Sean walked back to the woman's car with a Slim Jim, a thin piece of metal used to unlock car doors—more often than not by car thieves.

"Ma'am, I know this sounds silly, but I need to see your license and registration so I know it's your car. Is the registration on you, or in your glove compartment?"

"Oh, it's in my glove compartment and the door is locked!"

Danny could hear the panic in her voice from his seat in the car.

"Don't you worry a bit. I'll unlock it, and you can show me then. After you've had a minute to reassure Scooter," said Sean, while working the Slim Jim between the door and window.

Danny had to smile, probably his first smile of the day. *Sean was born to help older ladies.*

The lock came up right away, and Sean opened the door for the woman. She reached in for Scooter.

"There, my little boy. Everything is fine," she said, while the dog squirmed in her arms and licked her face, yelping as he did.

Sean reached in and popped her trunk open. "Would you like me to put those things in the trunk for you? You take your time with Scooter," he said.

Returning the now-calm dog to the car, the woman got her registration and showed it and her license to Sean. He barely looked at them as he apologized for making her bother.

"Routine, ma'am. You take Scooter home and have a good evening," he said.

She thanked Sean again, got in her car, and drove off. Sean put the Slim Jim in the trunk and returned to his seat.

"Fine bit of police work, Sean, if I do say so myself," said Danny. He was smiling.

"Jesus, it talks and smiles. What, did you call an exterminator?" asked Sean.

"It's almost nine. Why don't we get some dinner?" said Danny.

"Now this is more like it." Sean put his arm out the window and drummed on the roof with his fingers. "It's good when you're like this. Lead the way, driver."

"Wendy's is just up ahead," Danny said as he drove.

"Oh no, not Wendy's," said Sean. "There's a Burger King across the street. Let's go there."

"What's wrong with Wendy's?" said Danny.

"I just don't care for them."

235

Both men were thrown forward when Danny hit the brakes. "What? Are you telling me there is a fast food place that you don't like?"

"Just go to Burger King, please?" said Sean.

"Four years riding around with you, stopping to eat every two hours like I'm feeding an infant, and I just now find out you don't like something? What, may I ask, is wrong with Wendy's?"

Sean looked down. "They use square patties instead of round ones. It creeps me out."

Danny burst out laughing. "They creep you out. You'll put damn near anything that isn't moving in your stomach, but square patties creep you out. I love that!"

Sean folded his hands in his lap.

"Oh, we are *so* going to Wendy's, and I'm buying!" Danny pulled into the parking lot. He quickly backed into a space at the corner of the lot and got out. "Come on partner. This one is on me."

"Three double cheeseburgers," said Danny, taking them out of the bag and handing two to Sean. "I thought these things creeped you out, and you get two of them?"

"It's time to man up and face my fears head on," said Sean. "Besides, I'm starving."

The two men ate in silence for a moment. Danny felt like he didn't need to ever speak again. *If people would just stop talking*, he thought, *half the world's problems could be avoided.*

Sean drank from his Coke. "You want to tell me why you've been so quiet tonight?" he asked. "Until a few minutes ago, you hadn't said ten words since we started."

"Tell you the truth, I'm enjoying the quiet, Sean. Think we can just eat for a minute?"

Sean took a big bite of his cheeseburger and seemed to consider what Danny had said. "Is this about the fight you got into last night?"

Danny was glad it was dark, in case his face had flushed. "What? Who said I was in a fight last night?"

Sean didn't look at him. "Those bruises on your hand. First and middle finger, first knuckle on both." He pulled on the straw of his milkshake again.

Danny instinctively covered his injured hand. "I wasn't fighting. I bruised them trying to re-hang a closet door at the house. I took it off to sand it and I slammed into the door frame when I was putting it back on."

"You've got to be the worst liar in the world."

"What, you don't believe me?"

"Always look at a man's hands. You told me that just last week," said Sean.

"Well, bully for me. But you're wrong, Sean."

"I don't think so. Hitting a door like that, you'd do more damage than just those two knuckles. There's no scabs or scratches. Plus, you're shit at home fix-it stuff. I'd believe that *Carol* was trying to hang a door, but not you. You got those bruises connecting on a right hook."

Danny was both embarrassed at being caught, and proud of Sean at the same time. He took the last bite of his hamburger, and reached for his Coke in the cup holder.

"I gotta admit, Sean, I am impressed. That's good police work."

"It's good *detective* work."

"Okay, I'll give you that one." Danny sat quietly before continuing. "And yeah, I hit somebody last night."

"I know it wasn't Carol, either. If you had even tried to hit her, she'd have cleaned your clock. So, who was it?"

"You don't know?" said Danny. He wadded up the wrapper from his hamburger, and put it and his empty French fries packet in the bag.

"Actually, I figured it was your brother. You seemed pretty pissed off when the Chief was talking to us last night, and I figured you went straight to his house."

Danny got out of the car and threw the bag in the trash. "He's my stepbrother, and you think he did it too, don't you?"

Sean shook his head. "I didn't say that, and I don't know if he did or didn't. I admit, it sounded just like what you said he did, but I don't have any information beyond that. But if he put up a fight when you tried to talk to him, it doesn't look good."

Danny didn't respond.

"That's what happened, right?" Sean asked. "You went over there, and when you starting asking him questions, he got flustered, then lost it and started swinging at you, leaving you no choice but to defend yourself."

"That's not exactly how it happened. I knocked on the door, he opened it and I hit him. Then I left."

Sean did a double-take. "Come again?"

It was embarrassing enough to say it once. "You heard me, Sean. I'm not saying it again."

"Wha—" Sean interrupted himself with a quick laugh. "What are you saying? You hit the guy straight out? Jesus, Danny, cops get sued for a lot less than that."

"He's my brother, Sean. He's not going to sue me."

"Oh, *now* he's your brother. I don't care who he is, Danny. That's not how cops do things, especially you."

"I wasn't there as a cop."

"Oh, please, Danny. You went there, in your uniform no less, because you think he's a suspect. You, of all people, would *never* hit someone like that."

"You're making too big a deal out of this."

"No, Danny. You're not making a big *enough* deal out of it. You would never have done this before."

238

"Before *what*, Sean?"

"Before…last night."

"Now you're the one full of BS. You mean I wouldn't have done it before I got shot at, aren't you? You think it all has to do with PTSD."

"Well? You wouldn't have."

"Why don't you and everybody else just get off my case about that?"

"Nobody's on your case, Danny. I'm your partner. I probably care more about you than anybody else. And I'm just saying, you wouldn't have done that before."

Danny couldn't think of a response that made any sense. "Look, Sean, suspect or not, Tim is my brother and I lost it, okay? It wouldn't have happened otherwise, and it won't happen again. Can you let it go?"

Sean sat quietly, then shrugged his shoulders. "Yeah…if you're sure this was a one-time thing, I guess so."

"That's what I'm saying." Danny reached for the radio, fighting not to show the pain in his hand as he did so. "I'm going to check in." There were no calls waiting for them. Another quiet night. They should all be like this.

"How about Tim? You going to talk to him again?" said Sean.

"Yeah, when I arrest him."

"God, listen to you. Look, Danny, whether you go as a cop or his brother, you need to talk to him. Give him a chance to explain his side of things."

"I appreciate the advice, Dr. Phil," said Danny.

"He may have done it. If he did, I'll help you put him away, swear to God. But he's family, and you've got to give him the benefit of a conversation," said Sean.

"Okay, okay," said Danny. "If it'll get everybody off my friggin' back, maybe I'll talk to him."

"That's more like it," said Sean. Up ahead, the glaring lights of a 7-11 store reflected off the cars parked in front of it. Sean pointed to it. "Hey, they might carry Power Bars. Why don't you pull in?"

Chapter Thirty-Five

Tim got to the sandwich shop at 2:00 p.m., a half-hour before he and Danny were scheduled to meet. He wasn't sure his brother would show up, even though Danny was the one who'd suggested the meeting. But Tim didn't want to risk being late and find out Danny had come and gone. He got his coffee and stood by the cream-and-sugar station, drinking while waiting for a table to open up near the back of the room. When one did after about five minutes, he sat down facing the wall. He knew Danny would want to sit facing the door, constantly scanning the other people in the room: him, the person of interest Danny could control; everybody else, potential bad guys he'd need to watch. It was the way his brother operated. Always on, always a cop. Tim respected Danny for that. Danny was more aware of his surroundings than anybody else he'd ever known.

Staring into his mug, he twirled the coffee inside, daring it to reach the lip without spilling. He wondered what Danny wanted.

"Did you get me a cup?"

Coffee crested the top of the mug and spilled onto Tim's hand. He hadn't noticed that Danny was standing there. In awkward simultaneous movements, he stood up, wiped his fingers on his jeans, banged his knee against the table and extended his hand to his brother. "Danny. I didn't see you." He was surprised to see Danny in street clothes—assuming, without thinking about it, that he'd be in uniform.

Danny frowned at his brother's outreached palm. "You want to dry that off first?" he said, rejecting the handshake.

To Tim it felt like a called strike.

"I wondered if you would show up," Danny said.

"Why wouldn't I be here? At least in a public place I don't have to worry that you'll sucker punch me again."

"Did I do that?" Danny pointed to Tim's face.

Tim instinctively reached up and dabbed his black eye, still sensitive to the touch. If Danny was trying to hide the smirk on his face, he wasn't succeeding. "No, Danny, I ran into a door. Of *course* you did this. Want to tell me why?"

"Oh, so this is how you want to play it."

"Play *what* Danny? I haven't seen you in months, you come to my house in the middle of the night, punch me, and now you're playing some kind of game."

Danny continued to stand, glaring at his brother.

"Danny, sit, please. Look, I'm glad you want to talk. Hold on and I'll get you a cup of coffee." Tim started for the counter without waiting for an answer. Someone was already ordering, and he was happy for the extra time to compose himself. When he had paid for his brother's coffee and turned back to the table, Danny was still glowering at him.

"I assume you still like it black." Tim put the cup down, then sat. "What's going on, Danny?"

"You know *exactly* what's going on, Tim."

Tim had seen Danny angry before, but this was different. Danny had always contained his emotions, but he wasn't showing that kind of control now. "Well, just for the hell of it, pretend I don't know what you're talking about and tell me," said Tim.

242

Danny threw up his hands in resignation. "Okay, Tim. I'll tell you. I'm here because my partner and I arrested some homeless men who are somehow involved in an identity theft crime. Seems somebody borrowed money on some property that wasn't his. Got loans from a finance company, then deposited the money in a couple of bank accounts." Halfway through his answer, Danny had started speaking in a sing-song voice. "Sound familiar, or am I going too fast for you?"

"Sounds like what I did," Tim answered. Then the implication of what Danny was saying hit him. "Oh, man. And you think I did it."

"Well? If the shoe fits…"

"Danny, I swear to you, I know how it must look, but I didn't do this."

"Oh, I see." Danny's face was scrunched up and he nodded agreement. "It's just a *coincidence* that somebody else pulled the same elaborate scheme you pulled—"

"Come on, Danny—"

"Because there is *no way* you'd do it. You're a changed man, right Tim?"

"Okay, I probably deserve this—"

"*Probably?*"

"I didn't do it, Danny, I don't care what it looks like to you."

"Well, then, did you tell somebody else what you did?"

Caught without an acceptable answer, Tim turned red.

"Oh, that's right. You *couldn't* have told anybody else because you *promised* you wouldn't, right little brother?"

Tim took a sip off coffee. A waitress showed up at the table, and he felt like he'd been thrown a lifeline.

"Can I warm that up for you, honey?"

Tim quickly lowered his cup. "Yes, please."

"How 'bout you?" she asked Danny.

Danny continued to look at his brother as he answered, "No, thank you."

Tim was too ashamed to speak.

"You just going to sit there? I can do this all day, Tim, but sooner or later you're going to have to admit that you told somebody. Otherwise, I'm still looking at you as the person of interest."

Tim took a deep breath and plunged ahead. "Danny, I know how it looks, and I know you're still mad at me. But I'm telling you, I had nothing to do with that. I haven't had a drop to drink in almost three months."

Danny laughed. "I don't care if you haven't had a drink in three *years*. What the hell difference does that make?"

"Look, Danny, I only did it in the first place *because* I was drinking."

Danny put both of his hands in the air. "Oh, Tim. *Stop* it. I've had too much to drink before, too, and I didn't rob a bank."

"You're not an alcoholic, Danny."

"Okay, screw this. I don't care if you're an alcoholic or an acolyte. When you got caught, the main reason you didn't go to prison was that you promised you'd never tell anybody what you did or how you did it. But obviously you either did this crime or broke your promise. So, if it wasn't you, who did you tell?"

Tim mumbled his answer. "I told a guy at the center."

"I fuckin' knew it," Danny muttered, mostly to himself. He banged his fist on the table. "I *knew* you'd tell someone!"

"It was just one guy, Danny. I know it was wrong and I shouldn't have—"

"Oh, you think not? Jesus, Tim."

"Look, Danny, I'm sorry. I know you want more than that from me, but that's all I got. I've apologized to Dad—"

"And that makes everything just hunky dory."

Danny seemed ready to hang Tim for the crime without any more discussion. Tim leaned across the table. "And I've got to live with what I did to them for the rest of my life, Danny. If you want to hate me for the rest of *yours*, have at it. But I don't owe you shit. Mom and

Dad have let it go, and they're the ones I hurt the most. What the hell is it with you?"

Danny sat back in his seat. Tim could practically feel the burn from his eyes. "Okay, who did you tell?"

Tim unclenched his jaw, and tried to relax. "I went jogging with another client one morning."

"Client?"

"That's what they called patients at the program."

"Oh, that's cute."

Tim let it go. "I hadn't said anything to anybody up to then, and the guy was checking out later in the day. He thought I was this rich, spoiled kid. I know this sounds bad, but I wanted to show him that I wasn't some sheltered momma's boy."

"And what better way to do that than to break your word."

"Look, Danny. I said I screwed up."

"Who is he?" asked Danny.

"Just a guy." said Tim.

"He got a name?"

"Jorge."

Danny rolled his eyes. "Does he have a *last* name, Tim?"

"I don't know. Nobody used last names at the place. It's an AA thing."

"Where is he now?"

"You mean, where does he live?"

"Yes, Tim, I mean where does he live?"

"I can't say for sure. He used to live in the East Bay, but I think he lives in Napa now. I've seen him."

"You've seen him? Here in Napa?"

"Yeah, I ran into him on the basketball court, a couple of weeks ago, at Napa High. I stopped to see if I could get in a game and there he was. We talked a bit afterwards, but I don't know where he lives."

"Did you get his phone number, email or anything?"

"No."

"Have you seen him there since?"

"Today's the first time I've been back in town."

"I'll call New Beginnings. They'll have his last known address."

"They won't give it to you," said Tim. "The counselors stressed how everything was confidential there. Said they wouldn't open the doors, even for a federal warrant."

"And you bought that."

"That's what they said."

"I'll call them and find out."

Tim raised his cup, as much to think for a moment as to take a drink. "Look, I'm showing a house in a couple of hours, but I've got a little time before I go. You want to ride by the high school and see if Jorge's there?"

"Beats sitting here doing nothing." Danny stood up immediately. "This doesn't mean that I think you're innocent, Tim," he said. "If I find out you did it, I promise you you're going to prison."

Tim sighed. "The sooner we get this resolved, the better."

They left and walked to the car in silence. The layer of self-respect Tim had gained in sobriety dissolved, as though he'd been dipped in a vat of scalding hot shame. He remembered how he felt being wakened in a garage, passed out and shoeless. This was worse. This wasn't a stranger—it was his big brother.

Traffic was practically nonexistent, and Tim pulled into the school lot after just a few minutes. "How do we play this if Jorge is here?" he asked.

"I don't really know. Maybe we just watch until they take a break. You can introduce me as your brother, but don't mention that I'm a cop. We'll just have to see how it goes."

"I thought cops were supposed to know your every move. This sounds pretty loosey-goosey," said Tim.

"Yeah well, it's not like you see on TV. A lot of this is just playin' it as it comes, listening to your gut for the next move."

"Well, we're going find out soon enough," Tim said. He pulled up to the court and stopped the car. "Jorge told me he was here every day, and there he is."

Danny looked at the players and suddenly bolted upright in his seat. "Holy shit! The guy that just grabbed that rebound? *That's* Jorge?"

"He's got some moves, doesn't he?"

"Moves, my ass. That guy's a priest at my church. That's Father Morales!"

Chapter Thirty-Six

"Who is Father Mor—" Tim began, but Danny was already out of the car and jogging towards the court before he could finish.

"Danny, what are you doing?" Tim yelled, his arms stretched out across the roof of his car.

On the court, Morales was driving towards the basket, his back to the parking lot, and went up for an uncontested dunk. "Yes!" he said, pumping his fist as he snagged the loose ball. He beamed at the other men, then seemed to realize that they were all looking towards the parking lot and at the man coming towards them. Morales locked eyes with Danny, who—fists clenched at his sides—was almost at the court and walking laser-straight towards him.

"Morales!" Danny couldn't see anyone else, only the priest.

Morales paused for a second, then threw the ball hard, straight at Danny. He spun around and started running full speed in the opposite direction.

They say that when you see a bear or some other animal in the wild, the last thing you should do is run from it. Running away makes the bear think you are prey. Instinctively, bears chase prey. And these days Danny's rage popped out at the slightest provocation. When Morales ran, he stopped thinking. Deflecting the thrown ball without even looking at it, Danny took off—the chase now fully on.

"Stop, Morales!" His temples were throbbing.

A six-foot chain link fence fifty yards from the basketball court separated the athletic field from a wooded area. Morales reached the fence first and, without breaking stride, vaulted over. He stumbled when he landed but quickly regained his composure and kept running.

"Shit," Danny said to himself as he watched Morales clear the fence. He was no more than ten yards behind him. Danny placed his hands on the railing and attempted to vault over it, but his foot caught the top and he fell. Grabbing the top again, he pulled himself up and over. Dropping to the other side, he started to run again, but he'd lost distance. He saw Morales look over his shoulder at him, then veer to the left, behind a thicket of bushes. Danny could have sworn that Morales was smiling.

"Son of a bitch!" Danny muttered. He hoped to regain lost ground, but Morales was too fast and the vegetation too thick. He'd disappeared.

Coming out of the wooded area, Danny reached a clearing and three apartment buildings. No sign of Morales. Great. Danny didn't know which way to run. He paused, in part to catch his breath, then took a chance and ran to the building on his left. He was in predatory mode, void of reason

Unable to find Morales, Danny scrutinized the other buildings. He slowed to a stop, the trail cold, and kicked the ground. "Shit!" He walked in a small circle, scanning the area, hoping to catch a glimpse of the priest. He had to find him. He was so angry he couldn't think.

And then he heard it.

A voice, *his* voice, it seemed, but somehow unconnected to him, interrupted Danny's thoughts.

"Why are you chasing this man?" the voice said. "What are you doing?"

Danny stopped moving. The question caught him totally off guard, and he had no answer to it. *What am I doing? This is insane.* He shook his head as if to throw off whatever had taken him over. *I'm chasing a man—a frigging priest no less—for no good reason. And I'm a cop for God's sake. What is happening to me?* He scanned the area for any sign of Morales. He had no idea what he would do if he did see him, but he didn't know what else to do. He felt self-conscious, as though he was being watched. He halfheartedly began to jog back to the school.

Danny saw the basketball players, agitated and talking excitedly, as he approached the fence.

"There he is!" one of them said, pointing to him. Danny scanned the faces of the men on the other side of the enclosure. They seemed wary of him, as though he were a dangerous animal that might jump the fence and tear them to shreds, but they all had fight in their eyes. One of them was carrying the basketball, holding it at his chest, as if for defense.

Danny could feel the gas drain from his tank. Ten feet from the fence now, he didn't stop running as much as he lost resolve and stumbled to a stop. He put his hands on his knees, gasping for air, and stared at the ground. He hoped that stopping might take some of the fight out of the ball players. Still, he was in a potentially bad situation. *How am I going to explain this?* He stayed bent over, wishing for a do-over he knew he wasn't going to get.

"Hey! What the hell are you doing?"

Danny straightened and walked to the fence. "I'm a cop," he said. He pulled his wallet out of his back pocket and opened it to his badge, which he held up to the fence for the man closest to it to read.

"Son of a bitch," said the man. "He really is."

Danny put his wallet back and hoisted himself to the top of the fence. "Excuse me." He dropped down and the men stepped back, clearing a spot for his landing.

The man who examined his badge spoke. "We didn't know you were a cop. Father Morales told us you were trying to hurt him and said to keep you here. What the hell's going on?"

Before Danny could answer, he heard a man yelling in the parking lot. Everyone turned in that direction.

"Let go of the damn door!" It was Morales.

Tim was standing next to a Porsche, struggling to keep the car door open. Morales popped out of the driver's seat, and in doing so, hit his head on the edge of the door.

"Dammit!" he yelled.

"Oh, shit," Danny mumbled, then started running towards the car. The other men fell in behind him. Danny figured it was because he was a cop, and he was glad his face was hidden from scrutiny. He was the first one to reach Tim and Morales.

"All right, both of you, calm down. What's this all about?"

Morales snorted, "Oh, you're going to play cop now? Seriously?" He had a hand over his eye. Blood ran underneath it, down his cheek and onto his tee shirt. The situation was dicey at best, and Danny needed to get control of it.

Morales pointed to Tim and shouted to Danny. "He said you guys are *brothers!*"

"Yeah, we are. So?" Danny replied.

Morales uncovered his eye. "Look what he did to me!"

The point just under the eye from where the blood seemed to be flow was already raised and a nasty blue.

"Oh, man," said one of the men. "That looks bad." Several others offered their concurring medical opinions.

Danny figured it wouldn't take more than a stitch or two, if that, to close it up. "Did you do this?" he asked Tim.

"No. He kind of leaped out of his seat and hit the corner of the door full force when he did," said Tim.

"Oh bullshit. You kept me from closing my door, and when I got out, you pushed me into it," Jorge insisted.

"Now, *that's* bullshit," Tim responded.

"Will somebody tell us what's going on?" one of the men asked.

Danny ignored the question. He needed to break this situation up soon. "No one is stopping you now, Morales. I'm sorry you hurt yourself, but yelling like this isn't going to help."

One of the men gave Morales a tee shirt, which he used to cover his eye. The man then pointed to Tim's black eye. "Who hit *you?*" he asked.

"Stay out of this, please." Danny raised his hand for silence. This was not the time to complicate things with a discussion of his own transgressions. He turned to Jorge, made a sweeping gesture towards the Porsche. "Sorry to have inconvenienced you. If you want to leave, leave."

Jorge snorted. "Inconvenienced me? I'd call this more than an inconvenience. You had no right to chase me. You've been harassing me for weeks and I didn't want to deal with it again." Jorge crossed his arms, allowing the cut above his eye to bleed freely, and sneered at Danny, "I'll bet a judge will understand."

Jorge was probably right, thought Danny, but he couldn't play it that way and instead rolled his eyes. "First off, you should probably cover that eye. And no one is 'harassing' you. Tell a judge if you want, but he's going to have a lot of questions. You prepared to answer questions, Morales?"

The other ball players reacted as though watching a tennis match, looking from Danny to Jorge and back. "Somebody want to tell us what's going on here?" said one of them. "Why was a cop chasing you, Father?"

"Again with the Father? Please," snorted Tim asked. "You, a *priest?*"

Morales ignored him. "Look, I ran, but that's not against the law. *He* started chasing *me*. You want to explain why you did that?"

I wish I knew. Danny held up both his hands. "Look, nobody is running now or trying to stop you from leaving. No harm, no foul. I'd get that eye looked at, though. You're going to have quite a shiner there."

"You think this is funny. We'll see how damn funny it is when I report it. You had no right to chase me," Morales said, stabbing a finger at Danny. "When I finish with you, you'll be in a world of hurt!" Morales opened his car door and got in.

"You enjoy the rest of your day, Father. I'll see you in church," Danny said. Morales started his car, stepped on the gas, and pulled away.

Danny scanned the other's faces, all of whom seemed befuddled. "I guess the game is over," Danny said. "Tim, do you mind taking me back to my car?"

"Sure." He tossed off a quick wave to the others "Fellas. Guess we'll catch a game some other time."

Tim didn't speak until he and Danny were in the car, the doors closed. Brows furrowed, he looked at Danny imploringly. "You want to tell *me* what just happened?"

Danny didn't have an answer he wanted to share. His response was short and gruff. "It's complicated."

Chapter Thirty-Seven

Any time Danny entered a roomful of people, he always paid attention to their eyes. Eyes told him what the general mood was and who, if anyone, he should pay particular attention to. Most people were unaware when someone joined a group, or paid little notice other than a glance in the new arrival's direction. Danny passed over those individuals quickly. The ones who looked back at him, he scrutinized more closely. The majority of that group looked away quickly, not wanting to be seen staring. All in all, most crowds were benign, but you never knew.

As soon as he and Carol walked into church Sunday, two days after he'd chased Morales, he became aware that the tables had turned. A number of people were looking at *him*, as though awaiting his arrival. Some stole furtive glances, turning away quickly as soon as he made eye contact with them, but they were clearly checking him out. Others seemed to use that contact imploringly, looking, perhaps, for explanations for what they had heard. A few outright stared, several nudging the person next to them and pointing to Danny with a nod in his direction. Danny knew the question they wanted answered. He had nothing for them; he didn't know himself why he'd done what he'd done.

He peeked at Carol to see if she was aware of all the attention on him. Thankfully, she seemed oblivious to it. The two took their place in their usual second-row pew and rose when the organ began the processional. Danny glanced over his shoulder and could see the acolytes leading the procession, now only a few pews behind them. The procession drew audible gasps as it moved forward. When the first acolytes passed their pew, Danny glanced at the priests filing behind them. He couldn't believe what he saw.

To Danny's knowledge, Morales had never been part of the morning service, but there he was, walking besides Father Keenan on his way to the chancel of the church. Both men were dressed in their colorful priestly garments, their hymnals opened and voices raised in song. But in addition to his robes, Morales wore a large white patch over one eye, with tape holding it in place and crisscrossing his face. Danny scanned the church and caught the open mouths of other parishioners, fixated on the patch, some of them looking from it to him. He glared at the priest's uncovered eye, which was looking right back at him. The patch was complete overkill, worn for and achieving shock among the parishioners, and Morales was visibly delighted by the drama it created.

Carol gasped when she saw him. "You did that?"

"No, I wasn't around when it happened. I told you, he did it to himself," Danny replied. "And trust me, he doesn't need the dressing. His little boo-boo isn't that bad."

Still, Danny understood theater, and knew that Morales was on stage. This was going to be a long mass.

When the recessional hymn cued the end of the service, the priests began their walk out of the church, filing past Danny and Carol's pew. Morales and Danny glared at each other, a visual game of chicken. Once the recession party was a dozen or so rows on their way, Carol and Danny fell in behind them. The church began to empty.

"Everyone is staring at us," Carol said, leaning towards Danny as they walked.

Now she noticed.

"No, I'm pretty sure they're staring at me."

At the back of the church, Danny ignored Morales and smiled weakly at Keenan.

"Father," he said, taking Carol by the elbow and moving them both outside, toward the parking lot. Keenan let him pass with a wordless, expressionless nod.

"No, Danny. Let's go to the parish hall."

"You actually want more of this? Wouldn't you rather go straight home?"

"I feel like I'm wearing a scarlet letter, but I haven't done anything to be ashamed of and I'm not going to act like I have. What did you do, Danny?"

"Carol, I told you, I chased the man, but he injured himself—"

"Which never would have happened if you hadn't chased him in the first place. What were you thinking?"

"I told you, I wasn't."

When they entered the parish hall, no one spoke to them.

"You sure you want to stay?" asked Danny after a few awkward moments.

"Get us a cup of coffee," Carol said through gritted teeth. "I'll wait here."

When he returned, Carol was in conversation with a woman she knew from the altar guild. Danny had never felt very warm towards the woman, but could have hugged her then.

"Hi Betty," he said.

"Oh, Danny," Betty answered, acting surprised to see him. She turned back to Carol. "Well, let me know what you decide to do."

Every muscle in Betty's face registered disgust. Danny was surprised that the smile she offered him didn't make her cheeks crack. He sniffed near his armpit and moved closer to Carol. "Do I have body odor or something?" He grinned.

"She just asked me if I was going to stay on the altar guild. If we would be leaving the church." Carol's voice was flat.

Danny took a sip of his coffee. "Yeah. I say we finish our coffee and leave this party."

"No, she meant for good. She asked if we were going to stop coming to church here."

"Hey, even if I do have BO, it can't be that bad."

"You think this is funny, do you?"

Danny knew from the way Carol looked at him that his joke had been a bad idea.

"This because *you* hit a priest."

"Carol, I told you, I didn't hit him. But leaving the church or the altar guild is ridiculous."

"That's not the point. This is your fault, and you know it," said Carol. "I asked you to leave this alone after you talked to Father Keenan, but you wouldn't listen to me. You just had to go off and play the big-shot cop."

"Carol, that isn't fair."

Carol walked towards the door, put her coffee cup on a table, and looked over her shoulder at Danny. He sheepishly looked around to see if anyone was watching, put his cup next to hers, and followed her outside.

"What do you mean, 'it isn't fair'?" Carol hissed, continuing the conversation. "I'm your girlfriend, Danny. This is my church and I asked you to do something for me. I asked you to respect what the Father said to you and drop this, but you didn't. You only made it worse."

He knew she was right and was furious with himself, but he didn't like being verbally attacked either. He could feel rage take over him and, without thinking, he lashed out at her.

"Carol, I don't tell you how to teach. Stop trying to tell me how to do my job."

Danny caught himself immediately, and wished he could take the words back. What was getting into him lately? "I didn't mean that the way—" The look on Carol's face stopped him before he could finish.

Carol stepped back from him. "I—I can't believe you just said that."

The shame felt like a deep stain on his heart. "Carol, I'm so sorry. That was out of line."

"What's wrong with you, Danny? You beat up your brother, then a priest, and now you talk to me like that?"

Danny thought it wisest not to correct her this time.

Putting a hand to her forehead, Carol seemed to regain her composure. At least, Danny hoped she had.

"Danny, this just isn't like you. I don't know if you need to see the psychiatrist again or what, but I need some time alone to sort this out. Is there someplace else you could stay tonight? If not, I'll find someplace."

Danny couldn't form a response. He'd spent a recent night on the sofa, now she was asking him to spend another out of the house. He spoke as gently as he could. "Carol, I understand that you're mad, but I think that's a bad idea."

"It might be, Danny, but you've been acting differently lately, and I don't understand it. I need to be alone right now. Will you give me that, please?"

"Of course, whatever you need. I love you, Carol."

"I know you do, Danny. I hope you can figure what's happening to you."

Later that day, Danny called Sean and asked if he could bunk at his place for the night. Sean didn't grill him, and Danny thanked whatever God or karma was responsible for that small favor. The next day at work, neither man spoke of it.

Chapter Thirty-Eight

The plus side to working swing shift at this time of year was sunlight. With days getting shorter, being off during the day meant being able to do things outside while the sun was still up. This past week though, it hadn't mattered. Danny had spent most of his days indoors. Today he'd gone to a movie that started at 11:30 a.m. There'd been only one other person in the theater, which he found depressing. He couldn't remember if he'd ever gone to a movie alone or in the daytime. Now, just hours later, he couldn't recall the name of the film. He'd seen all the images on the screen, heard all the dialogue, but he just couldn't seem to process it. He was too preoccupied with the prospect that he was cracking up, or at least suffering from PTSD. With his shift starting in an hour, Danny had to shake these feelings.

"Couple more weeks of nights, and we'll be back on days. I can feel it, and I can't wait," said Sean. He bounced up the stairs from the locker room to see the duty officer, while Danny trudged behind him.

"I hope you're right. I'm ready to go to bed and get up when the rest of the world does," said Danny. He wondered if he was weary from walking up the steps, or from worry.

The two officers walked to the reception desk. "Top of the morning, Doris. Is the duty officer in?" said Sean.

"What morning? It's three thirty in the afternoon, and I'm going home in half an hour," she answered. "And yes, he's in, but the Chief wants to see you first, Officer Garcia."

Danny felt his stomach sink. "Why does he want to see us?"

Doris stopped typing, looked up from her keyboard and regarded Danny with exaggerated confusion. "'Us'? I didn't say, 'us,' I said he wants to see 'you.' Officer Rawlins, I'm sure the duty officer is awaiting *your* arrival with bated breath."

Danny could read the worry on his partner's face.

"It's probably nothing, Danny. I'm probably getting promoted over you and he wants to break it to you gently."

Doris rolled her eyes while continuing to type.

"Yeah, I'm sure that's it. I'll see you at the car," Danny said softly. Sean's joke did nothing to ease his anxiety.

Walking down the hall to the Chief's office was evocative of walking down the aisle of the church with Carol. Eyes he only imagined from people who weren't really there stared at him from both walls, and the feeling of shame returned. The visit to the Chief was going to be about Morales, that was a given, and he didn't know what he would—what he *could*—say.

As usual the door was open, and Danny knocked lightly on the frame. "You wanted to see me, Chief?"

The Chief looked up from his desk and over his reading glasses. "Garcia. Come in. Sit."

Save for the desk and chairs, the office was virtually empty. All the packed boxes that had been accumulating over recent weeks were gone. A coat rack, with a single sports coat on it, was by the door. Only one file, the phone, and the picture of his grandchildren remained on his desk.

The Chief pointed to Danny's chin. "Is that facial hair, Garcia?"

"Yes sir." Danny paused before sitting, resisting the urge to touch his chin. "Is that a problem?"

The Chief seemed to consider the question for a moment. His tie was loose, his shirt collar unbuttoned and his sleeves rolled halfway up his arms. Danny couldn't remember him looking this disheveled.

"Nah, what do I care? I'm outta here in two weeks. Grow it to the floor if you want. Do you know why I wanted to see you?" asked the Chief.

Danny started to say, 'No why?' but caught himself. "Yes sir. I suppose it's about me chasing a man."

The Chief took his reading glasses off. "That 'man' was a priest, Danny. You drove into a parking lot, jumped out of the car and started chasing a priest for no apparent reason."

While the Chief's account wasn't entirely accurate, Danny thought it best not to quibble over small details. "Chief, *he* started running as soon as he saw me. I had no choice but to chase him."

"No *choice*? Was there a crime being committed or did you have reason to believe that one might be? Was somebody in danger?"

"No, sir." Danny felt like an errant schoolboy.

"Someone wants to run from you, it may be rude, but if nothing's going on, you have no legal right to chase him. Maybe he suddenly felt like jogging, or heard his mother calling. You don't know."

Danny straightened up in the chair. "Sir, I know it doesn't look good—"

"I wish to hell you had thought about that before you did it." The Chief moved from behind his desk and sat on the front it, facing Danny. "And it turns out, that's just part of it."

"Sir?"

"The priest says you've been stalking him and accused him of extortion. You even went to the Bishop, in uniform and out of our jurisdiction, and tried to press the matter with him." Danny started to speak, but the Chief stopped him. He was rolling down and buttoning his sleeves. "Did you know I know the Bishop? It's not like we're friends, but I played in a golf tournament with him a couple years back. Hell, he baptized two of my grandkids."

Of *course* he did. The Chief *would* have to have a personal relationship with the Bishop. Danny tried to collect his thoughts before speaking. "Chief, I never used the word 'extortion.' Morales—the priest—tried to get money from a man at our church. The man was upset and approached me about it. I know he was telling the truth. This is going to sound a little crazy, given everything that's happened, but something about that priest isn't right. I think he's dirty."

"I see. And did you take this to your sergeant, or anybody else?"

Danny knew the question was both rhetorical and sarcastic. "I'm still getting information," he answered, without conviction. If a person Danny was questioning had said the same thing with the same lack of enthusiasm, Danny would have known he owned him.

"Getting information..." the Chief let the words hang in the air. "So, you took the word of a man from your church, who you just met, I believe, over that of a priest and a bishop. Then you pulled all that other shit, and you can't understand why it all might look just a tad bit bad to me?"

"Sir, I'm telling you, I've got a bad feeling about that priest."

"Yeah, okay, but chasing him? That's not the way to handle a..." the Chief made air quotes, "...bad feeling." He shook his head and chuckled. "Especially in front of a bunch of witnesses who all say it was unprovoked. The priest wants to file a restraining order against you."

The image of Morales's face in church, his smirk partially covered with the over-the-top bandages wrapped around his face, filled Danny's mind. "Sir, that's a crock—"

"I know that. He won't get the order if I can possibly stop it." The Chief pushed himself off the desk, walked to the window, and spoke with his back to Danny. "But somebody, and my money is on the priest, called the press and told them something was going on and that they should look into it. Said one of our cops has gone rogue and is harassing a man of the cloth." He faced Danny. "He actually said, 'a man of the cloth.'" The Chief snickered. "A reporter called me about it this morning. They want to talk to you."

"Sir, I'll tell the reporter that this isn't—"

"You won't tell the reporter shit, Garcia." The Chief walked back to his desk, stood tall and crossed his arms. You won't talk to him or anybody else. Not one word. Are we clear?"

"Yes sir."

"This priest may have a low flash point, but you've really pissed him off, and he is milking this thing to get back at you. I have no choice now but to take some kind of official action. This is not the kind of thing I want to be dealing with the last two weeks of my career."

"I understand, sir."

The Chief returned to his seat behind the desk and put his glasses back on. He picked up the lone folder. "This is your personnel file, Danny. You've had a helluva career up to now, which is why I'm not suspending you." Danny was shocked that suspension was even on the table. "However, I am taking you off patrol and putting you on a desk for a while."

Danny slumped in his seat. "Sir, if you give me a chance I can clear this up."

"It's a little late for that, Officer. You can have a chance, only it won't be on patrol. It'll be behind a desk. Do you understand?"

How could this be happening? "Yes sir, I do. When does this start?" said Danny.

"Right now." The Chief let Danny's file drop onto his desk. He took his glasses off and pointed them at Danny as he spoke. "I don't understand why you chased him. It was a rookie move to let your emotions get away from you like that. Why do you think you did it?"

Danny didn't think it wise to admit that he didn't know, that he'd just lost control of himself and started running. He was afraid the Chief would hear the voice in his head screaming, *It's PTSD! He's got it and he's screwing things up!*

"Sir?"

"You losing your temper like you did…is it an isolated thing? Does this have anything to do with the shooting?"

It wasn't isolated, Danny knew that, and he was beginning to realize it could be related to the shooting. How could he tell his superior officer that without putting his career at risk? *Damndest thing, Chief. Ever since I got shot at, I seem to be losing my shit. No telling what I might do out there.* "Sir, this is going to sound really crazy, but I think Morales may have been involved in that identity theft thing."

The Chief just looked at Danny for a moment. "No, it doesn't sound crazy, Danny. It sounds paranoid, like you've flipped. Why in the hell would you accuse a priest of that?"

"I know how it sounds. I don't have that much, and I'd feel stupid making a case to you now, but I'm almost positive I'm right."

The Chief put his glasses on the desk and rubbed his eyes. He buttoned his collar and pulled up the knot of his tie. "Danny, you're a good cop, and your instincts are usually right on the money. If you say there's a connection, maybe there is, but it's probably wisest to keep it to yourself. The identity theft crime is a federal case now, bank robbery, fraud and whatever the hell else it is, but what little I know about it, they definitely aren't looking at anybody from the clergy. You want to spend your time looking into this, you go for it, but you do it from your desk. You don't talk to anybody, I mean *anybody*, without clearing it with me first. And you are off patrol, understood?"

The Chief stood up. Reading it as a dismissal, Danny stood as well.

"Yes sir, I understand. Do I get to keep my gun?"

"Your what? Yes, hell yes. I said I'm not suspending you. You're just moving to a desk."

"How long am I on desk duty?"

"I haven't thought about that yet, but long enough that nobody will be up my ass asking why I'm letting a cop who chases a man of God for no reason back on the street. I also want you to take a couple of days off to think about all this." The Chief walked to the coat rack and put his sports coat on. "Doris made you an appointment to talk to the shrink tomorrow. She can give you the details. Go home, or wherever, Garcia. You're off the clock."

"Sir, do you think the shrink is really necessary?" Danny wished he could take the question back as soon as he said it.

The Chief looked at him for a moment without speaking. "I'm going to pretend you aren't talking right now, Officer. Take off your uniform and go home." With that, he left his office.

Danny hadn't moved since standing, and remained in place for a moment. "Yes sir," he said to the empty room.

Chapter Thirty-Nine

Dr. Hiakawa's receptionist averted her eyes when Danny walked into the office. She put her hand to her mouth—caught in the middle of a bite—and swallowed before speaking. Half of a sandwich and a pickle were on a plate in front of her. "Hello, Officer Garcia," she said behind her hand, "She's waiting for you."

Danny figured if he said, "Boo!" the poor girl might faint.

"Danny," said Dr. Hiakawa, rising out of her office chair when he walked in. "Good to see you again. I'm glad you're here."

Danny shook her hand. "I don't mean to be rude, but it wasn't my idea to come here in the first place."

Hiakawa smiled. "Please, have a seat."

Danny took off his baseball cap. "I've been sitting in the car, trying to figure out how it is I'm here for the third time in two weeks."

Hiakawa nodded. *Smiles, nods—she doesn't make this any easier,* Danny thought. "I thought about not even coming in, but I knew I'd lose my job if I didn't. Well, maybe not lose it, but get myself in deeper shit than I'm already in."

"So, you think you're in trouble," said Hiakawa.

"Are you serious? You know what happened. Although you wouldn't know that, in addition to being taken off the streets, my girlfriend threw me out."

"I'm sorry to hear that."

"She's just pissed, but she is plenty pissed."

Hiakawa picked up a file, and sat down in a chair across from Danny. "Why do you think she's angry with you?"

Danny stood, starting pacing the floor as he spoke. "I'm kind of a pariah at church, as you can probably guess, and Carol's paying for it. So, she's mad at me, which I totally understand."

"And this is because you chased the priest?"

"I think that's a pretty safe bet, yes."

"What were you feeling when you chased him?"

This was not a path Danny intended to go down. "What was I *feeling*? Seriously? Don't you think anybody just *does* stuff without stopping to think about how they *feel*?"

"Of course. I understand that you might not have considered it in the moment, but when you think about it now, what do you think you were feeling?"

"I don't know, a bunch of things. Sean…my partner?"

Hiakawa nodded. Danny wondered if she was always such a stimulating conversationalist.

"We arrested a couple of homeless guys a few weeks ago for stealing money—a lot of money, actually—and I thought my brother had done it."

"I don't understand."

Danny held up his hand to stop her. "When I confronted my brother, he told me it might have been a guy he'd met at rehab."

"I'm afraid I'm still not following you."

"We're getting there. Anyway, I didn't believe there really *was* a guy in rehab, I just thought my brother was trying to throw me off. Turns out the man he was talking about was Morales, the one I chased. He's a priest at my church who I am ninety nine percent sure has been trying to shake down some parishioners."

"Was he trying to shake you down?"

"No. He was trying to get money from a man in exchange for marriage counseling. Priests don't charge people for that stuff." Danny expected Hiakawa to start connecting the dots, but her expression told him it wasn't happening.

"The shakedown isn't important, except that it made me not trust Morales. My brother told him how he stole the money, and I think Morales copied it, to the letter."

This revelation didn't seem to enlighten Hiakawa at all. "Not the shakedown, I mean the stealing. When my brother stole all that money, he got sent to rehab. He met Morales, and told him all about how he'd stolen it, all the details. As soon as I realized my priest and Tim's guy were the same person, I knew I had him. *I knew* it!" Danny pumped his fist in the air.

"So, that gets back to how you felt when you were chasing him."

Danny had such a strong visceral reaction to her question, he wondered if he might have twisted an organ while sitting there. This is exactly where he didn't want the conversation to go, and she was taking him down the rabbit hole.

"Your Chief thinks you acted irrationally. He said considering the interactions you'd had with Morales, and the assurance you got from the Bishop that he *isn't* extorting anybody..." *Wow. She even knows about the Bishop.*

"...that chasing him showed bad judgment. He thought your reaction might be related to having been shot at."

"Being shot at? That's crazy."

"I'm just telling you what he said. He's worried that you might be suffering from post-traumatic stress disorder. Do you think that's possible?"

Danny laughed. "I think it's a load of crap. The two things don't have anything to do with each other." Danny felt lightheaded. He wondered if *he* had Wagon Eyes, and if Hiakawa knew to look for them.

"Do you get angry or irritated more easily since the shooting?"

Danny thought it probably wasn't a good idea to tell her about punching his brother. "No. What's your point?"

"Danny, you seem really averse to the idea of having PTSD. Why is that?"

"*If* I had it, which I don't, I think it's a safe bet that I'd be on my way out of the force."

"You'd quit your job?"

"Quit? Hell no, I'd be fired."

Hiakawa crossed her arms. "Really? Do you think that you're the first person in your department to be affected by something that's happened on the job?"

It had never occurred to Danny that another cop might have PTSD. "Oh. Who have you seen?" He knew she wouldn't answer.

"The department didn't send you here just to be diagnosed and then fired. If you have PTSD, my job is to help you formulate strategies for dealing with it. Counting to ten when you feel stressed out, for example. Most patients learn to regulate their impulse feelings and stop manifesting symptoms after a few weeks. Then they go on about their lives."

"Other officers have returned to duty after that diagnosis?"

"I've seen three other officers, two male and one female, and all of them returned to work. The only way that wouldn't happen is if you were abnormally compromised from the trauma you endured. Statistically speaking, that isn't likely. Your Chief just wants to make sure you're okay."

"Pardon me, but that's only one side of why I'm here." Danny leaned back in his chair. "I respect the Chief, but I think he sent me here partly because he needs to. He's got history with the Bishop, and he needs to show him that he's doing everything he can to make sure

I'm still a good cop. And let's be clear—a big part of the reason I'm here is because my brother detained the priest and he hurt himself in the ensuing scuffle. If that hadn't happened, nobody would think this was such a big deal."

"What do you think you would have done if you had caught the priest? If your brother hadn't intervened, what would have happened?"

That was a good question. If he'd still been lost in rage, he wasn't sure. "The same thing that *did* happen—nothing. I didn't do anything to him when I caught up with him, just talked. When Morales was ready to leave, he left, and I didn't try to stop him. I never actually *touched* the man. I'm here because he's a dirty priest, I'm about to pop him, and he wants to stop me from doing it. And the only way he can is to discredit me."

"You sound pretty sure of that."

"It's possible that I may be overstating the situation, but not by much." Danny paused. "So, where do we go from here?"

"The shooting was a textbook stressful situation, and stress has ways of showing up in other areas of our lives that we wouldn't expect," Hiakawa answered.

"You've read my file, right? My seven years on the force?"

Hiakawa held up his file.

"Is there anything in it about me ever making bad decisions? Does it read like I'm prone to being stressed out?"

"No, but you were shot at, Danny, and that has to be stressful."

"So, am I free to go back on patrol?"

Hiakawa hooked an errant lock of hair behind her ear. "I think what you're manifesting may be indicative of PTSD. I think we should talk a few more times before you return to patrol."

"Aw, Doc. You're *killing* me here. How long is this going to take?"

"Let's meet twice more in the next week, then we'll see where we are."

Danny couldn't believe the irony in this. He'd hated working nights, now he was fighting to get back on them. "Is there any way to make this go faster?" he asked.

Hiakawa stood, the folder still in her hand, and returned to her desk.

"Well, if there's a priest at your church you can talk to while we're meeting, that might help you process things more quickly. If you don't feel safe asking somebody at your church, maybe you could ask your brother for a referral."

"My brother? What would he refer?" asked Danny.

Hiakawa furrowed her brow. "A priest. He might know someone from another church you could talk to," said Hiakawa.

"What makes you think Tim knows any priests?"

"I thought you said he was a priest?" said Hiakawa.

"Hardly. Tim might know the name of a decent real estate agent, but he's no priest."

"But you said he and the priest from your church were in a drug and alcohol program together," said Hiakawa.

"Yes, I did." Danny usually tracked people pretty well, but Hiakawa had lost him.

"Well, that doesn't make sense." Hiakawa put the file back on her desk and tapped the top of it with her finger. "The church has its own rehab programs for clergy, and that's where priests go. If your brother isn't a priest, they wouldn't have been in the same program."

Danny sat back down in his chair. "No, I think you're wrong there. My brother went to a place called New Beginnings. That's where he met Morales, the priest from my church. I know Morales is a priest. I've seen him at Mass, and I know for a fact that my brother isn't."

"I don't know what to tell you, Danny. New Beginnings is not a place they send priests. Trust me. I've been a therapist for twelve years, and I've never heard of a priest, especially a Catholic priest, going anywhere other than a church-run program. It just doesn't happen."

"You're saying priests have their own alcohol programs, and nobody else gets in?"

"Well, the Force has its own programs."

"Cops do?"

"Yes, Danny. You don't think they'd put a cop in a drug and alcohol program with civilians, do you? It's the same thing with priests."

Danny was stunned. "I never thought about it. Tim is the only guy I know who's ever been in one."

"I guess you wouldn't know then. Anyway, take advantage of your time off the streets. I'm going to request this same time in three days. Does that work?" She extended her hand.

So, the meeting was over. "Yeah, sure, that's great," he said, shaking her hand. He left the office and started walking down the hall. If Morales wasn't a priest, what the hell was he?

Chapter Forty

Danny drove straight from Hiakawa's office to Carol's house, arriving twenty minutes before she got home from school. He didn't want to violate her asked-for privacy, so he sat in his car until she arrived rather than letting himself into the house. The mature oak trees on either side of the road provided shade and a sense of comfort that gave Danny the confidence he needed.

Carol pulled into the driveway, got out of her car, and walked towards him. Six feet from his open passenger window, she bent over to its level. "Danny," she said, "Why aren't you at work?"

Danny was looking for a clue as to her mood, but wasn't reading anything, and answered from behind the wheel. "It's a long story, and I thought I'd take the risk of explaining it to you face to face."

She didn't respond right away, and Danny felt himself sinking. "Carol, I'm so sorry. I miss you and I don't want us to be apart anymore."

Carol's face showed the light he was hoping for. "I'm glad you're here, Danny. Get out of the car and come inside."

Danny wanted to pick her up and carry her in, but decided that a heartfelt hug was probably best. He kissed her on the check. "I can't believe how much I miss you."

"I miss you too, Danny. I love you and I'm sorry, but I just needed some time. But why aren't you working? Is everything okay?"

"I'm not going in today, and I don't know if everything is okay or not, but I'm sure it'll all work out. Work is crazy, and I've got a lot of stuff I need to bounce off somebody. I'll explain everything inside."

Once in the house, Danny automatically walked to the fridge, but he hesitated before opening the door. Presumption seemed inappropriate, given his tentative place in the house. "Would you like some tea?" he asked. Carol nodded. He grabbed a couple of glasses from a shelf, poured them both iced tea from a pitcher in the fridge, and sat at the kitchen table. Carol had walked back to the bedroom. When she returned, having changed her blouse for a sweatshirt, he told her about getting reassigned to a desk and his visit with Hiakawa.

"I can't apologize enough for the way I've been acting lately, especially at church."

"It doesn't take much to trigger your anger recently," Carol answered. "Truthfully, I was completely shocked when you snapped at me at church, though. That just isn't like you."

The sting he'd felt when he'd lashed out at Carol felt as bad now as it had at the time. "I hope to God that never happens again. I'm really, really sorry."

"I know you are, Danny. I don't think you're a bad person, and I think seeing Hiakawa is a good idea, work-related or not. And the day shift is a great thing." She reached for his hand and gave it a gentle squeeze.

Her touch may never have felt better.

"Tell me about it."

Danny talked about his discussion about PTSD with Hiakawa. Carol seemed to accept Hiakawa's conclusions.

"I'm sorry you and Sean have caught the brunt of it." He paused for a moment. "Hiakawa said something weird about Morales. I know he's a really sensitive subject, but do you mind if I talk about him for a minute?"

Carol let go of his hand and crossed her arms, but her expression indicated permission. "Go ahead, Officer. Otherwise you'll want to leave and go tell Sean, and I want you right here."

"Well, in so many words, she said Morales might not be a priest."

Carol looked at him expectantly, as though for him to say more. "What do you mean, 'not a priest'? Of course he's a priest."

Danny explained what the doctor said. He felt the need to apologize for making what sounded like an audacious accusation.

"I believe you, Danny, but I'm shocked. I just can't believe someone would do something that deceitful."

"That's because you only see the good in people, and I make a living out of looking for the bad."

"Still, the thought that he might not be a priest is too much. How could he pull that off?"

"I have no idea. I just have to find out if he is or not."

Carol clutched her tea glass with both hands and rubbed her thumbs up and down the sides.

"What's wrong, babe?"

"Oh, Danny. I know I'm being selfish, but I just hate the thought of you going back to church and asking a lot of questions. I'm already uncomfortable there, and I hate that. I'm sorry—"

"I'm not going there, Carol, at least not now. Starting tomorrow, I'm riding a desk, and I thought I'd begin by Googling Morales and see what I find. I'd do it now but, tonight, I just want to be with you."

Carol stroked his arm. "You're right. You've got a whole day shift to do that. Right now, you are going to prepare a make-up dinner. Then you are going to clean up the kitchen, take me to bed, and do lovely, wicked things to me. After that, we'll hold each other and sleep all night. You can deal with Morales at work tomorrow."

Danny leaned towards Carol, kissed her, then kissed her more deeply. "That's a great idea. But don't you think we should skip straight to the sex and then eat?"

Carol cocked an eyebrow. "Why don't you put all that energy into cooking before that, stud? And I promise to make it worth your while."

Danny got out of bed the next morning before his alarm went off. Shaving in the shower to save time, he nicked his chin, cussed under his breath, then slowed down a bit. Still, he barely dried off before getting dressed. Putting on a suit—the office "uniform"—felt weird, but he didn't want to linger on the implications of having to do so. With two slices of buttered toast in hand, he bolted out the door before Carol got up. He'd written her a quick note which he'd placed on his pillow.

"Lots to do at work this morning," it began. "I really love you and I'm glad to be home."

Carrying a nearly empty coffee mug, Danny walked out of his office to get his third cup of the morning. "Good morning, Doris. Can I get you a cup of coffee?"

Doris didn't even look at him as she turned on her computer and put her purse in a desk drawer. "Officer Garcia. Did you get hit in the head or something? It's eight o'clock in the morning. What are you doing here?"

"Come on, Doris. You know I've been assigned days for a while. We're going to be working together, isn't that great? Heck, Chief said I should ask you if I need anything."

"Our Chief said that? Does he have any idea how in need you are?"

"So, no on the coffee?"

"I'll get my own, thank you. You boys always put in way too much sugar. What time did you get here this morning?"

Danny lied. "A few minutes ago." It would have felt funny to admit he'd arrived at 6:30 for an 8:00 shift. He walked to the kitchen and poured himself a cup.

Promising at first, Danny's Google search quickly hit a dead end. He started by visiting his own church's website. The "About Us" tab on the home page included tabs for Father Keenan, Morales, and another junior priest. He visited Father Keenan's page first, which had a large, full-body photo of him, his arms outstretched, standing in front of an altar. His bio was four or five paragraphs long and talked about where he was born, his family, and how he was called to "dedicate himself to the Church." It was brief but thorough, and ended with a list of his ministries, the organizations he'd worked with, and even his military experience as a young man.

Danny chuckled to himself when he visited the page for Father Morales, a third as long as Keenan's and, in comparison, an apparent afterthought. The picture was a black and white headshot. *If they'd taken another one from the side,* Danny thought, *they would have looked more like mug shots.* It said that Morales had been born in Honduras, but there were no details of his family or early life. He'd reportedly attended Seminario del Buen Pastor in Acapulco, Mexico before being ordained, but when Danny Googled the seminary, he found nothing. Morales's work history was limited to one church in Honduras, which also wasn't on the Internet. His only ministry outside the church had been working with the homeless.

Danny's next Google search led to the *Catholic Answers Magazine,* an online question-and-answer forum. The first entry, five years old, was from a woman named Debra and began: "I was wondering if there was a registry for priests in the US?"

Yes! thought Danny, *I should have started here.*

He read the reply from Leonard, a regular member of the forum group. It began with a link: *TheOfficialCatholicDirectory.com*. "Many parishes have a copy in their office. You'll probably have to read it there, though, as this is a necessary reference that they might not want to leave the office." Danny clicked on the link for the directory, which was described as the most authoritative resource available "for all 210 (arch) dioceses in the United States and around the world."

Jackpot! Danny clicked the link for the price. Three hundred and seventy-five bucks. *Dammit.* His shoulders slumped. There was no way the department was going to pay for such an expensive item, which Danny knew might not have any information of use to him, and he couldn't afford it himself. The only choice he had was to visit the church and borrow their copy. Given his history with Morales, that wasn't a comfortable option in his own church or anywhere in the diocese.

He spent the next hour trying different searches but, as he expected, nothing came up that he could use. Realizing he needed to bounce what he'd found off someone else, he left his office, emptied his mug in the kitchen sink, and told Doris he had to run an errand.

Doris glanced at her watch. "Yes, by all means, take a break. You've been here almost ten minutes. You probably need it."

Danny stood on the porch holding two cups of coffee when Sean answered the door. Still in his boxers, Sean groaned.

"Danny, it's eight in the morning. I just got to bed a few hours ago. Why are you here?"

"What, it's closer to eight thirty," Danny answered. "Besides, my partner worked his first night shift without me. I thought I'd bring you coffee and see how it went."

A scowl was all Danny got in response.

"Well, aren't you going to invite me in?"

"No, I'm not." Sean opened the screen door and joined Danny on the porch. "I've got company, and you'll scare her. Did you add sugar?" He took one of the coffees from Danny.

"Company? Isn't this a school day?"

Sean scowled as he took the lid off his coffee cup.

"And yes—four packs of sugar, just like you like."

"Needs more cream," said Sean, after taking a sip. "Seriously, why are you here so early? It's freezing out here."

"Well, you could invite me in—"

"Not going happen."

"In that case, stand here in your underwear and freeze. It's your call."

"Are you going to get to the part about why you came over here and woke me up anytime soon?"

Danny took a sip of coffee. "Sean, I've been on the Internet all morning trying to find out if Morales is really a priest or not. It turns out the church may have a registry listing all the priests, but you have to go there to look at it in person, and I can't exactly do that."

Sean crossed his arms and rubbed his biceps. "By 'there' you mean the church. You have to go to *your* church, where you're persona non grata, and ask to look at the registry to check up on *their* priest."

"Yes," Danny answered. "That's it. I could go to any church, actually, but every church within a couple hundred miles of here is part of the Bishop's diocese, and I can't risk having any word of what I'm doing get back to him."

"What is a 'diocese' exactly?"

"You know, his region. His territory. Every church from San Francisco to the Oregon border is his."

"And you think it would be a better idea for *me* to go to one of these churches and start snooping around."

"Exactly!"

Sean shook his head. "Danny, are you crazy, or is it that you just can't think this early in the morning? *I* can't go down there. I'm your *partner.* The Chief told you to back the hell off this thing. I get caught doing your dirty work, *both* our asses will be in a sling."

Danny knew he was right. He'd known it before he left the station and drove to Sean's, but he needed to float another idea past him.

"All right, Officer. What do *you* think I should do then?"

"I don't know. Why don't you ask your brother to do it?" asked Sean.

"Tim?"

"You got another brother I don't know about?"

"Why would I ask Tim to do it?"

Sean rubbed his biceps again, took a couple of steps in place. "Danny, it's a little chilly out here. Look, you said Tim may not have committed those crimes."

"I said he's no longer my only suspect."

"Yeah, well, I'm saying it then. The way he handled himself when you chased the priest means he's trying to help you. Why not ask him? And does he have to go to your church? Can't he go to one where he lives?"

Danny was thinking the same thing but wanted to hear Sean confirm it. "That's a good idea, Sean."

"Well, ask him then. I'm going back inside, see if I can do some snuggling with my girlfriend and warm up."

"Hey thanks, Sean. And that really is a good idea. I'm sorry I woke you."

"No you're not," Sean said, opening the screen door and walking back inside. "But that's what partners are for. Go get this Morales guy, Danny. You figure out a way I can help, let me know."

Chapter Forty-One

Once inside the house, Sara hoisted the bags of groceries higher on her hips. Looking over her shoulder, she used her foot to push the door closed behind her. At the sound, Tim looked up from his phone and mouthed, "Hello."

"Yeah, yeah," he said, returning to his call. "Tomorrow morning, first thing it is. No, no, I'll make it work. Sure. Okay. I'll call you afterwards." He ended the call and put his phone in his jeans back pocket. "Hi babe. Are there more bags in the car?"

"Yes, two. Thanks," said Sara.

Tim retrieved both and plopped them on the kitchen table. Most of the cabinet doors were open, and Sara was putting groceries away.

"Looks like somebody took the afternoon off," Sara said, motioning to Tim's tee shirt and jeans.

Tim glanced down at himself. "Yeah, I was supposed to be showing a house at four, but the wife's water broke and they decided it was smarter to go to the hospital than keep their appointment with me. Can you believe that?"

"The nerve. Was that work on the phone?" Sara asked.

"Actually…that was Danny," Tim answered tentatively.

Sara stopped and turned to Tim, a can of soup in each hand. "Your brother Danny?"

"The very one."

Sara's face was a concerned question mark. "Is everything okay?"

Tim leaned against the back of a kitchen chair and considered his answer. "Yeah—actually, it's *real* okay. He wants my help."

"How's that?"

"Turns out I'm not his number one suspect anymore. He wants me to go to a church here in town tomorrow and look for somebody in the registry of priests."

"Seriously? Are you going to do it? He's been such a jerk to you."

Tim appreciated that she was concerned for him. "Yeah he has, but I have to go. My big brother needs me."

Tim reckoned that churches were possibly used as much by recovering alcoholics as they were worshippers. The rooms that held Sunday school classes during the day hosted AA meetings at night, an interesting relationship and probably the only way AA could survive. The two populations didn't necessarily mix. Outside of going to AA meetings, he himself never set foot inside a church.

The basement of this church was home to a regular Wednesday night AA meeting Tim attended. He loved the building construction, the cornerstone of which had been placed in 1887. The roof was sloped like an old ski chalet, seeming out of place in Santa Rosa, where there had been measurable snow only a couple of times in the past hundred years. The maples in the front and ivy covering one side of the building were resplendent in brilliant fall colors. Tim silently acknowledged the gifts of a Higher Power and walked the short stone path to the office.

The building's architectural aesthetics continued on into the anteroom. The ceiling and walls were made from two-inch-wide redwood slats, fastened together without a nail in sight. Tim thought that most modern buildings were built with only efficiency and cost control in mind; this church was built when neither was a consideration—when all that mattered was that a church inspire awe in those worshipping God.

Tim rapped on the open office's doorframe. A woman looked up, lowering her eyeglasses on the chain around her neck as she did.

"Oh, hello," she said warmly. "How can I help you?"

"Good morning," Tim said. "This place is beautiful."

"Isn't it? I've been working here for eight years, and it still lifts my spirits every day."

"I'm Tim Harris. I'm trying to locate a priest I know, and I'm pretty sure he's at a church in this area." When Tim had told Danny he would help him, he'd stressed that he had promised Richard, his AA sponsor, that he wouldn't lie." Speaking to this woman now, he chose his words carefully. "I understand churches have a registry of priests, and I wondered if I could have a look at it."

"Hmm. Now that you mention it, I know it *used* to be here, but I don't think I've seen it in months." Turning to the bookshelves behind her desk, she ran a finger along the spines of the books there without finding it. She began to rummage through stacks of books on a table but again came up empty-handed. "I'm sorry, it doesn't seem to be here. If you want to tell me how to reach you, I can look for it and call you when it turns up."

"I might be able to help."

Startled by the voice behind him, Tim turned around and looked down at a nun, a small woman in her late sixties.

"Sister, I didn't hear you come in," said the woman. This is Tim..."

"Harris," said Tim. "I'm embarrassed. I'm afraid I'm not Catholic, and I don't know if I should shake your hand or just bow."

"Well, you could sell everything you own and give the money to the church," she said, "or we can just shake hands." She extended hers to Tim. "I'm Sister Ann."

Tim laughed, both disarmed and enchanted. . "I'll go for the handshake option now. It's a pleasure to meet you, Sister Ann."

She had a surprisingly firm handshake.

"It's a beautiful morning. Will you walk outside with me, Mr. Harris?"

"Please, it's Tim, and yes, I'd be happy to." He turned to the woman behind the desk. "Thank you for your help."

"My pleasure. Thank you, Sister." The woman put her glasses on and returned to her computer.

The nun folded her arms and put them in the sleeves of her robe. Tim realized Sister Ann may have been the first nun he had ever talked to. She led him to the door and out into the churchyard, and began walking the stone path towards the back of the church. "How can we help you, Tim?"

"Well, I understand you keep a registry of all priests here, and I was hoping I could look someone up."

"Who are you trying to find?"

It never occurred to Tim that he might be asked any questions. He just figured they'd hand him the registry and let him look. "His name is Jorge Morales."

Sister Ann walked without speaking for a moment, gazing straight ahead. She now stopped and stared Tim in the eyes. "How do you know this Father Morales?"

I never saw this one coming, thought Tim. "I… I really can't say, Sister. It's kind of awkward, but I have to respect his confidentiality." That seemed true, and safe enough.

"I see," said the sister. She turned and began walking again. The sunlight, partially filtered by the few leaves still on the trees, cast mottled shadows on her.

"Is there something wrong with my asking?" Tim inquired.

"There may be something wrong, but I don't suppose it's your asking questions. I've been expecting, hoping really, for someone to ask questions for a long time. Are you with the police, Tim?"

Tim's mind raced for an answer. Under the circumstance, both "yes" and "no" seemed to be somewhat true answers to her question. He mentally flipped a coin and took a chance. "Yes. I am."

"I knew somebody would ask about this someday, but I never guessed it would be the police."

Tim was winging it now. "Who did you expect?"

"Oh, I don't know, but I figured somebody in the church. I'm sorry that the police are involved. I've been praying about this for months now, trying to decide what I should do. I guess sending you here is God's way of telling me."

Tim waited for her to say more. Trusting his intuition, he said the first thing that popped into his mind: "Is it true?"

"That they aren't priests?" Sister Ann asked.

They?

"I don't know if I can say for absolute certainty," she continued. "The Bishop brought them all in to different parishes within a month or two of each other. He actually ordained them himself. All of them have very vague backgrounds and don't seem to know anything about being a priest, as far as I am concerned. All three are young, good-looking, and Latino."

"I see."

"Oh, they can recite mass, but any altar boy could do that after a few months of hearing the service over and over. I tried to look them up in the registry myself, but it seems to have disappeared."

"Have you talked to anybody else about it?" asked Tim.

"I've talked to Father Mumford—he's senior here—but he got uncomfortable and cut me off. I've gotten calls from nuns in the other two parishes, upset by what they think is happening, but you're the first outsider who's asked any questions."

She seemed to be lost in her thoughts. Tim decided not to interrupt.

"I've been a nun for thirty-six years and have known a lot of priests," she continued. "Something is off. What happens now, Officer?"

Tim let her mistake go. "I honestly don't know at this point. There are officers in other cities looking into this as well. I have to ask, how does someone who might not be a priest get the job?"

"It's not that kind of a position, Tim. We don't run an ad in the local paper or anything. Typically, church members and the Bishop work closely together to fill positions. If it's the senior priest at a church, the process is fairly extensive. A search committee is formed, and they can spend a year identifying priests from all over the country who might be a good fit. If it's a junior position, it doesn't take quite as long. Those positions could be filled with a new seminary graduate. Either way, once someone is identified, the Bishop makes the appointment and installs the new priest."

"Sounds like the church has a lot of openings," said Tim.

"Not necessarily. Sometimes, with junior priests, there isn't necessarily an opening as such. The Bishop can decide that a particular church has a need, create the position, and install someone."

"Why would he do that?"

"Any number of reasons. If the congregation has been growing, he might decide that another priest is necessary. Maybe the senior priest will be transferring or retiring in a few years, and he wants to bring in someone the congregants can get comfortable with before that happens. Sometimes, it's because a church decides to focus on a new outreach and needs someone to fill that role."

"And that's what happened this time?" asked Tim.

"In all three cases, yes," answered Sister Ann. "All were brought to the church at the recommendation of the Bishop and given the ministry of reaching out to the homeless. Do you mind if we sit, Tim? My right hip doesn't like me to be on my feet too long anymore." Sister Ann stopped in front of a bench that allowed for unfiltered sunlight.

She sat, closed her eyes and turned her face toward the sun for a moment, then patted a spot next to her.

Tm sat next to her. "What does the homeless ministry involve?"

"I'm not really sure," she answered. "The homeless rarely come to the church, so the priests go to them. I assume they try to get them in the system, help them get their lives back in order."

"Sort of like a social worker."

"I suppose. I haven't actually been involved, so I don't know exactly, and it's only been going on for a few months."

"Sister, this is probably a rhetorical question, but could the priest get personal information from the people they talk to? For example, their birthday, place of birth, social security number?"

"I don't see why not. If a priest asked you for that information, wouldn't you give it to him?"

"I suppose I would." Tim put his hands on his knees and pushed as he stood. "I appreciate what you've told me, Sister Ann. I just have one more question: How often does the Bishop create new positions on his own, without the church being involved?"

Sister Ann rested her hand on Tim's arm. "In the thirty-six years I've been with the church? This is a first."

Tim let what had just happened soak in before calling his brother. "Are you ready for this?" he said as soon as Danny answered.

"Ready for what? Have you been to the church?"

"Yes, and I just had a very interesting conversation with a Sister Ann."

"Did you look Morales up in the registry?" asked Danny.

"Didn't happen that way, but this is even better. Sister Ann's been a nun for over thirty years, and knows how priests are brought into a church. She never referred to Morales by name and never really said anything specific, but apparently there are *three* new priests around the diocese who are all young and Latino. She as good as said they may not be priests at all."

"She said *three?*"

"Uno, dos, tres."

"All I care about right now is Morales. She have any proof of this?"

"Mainly her years of knowing how things are supposed to work. She said she's never seen anything like this, and it sounded like these priests aren't right."

"'Aren't right.' You sound like a cop now, Tim." There was silence at the other end of the line for a moment. "She have any explanation for how these men are becoming priests?" asked Danny.

"Nothing specific. But, apparently, who becomes a priest in a church is ultimately the call of one man."

"The Bishop."

"You got it."

Chapter Forty-Two

After hanging up, Danny absentmindedly tapped a pencil on his coffee cup, and then stood up and walked to the Chief's office.

"Sir? Got a minute?" he asked.

The Chief was putting on his sports coat, his tie loose around his neck. "Come in, Officer. I was just leaving, but have a seat."

"I'll be quick," Danny said.

"What's on your mind?"

The Chief's body language shouted that he didn't particularly care, but Danny wanted an audience and so plunged ahead. He filled the Chief in on what he'd learned in the past day and a half. The Chief listened, interrupting with an occasional question, until he finished.

"Well, that's quite a story, Danny. I had an interesting conversation with the FBI myself, not an hour ago."

"Really? About the bank fraud? I didn't think they worked with locals once they rode into town," Danny said.

"They usually don't, but they wanted some background on the Bishop. And get this. They talked to him, and he is now a suspect."

"The *Bishop*? Seriously? Because of the nickel? I figured when they got deeper he'd be cleared."

"What made you think that?" asked the Chief, now seemingly more engaged in the conversation.

Danny shrugged. He couldn't tell the Chief that he thought Morales was the man the FBI should be talking to without having to explain his brother's criminal history and connection to the priest. "I don't know. He just doesn't seem right for it. Why does the FBI suspect he's the one?"

"They are a long way away from an arrest. Right now, they're just interested in him. Turns out the Bishop has some major money problems of his own. He's got a lot of construction activity going on in his district, or whatever you call it."

"I think it's a diocese," offered Danny.

"Whatever. The projects he's working on have involved some serious money, and it seems like some of it ended up in his personal account. It's going out of there pretty fast too, on vacations, cars, art and whatnot."

"Art and whatnot" sounded like an apt description to Danny. Most of the stuff he'd seen in the Bishop's home looked just plain weird, and people seemed willing to pay a lot of money for weird art.

"Anyway, the income has been drying up. Maybe it's the economy, but donations have stopped coming in, and the Feds suspect he's been doing a little check kiting recently. Not enough to prove he's guilty of stealing all that money, but enough to make it worth a closer look."

It was all he could do not to jump out of his seat, but Danny knew he needed to appear casual and relaxed. "Chief, this all makes a lot of sense to me, based on everything else I'm finding out. I'd like to talk to him myself if I can."

"The Bishop?" The Chief chuckled. "Danny, you're on desk for a while. Even Hiakawa agrees with that."

Danny got out of his chair. "Chief, I totally understand your decision and, to tell you the truth, I can't say that it's a bad one."

"Well, that's a relief to hear."

"No sir, I didn't mean any disrespect. I just think that the Bishop and Morales are tied together on all this, and I honestly think I can get the Bishop to flip."

"You think you can do that from your desk?"

"No sir, I need to go see him."

"Danny, do I have to remind you why you're on desk duty in the first place? You don't exactly play well with men of the cloth."

"I know, sir, but—"

"Danny, there is no *but*. You pull any crap again, and I'm going to take heat for it. I don't plan on my last couple of days on the job being anything but smooth sailing."

"Sir, I know I screwed up but I promise you it won't happen again." I'll take Sean with me, make the one call, then I'll go back to the desk. I'm not asking to go back on patrol, I'm just asking you to let me make this one visit to the Bishop."

It felt like the Chief stared at him for five minutes, but it was probably only five seconds. He turned towards the door. Danny thought he was leaving, but he stopped and spoke.

"Danny, do you have any idea how crazy it would be for me to let you do this?"

"I don't know, sir...plenty, maybe, but I think we're really close to Morales and the Bishop, and I think I can bring it home if I can talk to him face to face."

"And what makes you so sure you can make all this fall into place?"

Danny wished he could say more, but it was too complicated. "I just do, sir. It's right. I can feel it."

"You fuck this up even the slightest, Garcia, you'll be on desk for the rest of your life. I guarantee it."

"Understood, sir."

"This so goes against my better judgment. And you know the duty sergeant is not going to like this either. You pull Sean off night shift for one day, it'll blow holes in his whole schedule."

"Sean and I will do this during the day, and he'll still work his shift. I promise."

The Chief laughed. "You think Officer Rawlins is going to be okay with this? That's a long day, but if you think you can pull it off, you can go."

"Thank you, Chief. Sean will be okay. In fact, I'm going to call him now and see if we can go today."

The Chief replied with a quiet chuckle, and then turned and left the office.

Chapter Forty-Three

"So, how do you see this going down?"

"Hopefully without a hitch," Danny said, nervously adjusting a rear view mirror that was already aligned as he spoke.

Sean allowed a pause before speaking. "So... that's it? 'Hopefully without a hitch' is all you've got?"

"Well, I haven't worked it all out quite yet. It's got to be a clean call, or the Chief will be deep in my shit. I think we'll play it as it goes. I'll take the lead."

Sean seemed to let that soak in. "Okay, our plan is to 'keep it clean,' and 'you'll take the lead.' I guess that works."

"I might try and get under the Bishop's skin a little bit. You know, make him mad and maybe he'll let his guard down a little."

"You mean like I do with you sometimes?"

"Exactly. Can you lay a little smart-ass-Sean on him?"

"Say no more," Sean said, holding up his hand. "Does the guy know we're coming?"

Danny turned right on a street marked "No Outlet" and began a slight uphill drive. "Sean, what fun would it be if he was expecting us?"

The homes on the street immediately and unambiguously announced that this was a better neighborhood, as though a clearly marked line delineated "medium" from "high-priced" homes. There was nothing subtle about the transition.

"This is the bishop's street?" Sean asked.

"Makes you wish you'd gone for church work instead of joining the force, doesn't it?" Danny pulled into a driveway eight houses from the corner and parked. "We're here."

Sean examined the house through the windshield. "Holy shit."

"Yeah, I suppose it might be," said Danny, amused at his own joke.

"How much do you people put in the collection plate?"

Danny grinned and got out, and Sean followed him. A quick look through the garage door window revealed all three of the cars Danny had seen the first time: a Mercedes convertible, a Porsche 911, and a Toyota. Danny figured the odds were good that the Bishop was home.

"Wait till you see inside the place. It'll blow you away." Danny pushed the doorbell, which responded to his touch with the sound of four ringing church bells.

"That's a little over the top, don't you think? Sean asked.

"Don't be intimidated, Sean. Remember, this guy maybe rich and powerful, but you can have him thrown in jail."

"Yeah, sure, and that's all well and good, but he can have me sent to hell."

The partial opening of the door interrupted their exchange. The butler's face, at first a placid mask of inscrutability, momentarily registered fear when he saw Danny. He regained his composure quickly and began shutting the door as he spoke. "I'm sorry, the Bishop isn't in right now. I'll tell him you stopped by."

Danny pushed against the door, opened it, and walked into the foyer. "That's okay. We don't mind waiting."

"I'm afraid that's not possible," the butler said, his voice at a higher register.

"Martin, isn't it? Seriously, we don't mind the wait."

Visibly flummoxed, Martin looked at both officers, then abandoned them to head down the hall towards what Danny knew was the Bishop's office.

"You coming in?" Danny said to Sean.

"This is going well. Is this your idea of a clean call?" Sean tentatively walked in, looking around as he did.

"His office is down the hall. I'll bet Martin is announcing us now." Danny proceeded in that direction, relieved that Sean was following.

Danny placed his hand on the doorknob to the closed office, and the officers silently nodded to one another. Danny thrust the door open, and they burst in.

Martin stopped speaking in mid-sentence when they entered and frantically looked back and forth between the two officers and the Bishop. Danny thought him damn near apoplectic.

The Bishop rose from behind his desk. "Seriously?" he roared. "You think you can just barge in my office like this?"

"Afternoon, Bishop. I don't think you've met my partner, Officer Rawlins. Officer, the Bishop."

The Bishop's bulging eyes reminded Danny of a cartoon character, and he wondered if they might pop out of their sockets and roll across the desk. The image made it hard to suppress a grin as he walked to the chairs in front of the desk.

"I hope you have a warrant, because if you don't—"

Danny interrupted him. "We don't have a warrant. We just want to talk, and your man let us in."

"That's not true, sir!" Martin pleaded.

"It's okay, Martin." The Bishop picked up the phone, simultaneously looking through his Rolodex. Danny reached across the desk and depressed the call button, and then gently but firmly took the phone out of the bishop's hand and hung it up.

"Bishop, talk to me first. If you still want to call somebody when we finish, I'll dial the number for you." He motioned for Sean to take the seat next to him.

Sean was standing with his hands on his belt, open-mouthed. Danny wished he could have frozen time, reassured his partner that this was okay, but he didn't want to stop the momentum.

The Bishop shook with anger. "Are you *crazy*? Do you have *any* idea who I am or what I can do to you? You've just ended your career, Officer." With that, the Bishop seemed to calm down, and he sat. "This may be your last official duty as a policeman, so please, say what you have to say."

"What do I do, sir? Do I bring tea?" Martin stammered. Still standing by the door, he rocked back and forth on his feet like a small child trying not to wet his pants. Danny felt sorry for him.

The Bishop inhaled deeply before dismissing him. "Thank you, Martin. The officers won't be here that long and we don't need anything." Turning back to Danny, he said, "I'll give you one minute before I pick up the phone again, and this time, I'm calling my good friend, the Chief of Police."

Not quite the way the Chief described the relationship, thought Danny. "I'll answer in a sentence. We're here because the Feds found five cents of stolen money in your bank account."

"I have several bank accounts. What possible difference does a nickel make?"

"I know, I know, it sounds crazy. But somebody stole three hundred thousand dollars from several finance companies, and for some reason they put a nickel of it in your account. Until the FBI can make sense of the whole thing, that five cents makes you a person of interest. Real interest. Plus, you're also going to get arrested for having three fake priests in your diocese. Well, I guess the police may not care about that, but I'll bet your bosses will have something to say about it." Danny paused, turned to Sean, and pointed to his wrist. "How's my time?"

Sean looked at his watch. "I think you've got about twenty seconds to spare, partner. Were you keeping track, Mr. Bishop? Because I think my partner beat the clock."

Ah, Sean at his mocking best, thought Danny.

The Bishop, expressionless, looked back and forth between the two men. Then he burst out laughing and couldn't seem to stop.

"You're taking this better than I would have thought, Bishop," Danny said.

The Bishop waved him off and kept laughing. "Oh, I'm sorry, let me catch my breath."

Danny looked at his partner, who just shrugged. "Want to tell us what's so funny, your Excellency?" asked Sean.

"You're really trying to insult me, aren't you? 'Your Excellency.' 'Mr. Bishop.'" He laughed again. "You think you've got me, don't you? Well, I can't believe how badly misinformed you are, and how naïve as well."

"And how's that, sir?" asked Danny.

"Even if I had a *dozen*—what did you call them? Fake priests?— and I don't have any by the way, there's no way I'd be arrested for it. It would be a church matter. And the church, gentlemen, is not going to let one of their own, certainly not a bishop, twist in the wind. At the absolute worst, I'd get a slap on the wrist behind doors that were so tightly closed no one would know about it, and then I'd get transferred. I'd still be a bishop, and things would go on as before. Not even a hiccup. Danny, you really *are* new to the church, aren't you?" He began to laugh again.

"Well, the Feds like you enough for stealing the money that they talked to you about it," Sean said.

"'The Feds *like* me?' You sound like a TV cop, young man. And for your information, they didn't talk to me because they 'like me' for anything. They never seriously considered me at all and left after about a fifteen-minute conversation. Which, by the way, was largely about things going on with the building projects in the diocese. One of the officers is a parishioner in one of the Santa Rosa churches."

"And you believed that they didn't like you for the crime?" Danny asked. "You think that they left here so soon because they knew you were innocent?"

"Oh, now you want to make me second guess myself?" The Bishop stood and pointed to his office door. "I really do have a lot to do, including calling your Chief. Maybe on the drive back to Napa, you should start planning your next career move."

Danny looked at Sean, raised his hands and let them drop back in his lap. "I think he beat us, Sean. I think it's over for us both. We may just be finished as officers of the law."

"That's too bad, because my girlfriend gets really hot when I come home in a uniform." Sean looked back at the Bishop. "Oh, sorry, your Eminence."

"You're very amusing," the Bishop replied, the disgust thick in his mouth. "Get the hell out of my office."

Danny and Sean stood and started for the door. Just before walking out, Danny turned to face the Bishop. "There is one more thing about the Feds, though."

"Well save it for the boys back at the station and get out."

Danny ignored him. "The Feds don't like it when they can't solve a crime, so whether or not they *were* looking at you for stealing all that money—rather, if they *liked* you for it—they'd probably look at your personal bank records, see if anything shed any light on their case." Danny spoke slowly, as though to a child. "They wouldn't need a warrant to do it either, because that's where they found some of the stolen money, that nickel I mentioned earlier. That measly little five cents gives them permission to tear your books apart and look at all your financial activity as far back as they want to go. And, trust me on this, they are desperate to find something to explain this. So, it would be natural to look around. In your account, I mean."

The Bishop rolled his eyes. "And why should I care about that?"

"I don't know, they have accountants look at that kind of stuff. I mean, it can be really complicated for anybody else. Anyway, what kind of things do you think they *could* find if they looked around?"

Danny could practically see the wheels turning in the Bishop's head.

"Seriously, want to guess?" Danny asked.

"Can *I* guess?" Sean asked.

Danny nodded to his partner. "Of course you can, Officer Rawlins. Take a wild stab at it."

Expressionless, Sean began. "I'm no expert on it or anything, but I understand that if somebody is in trouble, sometimes they write bad checks, moving money from account to account quickly, so that imaginary money is covering debts that otherwise would come to light. I think it's called *check kiting*? And if there were large sums of money going from the building funds of the church into *your* account, they'd probably match that against Visa statements and look for unusual expenses that the church had paid for. You know, things like travel and art. By the way, that's an impressive collection you have. Anyway, that's what *I* guess they'd do."

Danny wagged a pointed finger at Sean. "Wow. He's impressive, isn't he? And I'll bet he's exactly right, Bishop. If they did look and found out you were playing fast and loose with the church's money? They might think it was a motive to steal. And they would *like* you for it." Danny chuckled and shook his head, "Man, then they are like a pack of wolves tearing apart a fresh kill. They'll devour it all. If they found anything weird going on with the church's money, they'd probably nail you for it, just 'cause they could."

The Bishop sat down in his chair. Danny could practically smell the fear oozing from his pores. "That's ridiculous," said the Bishop. "That's all pure speculation, and besides, the church would never prosecute."

"Oh it's definitely speculation. We're just talking. But if they were to look and *did* find any of that, the courts wouldn't have to wait for the church to press charges, because the bank would, believe me. *Then* you would go to jail."

Danny could almost see the color drain from the Bishop's face. "Assuming there was any truth to these accusations, and I assure you there is not, what would make this go away?" asked the Bishop quietly.

"Away?" asked Danny. "You mean like a 'Get out of Jail Free' card? I don't think it would just go away. I think something would happen to you besides getting your wrists slapped behind a tightly closed door. Funny thing is, I don't think you stole anything. Neither does my partner."

"Then it's your duty as sworn officers to tell them."

"*Tell* them? I don't think I can tell them anything, unless I can point to an alternative suspect. Do you think one of your," Danny made air quotes, "fake priests could have done this? Maybe the one in Napa?"

"Morales." The Bishop muttered as though he was chewing on something bitter.

"Yeah, Father Morales. He's probably the one the Feds really want. Somehow he got the social security numbers of a dead guy and a couple of homeless men, and stole three hundred thousand dollars using their identities." Danny shook his head and chuckled. "He tried to steal a million, but it didn't quite work out. Anyway, I wonder if he put the nickel in your account as a joke or if he has it in for you? Either way, at this point, I don't think the cops even know Morales exists. Unless something happens that brings him to light, I'll bet he walks—and that nickel becomes a giant 'Fuck you.' Thing is, the only way I can help you is if Morales gets arrested. It doesn't even have to be for this crime, just something that gets him locked up for a little while."

"How would it help me if you arrest him?"

"I know you and I don't have the best relationship, Bishop, but you're going to have to trust me that it will. Three hundred thousand dollars is missing, and a lot of people want somebody to get arrested for it, and quick. If you help us get Morales arrested, it can only help you."

"And all you need is a reason," the Bishop said.

"That would do it. Has he done something you know about?" asked Danny.

The Bishop ignored the question. "Would he have to be proven guilty, or just arrested?"

"Just arrested," said Danny. "What do you have in mind?"

The Bishop ignored the question. "This sounds like amateurish police work, but if I can help, I'm always willing to be of service."

So civic-minded of you, thought Danny.

"I'd like to help you find the man you're looking for, and if it'll save me an unnecessary inconvenience, all the better. But I'm going to have to talk to my attorney first, and I'm sure he's going to want some kind of guarantee about how it will work out for me."

Danny looked at Sean, who nodded and shrugged approval.

"I think something that would get Morales arrested would show people that you were trying to help. Talk to your attorney. You give us a way to arrest Morales, we'll help you. Meanwhile, you don't talk to him at all, about anything. I find out you did, I'll do everything I can to make sure you don't get any help from anybody. In fact, I'll do all I can to make sure you take the fall for the whole thing."

"You're bluffing. You can't do that." The Bishop's voice lacked conviction.

"Maybe not, but if all that other stuff my partner talked about turns out to be right?" Danny exhaled loudly, shaking his head as he did. "Figure out how we can arrest Morales. With your help, I'll pick him up myself, tomorrow afternoon."

The Bishop sunk in his chair, his brow furrowed. "Afraid that's not going to happen," he said. "Morales was uncomfortable with you stalking him, accusing him of extorting a parishioner, and asked me to help. The best way I could do that was to send him someplace way out of your jurisdiction. He didn't mind moving if it got you out of his hair, so I transferred him to a parish in Ukiah, two days ago."

"He's there now?" asked Danny.

"Afraid so," answered the Bishop.

Danny rubbed his palms. "Tell you what, Bishop. I don't care if it's the Ukiah police that do it, you just give us a good reason to arrest him."

"I think I can deliver on that. I'll have to talk to my attorney and make sure I can do this without getting hurt, but I'll bet Morales has a good reason with him right now."

"Wait, wait," Danny muttered as they walked off the porch.

Sean whispered, "I know." They opened their doors at the same time, got in the car, and closed them. Then they erupted.

"YES!" said Sean, high-fiving Danny. "Was that fun, or what?"

"Oh, man. I think he knows he's all jammed up."

"I thought the bad guys were supposed to come out at night, but it's..." Sean checked his watch, "just after one, and *that* is a bad guy."

"That he is, partner."

"Hey, I don't mean to tell you how to be a cop and all, but we were cutting it pretty close to the bone in there," Sean said quietly.

"How's that?" asked Danny.

"You said the Chief told you to behave. You were pretty loose with what the Feds are up to, which I doubt they would have liked, and we were darn right insulting to the Bishop. If this hadn't gone our way—"

"Yeah, but it did, Sean. Far as the Feds go, I never stated anything for a fact. And you heard the Bishop—he just wants to help."

"Yes, but you're usually way more reserved and by the book. This was pretty wild west, especially for you. I mean, it was fun and all, but damn."

"You're right, but I just don't feel like playing some long, drawn-out game."

"I just want you to be careful. This could get you in a world of hurt. Hell, it could get *me* in a world of hurt."

"I don't know, Sean. To be honest, I've been thinking a lot since seeing the shrink. Maybe getting shot at did change the way I see things and do the job. I don't think I'm dangerous, just more direct. Besides, we know Morales is dirty, and I just want to get him."

Sean seemed to take this in, and then shifted in his seat. "Still, I don't see how getting Morales arrested for something unrelated is going to point to him as dirty for the ID thing, though. Won't he have to do something stupid to trip up?"

"Remember, my brother has some experience in this field. He said if we can get him arrested, it'll lead him straight to the identity theft thing."

"Your brother said that?"

"Yup." Danny couldn't help but grin.

"Your brother, the real estate agent, who isn't a cop."

"Sean, you worry too much. Tim said this would work, and I believe him."

"Either way, the action's going down in Ukiah, and we can't be part of it."

"Who says we can't?"

"Who *says*? Well, our Chief, to start with. Probably theirs too, since it's way the hell out of our jurisdiction. You need anybody else?"

"Sean, I wish it was going to happen in Napa, but it's not. That doesn't mean I can't be part of it, I just can't do it officially. But trust me, we'll be there."

"*We*, Kemosabe? And how do you suppose that's going to happen?"

"I don't have any idea, Sean, but that is one dance I have no intention of missing, and I know you feel the same way. Tell you what. I appreciate all your help, and I'm going to take us to a Burger King and buy your lunch. Anything you want."

Sean seemed to consider the offer before speaking. "I'm not that easy, Danny. This is going to cost you *two* trips to Burger King."

"Have it your way, Sean."

Chapter Forty-Four

When Danny called and asked if he had any idea where Morales might go in a new town, Tim drew a blank. Then it hit him.

"Actually, he likes to hang out in gay bars," he'd told Danny.

"I thought he quit drinking?"

"Well, he still likes bars, said that's where the fun is. Can the Napa police find out if there are any gay bars in Ukiah? That's about the only place I can think of."

"I'll have to figure out a way I can ask without anybody wondering why I'm asking, but I'll find out," replied Danny.

"Can't you just send the police to the church he's been assigned to?"

"No. If this goes down at a church, they'll treat Morales differently. He needs to get arrested when he's not wearing a collar, and a bar would be the perfect place. Besides, I want to be there, and I can't risk going to a church."

Danny called in sick the next day, the first time in his career. He figured that, given that he was riding a desk, no one would care that much. He picked his brother up later that afternoon. He told Tim that the Napa cops had learned that Ukiah didn't have any bars that were exclusively gay, but that there were two that gays and lesbians frequented.

"Is your partner going with us?" asked Tim.

"I was going to ask him, but the more I thought about it, the more I thought it would be better if I didn't. I'm not sure how this is going to go down, and I don't want Sean to have to lie on my behalf if it goes badly."

"Are you sure you want to do this? You could figure out another way."

"Yeah, but if the Bishop changes his mind about this, he could kill any chance we've got. Unless you want out, it's on."

"Then let's go to Ukiah."

The brothers talked strategy as they drove.

Morales was not in the first bar they checked. The second was a restaurant with a lounge that had a happy hour from 5:00 to 8:00 every night. When they arrived, they checked out the parking lot, and Danny called the police. Tim got out of the car and circled the building before going in, checking for the location of all the exits.

"Good evening, and welcome to Spanky's," a cute twenty-something hostess greeted Tim as soon as he walked in. "Do you have a reservation this evening?"

The lounge area had a couple of chairs sitting opposite a love seat and several taller bistro tables. Tim spotted Morales standing with a half dozen other men around one of the tables. Taller than all of them, he was easy to spot.

"No, I'm not having dinner, I just came by for something to drink."

"Okay," the hostess responded, all smiles. "It's happy hour till eight. All well drinks and appetizers are five dollars."

"Thank you." Tim headed straight to Jorge.

Morales said something to his companions who laughed in response. As Morales took a drink from his beer, Tim made eye contact with him. Morales' laughter stopped immediately, and his eyes narrowed. As Tim walked up to him, Morales stepped away from his group.

"Hi Jorge. I mean, *Father Morales*. Come here often?" Tim's face was one big smile.

Morales glared at him. "College Boy. I hope you didn't come here to fuck with me. I'd hate to kick your ass in a public place."

"No, it's happy hour, right? If I was going to fight, I'd at least wait till after eight."

Morales didn't react to Tim's joke. "What *are* you doing here?"

"I came to talk to you, Morales. I didn't like the way things ended with us last time and thought I owed you an apology. So, here I am."

Morales took a swig of beer. "You came to Ukiah to apologize? How'd you find out I was here?"

"You mean this bar, or the town? I heard you got transferred to a church up here and, to tell you the truth, I started bar-hopping, hoping I'd run into you."

"Can I get you something to drink?" The woman speaking to Tim was dressed like the rest of the wait staff, in black jeans and a white shirt. Her blond hair was pulled back in a ponytail.

"Yeah, I'll have an iced tea," said Tim, "and bring him another beer. You want another one of those?"

"Why not," answered Morales, "if you're buying."

Tim nodded, and she walked away.

"So you're telling me you drove up here to say you're sorry," Morales said.

"That's pretty much it," Tim replied, staying just on the edge of the truth. "When did you start drinking again?"

"I never signed up for the whole sobriety thing, but I'm not really drinking. Just a couple of beers now and then, especially if I can get a chump like you to pay for them."

Tim thought Morales' breath smelled like more than just a couple of beers, but it didn't matter to him and wasn't worth pressing. "I really am sorry you hit your head on your own car door like that. It must have really hurt, and with all that blood and everything. Well, it's just too bad."

"Is that the apology you wanted to make? What the hell is wrong with you?"

"It didn't sound all that good when it came out, did it?"

"You drove all the way up here for that? Jesus, your whole family is crazy." Morales drank more of his beer. "Speaking of family, what's up with your brother? He get thrown off the force yet?" asked Morales.

"No, actually, he's working on a stolen identity case. Did you hear about it? Somebody took a loan out on some properties, almost exactly like the crime I told you *I* committed, and most of the money has disappeared. But whoever did it transferred a *nickel* of it into your boss's account—the Bishop?"

"You don't say."

"Yeah," Tim continued. "My brother originally thought I had done it again. I mean, I don't blame him. It was just like my crime, and who else would he suspect? But then I mentioned that I had told you all about how I did it. You remember, when we were in rehab."

"Cut the bullshit, Timmy. If you're here to accuse me, you're barking up the wrong tree. I don't remember much of what you told me. I *do* remember you saying that with identity theft there is no way anybody can figure out who did it."

"That's pretty much true," said Tim. "The only way somebody is going to get caught is if they do something stupid."

"Is that how you got caught? Doing something stupid?"

Tim chuckled. "Yeah, afraid so."

"Here you go, gentlemen," said the waitress, handing Tim his tea and Morales the beer. "Do you want to start a tab?"

Tim reached in his pocket and pulled out a twenty. "I don't know if I'll be here that long, but thanks. Keep the change."

"Thank *you!*" The waitress held up the twenty in acknowledgement of the large tip.

"Pretty generous," Morales said. He finished his first beer and put the empty on the table.

"Yeah, well, I don't know if I'll ever be here again. Might as well make a big splash, in case they talk about me when I'm gone."

"What'd you do?" asked Morales.

"Excuse me?"

"To get caught. You said you did something stupid and got caught."

"Aw, it's too embarrassing," Tim replied. "It was really bad. Besides, I had to promise I'd never tell anybody." Tim took a sip of tea and checked out the room, as though soaking in the scene. He nodded his head in time to a song coming from two wall speakers behind the bar.

"I told you at the program that I'd never tell anybody," Morales said.

I didn't believe it then, and I don't believe it now, thought Tim. "It's too embarrassing. You'll just laugh, and I wouldn't blame you."

"Try me. Just tell me where you went wrong."

"What, you worried you might have made a mistake, Morales?" Tim could see Morales grinding his jaw.

"I told you, I didn't do anything. You can let go of any ideas you got that I did." Morales' face relaxed. "I'm just asking you how you screwed up. Your answer doesn't leave this bar."

"Oh, I don't doubt that." Tim wondered if his AA sponsor, Richard, would think that sarcasm counted as a lie, but at the moment he didn't really care. This was fun. "I have to confess…I didn't quite tell you the whole truth at rehab." He took another sip of tea, enjoying stringing Jorge on a little bit. "The truth is, I got a notary's license using some dead guy's name after stealing his ID, just like I told you. But then I chickened out on the second ID and decided it would be better if I stole my dad's identity, took a loan out on his property, and then paid it back before anybody knew about it."

Morales seemed perplexed. "You've got to be kidding. That makes no sense to me. Why would you do that?"

Tim drank more tea and motioned towards the group Morales had been talking to. "Are these friends of yours?"

"What? No, I just met them. Who cares? I want to know why you did what you did."

"Oh, right. Yeah, I can't really say that it makes any sense to me now either, but at the time it did. I *borrowed* more than I actually needed, so that I could use some of it to start paying back the loan. I took enough to get me out of debt, and figured the cushion would give me enough time to get a job and pay the rest back."

Morales laughed. "Damn, man, no wonder you got caught. That's just plain stupid."

"Oh, that's not what got me caught."

"What did?"

"Before I stole the money, I opened an account at a local bank in my dad's name. The day after the big heist, I went in to make a withdrawal. I've got to admit, I was nervous, big time." Tim stopped talking, just to mess with Morales.

"Okay. So, what happened next?"

"What happened next was that the teller asked for my ID. I was ready for that, and had made one with my dad's info but my picture on it."

"So you handed her an ID with a birthday that made you, what, fifty, sixty years old?" That *was* pretty stupid." Morales held up his nearly empty beer for the waitress to see. "You're buying me another beer, College Boy."

"My pleasure. No, it had my birthday on it. That wasn't the stupid part. I put the fake ID in my top pocket so I could get it without having to go through my wallet. I was nervous, like I said, but I was also still pretty drunk from the night before. Too drunk. So, when she asked for my ID, I reached in my pocket, pulled out my wallet, and gave her my real one instead of the fake."

Morales nearly choked on his beer. "You did *what?*"

"Yup. Totally forgot the one in my top pocket. She looked at it, my withdrawal slip, then told me to hold on a minute, she just needed to get the money ready. Then she went straight to the manager's office."

"Who called the cops!" Morales started laughing.

"Who called my *dad*," Tim corrected him. "Talk about a small world, my dad had gone to college with the guy in Berkeley and was in the same frigging fraternity with him. And now they're fellow Kiwanians. The bank I was in was in Santa Rosa, and Dad lives in Napa, but the manager picked up the phone, called him, and told him what was going on."

"Holy shit. You *did* screw up!"

"Did I ever! The manager comes out, tells me he's called my dad, who's on the way there, and unless I want to get arrested sooner than later, I should wait in his office. I didn't know until after rehab that neither of them had any idea what I'd done, but they both concluded that I'd probably broken a law or two."

Morales put his hand on Tim's shoulder. "And I thought you were a bright guy!"

The waitress walked up and Morales took the beer from her. "Whoa—that was quick." He pointed to Tim. "He's buying again."

Tim handed her a ten this time. "Sorry, I spent all my show-off money."

"That's okay, she said. "Ten still leaves a nice tip. You guys need anything, let me know."

Tim waited for her to walk out of earshot, and then continued. "So my dad shows up, and he and the manager talk for a few minutes. Then my dad comes out, tells me he told the manager that *he'd* taken out the loan. Dad instructed the bank to return the money to the company I'd borrowed it from, which charged dad a 25% early repayment penalty. Dad paid that as well. He said he doubted the manager believed any of it, but he was dad's friend, and dad's story was enough to cover any wrongdoing, provided I never talked about it and never set foot in his bank again. My dad then tells me that I'll be paying him back the penalty, and he's taking me straight to rehab. Not even home for a toothbrush first."

"Oh Timmy, you couldn't have made that story up. So, you actually never got arrested, never went to trial, nothing. You got off scot-free."

"Well, I could probably still go to prison for it. I don't think my dad or the banker wanted to know exactly what I had done and they didn't ask. You know, that whole 'plausible deniability' thing. None of that really matters now, because I told the police everything before coming here."

"Bullshit. You got away with it, why would you do that?" asked Morales.

"I told them you were the man they were looking for now, and they agreed to give me immunity if I'd help them arrest you for it. I mean, you stole a lot more money than I did, and they really want to put you away."

"Except that I didn't do it, and nobody can prove otherwise. But if I had, I would have to do something stupid, like you did, to get caught."

"True. And you did everything right when you took out your loan. But you screwed up something else."

Morales just stared at Tim.

"You put the Bishop in a pretty tight spot when you gave him that nickel. My brother can't figure out why you did that, but it gave the Feds the only break they have in this. It's obvious to Danny the whole three hundred thousand dollars came from the loans you took out—"

"How many times do I have to tell you? I didn't do it." Morales' voice rose.

Tim thought Morales sounded more like he was pleading with him than denying anything. "Right. Anyway, the Feds decided, as long as *some* of the money was in the Bishop's account, to look around in his records. They didn't find squat about the three hundred thousand dollars but what they *did* find is that the Bishop has been mixing the church's money with his own, which your deposit indirectly brought to light. If they can't find out anything else, they may send him to prison for that, just out of spite. Ain't that some shit?"

Morales' only response was a hard glare.

Tim slowly drank from his tea, chewed and swallowed a few ice cubes, and scanned the room again. He glanced at Morales out of the corner of his eye as he did so, and he could see that the man was uneasy. "It turns out that the Bishop does *not* want to go to prison, although I guess that's no surprise. So, my brother made a deal to clear the Bishop's name if he'd help the cops catch you."

"You think this is all real funny, don't you, College Boy?" Some of the patrons who had been discreetly eavesdropping dropped all pretext of discretion as Morales got louder.

"Well, just a little, maybe. Anyway, they got to talking and the Bishop mentioned his Porsche, and how you haven't returned it to him despite his asking you several times. Danny asked if you might have stolen it. If the Bishop thought you did, he could file a police report and you'd get arrested. When Danny explained that part, the Bishop realized you *had* stolen it and filed the report." Tim wasn't sure if Morales looked confused, scared or angry. "My brother wanted to be the one to arrest you, but Ukiah is out of his jurisdiction."

"Bullshit. I didn't steal that car and there's no way they can prove otherwise."

"I don't think anybody cares if you really stole it or not. I know my brother doesn't." Tim looked around the room for the side door. His walk around the restaurant had revealed three exits—the front, back, and one off the lounge. He hoped Morales would run out the front and straight to the Porsche and the police, but had to plan for what to do if he didn't. "But if you just get *arrested* for stealing it, they'll take fingerprints. And if your prints just *happen* to match the prints of the notary on the loan document that was used to steal the three hundred thousand dollars...you know, from the fingerprints of all the notaries that the state has in a file somewhere...well, you're toast."

Tim had heard the expression "white as a ghost," but it had never occurred to him that anybody actually turned that color, especially someone dark-complected. He thought Morales looked a little more gray than white, but the cliché wasn't too far off.

"You're trying to set me up!" Morales sputtered.

"That's part of it. I'm here to do two other things as well." Tim casually stepped between Morales and the side door. "One is to keep you occupied while the police locate and go through your car, which they're probably doing now."

"The police are here now?" Morales's eyes widened beyond what Tim would have thought physically possible.

"I imagine," answered Tim. "I think they got an anonymous call, just before I walked in, telling them the stolen Porsche was in the parking lot. I'll bet they're out there now, checking it out."

Morales looked around the room as though looking for a way out of all this, then shoved Tim aside and plowed through the crowd, hurrying towards the front door. He burst outside and started yelling. "Hey! That's my car!"

Danny had been listening to some talk show on the car radio while he watched the restaurant. The Ukiah police had shown up a few minutes earlier and were checking the outside of the Porsche with their flashlights. He was startled when Morales burst outside. Even though the door was only 75 feet or so away, Danny used binoculars, just to make sure. "Hello, Morales," he said. "I was hoping you'd play it this way."

Tim followed Morales to the front door, just closely enough to watch him. He spoke to Morales under his breath. "That's it. Go to the police and start yelling at them."

"Get the hell away from my car!" Morales yelled. He started running towards the parking lot, and the officers looked up at him. One of them shined his flashlight in Morales's direction. Jorge stopped in mid-stride at the sight of the light, turned around, and ran back into the bar.

"Dammit!" Danny said, more noisily than he intended. He looked towards the officers, who glanced in his direction, and quickly turned his face away from them. *I can't blow this now.* He looked at his watch's secondhand. Danny had to hope that Morales would try to exit through the back door. Meanwhile, he had to wait fifteen long seconds before making his next move. It was a weak plan, but it was all they had.

Tim saw Morales running back into to the bar. *Damn!* He moved to the side door of the bar and planted himself in front of it. He crouched down like a tackler on the line of scrimmage, guarding it when Morales came back in. "Out the back, out the back," he muttered to himself.

Morales started in Tim's direction and locked eyes with him. "Out of my way, asshole!"

Several people turned to see what was going on.

"You're not going anywhere, Morales."

Morales glanced at the people staring at him, and then turned and headed for the back door. He pushed the emergency exit bar, flinging the door open, and stepped out. Tim was right behind him. As soon as Morales was outside, Tim leaped. Morales was almost too far away, but Tim caught him by the ankles and tackled him. Morales rolled onto his back, wrested his legs free, and kicked Tim in his head.

CRAIG SMITH

The blow stunned Tim, giving Morales enough time to pin him to the ground and hit him in the face. "You've fucked with the wrong man," Morales said, hitting Tim again.

For Tim, it seemed to happen in slow motion, and the blows hardly hurt at all. *That's it, Morales,* thought Tim. *Knock yourself out.*

Looking at his watch, Danny ran towards the two cops who were searching the Porsche, reaching them just as fifteen seconds had passed, as he and Tim had planned. "Officers! There are two big guys in a fight behind the bar. Looks like they might kill each other."

Danny had their attention. "Around back?" one of them said, pointing towards the restaurant. He and his partner barely waited for Danny's answer before running in that direction.

"Yes sir," Danny answered, although the men were already in full run.

The sight of the cops taking off triggered something in Danny. He felt flushed as his adrenalin started coursing through his body. His rage was immediate, and almost knocked him off balance. *Your ass is mine, Morales!* He began to run after the officers. He wanted in on this, could taste it. His brain shut down as his body took over. He was an animal, in pursuit of prey.

Then he heard it. A woman's voice, deep in his head. "What are you feeling, Danny?" It was Hiakawa's voice, and it stopped him dead in his tracks.

"I feel rage," he spoke out loud, answering the imaginary voice. *I feel an all-consuming rage. I can't think. It's as if I've checked out and someone or something else has taken over my body. I don't know why I'm running, or why I'm so angry.*

Danny stopped moving so fast that inertia almost toppled him. In that instant, he got it—*this* was PTSD. *He* wasn't running: his response to getting shot was running, and for the moment, it was controlling him. Except that, this time, he caught himself before he got carried away.

Danny watched the two officers as they turned the corner and vanished behind the restaurant. *This isn't my fight anymore,* he thought. *I don't have to do this.*

Tim didn't see the cops until they pulled Morales off him. He could taste his own blood in his mouth. Morales had hit him repeatedly before the officers intervened, and Tim had just let him.

The officers held Morales from behind. Fighting to free himself from their embrace, his eyes never leaving Tim, Morales could only sputter his outrage. "He's trying to set me up! He started this. Let *go* of me, dammit! I haven't done anything."

"Calm down or, so help me, I'll Taser you," one of the officers said. That seemed to get Morales' attention. He looked at both cops, then stopped squirming. One of the officers held his arm in a way to immobilize him; the other one bent over Tim.

"Did you start this?" he asked.

"I never threw a punch," Tim answered calmly.

"Speak to the cops in an even voice," Danny had instructed Tim earlier. "They'll listen to the one who is the most in control of his emotions."

"That is such bullshit!" Morales started struggle again, but the officer containing him had him under control.

"I want to see ID from both of you," said the officer talking to Tim. His badge identified him as Patrolman Robertson.

"Mine is in my back pocket. May I get it?" Tim got up from the ground. He thought Danny would have loved how compliantly he was acting. "I don't know Father Morales that well." Neither officer had mentioned names, and Tim wanted to make sure the officers knew who they had contained.

"*Morales?* Are you Jorge Morales?" The second cop wanted to know.

"This isn't right! You can't do this!" Morales had stopped resisting, but his voice was still loud.

"We came here investigating an alleged car theft that you've been accused of," said Robertson.

"I didn't steal that car! This is a setup."

Robertson shined his flashlight in Morales's face. "Well, some credible people are accusing you of it," he said. "A warrant for your arrest was emailed here about an hour ago, and the sender thought you might be here. Then we got a call fifteen minutes ago confirming that the Porsche was in this parking lot. Somebody wants you locked up. If this is a setup, you've made some powerful enemies."

"But I'm telling you, I *didn't steal it!* That car belongs to my boyfriend."

"Whoa, *whoa*," said both of the officers, almost simultaneously. "*Way* too much information for us," Robertson continued. "We were told it belongs to a bishop. You can call your boyfriend from the station and see if the two of you can work it out. Until you do though, you're going to jail."

"You think you're so fucking clever, College Boy, but I'll get you for this! Just wait," Morales hissed at Tim through gritted teeth.

The officer holding Morales handcuffed him.

"What are you doing in Ukiah, Mr. Harris?" Robertson looked at Tim's ID as he spoke.

"I came up here with my brother. He's got some business in town and dropped me off here. I saw Morales in the bar. I know him from way back and started talking to him."

"And you ended up, fighting."

"This'll sound crazy, but I tried to apologize to him for something that happened a while back."

"You are so full of shit," Morales's voice started to rise again.

"I don't think Father Morales accepts your apology. Are you okay?" Robertson asked.

"My eye hurts but I'll be fine. Thanks for your help."

"Look, we don't like bar fights in Ukiah. I don't care who started this, I don't want to see you again while you're here or I promise I'll lock you up. Is that clear?" Robertson kept his flashlight beam on Tim's face, just below his eyes, as he spoke.

"You have my word, Officer." Tim was completely comfortable that he was telling the truth.

"Do you need a ride somewhere? I can call you a cab."

"No, thanks. I'm supposed to meet my brother soon anyway."

Robertson turned back to his partner. "Let's get this one back to the car. Father Morales, we're taking you to jail now." Robertson officially arrested Jorge for auto theft and began reading him his rights.

"This isn't over yet, Tim." Morales growled as he was being led away.

No, I suppose it isn't. Alone now, Tim couldn't stop grinning.

Danny saw the two officers emerge from behind the restaurant, leading a handcuffed Morales with them. He watched them put him in their cruiser and drive away. A few minutes later, Tim walked out of the restaurant. As he got closer, Danny could see that the front of his shirt was covered in blood. And that he had an ear-to-ear grin.

"It looks like you got the worst of that one," he said. He and Tim hugged, slapping each other on the back.

"I sure did," Tim said, his eyes sparkling. "It went just like we planned."

"You look like shit," Danny said, a smirk accompanying the remark. "Thanks, man. You did a great job. I really owe you one."

"Tell you what." Tim put his arm around his brother's shoulder. "Let's call it even, and let it go at that. Okay?"

Danny laughed. "You've got a deal, brother. We're even on everything. Come on, get in the car and I'll take you home."

Chapter Forty-Five

Morales was fingerprinted and photographed at the time of his arrest. There were no outstanding warrants against him, nor a prior arrest record. After spending the night in jail, he was exonerated of the auto theft charge when the Bishop suddenly remembered that he had lent Morales the Porsche.

"No offense, Father, but how do you 'forget' that you lent someone your car?" the on-duty sergeant asked the Bishop when he appeared at the station to withdraw the accusation and take custody of Morales.

The Bishop showed no signs of embarrassment, and answered the policeman as though addressing a child. "Is it against the law to forget something, Sergeant?"

"No, it just seems unusual, that's all."

"And is it your duty to interrogate everyone who walks in the door?"

"No." The sergeant glared at the Bishop.

"Well then, do you suppose you could stop the questions and release Father Morales?"

"*Dick,*" the sergeant said under his breath, as he began to walk to the cell area.

"Sergeant, before you go," another officer had his hand over the mouthpiece of his telephone, "I'm on the phone with the Chief's office. They want us to run Morales's prints against all the prints the state has on record, not just those with prior arrests, before we let him go."

"Seriously? *All* prints?" The sergeant looked at the Bishop with a smirk on his face. "Sixteen years on the job, I've never heard that one. I'm awfully sorry, but your boy is going to have to sit in his cell a bit longer, and you're just going to have to wait. Would you like some coffee or something?" The sarcasm in his voice could not have been more obvious.

The more extensive fingerprint search revealed a positive match with one of the state's newest notaries, who had just days before approved loan documents totaling $1,000,000. Smiling broadly, the on-duty sergeant informed the bishop that, while the auto theft charges had been dropped, Morales was now a suspect in an identity theft case, and a felony charge for fraud was entered.

Morales had very little to say when questioned by the FBI, even after an attorney, secured for him by the church, encouraged him to cooperate.

"That nickel was your downfall," one of the agents questioning Morales had said. "Why'd you do it?"

Morales had only smiled. While the circumstantial evidence against him was strong, the only thing that could be proven was that he had illegally notarized documents. Finally, he agreed to plead guilty to that. He also agreed to "see what he could do" to get the stolen money returned, all of which was anonymously wired into his attorney's account a few days after that. Tried and convicted, he received a five-year sentence with the possibility of time off for good behavior. He never admitted to the crime and never spoke to the Bishop again.

Before the Bishop was charged with anything, vestry members in the diocese came forward to explain that there had been a lag on the church's part in reimbursing him for legitimate expenses from the five building projects he was overseeing. They went on to say that the irregularities in the Bishop's personal account were due to mismanagement on their part, not his.

"This is very embarrassing for us," one vestry member told the authorities. "But the Bishop didn't do anything illegal. I can imagine how it must look to you, but the fault lies with the vestry."

The Chief looked from one vestry member to the next. "You all agree on this?"

"Yes sir," said their spokesman.

All of the Bishop's debts, including those that appeared to be personal, were made good. Within a month, he was transferred to a diocese in Southern California: one with more churches, more congregants, and a much bigger budget. It was, to Danny's amazement, an apparent promotion, just as the Bishop had predicted—and if he'd even *had* his hand slapped, Danny missed it.

The day after the events in Ukiah, the Chief announced that two new hires had been vetted and would be joining the force. Two weeks after that, Danny and Sean left the swing shift and returned to days.

Able at last to admit that he was suffering from PTSD after being shot at, Danny continued to see Dr. Hiakawa for a couple of weeks. In her final report, she stated that he had learned to recognize the triggers that led to his chasing Morales and could return to active duty. The Chief's last official act was to promote Danny to detective.

"Did you hear somebody at the door?" Danny hollered from the kitchen.

Carol walked in, putting in her other earring. "No, Danny. Nobody is at the door. You're so *nervous*, like we've never had company before." She walked up to him and turned the collar of his rugby shirt down in the back, and kissed him on the cheek. "I like you better without the goatee. You look more like the man I know and love. Thanks for shaving it off."

Danny rubbed his skin. It felt more like he'd shed a false skin than shaved. "You're welcome. I guess I *am* nervous, but it's a big night." He held her at arm's length. "You look great tonight, Carol. I'm so happy to be with you."

The doorbell rang. "*That's* somebody at the door. I didn't think anybody was coming till seven thirty?" said Carol.

Danny looked at his watch. "7:29. Let's see who's so punctual."

Danny opened the door to find not only Tim and Sara but Sean and a woman as well. "Come in, come in. Did you all meet?" asked Danny.

"In the driveway," answered Tim. "But I haven't met Carol," he said, extending his hand to her.

Sean made a great show of introducing his date to Danny. "And this is my girlfriend, Sam."

"Sam, a pleasure to finally meet you," Danny said, shaking her hand. "Please don't take this wrong, but you are, fortunately, older than I expected."

Sam twisted her mouth and hit Sean in the arm. "How old did you tell him I was?"

Sean threw up his hands in his own defense. "I'm not sure I ever told him, but for some reason, he thought you were in high school."

"Oh and you had nothing to do with that," Sam said.

"I might not have corrected his error," said Sean.

Sam turned to Danny, "Sean always speaks highly of you, but he likes to tease. You should never take what he says at face value."

"And *that's* coming from a doctor," said Sean.

Danny's jaw dropped. "You're a doctor?"

"A pediatrician," answered Sam. "He really didn't tell you anything about me, did he?"

"I can't believe you, Sean," Danny said. "I'm really going to miss working with you every day. But I'll get over some parts of it quickly."

"Oh, you say that now, Officer Garcia, but you'll be trying to get back on patrol duty and partnered up with me in no time."

"Yeah, I'm sure. Anyway, it's a pleasure to meet you, Sam, but I'm pretty sure you're too good for Sean."

"Hey, I'm standing right here," said Sean.

"Tim, can you help me get drinks?" Danny pointed towards the kitchen.

"Lead the way," his brother answered.

Danny took drink orders from his guests. Once in the kitchen, he lowered his voice. "Look, I wanted to ask a favor of you."

"I've got something to talk to you about, too. What's on your mind?" asked Tim.

"No, you go first."

Crossing his arms, Tim leaned against the kitchen counter. "Well, I've been thinking about this for a few weeks now. I'm probably going to give up real estate."

"What? You're kidding," Danny said. "I thought things were going great?"

"Yeah, well, I'm selling a lot of houses—"

"And you've paid back all your debts, including to Dad."

"I did."

"Why would you want to quit?"

Tim shrugged. "Real estate is going well and I guess I'm good at it, but I just don't enjoy it that much. Every time I sell a house, all I feel is relief that it's over. There's no joy in it. It's just a job."

"But you help people find a home. You told me about a couple that didn't think they could ever afford a house, and you found them something they really liked in their price range. That's gotta feel good."

"It does, but it isn't enough. I need to feel challenged and like I'm *really* helping people."

"Can you grab a bowl from the cabinet above the stove and empty that bag of chips in it?" Danny opened the refrigerator and took out a three-bowl serving dish. "I don't know, Tim. This is a big decision, but I guess if you aren't happy…"

Tim emptied the chips into the bowl. "It's not that I'm unhappy, I just don't feel like I'm contributing anything. Sure, I help people find a house, but it doesn't feel like the world is any better because of it. I want to feel like I'm doing something important, like you do."

Danny took two beers out of the refrigerator and held them up to Tim. "You cool taking these out to the living room?

Tim chuckled. "Sure. Thanks for asking, though."

"There are steins in the freezer. What, you want to be a cop?" Danny chuckled.

"Well, yes."

Danny did a double take. "Are you serious?"

"Yes. I've thought about it since we went to Ukiah. I think I'd like it. I think I can do some good."

"Tim, I don't know. It's not like that all the time. In fact, ninety-five percent of the time, it's pretty boring."

"Well, real estate bores me one-hundred percent of the time, so that would be an improvement. Look, Danny, I'm not going to quit my job tomorrow, but I'm serious about this. I'd like to do a few ride-alongs with some officers, take the test for the academy. I might decide that it's not for me, but I'd like to check it out."

Danny looked down at the floor for a moment. "Tim, the way we did things in Ukiah—the way *I* did things in Ukiah—that wasn't good police work. That was rogue cop stuff. I mean, the end was good, Morales got what he deserved, but I was *way* out of line in the way I handled it, dragging you into it and all."

"Hey, I could have said no. I wanted to do it."

"Still, it was a bad decision on my part," said Danny.

"Yeah, but you were right. The Bishop did change his mind, and if we hadn't acted when we did, Morales might have gotten off completely—with the money no less."

"So I got lucky."

"No, Danny, you were right, period. I know you're worried about the post-traumatic thing, but you said you're getting a handle on that. Besides, you'll make a great detective."

"I just don't want you to think that what we did, and all that excitement, is what being a cop is all about, because it isn't. If that's what's leading you to this decision, you'd be making a mistake."

"It's not, Danny. I know we crossed a line getting Morales, maybe a bunch of them, but you've helped a lot of people over the years, and that's what I want to do. If I do decide to become a cop, I want to do the job the way you do it."

Danny couldn't help smiling. "Tim, you've got to be crazy to want to be a cop. Anybody does. But if you really want to go down that path, I'll help in any way I can."

"Thanks, Danny. That's all I ask. Tim picked up the beers and pointed them towards the living room. "Should we head out?"

"Yeah, but first I want to ask you something."

"Oh, I'm sorry, you said that." Tim leaned against the counter. "What's up?"

"Well, Carol and I are getting married."

Tim was quiet for a moment, then put the beers on the counter. "Son of a bitch. That's great, Danny!" He gave his brother a bear hug. "When's the big day?"

"We've got to work all that out, but it's going to be fairly soon. Carol wants to do it right, so it's going to be a church wedding."

"Do Mom and Dad know?"

"Not yet. I haven't even told Sean. We're having brunch with the folks, tomorrow. Point is, I'm going to need a best man, and I wondered if you'd stand up for me."

Tim didn't answer right away, and began to tear up. "You want me to be your best man?"

Danny put his hand on Tim's shoulder. "Seriously? I can't think of anybody I'd rather have standing next to me. It would be an honor if you'd say yes." Danny wiped a tear away from his own eye, and then sheepishly added, "But we can't be crying during the ceremony."

Tim hugged his brother again. "Hell yes, I'll do it. You have no idea what this means to me. Thank you, Danny."

"It means just as much to me, Tim. I'm really glad you're back in my life."

"Hey, we're dying of thirst out here," Sean called from the living room.

Danny rolled his eyes. "Come, little brother, let's take him his beer and tell them the news."

"Yeah, okay. I'm glad we're family again too, Danny. I've really missed you."

Tim and Danny returned to the living room and handed out the drinks. Danny raised his glass. "Thank you all for being here tonight. It's hard to believe that some of us have never met. You all mean a lot to me. Well, not so much you anymore, Sean, lying about a doctor like that. But seriously, I'm glad you're here."

"Are you going to be all sentimental like this all night, or do we get to eat and drink fairly soon?" said Sean.

"All right, smart ass." Danny motioned for Carol to join him, and then he put his arm around her. "You can eat and drink all night, but—first—we have an announcement to make. Carol and I are getting married, and we wanted you to be the first to know."

"Danny, it's more like you're the *last* to know. We've all had our money on this for a long time," Sean said. "Seriously, congratulations, partner. I'd like to propose a toast to the happy couple: The beautiful, intelligent, sexy Carol, and Danny—the guy I made look good on the job for four years. May you live long, happy lives together."

To the Reader,

I hope you enjoyed reading *Lies That Bind*. It's probably true that authors put a little of themselves into every character, both good and bad, and I am guilty of that as well. It made it a fun project for me.

Danny and Tim will be presented with challenges that will alternatingly bring them even closer together, and also pull them further apart, in the second book in this series *Wines That Lie*. If you have any feedback on *Lies That Bind*, things you liked or didn't like, let me know at craigsmithauthor@gmail.com or visit craigsmithauthor.com.

Ultimately, you, the reader have the power to make or break a new book. If you have the time, here's the link to my author page on Amazon (amazon.com/author/craigsmith). Whether you liked the book or not, it would mean a lot if you would write something.

I'd also like to thank the members of my writers group, who know these characters almost as well as I do: Linda Andereggen, Lorraine Babb, Carlos Chaves, Jean Holroyd, Charles Markee, Mark Piper, and Florentia Scott. Special thanks to Debbie Augustine and the team at Augustine Agency for the book cover design and enthusiastic support. Melissa Peterson from Classic Photography made me look pretty darn "authorly" in the cover photo. My lifelong friend, former roommate, and sometimes traveling companion, Selene Cameron Green, provided editing. Finally, to the dozens of folks who read and critiqued *Lies That Bind* along the way. Your input and suggestions kept me on track every time I wondered off.

With gratitude,

Craig Smith

CPSIA information can be obtained
at www.ICGtesting.com
Printed in the USA
LVOW03s2312061217
558938LV00009B/232/P